CHARLES EGAN was born in Nottingham, England, of Irish parents.

When he was five, the family returned to Ireland, as his father had been appointed Resident Medical Superintendent of St. Luke's, a psychiatric hospital in Clonmel, in County Tipperary.

Every summer they visited his father's family's farm, outside Kiltimagh in County Mayo for a month, where his grandmother and uncles spent many evenings, talking about family and local history.

The family subsequently moved to County Wicklow, where he initially attended the De La Salle Brothers School in Wicklow town. He then went to the Jesuits' Clongowes Wood College (James Joyce's alma mater), and subsequently studied Commerce in University College Dublin, graduating in 1973.

After an initial career in the private sector, including Marubeni Dublin, (where he met his future wife, Carmel), he joined the Industrial Development Authority (IDA) in Dublin. After a few years, the desire to be his own boss, led him to resign and set up his own business, which ran for 30 years.

Apart from business, his main interests are history, film and worldwide travel.

D0723790

Also by the author

The Killing Snows
The Exile Breed

COLD
IS THE
DAWN

CHARLES EGAN

SilverWood

Published in 2017 by SilverWood Books

SilverWood Books Ltd
14 Small Street, Bristol, BS1 1DE, United Kingdom
www.silverwoodbooks.co.uk

ISBN 978-1-78132-659-6 (paperback)
ISBN 978-1-78132-660-2 (ebook)

British Library Cataloguing in Publication Data
A CIP catalogue record for this book is available from
the British Library

Page design and typesetting by SilverWood Books
Printed on responsibly sourced paper

'Mayo! Mayo! To mourn thy dismal fate is indeed poor consolation. Throughout the length and breadth of the county, it is one vast howling wilderness.'

Telegraph & Connaught Ranger
County Mayo, December 1848

For Carmel

Preface

1848 and 1849 were tough years for Europe. But Ireland was worse than any.

In 1848 the blight, which had almost disappeared in 1847, came back in full force, right across the country. Famine, which had never really gone away, intensified to a shocking climax in 1849.

Emigration intensified too. Most travelled to the traditional destinations of Great Britain and North America, but conditions in both worsened, in different ways.

England, along with the rest of Europe was suffering its own shortages. The financial crash of late 1847 had thrown many hundreds of thousands out of work. In English mines and mills, rising unemployment caused riots. Much of the violence was targeted at poor Irish emigrants, who were accused of stealing English jobs. Homeless and jobless, they squeezed as best they could into the slums of British cities.

Of an estimated two hundred thousand Irish navvies working on the railway construction in 1847, one hundred thousand were without work by the middle of 1848. For the labour contractors on the railways, many of them Irish, this was an excellent opportunity to exploit hungry Irish workers.

Another factor in 1848 was revolution, which broke out in many European countries. France, Prussia, Austria, Hungary, Denmark and Sicily were all rattled by revolt. In London, the Government was terrified of a similar revolution, either through the Chartist Movement in Great Britain or the Young Ireland Movement in Ireland itself.

The Government faced down Chartism, and it slowly faded away. The Young Ireland Rebellion in Tipperary, was very limited, and put down by a few hundred police in a single day. But none of this quelled the Government's fears, and they were convinced revolution might break out any time, either in the English cities with large Irish populations, or in Ireland. The British Army was over-extended, with fifty thousand troops in Ireland alone, awaiting another rebellion which never came.

Across the Atlantic, the exile faced different challenges. The forest industries of the Canadian provinces had been badly hit by the 1847 collapse. Widespread unemployment across Quebec and Ontario, meant there was no work for the Irish, even if they had survived the coffin ships on the Atlantic, or the quarantine stations of Quebec and Montreal. Hunger, fever and cold killed many thousands of the emigrants. Thousands more made their way south into the United States, dying as they went.

The 1847 crash did not hit the United States so hard. This was because the country had a huge surplus of food, much of which was exported to the starving countries of Europe, mostly for cash, and some for Irish relief. Very few Irish worked in American farming though, and other employment could be erratic. 1840-1860 was a time of heavy railroad construction, but this was liable to be terminated at very short notice, throwing thousands of men out of work.

As in Britain, the Irish squeezed into the slums of American cities. For the most part, Irish men took the heavy, unskilled labouring jobs. Along the waterfronts in New Jersey and New York, there were thousands of Irish stevedores, which resulted in bitter battles for union recognition and Irish control. In the anthracite mines of Pennsylvania, the late 1840s saw a similar struggle for better conditions and Union recognition. But a series of strikes and lock-outs ended in defeat for the miners.

Then, in 1849, cholera appeared. For once, Ireland was not alone in its suffering. The Asiatic cholera killed tens of millions as it spread around the world. It was a new type, and few had immunity to it. Millions died in the crowded cities of Europe and America. England and the United States suffered appallingly.

But Ireland was already on its knees.

Luke's Family and Locations

Luke Ryan
Winnie, his wife
Liam, his son
Michael, his father
Eleanor, his mother
Pat, his younger brother

Murty Ryan, Luke's uncle
Aileen, Murty's wife
Danny, their eldest son
Murtybeg, their youngest son
Nessa, their daughter, deceased
Brigid, Nessa's daughter, adopted by Eleanor

Sabina McKinnon, Luke's aunt
Ian McKinnon, Sabina's husband, deceased

In County Mayo, the East Mayo towns of Kilduff, Knockanure and Brockagh are fictitious, as are the settlements and mountains around them. The county towns of Castlebar, Claremorris, Westport, Ballina and Louisburgh are real, as are the Ox Mountains, the Erris peninsula, the Partry Mountains and Mweelrea, together with the settlements within and around them.

All the English railways, cities and slums are real as described. In Pennsylvania, the mining town of Lackan is fictitious. All the other towns in New York, New Jersey and Pennsylvania are real.

Fr. Peter Ward's letter to The Freeman's Journal is genuine, as is Dean Callanan's letter to the Dublin Evening Packet.

A note about italic use in this book. Where the dialogue is in italics, the character is understood to be speaking in Irish.

Prologue

Cold fear.

For the rest of her life, Eleanor would remember that first baffled moment of startled bewilderment, leading to an awful surmise, and then to the appalling certainty.

She grasped her daughter-in-law by the arm.

'Easy, Winnie. Stay easy.'

'It cannot be,' Winnie whispered. 'Not again. Not so soon.' Her face was pale.

'It is,' Eleanor replied. 'There's no doubting it.' She felt the need to vomit, but did not. The shock had hit her with brutal force.

Winnie stared at the putrefied potatoes on the table, both cut open to show the dark purple rims, deepening to a sodden wet black at the centres.

'But...not all...'

'The most of them,' Michael said. 'I've dug up and down and across the big field. There's damned few left, and I reckon they'll rot soon.'

'There's the ones in the loft,' Eleanor said. 'It's as well we dug them in time.'

'They've rotted too,' Michael said.

'They couldn't...'

'They did. Can't you smell it?'

Eleanor sensed the cloying sweet smell. Why had she not noticed it earlier?

'But the high field...?'

'Little enough, you'd find there.'

She steadied herself on the table, shaking her head.

'It's back, so.'

'It is. The blight is back, and the crop is gone.'

Chapter 1

Morning Post, London. July 1848:
Imperial Parliament, London. At Belmullet, 140 families
were turned out by one landlord, and 700 persons turned
houseless upon the high road. From the estate of Lord
Lucan, in the poorest part of Mayo, 1,200 evictions took
place. George Scrope, Member of Parliament, condemns the
evicting landlords of County Mayo.

Michael made to the door, taking the spade. The women stayed behind.
Outside, a grey, knee-high mist had settled over the potato field.

'*Will he find anything?*' Winnie asked, slipping into Irish.

'*Not much,*' Eleanor replied. '*He knows that as well as we do. He's only
working out his anger.*'

'*And fear?*'

'*I don't know about that. We might have money enough with Pat working in England and Luke in New York. Who knows? Still it's a matter of
pride. Having to rely on our sons for money – it's not easy for any man.*'

Liam was crying. '*It's the noise we're all making,*' Winnie said. '*It's time for
his feed anyhow.*'

She brought him into the kitchen, rocking him gently. She opened her
blouse and gave him to suck.

'So what now?'

'*It's like I told you before,*' Eleanor said. '*Us women, we're hard because
we have to be. You've lived through hunger before. And what do you feel?
Pity for the dying. Disgust at the rat-eaten bodies. The fear of death. Many
times, I have felt these things, and then I can't think. But we must think
plainly to see what is vital to us. Even when our babies die, we cannot allow
our feelings dim our reason. So now we go cold. Cold in our heads, and cold
in our hearts. Otherwise we lose all charge. Are you cold?*'

For some time, Winnie said nothing.

'*I am,*' she said at length. '*I have the understanding of it now. Our
families come first.*'

'*They do,*' Eleanor said. '*Always.*'

Then there was only the sound of the baby feeding. When he had finished, Winnie rocked him until he fell asleep.

'*I'll just put him in the back room.*'

Eleanor took the rotten potatoes from the table and threw them on the turf fire, where they sputtered as they burned. Winnie joined her by the fire, but neither spoke.

Brigid came into the kitchen rubbing the sleep out of her eyes. Puzzled, she looked from one woman to the other.

'*She knows there's something wrong,*' Winnie said.

'*She does,*' Eleanor said. '*Now come on, we've work to do. Let's clear the loft.*'

Winnie went outside and took in a bucket and shovel. Eleanor climbed into the loft. Winnie passed up the shovel and bucket, and followed up the ladder. Most of the potatoes were black. Some had turned to slush, and a viscous fluid was seeping across the floorboards. Eleanor took a bucket and filled it with the foul-smelling potatoes. Winnie took it down and dumped it outside. Brigid held her hand to her nose, her face wrinkled with disgust.

At last Eleanor joined Winnie. She could just see Michael sitting at the top of the field, smoking his pipe. Slowly, the mist above the potatoes burned off in the sun, but the rotten stench remained.

Later the women joined him. Winnie carried the baby in a shawl tied around her back, while Brigid sat at the edge of the field, watching. Many of the potato stalks had blackened. The mist had disappeared.

'What of the high field?' Eleanor asked.

Michael knocked his pipe on the rock to clear the ashes.

'Come, I'll show you.'

The two women followed him to the high field. It was no more than a few tiny ridges of potatoes below the rath. Here some of the stalks were green, and a few of the potatoes that Michael had dug were firm and clean.

'There's no sign of these ones rotting anyhow,' Winnie said.

'They will,' Michael said. 'Look here.'

Under the leaves, there was a white, down-like substance.

Eleanor rubbed her finger on the leaf, and looked close. Again, she felt the shock in her stomach, but calmed herself quickly. Go cold.

'It's blight right enough.'

'It is,' Michael said.

'But let's get these ones out while we have the chance.'

'We can try, if ye want.'

Eleanor went to the lower field and picked up two hessian sacks. They filled the sacks with the few firm potatoes and carried them back to the house, where they were stored in the loft.

But she knew they were working to no purpose. A day or two in the loft, and they too would rot.

That afternoon, she walked up towards Kilduff. There were men and women in the fields on either side of the road, digging potatoes. As she walked, she heard a weird keening sound. She had heard that sound before at funerals, but this was different. These people were keening their own funerals.

When she arrived in Kilduff the line at Dillon's was shorter than she had expected. A few women stood outside, all gaunt with hunger. Then a woman ran out of the shop. She was weeping.

The women in front turned to Eleanor. '*The price is up,*' one said, '*there's not many that'll afford it.*'

After a few minutes, Eleanor entered the shop. 'Fourpence per pound,' Dillon said, before she even opened her mouth.

She gasped. 'But that's four times the price…'

'Take it or leave it.'

Eleanor was undecided. Then she thought it better to take a small quantity, even less than a quarter of what she normally would. As she walked back, she saw a family kneeling outside a mud cabin, scrabbling through a heap of rotten potatoes. She went on.

When she arrived in Carrigard, she placed the bag of corn on the table.

'So *little?*' Winnie asked.

'*The price has gone up four times. At these prices, we might have to start eating our own, whether it's full grown or not.*'

That night, they ate corn with turnip. Eleanor had decided to leave the new potatoes for a few days. There was no point in sickening themselves on hidden rot.

Dinner was quiet the next evening. Again, they fed on corn and turnips. The potatoes in the loft were rotten.

'They looked well enough when we dug them,' Winnie commented.

'Yes,' said Michael, 'but the rot was there, only waiting to show itself. This is '46 again. '42 too. There's nothing left. Not a damned thing.'

'And what of the ones from last year?' Eleanor asked.

'Still sound,' Michael said, 'but we should keep them for next year's seed.'

'Is it worth keeping them, if the crop will only rot next year?'

'We must try,' Michael replied. 'What else can we do?'

'There's the hens. We could kill them. Then we wouldn't have to keep feeding them. Yes, we'd have no eggs, but we could eat their feed ourselves.'

'They won't last long,' Winnie said.

'No,' Michael said, 'but we've still some flitches of salted beef left. It won't be enough though.'

'We may kill the pig,' Eleanor said, 'and won't it be strange? Not able to buy corn but living on meat.'

'And what of the horse?' Winnie asked.

'We'll eat it last,' Michael said. 'The donkey too. But one thing's for certain, we can't leave any animals outside. We'll have to bring them in or they'll disappear. As for eating, we'll stretch them out long enough. But we'll have to sell something for the rent, and I'm not sure we'll have enough corn if we eat it ourselves.'

They drove the animals inside, and tied them to the rings under the loft, away from the kitchen. There was a smell of animal sweat, and soon a stink of dung. Michael spread straw over it.

'We'll dig it out in the morning,' he said.

'I thought we were finished with this kind of thing,' Eleanor said.

Michael sat back at the table. Brigid sat close to the fire, playing with a straw doll.

'So what now?' Winnie asked.

'We'll have to write to Pat in England,' Michael said, though Eleanor knew from the tone of his voice that he would not write any time soon.

'Don't forget I'll be sending money to ye from America,' Winnie said.

'I'm sure ye will,' Eleanor said, 'though I don't like that it has to be that way. And anyhow, it'll be months till we'd have it.'

'I know,' said Winnie, 'but sure what else can we do?'

The women were alone in the kitchen the next morning, as Michael had gone to the rath, where he could overlook the cornfield, and protect the growing crop against theft.

'*There's no choice now,*' Winnie said. '*It's America for me, whether I like it or not. It's where Luke is, so I have to go.*'

'*You're right,* Eleanor said. 'We've bought the ticket. We have his address. There's only the hunger here, so why stay. Anyhow, you can get work in New York or Jersey City.*'

'*Working as a bridget in one of their big houses?*'

'*Any work you can get.*'

Brigid was fed on chicken and corn. Winnie fed Liam by breast. Eleanor was thankful she could do so. She had heard of women whose babies had died in famine, but knew that this was only in the last stages of starvation.

She would have to cut back on what the rest of the family were eating, and all their reserves of food, either in storage or on the hoof, would have to be guarded. The turnips were dug, and brought inside. By now they were guarding the cabbage patch, but since it was beside the house this was not difficult.

Eleanor went up to Kilduff to buy more corn. Just outside the town, a woman's body lay face down in a ditch. She knelt beside her, and turned her over. She listened. There was no breathing. She walked on to the town. At the priest's house, there was a line of people, where Father Reilly was giving out soup. She made her way to him.

'Delia Loughney is lying dead out the road towards Carrigard,' she whispered to him in English, knowing few others would understand.

'I'll see to it,' he replied, blankly.

In Dillon's the price had dropped, but it was still expensive.

When she returned, Winnie was sitting at the table with Liam and Brigid. There was a letter.

'*Where's it from?*' Eleanor asked.

'*England.*'

Eleanor examined the stamp.

'*Pat then.*'

She slit the envelope.

'*Look at this. Three pounds.*'

Winnie took the notes, wide-eyed.

'*But why? We never even asked him.*'

'No, but he'd have known, wouldn't he? He'd have heard all about the potatoes and that we'd be needing money.'

'*But how?*'

'*Sure by now they'll know all about it, up the length and breadth of England. And they'll have had their own blight, they'll know full well what's happening.*'

She slipped the letter to Winnie.

'*Here, you read it, and tell me what he says.*'

Winnie glanced through it.

'*Just what you've said. He'd seen blight in England, and thought we might be needing the money.*'

'*Anything else?*'

'*Not much. Just that he's working well with Danny.*'

'*Does he say anything about that* Irene *woman?*'

'*Nothing at all.*'

The next morning a letter arrived from Castlebar, addressed to Pat. Eleanor gave it to Michael.

'Should we open it?' she asked.

'Better not,' Michael said. He re-addressed the envelope to Pat in England and Eleanor took it to Kilduff to post. There was the usual line of ragged people outside Dillon's, but she did not join them. There was no line outside the post office.

*

That night, she took her turn in guarding the cornfield. There was a half moon, and a slow breeze whispered through the trees.

She was startled by a figure moving towards her.

'*Who's there?*' she shouted.

''*Tis only me.*'

'*Winnie! You gave me a fright.*'

'*Sorry. It's just how I couldn't sleep.*' She sat on the flagstone beside Eleanor. '*I keep thinking about this America business. We've written to Luke last month, like he asked us.*'

'*I know.*'

'*We never said anything of blight. He'll be thinking there's no reason to send money, or very little if he does. Maybe we should write him another letter?*'

'*Arra, will you stop being silly. He'll have news of the blight far faster than any letter of ours. It'd only be a waste of money on a stamp to be telling him what he'd already know, and your last letter he'll have soon enough, so he'll know when to be awaiting you.*'

Sometime later, Michael arrived to take his turn, and Eleanor and Winnie walked down to the house. The moon had set, and vague streaks of green and red flickered above the Mountain.

'So how are you planning on getting to Westport?' Michael asked the next day.

'Walking,' Winnie answered. 'How else?'

'We can't let you do that. It's too far with a baby, and unsafe with the times that are in it.'

'I'll take her across,' Eleanor said.

'How?' Michael asked. 'With the donkey and cart, is it?'

'Well, why not?'

'Why not! The donkey wouldn't get out of Kilduff. They'd have him for meat.'

'What then? What the devil can we do?'

'I'll take her over.'

'You could be attacked too, you know,' Eleanor said.

'I know, but at least a man would have better chances.'

'Well, let's the three of us go.'

'And leave the farm unguarded, is it? No-one to feed the hens, neither.'

'We could ask Kitty down. She's great enough *grá* for little Brigid. Ever since Nessa died, she's almost been like a mother to her. She'd move in here if she could.'

'Maybe, but would that drunken husband of hers allow it?'

'I doubt he'd much care,' Eleanor said.

Eleanor went to visit Kitty. She left early, preferring to meet as few people as possible. As she walked, she saw the villages strung out along the Mountain. Most were half abandoned; ruined cottages where families had died or emigrated. At *Gort na Móna,* she saw the tumbled ruins from Lord Clanowen's evictions the year before, a day that would live in her memory.

She reached a cluster of houses on the edge of the Mountain. Eleanor herself came from the Mountain, and she had a vague memory of this area from twenty years before. There were two ruined houses, brambles and weeds growing alongside and through them. Three houses were left standing. A ragged woman was standing outside one of them.

'*I'm looking for Kitty Brennan,*' Eleanor said.

Wordlessly, the woman pointed her to the next house. Eleanor knocked.

When Kitty answered, Eleanor saw at once the gash on one side of her nose, but said nothing. She explained Winnie's plans.

'*Winnie leaving?*' Kitty gasped.

'*But sure you knew that,*' Eleanor said.

'*Maybe I did, but I didn't want the knowing of it. When do ye want me?*'

'*She's leaving in two days' time. The night before would be a good time to come.*'

'*I'll be there. Ye can rely on it.*'

Eleanor walked back down the Mountain. The sun was well up by now, and she noticed that not all the fields were blighted. It was a patchwork – some tracts, larger or smaller, totally blighted, with many fields and farms between with no blight at all.

She mentioned this to Michael and Winnie that night.

'It won't last,' Michael said. 'Sure the potatoes we took in the other day, they're gone. No, the blight is here and it's going to have a clear run at the potato fields, every damned one of them.'

When Kitty arrived, the gash had healed a little, but her cheeks were bruised.

Michael was furious. 'That's one right bastard of a husband you have.'

'Don't I know it,' Kitty said. 'Sure what choice do I have?' She pointed to the bruising. 'And this was when he heard I was spending a few days with ye.'

'But he let you go,' Eleanor said.

'He did. But only after I had boiled a pot of porridge for him. He had a sack of potatoes too, though I'd say there'll be few enough for the eating.'

Michael and Eleanor drove with Winnie to Westport.

As they left, Kitty's eyes were brimming. Eleanor remembered the impossible love she and Luke once held for one another. But it was all too late. Kitty had already married Fergus. Still, she reflected, Luke had married an able woman, and an agreeable one at that. Kitty knew that too, and the strong friendship between her and Winnie was something Eleanor had never expected.

Kitty stood out on the road, waving to them. A cart full of cadavers followed them towards Kilduff. Three emaciated women followed. Eleanor did not recognise them, but their sunken faces would have changed the look of them.

Kilduff itself was quiet. As they left the town they passed two corpses on the roadside. Many times, they saw feral dogs.

There was little said on the journey. Winnie had Liam in her arms, and tried to rock him to sleep. Eleanor did not want him to see the ghastly sights on the road. She tried to cover his eyes with her shawl, but he kept tearing it away. In the end, she told herself that he was too young to understand. Perhaps.

Still, the blight was incomplete. In the few green fields, wan, wasted families dug desperately. But most fields were blackened, the pungent aroma of blight coming from them, and the unnerving sound of keening.

Close to Castlebar, they overtook gaunt people walking towards the town, some carrying children on their backs, or in turf panniers on their donkeys. Once they passed a donkey carrying a child on either side. One was dead.

Eleanor thought perhaps they should have offered at least one family a place in the cart, but realised as soon as she had thought it that they could have fever.

Castlebar was as filthy as ever, open sewers running brown and green. The town was crowded with donkeys and carts drawn up along the streets. Most carried families with many, many more children.

'So many donkeys,' Winnie exclaimed. 'I'd have thought they'd all be gone for eating by now.'

Michael steered the cart away from the workhouse, avoiding the desperate crowds.

As they left Castlebar, Winnie lay down.

'*I'm tired, mother,*' she said. '*I slept little last night.*'

'*Why didn't you?*'

'*Arra, I don't know. Was it fear? Or maybe the thought of leaving ye all.*'

'*Would you stop being silly,*' Eleanor replied. '*You've got Luke waiting for you on the other side.*'

Within minutes, Winnie was asleep. Eleanor lay back on the sacks alongside her. She closed her eyes, but she did not sleep.

She listened to the crunching of the wheels on the gravel, as Michael drove the donkey. He was a strong man, no doubt about it. Still, what could he do now? What could either of them do? Luke had gone to America, Winnie was following with little Liam, and Eleanor was certain that none of them would return.

Then there was Pat. For many years, she had thought that he would be the one to take over the farm and the quarry, when Michael was no longer able for either. Now he was in England, working with Danny, and she was certain that he would never return. Then she and Michael would have no sons on the farm.

She dozed for an hour. When she awoke, Winnie was leaning on her elbows, looking at her.

'*What were you thinking,*' she asked.

'*I don't know,*' Eleanor said. '*I was half asleep. I was just thinking of all the family, most all of Luke and yourself. It won't be long now. Time for Liam to meet his father.*'

'*Indeed.*'

The cart swayed as one wheel dropped into a hole in the loose gravel. The baby awoke.

'*And look at him,*' Eleanor said. '*The nose of his father, that's for sure.*'

'*I think you're joking,*' Winnie said, as she gave Liam her breast.

Eleanor laughed.

'*Who knows? But there's one other thing on my mind. What about Pat? And what about this Sarah Cronin? I've always thought they were very close.*'

'*They are,*' Winnie said. '*I've little doubt of that.*'

'*Do you think they'll marry though? That's the question, isn't it?*'

'*I don't know,*' Winnie said. '*It all depends on Pat now. What will his station in life be? That's what her mother will be thinking.*'

'*I think you're right,*' Eleanor said. '*But will he stay in England working with Danny, or can he get a good opening here in Mayo? Or Dublin even?*'

'*Hard to say,*' Winnie responded. '*If he comes home, they could marry, but why would he come home? If he gets a place clerking with the County like he was before, then he'll come home and they'll marry for certain. Otherwise he'll stay in England.*'

'*But if he stays working with Danny, would Sarah go to England?*'

'*Who knows?*' Winnie said. '*And that's the real question, isn't it?*'

The cart had stopped.

'What's wrong?' Eleanor asked.

'Would you have a look at this?' Michael replied.

Eleanor and Winnie sat up. Around them was a scene of devastation. There were houses, some fully flattened, most with broken walls, the roofs either collapsed or burnt. Listless creatures were picking through the ruins.

A few soldiers stood by, looking quite bored. There were more sitting alongside a ruined rafter, playing cards; their guns stacked beside them.

'Oh, Mother of God!' Eleanor exclaimed. 'What have they done? What in God's name have they done?'

'Maybe someone can tell us,' Winnie said.

'No,' Eleanor answered, shaking her head in horror. 'Let's just get you to Westport.'

Michael flicked the reins. They drove on in silence. Along the side of the road there was the debris of the eviction – broken furniture, abandoned carts, farm implements too heavy to carry. All the shattered wreckage of an undeclared war.

But Eleanor was already thinking of other things. Sarah was still on her mind. Sarah lived in Westport Workhouse, where her mother worked as Matron.

As they neared Westport, the traffic on the road became heavier, as hundreds trudged the side of the road. Even in the ditches, the evictions went on, as policemen woke sleeping families and forced them to keep walking.

Some had donkeys. As before, many of them carried panniers containing young children, ribs protruding.

They passed one older boy riding a donkey, travelling on his own. His hands and arms were shrunken, his feet blue and horribly swollen. It was clear to Eleanor that he could not control the donkey.

'He'll have no chance of getting inside the workhouse,' Eleanor said.

'Not a hope in hell,' Michael said.

A man stood by a wall, staring hopelessly at the pathetic scene. Eleanor asked him what had happened.

'Lord Lucan's *evictions*,' he answered. '*Kilmaclasser and up by Kilmeena and down towards Islandeady. Dozens of evictions, hundreds, thousands, the Lord knows how many. Lucan has crucified us.*'

They drove towards Westport. Now the line of trudging people had become continuous. They slowed to a walking pace. At Westport, Michael led the donkey, forcing their way through the throngs of animals and humanity, and across to the docks.

When they arrived, Winnie and Eleanor shoved their way through the crowd outside the shipping office, leaving Michael to guard the cart.

The clerk brought his finger down the names.

'A hundred and thirty from Mayo, you know.'

'A good number,' Eleanor said.

'Ah yes, here it is. Winifred Ryan from Kilduff, that's it.'

'It is.'

'It's leaving tomorrow on the tide, about noon time.'

They left.

'So where now?' Michael asked.

'The Workhouse,' Eleanor said. 'Let's visit Sarah.'

'The Workhouse! Are you mad?'

'We can try it at least.'

'We won't get near it.'

He tapped the donkey. As they drew closer, the crowds got denser and denser. Soldiers were keeping order, lined along the outside of the workhouse. Michael stopped and tied the donkey to a rail.

'Here, I'll go,' he said.

'Be careful,' Eleanor said. Already she was feeling doubtful about her idea. The soldiers disturbed her. What was this? A war? Did it take a whole army to control Mayo?

It took a long time for Michael to return.

'Well, what happened?' Winnie asked.

'I got all the way to the gate. Had to ask this soldier fellow – an officer, he was – to let me forward, and even then, there were inmates inside the gate keeping the people out. Anyone trying to climb the gate, they just pushed them back with sticks. But I got close enough to shout a message to one of the guards – told him I was looking for Sarah Cronin, and he heard that right enough. So he went off, returned in a minute and said no one was allowed near the infirmary. I told him Sarah wasn't working in the infirmary, but he wouldn't have any of it.'

'I didn't think Sarah was working in the infirmary, right enough,' Winnie said.

'Neither did I,' Eleanor answered. 'I'd understood she was in some class of clerking, but maybe she's not. I know with her mother being Matron and that, she'd be in the infirmary often enough. Maybe Sarah was working there too.'

'That would be dangerous,' Winnie said.

'It would. I hope she hasn't got fever.'

'We can only pray.'

Michael untied the donkey, and backed the cart into the road.

'So where now,' he asked.

'We'll have to find somewhere to stay the night.' Eleanor said. 'Not back the way we came though.'

'You're right,' Michael said. He flicked the reins and followed around the side of the docks until he picked up a road heading west, with Clew Bay on their right. Half way between the coast and a small island, a three masted ship was under sail, a long bowsprit extending from the prow, seagulls wheeling behind it.

'It might well be yours,' Eleanor said.

'It might, mother.'

'What does it say there along the front?'

Winnie squinted, holding her hand to shield her eyes against the setting sun.

'Vega. It's the Vega.'

'And below?'

'Philadelphia. That's where it's owned, I'd say.'

'A good-looking ship, in any case,' Michael said.

They looked for somewhere to bed down. It was clear that no one wanted to take them in.

'Disease,' Michael said. 'They're terrified we'd have fever.'

'I wouldn't blame them,' Eleanor said.

At length, one farmer brought them to an outside shed where there were no beggars sleeping.

'There's enough hay, so ye may rest easy,' he said.

'We will,' Michael replied.

Next morning, they drove back to the quays. The Vega had berthed.

The crowd of people at the quayside were very different to those outside the workhouse. These people were not starving, though many were weeping.

Michael unloaded Winnie's packs. A group of three girls were waiting on the quayside. They were better dressed than most. One broke away and came over to Winnie.

'*Oh, would you look at the little baby,*' she said. '*Is it a he or a she?*'

'*A he.*'

'*Is he coming too?*'

'*He is,*' Winnie said. '*Just the two of us.*'

'*Why don't ye travel with us then, yourself and the baby?*'

'*What are you on about,*' one of the other girls said. '*That little scamp would keep us awake all night.*'

'*Arra, would you stop that kind of nonsense,*' the first girl said. '*He'll be well looked after between the lot of us. How old is he?*'

'*Nine months,*' Winnie said.

Already there were whistles blowing. Eleanor was surprised when Michael took Liam and kissed his forehead. She was even more surprised when Michael handed the baby to her, and hugged Winnie tightly.

'Make sure to come back and visit us,' he said, 'and make sure to bring that husband of yours with you.'

'I will,' Winnie said, 'I promise.'

She boarded the ship with the three girls. Eleanor bit her lip. How long would the ship really take to reach New York? And when would they return? Winnie had promised, but what of that? They would never return, Luke neither.

Her eyes were wet. *Go cold. It can't be helped.*

They stood on the dock with the crowd, waving, as Winnie waved Liam's tiny hand from the deck. Then the ship was moving. It sailed out through the islands of Clew Bay and into the Atlantic Ocean.

Chapter 2

The Pilot, Dublin. August 1848:

Shrule, Co. Mayo. Blight in 1848! 450 houses levelled. From Michael Phew, Parish Priest. It is awful to know, as I do, that within the circumference of four miles in this district, that there are no less than 450 houses levelled within the last three months, and the families residing in these houses were tossed out of them, and are now to be seen by the ditches and roadsides without any shelter in the shape of a cabin to keep them warm by day or by night, and without even half enough to eat, looking like spectres, moving skeletons, crawling along the highways. May the great and merciful God commiserate with them in their wants!

Eleanor and Michael made for home. He took side streets to avoid the workhouse. Many were open sewers stinking with shit and piss, but even so, families sat or slept along the walls at the side.

They cleared Westport, driving out the road towards Castlebar. As they passed the wall surrounding Lord Sligo's estate, Michael pointed out where their convoy had been attacked a year or two before, as they had returned, carrying relief corn from the Westport docks, to the soup kitchens in Kilduff.

'You never spoke much about that,' Eleanor observed.

'Maybe I didn't want to. It's a hard thing fighting starving men and women.'

'But if you hadn't fought them, the corn would never have made Kilduff, and our own people would have been starving. Wasn't that the way of it?'

'True for you,' Michael said. 'But it was a savage battle, I can tell you. One fellow near killed me with a rock, but Luke got him first.'

Outside Westport, most of the houses between the wreckage were mere mud cabins. The people were digging potatoes in the afternoon sunshine, but while a small number of fields were untouched by blight, most were already black. Eleanor thought there were more blackened fields than when they had come in, but perhaps she was imagining it.

What kind of people were these? The kind of starving men and women who had attacked the Kilduff convoy. No different here than all around Kilduff though, or Carrigard either. They were not even tenants, she guessed, and doubted that any could read or write, nor sign their name beyond an 'X'. Not to say that she herself could read well, not like the rest of her family. Eleanor herself came from the Mountain, and there was little call for reading or writing there. But, as with so many around Carrigard, these people here would never even see money. Their small ridges of potatoes were all they had, and rent was paid in labour, not in cash. And now the potatoes were gone; once again, they had nothing.

Beyond Westport, it was raining. 'Let's shelter a while, Michael,' she said.

Among the shattered houses, they spotted one where the roof had collapsed in the centre but still clung to the walls at the gable end.

'In here,' he said.

It was dark inside and Michael stood at the splintered window, holding the donkey. As Eleanor's eyes became accustomed to the dark, she realized there were people inside. One woman and four children. A heap of rags lay in the corner. She could hear the squeaking of rats, and smell the stink of rotting flesh.

'*Ocras,*' the woman murmured. Hunger.

But Eleanor knew they had little to give. Did they provide charity, or did they protect themselves? A hard question.

'*What has happened here?*' she asked.

'*The agents of* Lord Lucan,' the woman whispered. '*They would have us here no longer. They drove us from the houses.*'

'*A terrible thing.*'

'*Worse than terrible. A violent afternoon, wet and windy, and the night the same. I lost one of my daughters that night. But when the tumblers had done their work, we crept back in here and stayed since. And now my son. He has died too.*'

'*God help us all,*' Eleanor said.

They left before the rain had stopped. Eleanor could no longer bear being there, though she did not want to upset the woman by leaving too soon. But they had to.

'We didn't leave them any food,' she said.

'That's right, we didn't,' Michael said. 'We've little enough of our own.'

'I know.'

In Castlebar, they saw the same scenes as in Westport, as wasted people slogged towards the workhouse. There was much military activity in the town, far more than before. The military barracks was heavily guarded.

'It wasn't like that, and we going out,' Michael said.

'No indeed,' Eleanor said. 'I wonder why it is now.'

More dead bodies in the streets. Even more out the road towards Kilduff. The rain had cleared, and at last the sun came out, steam rising from Michael's shirt.

It was dark when they arrived in Kilduff. A waning moon hung in the sky. No more bodies in the streets, though perhaps it was just too dark to see them.

In Carrigard, the house was warm. Kitty held her finger to her lips.

'She's asleep, don't be waking her now.'

She took three cups and a bottle of *poitín*.

'There's strange news afoot.'

'What's that,' Eleanor asked.

'There's revolution,' Kitty said. 'The country is in rebellion.'

Michael looked up. 'What's that you say?'

'Revolution,' Kitty said. 'They're all talking of it. There's desperate fighting going on in Tipperary and Kilkenny, thousands of people fighting the police and army. They're burning the trains, and there's places the army is refusing to fight.'

'Is it war?' Eleanor asked.

'It is. And it'd be more of a war if the army would stand and fight.'

'Who told you all this?' Michael asked.

'We went up to town yesterday, Brigid and myself. The cattle drovers, they're talking of nothing else. They're saying Dublin is to be taken over too. They're wanting change in the government. They're saying we won't have to pay any rent anymore.'

'I wish I could believe that,' Michael said, 'but I don't think I'll live to see that day. I saw enough of '98. They slaughtered us then, and they'll slaughter us now.'

The day dawned bright, with a near cloudless sky.

Over the shoulder of the Mountain, Nephin stood sharp; brown against blue. Kitty and Eleanor stood outside the half door.

'*I'd better go home, and feed the brute,*' Kitty said. '*I don't know that he's able to cook for himself, the state of him.*'

Eleanor handed her a groat.

'*Fourpence might help.*'

'*Arra, not at all. Sure it was a pleasure feeding little Brigid, and having the odd bit of your food.*'

But Eleanor insisted. Kitty took the coin, and left to walk home to the side of the Mountain.

Eleanor went up towards the cornfield to call Michael for his breakfast. She was surprised to see him scything.

'I thought we'd better make a start, seeing as the day that's in it,' he said. 'We mightn't get more days like this.'

The corn was harvested rapidly. It was now the only immediate source of food on the farm. The weather was warm and continued so. Every morning, Michael was up before sunrise, and Eleanor accompanied him. Mostly, it was Michael who scythed the corn, but sometimes he would pass the scythe to Eleanor while he rested.

She carried Brigid up to the fields, lying her in a blanket, where she slept till sunrise and played most of the day. She, at least, thought it was all fun, chasing the frogs that leapt out ahead of the scythe.

They worked long hours, from sunup to sundown. As the scything progressed, the sheaves of corn were stooked, and before the harvesting was finished, the early stooked corn was already being threshed.

Every night, one of them stood guard high up by the rath, where all the fields and house could be seen from one single vantage point. As the weather continued warm, the nights were clear. On one occasion, Eleanor thought she saw movement in the fields, but when she came closer, there was no one there, or perhaps there had been, but he had left. She slept late that morning, leaving Michael to work on his own.

She was proud of Michael's strength as a scytheman. Most men could manage a half acre a day, but Michael cut half as much again through the long, long days. Whatever his age, he could still work hard. When she was younger, he used to entertain her with stories of working with other Mayo men on the English harvests, during the time of the French wars.

And then it was over. The corn was saved. That night, the rains started.

'And, by God, that was good timing,' Michael said.

The corn too was taken into the house where it could not be stolen. Michael decided they should keep it, and pay the rent using the money from Luke and Pat. Eleanor knew the high price of corn had tempted him to sell some at least of what he had, but that would destroy their own food reserves. For the next months, they must depend on Pat. It was hardly a month since Luke's last letter with the remittance, most of which had been spent on Winnie's ticket for New York. She doubted there would be another letter from America for some time. Either way though, their own food reserves and their reserves of cash meant that the family would not starve.

She thought again about Michael's insistence on always paying the rent, regardless of any other calls for cash. What would happen if they refused? Was Mr. Burke in a position to do anything about it if they did? Or would he be ruthless enough to evict them? In the end, she knew she had no say in the matter. Michael would pay the rent, and there was no question of their being evicted.

29

But if the Ryans were secure, they lived in an ocean of increasing horror. Yes, there were other families who were receiving remittances from England and America, but these were few, and with many of them the few shillings received could never be enough.

The stories filtered back to Carrigard in different ways. Whenever Kitty came down, she brought desperate stories from the Mountain and the farms around. On one occasion, Michael walked five miles to Knockanure to buy a spade handle. She guessed that he was only walking off his own powerlessness. When he returned, he was quieter than before and would not discuss what he had seen or heard, either in Knockanure or on the road.

But the early talk of revolution had died down. Kitty did not mention it again on any of her visits, but that was not surprising since she lived well out of town, and was not close to sources of news. In any case, starvation around the Mountain was worse, and people had other things to think of.

One morning, when Eleanor was in Kilduff, she called into McKinnons' on her way home.

The bar was dark, with a candle burning at either end of the counter. Four men sat around a table by the far wall, smoking at clay pipes with their drink. It was warm, and the fireplace was empty, stacked sods of turf alongside.

Sabina looked morose. This surprised Eleanor. Michael's sister was not one to be easily put down. She handed Eleanor a gin, and waved away Eleanor's coin.

'Not that there's much other business,' she said. 'The fellows down the end, they nurse their pints all day. All they talk of is the rebellion in Ballingarry, and I'm sick of it.'

'I'm sure you are, but we hear nothing.'

'*Arra* what. They were all on about it for weeks, they're much quieter now. Damned if I know what's happening.'

There was less need for Eleanor to go to Kilduff now. They had enough corn for now, but sometimes she bought a few pounds at Dillon's, if only to listen to the talk of the women around her. In many ways, it troubled her, and even put her at risk of fever. Still, she had to keep abreast of what was happening in Mayo, and through the women's gossip, she heard the reality of famine.

The failure of the potato had caused outright panic. The appearance of the potatoes in June and July had brought back confidence, but the total blight of August resulted in terror. Many people resigned themselves to death, but others fought for life.

She knew too that all the workhouses were either penniless, or close to it. She heard that roadworks for Famine Relief had started again, but it was as nothing compared to what it had been in the winter of '46. Starvation was back, and with it, fever. Week by week, the number of deaths climbed. Now, she heard no one was being buried with coffins, and very few were even buried in churchyards. The priests tried to bring more corpses to trenches within consecrated ground. But, as the level of deaths soared, these too were filled, and new trenches were dug out along the Castlebar road, and hastily blessed. And still, the death carts clattered past Carrigard, jangling her nerves.

The women in the corn line were panicked by fever, and often no one would even approach houses or cabins where it was known to be present. Families died in total isolation. Sometimes the houses were tumbled over them, sometimes they were not. Many were buried in ditches and bog holes by people who were too scared to give them a proper burial. The rats feasted on the remains. She did not need the women to tell her this. Every time she went to Kilduff, she heard the squeaking from the ruins of the cabins, and from the ditches along the road where bodies and skeletons still lay.

And the flight from the land went on. Hordes of people passed through Kilduff and Carrigard.

'Erris and Achill, that's where they're all coming from,' Sabina said one day. 'Partry too, I've heard.'

'You're right,' Eleanor said. 'And you know what I'm thinking, there's many out there who'll never make Dublin, let alone Liverpool.'

'There's many won't even make it out of Mayo.'

She lay awake that night, listening to the wind rustling the leaves among the ash and birch trees.

Sabina was right, she thought. *And it's not just young people that are fleeing. Now the babies and old people escape with them. They dream of America, but there's crowds of them will never get that far, nor nowhere near it. Even if they make it to the ports, the fever ships are waiting; death stalks the ocean trails. Oh God.*

Were they the guilty ones? They were guilty of nothing. What difference does it make to You? What difference did it ever make to You? Guilty or not, they'll suffer Your anger and pay Your price.

Oh, to hell with it, I'll have to stop thinking like this. It only upsets me.

Chapter 3

Manchester Times, July 1848:
Liverpool. Several thousand special constables have been sworn in, and for the last few days the police have been exercised in the use of firearms, in addition to the sword exercise, and, liking the task, have attained great efficiency. About 600 additional policemen have been appointed. The additional soldiery who have already arrived are the entire regiment with the exception of one company of the 9th Infantry, three companies of the 31st Infantry, and three or four troops of the 4th Royal Irish Dragoons. A brigade of artillery has also arrived from Chester; and an official communication has been received that another body of 1,000 men will arrive here direct from London. Several hundreds of the servants of the Dock Trust have been sworn in as special constables, and a strong extra guard has been placed around the docks. Several thousand stand of arms have been received from Chester.

Danny was dead.

Pat was stunned. Since he had come to England again some months before, he had been working with his cousin, and he knew Danny as a ruthless man. Scrupulous too. Yet here he was being told that Danny had had an accident on the railways. That such an accident could have happened on the Manchester & Birmingham Line was bewildering for two reasons. First, none of Danny's contracts were on that line, so why was he there? Second, it had happened on one of the longest straights in England. How could Danny have fallen under a train that would have been visible for miles? Had he been drunk or what?

It fell to Murtybeg to identify Danny's corpse, but he asked Pat to accompany him. As the clerks went on their eleven o'clock break, they stepped outside, and flagged down a hansom cab.

'You've no idea how thankful I am,' Murtybeg said. 'This is not going to be easy.'

'I know,' Pat said. 'Your own brother...'

'Yes, it's rough. Not that it'd be much easier on you. Still, I think you're more used to this kind of thing than I am.'

'Because I lived longer in Mayo?'

'Perhaps. But still, we've both got to face it. Danny killed himself.'

'But how can we know that?'

'We can't know for sure. The police say he stood out on the track, straight in front of the train, as if he knew what he was doing. Leastwise, that's what they say the driver said.'

'He would say that, wouldn't he?' Pat said. 'Do you believe him though?'

'I don't know,' Murtybeg said, 'I'm inclined to believe him. It's like I told you, Danny was under giant pressure, between the business and Irene.'

'Yes,' Pat said, 'even I knew that.'

'That woman, she had him where she wanted him. That's what it was. Danny knew he had no chance. He had to marry her, and that was an end to it. If he tried anything else, she'd bring the business down. You know, Pat, it's a strange thing when you think about it. Most men might look forward to marriage, and with good reason. But Danny was terrified of it.'

'It's hard to believe,' Pat said.

'Hard enough. We all thought of Danny as a right tough fellow, but I don't know, these tough men are never quite what they seem.'

'I know. I've met fellows like that. Hard as nails on the outside, but it's all for show. Hiding what they really are.'

'You're right. But, like I say, there were other burdens on him.'

'Like what?'

'The Manchester & Salford Bank. He was in some kind of trouble with them, but what it was, I've no idea.'

'I didn't know that.'

'For God's sake, Pat, do you not see what's under your own eyes.'

'I haven't been here as long.'

'I know. But I think there was worse than that.'

'What, in God's name, could be worse?' Pat asked.

'That Inspector fellow who kept calling.'

'Wasn't that about the killings on the railway works?'

'It was.'

'But sure that was nothing to do with Danny. Surely you're not saying...'

'That's just what I'm saying, Pat. I think Danny was more tied up in those killings than we thought.'

'Danny!'

'Even worse, I reckon the Molly Maguire gang was part of it.'

Pat sat back in silence, looking out at the streets of Stockport. There were beggars on every corner. Irish? What else?

What Murtybeg said had really stunned him. Had Danny really been in trouble with the Bank? And with the law? Working with the worst Irish gang in England. Impossible.

They were coming to the morgue.

They paid off the cabbie and went inside. The mortuary attendant brought them down a long corridor and opened a steel door into a long, white-tiled room. Light poured in through six windows along one wall. Along the other wall were six benches, two with uncovered cadavers, one male, one female. Two canvases covered more cadavers, feet protruding. Each had a label tied to a toe. On one bench, there was only one foot, bloodied and broken. The label read 'Daniel Ryan. Male.'

Even with all he had seen of famine in Mayo, Pat was not prepared for the shock when the canvas was whipped back. Danny's body was shredded and covered in dried blood, turning brown. What remained had been pushed together to give some appearance of a human form.

'It's what happens to all of them,' the attendant said. 'Step in front of a train and they think it's all over, just like that. What they forget is what happens to the body afterwards. The train takes hundreds of yards to stop, and rips them to bits as it does.'

'You think he killed himself?' Murtybeg asked.

'That's what I heard. It's what the driver said. He just stood out between the tracks, of his own free will.'

Murtybeg slumped forward, but caught the edge of the bench and steadied himself.

'How did you know his name?' Pat asked.

'There was a contract of some sort in his pocket, with his name and address on it.'

'Where is it now?'

The man shrugged. 'The police might have it.'

'No letter?'

'None.'

Murtybeg was weeping. Pat wondered how long it was since he had last done that. Not since they were children. Or was it? He remembered the time he had brought Murtybeg to Knockanure Workhouse to recruit inmates as railway navvies. Murtybeg had broken down on that occasion, but the sight of the mass grave at the back of the workhouse was enough to break any man who was not used to it.

He put his arm around Murtybeg's shoulder.

'Come on, Murteen. Time to go.'

'You haven't identified him,' the attendant said.

Murtybeg couldn't speak, but simply nodded his head.

'That's Daniel Ryan right enough,' Pat said. 'No doubt about it.'

The man took a pen, dipped it in ink, and handed it to Pat.

'Sign here.'

Pat signed. He passed the pen to Murtybeg, took his hand, and brought it to the paper.

'Just here, Murteen.'

Murtybeg signed, and they left.

Pat hailed a cab.

'Well, what do you think, Pat?' Murtybeg asked. 'Did he fall, was he pushed, or did he do it himself?'

Pat shook his head in bewilderment. 'There's only one answer, Murteen. He did it of his own wish. But damn it to hell, I still find it hard to believe.'

Murtybeg said nothing more and was silent all the way back to Stockport.

Dinner too was a silent affair. Murtybeg said little, beyond confirming to Irene that he had identified Danny's corpse. Pat was thinking of their shock when the attendant had shown them the corpse. Did men like that enjoy the drama of that moment. A body torn asunder under a train. Many a tougher man would have found it hard to take the sight of a train-kill. Worse than the fever dead in Mayo? Perhaps.

But he was thinking of other things too. He could not take his eyes off Irene. Yes, she was a good-looking woman, with a striking figure, and the black dress highlighted her figure far more. Once, he thought he saw Murtybeg looking at Irene in the same way, but dismissed it from his mind. Murtybeg had been too overcome by the day's events.

But what of Irene? No tears! He had always reckoned her a tough woman, but this poise, this self-control, was something he had never seen in a woman before. Coldness in the face of death.

Had Danny really been frightened of her? He had reckoned Danny as being a tough man, and Irene was surely tough too. A match made in heaven? Perhaps not. He could think of marriages that were poisoned because both husband and wife had been like that, and could never agree. What Murtybeg had suggested was different though. Irene was the tougher one, and she had controlled Danny in a way that drove him to kill himself.

There was another factor though. Danny's parents had left him. Murty was Danny's own father – Murtybeg's too – and he held that the way Edwardes & Ryan was being managed was wrong. Immoral, even. He saw the way Danny and Irene were importing cheap, starving Mayo labour from the west coast of Ireland. In the end, Murty had not been able to take it, and working with the Gilligan gang on the Leeds & Thirsk railway was far preferable to working with Edwardes & Ryan, Danny's own business. That must have been a real slap in the face for Danny.

And Murtybeg, for that matter.

After dinner, Pat and Murtybeg stayed behind.

Murtybeg fetched two glasses from the cupboard. Crystal glass, as Pat noted. Waterford perhaps? Danny had been trying to create an impression, essential, as he had understood it, to a man who was rising in the world as a labour contractor on the railways.

Without asking, Murtybeg poured brandy. His hands were trembling, and the neck of the bottle rattled against the glass as he poured. He handed a glass to Pat.

Pat sipped at it. Even with no knowledge of brandies, he knew it was of a high quality.

'I'm sorry,' Murtybeg said. 'That all gave me a hell of a shock.'

'I know,' Pat said, 'Sure I wasn't much better myself.'

'And father and mother. One way or another, I'm going to have to tell them. I'll have to write.'

'What'll you say?'

'Just that Danny met with an accident. We don't need to say any more.'

'It'll be a terrible blow to them.'

'I know,' Murtybeg said. 'Father is strong, though. But Mother? You know how feeble she is.'

When Murtybeg had finished, Pat wrote to Michael in Carrigard, only saying that Danny was dead, without any further information. As he was writing, Murtybeg sat on a chair by the empty grate. Then he gulped back the rest of the brandy.

'I'm going to bed,' he said.

'I'll follow after,' Pat said.

At last, he finished the letter. Then he went and stood outside the house, staring at the stars over the viaduct and the mills.

What was his future now? Could he work alongside a woman like Irene? Could Murtybeg?

The next morning, Pat was surprised when Murtybeg told him there was to be a meeting with Irene in the boardroom. He was more surprised to note that Irene sat in Danny's seat. She was still dressed as a widow. But she was no widow. She and Danny had never married.

Murtybeg made to speak, but then said nothing.

'Well,' Irene said, 'back to business. Let's see what the figures are looking like now. Pat – you've been going through them, haven't you? Eighty men gone. What's our nett outgoings now? Are we still losing cash?'

'We are,' Pat said. 'The drop in prices on the Anderson contracts will be more than we had supposed.'

'I know,' she said, 'and we've another problem too. The loan is on overdraft only. The Manchester & Salford could call it in at any time.'

'Danny never told me that.'

'Perhaps he didn't want you to know.'

'So what should we do?'

'There's only one thing we can do. Let more workers go. Will you see to it?'

'I'll have a word with Johnny Roughneen straight away.'

Murtybeg had said nothing. He was staring at Irene in an odd sort of way. Wondering perhaps at how a woman could control her grief like that. Or have none.

At Danny's funeral, Irene put on a superb performance. Again, she was in black. Her dress was tight, and she wore a black, translucent veil, swept back with her long hair.

Pat was a little surprised that she could weep after all, but was it genuine? She sat in the front pew, accepting condolences alongside Murtybeg and Pat – the line went on forever.

He thought it odd that she could do all this in a Catholic Church. Perhaps it was all a front. Many of the men and women in the line were sub-contractors to Edwardes & Ryan, and Pat had little doubt they were concerned about the future of the business.

There were others too. Roy Anderson was there. He was a larger contractor in the Manchester area. He was the man who had given Danny his first contract in 1846. How Anderson & Co. might be doing in the present market was an open question, but Anderson did not seem to be concerned. He was the one who had reduced prices to Danny. He did appear to be genuine in his sorrow though.

Murtybeg's parents had not been there, but as they carried the coffin down the aisle, Pat saw Murty usher Aileen into a pew at the back of the church. Murty nodded to them as they passed. After they had lowered the coffin onto the hearse, Pat found them in the crowd. Roughneen was already talking to them. He went across. Aileen was weeping. Pat embraced her.

'I'm sorry we're so late,' Murty said. 'The trains were running late, and with this crowd, it was near on impossible to fight our way into the church.'

'I understand,' Pat said.

Murty took his arm, as they made their way out of the crowd.

'How could this have happened, Pat?' Murty asked. 'Danny was careful, not a man for accidents.'

'It was no accident.'

Murty's eyes opened wide. 'Murder!'

'Madness, more like, Danny killed himself.'

Murty's chin dropped. He took some time to compose himself.

'Killed himself?'

'Yes.'

'But why…but how could they know?'

'We can't be certain,' Pat said. 'That's what the train driver said, I understand.'

'But why in hell…?'

'Sure you know enough about it yourself. The markets are dropping, the railways are cutting back, the business is in a tough way. That's if Danny showed you what was going on. I know you had some idea, but from what I hear, there were other things too. The Manchester & Salford Bank – there was a lot of money owing.'

'But did no one know about this?'

'Irene did. And I reckon she was another burden on him.'

'A burden?'

'One hell of a burden. He was just a few weeks from marrying her. Murtybeg reckons he wanted out of it, but he couldn't see how.'

'But why not?'

'Who do you think is running the business? And always was, ever since she arrived.'

'A tough lady, eh?'

'Damned tough. But sure we always knew that.'

'So what now?'

'God only knows,' Pat said. 'But tell me this. Aunty Aileen? How's she taking it?'

Murty turned away from him for a moment. He turned back, not looking at Pat.

'Well, you know what Aileen's like. Do you know, she hasn't said a single word since we left the house? No crying, just hush.'

Murtybeg ran over.

'Would you come over, you two. We've been looking for you everywhere.'

They returned to where the cortège was forming and mounted the carriage behind the hearse. Irene and Aileen were already sitting side by side in silence. Pat observed Aileen closely, all the way to the graveyard and during the interment. He knew the silence was only a passive surface hiding the turmoil beneath.

But what was Irene thinking?

*

Murty and Aileen stayed in the hotel beside Stockport Station. The next morning, Pat and Murtybeg joined them for breakfast in the hotel.

Again, Pat embraced Aileen. 'I'm sorry, Aunty Aileen.'

'*He was my son,*' she murmured in Irish. '*Whatever he's done.*'

Murty looked up, surprised that Aileen had spoken. '*He was, alanna,*' he said. '*He was our son.*'

They sat down to breakfast.

'How are you finding the Leeds & Thirsk?' Murtybeg asked.

'As good as can be,' Murty answered. 'As you know, I'm working as a clerk with Gilligan and the lads. They ask no labour of me, though sometimes I give them a hand out with the shovelling. Nothing near as fast as those fellows though. Not at my age.'

'Your age?' Pat asked.

'Sixty. Sixty-one close enough. Who cares?'

'You're better than most, so. There's many a navvy would be well past it by that age.'

'Me too,' Murty said. 'Still, digging the potatoes back home gave me some amount of practice. But I'll never know how those fellows can keep going the way they do. They're all powerful men. There's only one snag though. Our contract on the railway will be coming to an end. We're hoping that Gilligan will be able to get another one for us, but who knows.'

Murtybeg looked at him in alarm. 'But could ye get another contract with Brassey? That's the question, isn't it?'

'It is. There's talk of contracts in and around Bradford, but I don't know if they'd be Brassey contracts. And if they're not, we'd not be able to work as a gang in the way we're used to. And there sure as hell wouldn't be any call for a clerk.'

'Yes,' Murtybeg said, 'it could be a difficult state of affairs.' He leaned back in his chair. 'Would you not come back working with Edwardes & Ryan? I know it's a hard thing to say, but Danny's gone. Wasn't it him you had the differences with?'

'Him and his woman.'

'But I'll be running the place now.'

'Will you?' Murty asked. 'Will you really? Will you end up the kind of man that Danny was? Or will that damned bitch of a woman break you too?'

For some days now, news had been trickling across the Irish Sea. Blight again? That was hardly surprising. There was already blight in the English potato crop, and Pat knew at some time it would have to arrive in Ireland. He was sending money to his own family, three pounds a few weeks ago. In some ways that settled his conscience. But what about all the other people around Carrigard and Kilduff? Who knows? And the rumours now were frightening.

He walked into Stockport and bought another money order for two pounds to send to Carrigard.

Should he be sending so much, though? Could he really afford it?

Could he afford not to?

But the Famine was not his only concern. Danny's suicide would change Edwardes & Ryan. That was for certain. The thought of working under a woman like Irene disturbed him even more than before. He suspected there would be some kind of power struggle within the business. The question was – would Irene or Murtybeg come out on top? And even if Murtybeg won out, how could he do it? He would have to be rough to take on a woman like Irene. What kind of man could do that? Could Pat work under Murtybeg in the future?

He decided to wait it out, and see. But then a letter arrived that changed everything.

Murtybeg handed it to him.

'Castlebar and Kilduff. It's been redirected.'

Pat took it. 'Looks like father's writing underneath.'

He slit the envelope open.

'It's from Gaffney.'

'The fellow we met in the Union in Castlebar?'

'That's right. Seems from his letter he doesn't know I'm in England though. He's heard I lost my job at the Union in Knockanure. That's why he wrote to me at Carrigard. He's offering me a post in Castlebar.'

'In Castlebar!' Murtybeg echoed.

'Well, based in Castlebar perhaps. They're looking for someone to ride around the County and make reports back to Castlebar. He wants someone to talk to the Unions, talk to the priests, and observe.'

'Observe? Strange word.'

'That's his word. He wants someone who's not afraid to go into cabins, and see how the people are. Report back on hunger, fever, crops, burials, evictions – anything and everything. And I must say, the money isn't bad either. Three shillings a day, by God.'

'That's far less than we're paying you.'

'It is,' Pat said, 'but even so, it's a good wage, and I'll be able to help father on the farm.'

'But why you? There's many another in Mayo would jump at it.'

'He doesn't say anything about that. Still, I'm guessing it's because he knows me already from all the times I've met him and knows I've good practise at clerking in Knockanure Union. I think too, the fact that I'm Luke's brother would have weighed in his thinking. He knew Luke well.'

'So what will you do?'

'I'll think about it.'

Once again, Pat was torn. In some ways, he had come over to England against his better judgement, especially in view of Danny's ways of working. In the end, he had adjusted to this and had compromised in the very same way as Murtybeg had. He thought back to the navvy's moll he had once met in a shack on the railway. '*You're no better than the rest of them,*' she had said, after he carried out Danny's sackings. She had been right. Had he compromised too much?

Irene was still in his thoughts. He was beginning to think, much as he and Murtybeg might resist, she was going to be the real power in Edwardes & Ryan. In many ways, she was at a disadvantage as a woman, since the rough-cut contractors and railway negotiators would not deal with women. But she had Murtybeg and Pat to do that. Roughneen and Lavan too. As against this, her tough negotiations with the horse dealers, the timber merchants and the other traders who supplied Edwardes & Ryan showed a ruthlessness that few men ever expected, but that Pat and Murtybeg knew all too well. Danny too, before he had killed himself.

There were other good reasons for accepting Gaffney's offer.

Carrigard was one. He would be needed on the farm, if not now, later.

And Sarah was another.

Before he left Ireland, they were beginning to plan their lives together. Now, she was in Mayo, and he was in Stockport. Sarah was an attractive woman, there was no doubt about that. Would other men see her in the same way? Most certainly. If he really wanted to win Sarah, he would have to return.

There was one single reason against returning.

Gaffney wanted Pat to observe Mayo, and Pat was frightened of what he might observe.

For a few days, he thought about it, and discussed it with Murtybeg, who had been sworn to secrecy. At length, he decided for Mayo and wrote to Gaffney, indicating his acceptance. Within a week, he had a reply confirming his position.

He wrote to his mother and father to inform them he was returning, and a similar letter to Sarah in Westport.

Irene, when he told her, did not seem in any way concerned. Pat knew that Murtybeg was the one who was really worried. As long as Pat was with him, he had some strength against her. With Pat gone, it would be hard to predict how matters might turn out between Murtybeg and Irene.

41

The next day, matters changed again. He received a letter direct from Sarah. He saw from the date that they had crossed in the post – she had written to him on the same day as he had written to her. He opened it in pleasant anticipation, but what he received was a shock.

Sarah's mother, Mrs. Cronin, was opposed to any further contact.

As head Matron in Westport Workhouse, she saw Sarah's future in better terms than being married to a railway labourer. It appeared, that while Mrs. Cronin might have once been satisfied with Pat, that was when he was a clerk in what, at the time, was a permanent position. But his salary as a clerk in Knockanure Workhouse had dropped according as the workhouse moved closer to bankruptcy. It would be impossible to explain all that to Mrs. Cronin. He was earning far more with Edwardes & Ryan than he could in any clerical position in County Mayo. Nor was he a labourer, as Sarah herself pointed out in her letter, but it was impossible to convince Mrs. Cronin of this.

Now Gaffney had invited him back to Mayo in a good position. The only problem was that Pat suspected that this would not be a permanent position. Then what future would there be when he was no longer a clerk in Mayo? Return to England? Or farm again in Mayo? Either way, Mrs. Cronin would not consent, that much was clear, and Pat could not expect Sarah to go against her own mother.

He decided to say nothing to anyone. He was too hurt to think clearly.

Next morning, Murtybeg accompanied him to the station in a cab.

'Don't you have work to do?' Pat asked.

'I'm sure Edwardes & Ryan can do without me for an hour.'

'I wouldn't know about that. That woman'll have taken it over – lock, stock and barrel – if you're away too long a time.'

Murtybeg slapped him on the back.

'Well, thank God, we're still able to laugh.'

At the station, a troop of cavalry stood across the street. They were being led by an officer, who wore a blue uniform with red piping, a Maltese cross on his shako. He was riding a tall chestnut horse, which pranced forward and back. Nervous perhaps? The officer made no attempt to control it, though the horses behind all stood in line, unmoving.

'Who the devil are they?' Pat asked the cabbie.

'Those fellows, sir? That's the Cheshire Yeomanry.'

'What are they doing over here so? Aren't they based in Chester.'

'Oh, they are, but these lot, they'll be the Stockport Troop. They're based right here. They're well spread around, the Cheshires are. They keep them in reserve so as to send them in whenever there's trouble. They were in the

Peterloo massacre. A savage lot. Pack of bloody murderers.'

'That was all a long time ago,' Pat commented.

'Twenty or thirty years, who knows? They'll never be forgotten for it though. And whenever there's trouble – Liverpool, Manchester, Bradford, Leeds or wherever – they'll have those fellows in. They're off back to Chester now, I understand. Something to do with revolution in Ireland.'

'Just because you know my accent...'

'No, sir, it's what they're saying. It's all over town. Though for my tuppence worth, I reckon it's just an excuse to get them nearer to Liverpool. There's talk of rioting there too.'

Murtybeg paid off the cab, and they walked around the horses and into the station.

'Was he serious?' Pat asked.

'What?'

'That bit about revolution in Ireland.'

'Damned if I know, though he seemed to know enough about it.'

Pat bought the ticket. They both walked along the platform. Pat stepped into the carriage and stood by his pack inside the door.

'You take care of yourself, Murteen,' he said. 'And watch your back.'

'I will.'

The train pulled out towards Manchester. The Manchester & Birmingham Line. The one that killed Danny. Let's not think about that.

In Manchester, he changed for Liverpool. He settled into a comfortable carriage for the journey.

Going home to Mayo at last. Soon to meet the family. He knew his remittances had been vital, but what of the price of corn? Did they have enough to last out the winter?

Lime Street Station. Liverpool at last.

As the train came to a halt, he was not surprised to see more of the Cheshire Yeomanry disembarking from an open train on the other side of the platform. What did surprise him was the artillery; with horses yoked up to the gun carriages and the ammunition caissons. Already, a crowd was gathering around them.

'That'll sort the bloody Irish out,' a woman in front of him said. 'They'll have enough of their bloody revolutions by the time our fellows are finished with them.'

Pat did not reply. He had no desire for his accent to be recognized.

One of the women tapped a young yeoman on the shoulder. 'When are ye sailing?'

'We're not sailing at all,' the soldier replied. 'We're for Liverpool, not for Ireland.'

'Liverpool? Are you mad?'

'You don't have to go all the way to Ireland to find Irish rebels, you know. There's plenty of them here in Liverpool. But don't worry. They've thousands of us out at Everton. We'll sort out the Irish Clubs. Show them who's top dog in Liverpool.'

The woman laughed in scorn.

'Better be careful. The Afghans had ye running. And Liverpool's a tougher nut to crack.'

Pat walked towards Vauxhall, thinking. Thousands of troops in Liverpool. The city under military rule. Was this a war? Against who? The Liverpool Irish? Or Liverpool itself? Was England's second city such a danger to the Crown? It made no sense.

He decided to stay in Buckleys'. When he had come over, he had stayed at Brown's Temperance Hotel. But that was last May, and all had thought that the blight was gone, and the Famine was disappearing. But now, it was back in full force. Every penny would be needed when he got to Mayo. No, there was no way he could waste money on the comforts of Brown's.

There was another factor in his thinking too. If Gaffney wanted him to 'observe' County Mayo, he might as well get used to doing it. Even at hundreds of miles remove, Buckleys' was as good a place to start as anywhere.

As it certainly was. It was as disgusting as he expected. He went into the dining-room, but the pigswill he was served, sickened him. He forced himself to eat it, but spoke to no one. From the accents, he could hear enough of Mayo around him. Almost all were speaking in Irish too. Most were desperately thin. Were these the people the yeomanry had to control in Liverpool? These were the men who would work the railways, if they could get work. But many more would end up in the squalid courts and cellars of the Liverpool slums all along Scotland Road, and the Manchester slums of Ancoats and Little Ireland.

Next morning, he went to the George's Dock, and walked towards the ticket office.

A war steamer was docked close by. A group of soldiers were leading horses off the ship, more standing aside, watching them. Dragoons! He knew from passing through Liverpool before, that this part of the docks was for Irish shipping. Were they coming from Ireland? Why?

One was standing apart, smoking a pipe. Pat stood beside him.

'Come from Ireland, are ye?' Pat asked.

'Aye, and damned glad to be leaving it.'

'Dublin, was it?'

'Dublin! How I wish it was Dublin. We never got near Dublin. Mayo, that's where we've been. Never got out of it.'

'Mayo,' Pat exclaimed.

'Aye, and I have never been in a more cursed county.'

'I know,' Pat said. 'I'm from Mayo.'

The soldier looked up in alarm. 'Oh look, mate, I'm sorry...'

'No need,' Pat said, 'I know what you mean.'

'It's just that...with you looking all respectable and that.'

Pat laughed. 'I'm glad someone thinks so.'

'There weren't many in any kind of decent clothes in Castlebar. Rags – that's all they wear. Doesn't even cover their decency.'

'I know,' Pat said 'and it's getting worse, from all I hear.'

The unloading of the horses had finished.

'Tell me,' Pat said, 'what's this about revolution in Ireland. Is it all stories?'

'I couldn't tell you that, rightly,' the soldier answered. 'For myself, I think it's all stories. After all, if there was a revolution, why would they be sending us home to England, and why would they be sending the Scots Greys to Mayo? There's no talk of revolution in Mayo, that's for sure.'

'There's talk of them sending the Cheshires over though.'

'All talk, I'd say.'

A convoy of six carts arrived alongside the ship, carrying sacks. One of them had burst and was trailing corn along the quay.

Pat discovered that the HMS Orion was now to take forty of the Scots Greys to Westport, and on to Castlebar. At first, he thought the corn they were loading was for soup kitchens in Mayo, but it turned out that this was not the case. The corn was only bound for the military depot in Castlebar and for constabulary stations around the county.

For what? Who were the army fighting in Mayo?

He went to buy his ticket.

'Any tickets for Westport?' he asked.

'None. The military have them all taken.'

'Dublin so?'

'Cattle boat or Kingstown?' the clerk asked.

'What?'

'The Kingstown boat is the steam packet and it has no cattle. I'd advise you to go that way.'

'I wasn't thinking to go the cattle boat anyhow.'

'I didn't think you were.'

'What's the difference?'

'A shilling more. Shilling and four pence total.'

'Fine so,' Pat said. 'Kingstown.'

He put down a half-crown and took his change.

'The Arlene,' the man said. 'Fourth along on your left.'

Pat found the Arlene and walked up the gangplank. It was a single funnel vessel, streaming dirty black smoke. There were three masts, but all sails were furled. A red ensign flew from the rear.

The crossing was a quiet one. It was crowded inside, but he found a single seat at a table with three other men. They were talking about the revolution. Pat said little, but listened. As far as he could deduce, it had centred on Ballingarry, a mining town in Tipperary or Kilkenny. But for all their excited discussion, they seemed to know little more. Nor were they too concerned about any question of famine.

He went out on deck and walked towards the front of the ship. There was a strong breeze from behind, and, despite the time of year, it was cold. He had only been a short time in England, but already Ireland was a foreign country to him. He had never expected all the talk of revolution, but Mayo concerned him more. The potatoes had failed again, and Mayo would be starving. The lack of concern among the other passengers unsettled him. Did they not know? Or did they not care?

Chapter 4

Manchester Times, August 1848:

Serious disturbance at Ashton. A policeman killed. Last evening, about 12 o'clock, the town of Ashton was thrown into consternation and alarm by a report that Chartists were intending to rise in insurrection at that hour, and from what occurred, it would appear that the report was not without foundation. About 10 minutes before 12, Police Constable James Bright was passing down Bentinck Street, and, when about 50 yards below the Chartist room, he was shot in the breast by some person at present not known to the authorities, although he must be known to at least 50 persons who were in company with the assassin, most of whom were armed with pikes or guns, and all were more or less armed with warlike weapons of some kind or other.

In the weeks following Pat's departure, Murtybeg found himself in an ever more impossible situation. Without Danny or Pat, he was the only Ryan in the business, and even his parents lived in Yorkshire, on the other side of the Pennine Mountains, leaving him alone in the evenings with Irene and the maid. They shared a large house, built for many more. It was almost as if they were man and wife. Perhaps people thought that, but Murtybeg did not care.

Edwardes & Ryan were doing better than before. They won more contracts, including many contracts that Murtybeg had not expected. He did the pricing, but they had to be cleared through Irene first, who gradually started to do some of the pricing herself. When contracts were won, he did not complain, and when Edwardes & Ryan won a large contract in Bradford he was stunned, but relieved.

He himself had done the pricing, and he knew they had strong competition. The contract was on the Colne Extension running west out of Bradford to connect the Leeds Bradford Railway with the East Lancashire. It was a Mackenzie contract. Three days after Danny's funeral, Murtybeg himself had travelled to Bradford to negotiate the details with a Mr. Ackroyd, one of Mackenzie's senior managers.

Mackenzie was one of the top three contractors in Britain, along with Brassey and Peto. The ease with which Edwardes & Ryan had won the contract was surprising.

He was checking through a far smaller quote for Andersons, when he saw something most odd.

He had done the pricing himself, costing out labour, materials, overheads and a margin for profit. The total came to £520.

He had then sent it out to Roughneen to double-check all the figures. What he had received back, was a new quote in someone else's handwriting. The total now came to £572 – ten percent higher than his own quote. He checked through the detailed figures. Every single one had also been increased by ten percent. Of his own quote, there was no sign.

Roughneen came into the office on other business.

'Johnny, I want a word with you.'

'What's that?'

'This quote. I sent it out to you to check through. Mine seems to have gone missing.'

'Miss Miller's orders. All the prices are to be jacked up.'

'But the wages and materials are supposed to be at cost.'

'So?'

'Have we put up the wages?'

'Of course, not.'

'Well then?'

'I just did what I was told.'

'Well, I didn't tell you.'

Roughneen was downcast.

'Sorry, Murteen.'

Murtybeg approached Irene that afternoon.

'So what's this all about?' he asked.

'Increasing our margins. You do want to make a profit, don't you?'

'Of course. But that's only after actual costs.'

Irene leaned back in her chair. She glared at him, haughty and arrogant.

'Look, you just do your job and I'll do mine.'

Over the next week, Murtybeg saw three more quotes increased by similar margins, but said nothing. Then, one day, he was working through a ledger, totalling outgoings. One single entry stood out starkly. To Nicholas Whittle, Anderson & Son. £50. Cash.

Now all was clear. He stood in front of her desk, furious.

'This is bribery.'

'And what of it?' she asked.

'It's not the way Edwardes & Ryan do business.'

'It is now.'

'Look, I want none of this. Even Danny wouldn't do this. And it's got to be stopped. This is our business, not yours.'

'Is it?'

He decided to consider matters for a few days. At some point, he would have to confront Irene on policy, but first he decided to visit the Mackenzie site in Bradford again. There were technical issues to be resolved.

He travelled into Manchester Piccadilly and bought a ticket to Bradford, and a copy of the Manchester Times. As he settled into his seat, the first item he saw related to riots and a murder at Ashton-under-Lyne. Astonished, he read the details. It had been a violent riot, and a policeman had been killed.

Killing a policeman, how could they do that?

The train stopped at Ashton, twenty minutes later. An older gentleman settled in the seat across from Murtybeg. He wore a long morning coat over a chequered waistcoat. Carefully, he took his top hat off, and placed it on the seat beside him.

'It's a dreadful business, this rioting,' he said to Murtybeg.

'I've only just read it,' Murtybeg said.

'Absolutely shocking.'

'I never expected violence like that.'

'One doesn't, does one. Though with the country the way it is, anything is possible. Where are you going yourself, young man?'

'Bradford,' Murtybeg answered. 'I pass through Ashton, and here I am reading about it. What do you know yourself?'

'Everyone's talking about it. This country is in a state of war. They've got a troop of cavalry in, I hear. I doubt whether that will be sufficient to keep order though. The police are over-stretched too. The rumours are they'll be bringing more of the Yeomanry from Chester. They say there's hundreds of them, these damned Charter fellows, trying to overturn parliament. And the revolution is not just in Great Britain. There's revolution all over the world. Paris is in a desperate way, I hear.'

'Yes,' Murtybeg said, 'I'd read that.'

'Spain, Naples, Frankfort and the rest of the German Confederacy, they're all up in arms. Ireland too. You're Irish, I would say?'

'I am' Murtybeg replied,' but I can tell you, I am not into this kind of thing. I was never one for the Charter anyhow.'

'I am not that kind either. Far too revolutionary, if you ask me. Votes for all men, we can't have that kind of thing, can we? Votes should be confined to property, not every damned ruffian in the country. And they say they're peaceable, but now they show their true colours. It's all to do with this O'Connor fellow, Feargus O'Connor.'

Murtybeg looked out the window. The train was beginning to climb towards Woodhead Tunnel.

'It's as you say,' he said, 'they should limit the vote to property.'

'A man of property, are you?'

'Indeed,' Murtybeg answered. 'Edwardes & Ryan, we're labour contractors. We work for the main contractors – Brassey, Mackenzie and the like.'

'Men of the top rank and reputation.'

'They are.'

'A good business then?'

'It is. Last year was shaky, but it seems the panic is over.'

'Let's just hope another panic doesn't begin. With all this talk of revolution, the financial markets are most unsteady.'

After passing through the tunnel, they were drawing into another station. Two young men joined the compartment. Despite the time of year, they both wore canvas overcoats over knee-high leather boots. They too were talking about the Ashton riots.

'It's all these bloody Irish,' one of them said. 'O'Connor and his damned Repealers. They're taking over the Charter. They should send them back to their own bloody country. Why should our rates pay for their damned laziness, when all we get in return is revolution? Shoot the lot of them, that's what I say.'

The old man took his top hat from the seat and held it on his knees. Neither he nor Murtybeg said anything. It was more than enough to listen to the endless hatred from the other two. He tried to ignore them.

He went back to his newspaper. In Ireland, many arrests had followed on from the Ballingarry Revolt, and it was said that most of the ringleaders had been arrested.

Liverpool was still a dangerous city. Thousands of troops and constables were keeping order in one of the most Irish cities in England. But what about Bradford?

As they arrived, the two young men disembarked quickly.

'I'm sorry you should have to listen to that kind of bilge,' the old man said. 'I thought it best we not talk while they were in the carriage.'

'You're right,' Murtybeg said. 'With my accent, God knows what would have happened.'

The older man shook his hand.

'It was most agreeable meeting you in any case, and I hope what you were saying about the railway business is true. Good luck with it all anyhow.'

Murtybeg took a cab to the Mackenzie office.

Crossing Kirkgate disgusted him. The rotten stink of sewage mixed with the phosphoric smoke pouring from hundreds of chimneys, came close to making him vomit. Was it worse than any other districts in other English towns? Vauxhall? Ancoats? Could Bradford be worse?

Ackroyd showed him in.

'I'm delighted to see you again, Mr. Ryan.'

'Delighted to be here, too,' Murtybeg said.

Was Ackroyd too friendly? Had he been bribed too?

'Which way did you come?'

'By cab. Straight down from the L&Y at Mill Lane.'

'Across Kirkgate?'

'Yes'.

'They've had quite a bit of rioting you know.'

'I know. I hope you've had no troubles here.'

'It was difficult enough to get to work some days. They had an armed guard on the office for a few days though, so we were safe enough when we got here.'

The two men worked through the contract, discussing the labour requirements, quantities of muck to be removed in the cuttings, and many other things. It was some hours before they finished.

Ackroyd stood.

'It's always a great pleasure to work with you, Mr. Ryan. Do return, we're always happy to see you.'

'Indeed,' Murtybeg said.

Yes, he thought, as he left. He's the one. He's been bribed, no doubt about it. And I haven't even been told.

It was getting dark. He found a small inn and stayed there for the night. Next morning, he walked out the early stages of the Colne Extension, picturing all the work required in his own mind.

Six men were working, hammering stakes into the ground and linking them with rope. Just beyond, a man was taking a sighting as another held a post some distance away. Murtybeg remembered the days when the Ordnance Survey had been working around Carrigard. What was it? Ten years ago? That was when McKinnon had come to Mayo and married Sabina.

He walked to the first surveyor, who turned out to be friendly, and delighted that someone should be interested in his work. Within a few minutes, Murtybeg had sufficient information, including the width and breadth of the cutting and the depth of the clay to be removed at a number of points along the length of it. It was sufficient to give him a rough idea of the contract, and it confirmed Ackroyd's figures and his own.

When he returned to Kirkgate, he waved down a cab and returned to the Lancashire & Yorkshire terminal. It was unnaturally quiet.

He walked to the ticket desk. 'Single for Manchester.'

'I'm sorry sir,' the clerk said. 'All the Manchester trains are cancelled.'

'Cancelled?'

'Something to do with the riots. The army is out at Ashton. I think they're worried the Chartists might cut the line, and there's all sorts of stories about Manchester too.'

Murtybeg walked out again, cursing his luck, the Chartists and the army. Now he was caught in Bradford.

He reconsidered the matter. He was very close to where his parents lived outside Leeds, and where the Gilligan gang worked. He could visit, and still return to Stockport the following evening. But would the trains on the Leeds & Bradford line be running today? There was only one way to find out.

He looked for a cab to go to the Leeds & Bradford station, but there were none. He began to walk back in the direction he had come. Again, he thought, it was very quiet. Being a Sunday, there were few men working.

The silence was shattered by a sound of screaming. Several police officers were coming towards him, dragging a man with them. They were being followed by a large and angry crowd. He began to retrace his steps, but another mob was forming behind him too, and quickly he was engulfed in the yelling crowd.

The policemen were being attacked. Their helmets were knocked off, and one of them had his coat and shirt ripped off, until he was stripped bare to the chest. Most of the assailants were women, and it was with a sense of surprise that Murtybeg realized that they were shouting in Irish. Many of their accents were clearly from the West. They began to throw bricks and broken paving stones at the police, some of which hit the prisoner and other rioters. Then the police were down, and the women caught hold of the prisoner and pulled him back out of sight.

Then, a brick hit the top of his forehead, and he fell. Concussed for a few moments, he returned to consciousness, with a vicious pain in his head. He felt blood on his forehead. He took out his handkerchief and dabbed at his wound. He crawled onto his hands and knees, and looked around him.

The clamour was less, as one woman took control of the situation. She kicked and hammered at the police, encouraging the other women to do likewise. Soon afterwards, she was captured by the police, and they carried her away, still screaming. People were going down under the shower of missiles, some of whom appeared to be badly injured.

More police arrived. Incredibly, they were carrying sabres. Across the road, a group of dragoons had appeared. They sat on their horses without moving. Murtybeg realised the danger. He stood up and staggered away. Still weak, he pulled himself into a doorway.

The police charged the crowd again, waving their sabres, but again they were beaten back. Then the dragoons moved slowly forward, and the crowd began to disperse.

As order was restored, he left the shelter of the door. Going around through filthy back streets, he managed to evade most of the remaining crowd, as well as the police and soldiers.

When he reached the Leeds & Bradford Station, the bleeding had stopped. He stared at the bloodied handkerchief. How much blood had he lost? He felt his forehead again, but there was no severe pain, and he guessed that his skull was not broken.

He made his way to the ticket office. The ticket glanced at him.

'Caught in the riots, sir?'

'Yes, and may God damn them all to hell.'

It struck him at once that his accent would have given away the fact that he was Irish. For a moment, he thought the clerk might try to have him arrested, but the moment passed.

'Where to, sir?'

'Leeds.'

'You're lucky, sir. There haven't been trains for hours now. There's one leaving for Leeds in ten minutes though. Platform Two.'

Murtybeg took the ticket and boarded his train. He was thankful to find an unoccupied carriage. He had no desire to have people staring at him and questioning where he might have been.

He could not believe what he had seen. Bradford was a city at war.

He arrived at Leeds Station, and two hours hard walking brought him to Bramhope. Sometimes he travelled by road, sometimes along the new tracks of the Leeds & Thirsk. At times, he was faint, and could feel a swelling on his forehead, but he walked on and asked his way to the house where the Gilligan gang were staying. Jim Doyle answered his knock.

'Murteen! Come in, come in.'

The rest of the gang were at dinner, together with Murty. Gilligan stood up and came to shake his hand. 'My God, you look rough. What happened?'

'Nothing much,' Murtybeg said, casually.

Aileen was not at the table.

'Where's mother?' he asked Murty.

'Just resting. Don't you be worrying about her. What about you?'

'I was caught in the riots.'

'Riots?' Gilligan exclaimed. 'What? Where?'

'Bradford. Haven't you heard?'

'Oh, Bradford, is it? We'd heard stories of fights right enough, but not what you'd call a riot. Was it as bad as all that?'

'It surely was.'

'So who was doing the fighting?'

'It was those damned Chartists again. The peelers arrested some fellow, but the mob wasn't having it, and they took them on.'

'But...what in the name of God were you doing in Bradford?' Doyle asked.

'We've a new contract there. Surely you know...?'

'Not yet,' Gilligan answered. 'I'm sure you'll tell us all about it. But first, what about the riot?'

Murtybeg recounted all he had seen of the riot.

'Dragoons,' Doyle exclaimed, at length. 'They brought in dragoons for women and children.'

'They had to,' Murtybeg answered. 'They're tough women in Bradford, I can tell you.'

'And Bradford isn't the only place,' Gilligan said. 'There's talk of a rising in Liverpool. They've thousands and thousands of troops there.'

'I know,' Murtybeg said, 'I've read all about Liverpool. Ireland too.'

'*Arra*, what kind of rising was that?' Murty said. 'Nothing like '98, they weren't that kind of men. But what can you expect, a gang of coalminers, what would they know? And their leaders, soft fellows, poets and the like. And this Smith O'Brien fellow, a landlord! Was he even on their side? Did he betray them, that's what I'm asking?

But Murtybeg was thinking of other things.

'But...how's mother?' he asked again.

'You'll see soon enough,' Murty said. 'She was quiet enough before, but God, Danny's death has rattled her. I don't know what I'm going to do with her.'

Gilligan spoke. 'I don't know what to say. Danny dead. I could never understand it. Your father, he says Danny killed himself.'

'I've no doubt of it,' Murtybeg replied. 'We went to the morgue – Pat and myself. The story was that Danny had just stood up between the rails facing the engine. I saw what was left of him. That could only have come about by being dragged along under the train.'

He looked across at Murty.

'I'm sorry, father.'

'No need. Whatever grief there was ever in me, it's all burnt out this long time.'

Murtybeg spent the night on the floor in his parents' room, wrapped tightly in his greatcoat, and a heavy blanket wrapped around that.

Murty woke him the next morning. He and Aileen were dressed.

'Come on, Murteen, time for breakfast. The lads will be going out in half an hour.'

Aileen said nothing. Murtybeg was more concerned than ever, but what could he do?

'So what of Pat?' Murty asked him. 'How's he getting on, with Danny gone?'

'He's gone back to Ireland,' Murtybeg said. 'I didn't like saying it last night.'

Murty was quiet for a few seconds.

'Gone back to Ireland? What the devil would he do that for?'

'He's got some job with the County back in Mayo, though I'd reckon that's not the only reason. There's some girl he fancies in Westport too.'

'Ah yes,' Murty said. 'I'd heard tell of that.'

When they went down, the others were already at their breakfast.

'A hard day ahead, lads?' Murtybeg said.

'Hard is right,' Doyle said. 'Gilligan here, he works us into the ground, didn't you know?'

Murtybeg laughed. 'And he'll work ye for a long time yet, I've no doubt of that.'

'If he gets the chance.'

'What do you mean?'

'It's like this,' Gilligan said. 'A lot of the heaviest work has been done already, all the way from here into Leeds. They're saying it'll be finished in three or four months. The tunnels are near done, and that's the snag.'

Murtybeg was puzzled.

'Why's that?'

'They want to keep the tunnellers as a gang. The Donegal fellows, that is. I can see why. They've no work for them, so what they're aiming to do is to put them working on the cuttings. Not their kind of work, but at least it keeps them as one, until another tunnel comes up. And until it does, there's many of us fellows being let go.'

'So where will ye go?'

'Well, there's one thing for sure and certain, we're not going back to Ireland. It's in a desperate mess. Utter starvation.'

'Don't I know.'

'No, we're going to have to stay here. Like yourself, we're looking at Bradford. The only question is – can we get work with Brassey? If not, we won't hang together as a gang.'

Murtybeg looked across at his father. If they could not stay together, then there would be no need for anyone doing their paperwork. And where would that leave Murty? As a labourer? A navvy?

And what of Aileen?

A bowl of porridge was placed in front of him. He took the buttermilk from the centre of the table and poured. Doyle was talking.

'What of this business you have in Bradford, then? Is that through Edwardes & Ryan?'

'It is,' Murtybeg answered.

'But how are you managing without Danny?'

'I'm dealing with Mackenzie's direct. One of his bosses.'

'You got the work easy enough.'

'We did.'

'Still the cheapest on the railways?'

'We must be.'

Murtybeg was thinking of the question of bribery, but no need to mention that.

'And still using fellows from the far end of Mayo?' Gilligan asked.

'No need,' Murtybeg answered. 'There's plenty of fellows in Bradford.'

'And how do you think Bradford is for wages?' Doyle asked.

'They'd be low, that's for certain, but I don't need to tell you fellows that. You know how they live in Bradford, and if you don't, sure it's just like in Leeds. If I were in your shoes, it isn't Bradford I'd be looking at, unless you can find Brassey contracts there.'

'I think you're right,' Gilligan said, 'and there's the real nub of the matter. What will we do if we can't get work with Brassey? Work with Edwardes & Ryan, is that it?'

Murtybeg hesitated.

'I think ye'd be better off with Brassey.'

Gilligan stood and pulled on his donkey jacket.

'Well, I've no doubt we'll meet again, Murteen,' he said. 'In Bradford, I'd say, unless we all end up back in Ireland again.'

'No way are we going to do that,' Doyle said. 'The blight is back, and we all know what that means. The only thing waiting in Ireland is death.'

Soon afterwards, Murtybeg left to walk back to Leeds. Then he took the short train journey to Bradford. Crossing the centre of the city from the Leeds & Bradford Station to the Lancashire & Yorkshire Station, he passed close by Adelaide Street and Manchester Road. The mills were open, but there were very few on the streets, except police officers and mounted dragoons. As he walked, a woman turned and spat at him. A dragoon raised his sabre, and she scuttled into a nearby lane. The man smiled at Murtybeg.

'Glad to be of service, sir.'

'Indeed,' Murtybeg said and walked on. It was as Danny had said. It was always best to dress well. Even the army knew who their betters were.

He bought a ticket at the station, and sat in his carriage, brooding.

England in revolution! Yes, there had been riots in Manchester, Danny had spoken of that before he had died. Now, he too had seen it with his own eyes. The violence in Bradford had shocked him. And what of Liverpool? The newspapers said it all. Thousands of troops keeping order, the government terrified of an uprising in Liverpool, more violent than the one in Ireland. And yes, Ireland was quiet, but why? Tens of thousands of troops. Was that what it took to keep Ireland down? Martial law?

But there were other matters to consider closer to home. Irene. It would be a bitter battle for the control of Edwardes & Ryan. Her ways of doing things horrified him. Bribery? Was that the price of successful business? Could he handle that kind of business and hide it from the authorities, so that he did not end up in prison himself?

He had little doubt that at some time they would join battle, and he would have to win. To do that, he would have to be even more ruthless than Danny. More cunning too. Could he do it? Or would he end up a common labourer on the railways? A mere Irish navvy.

That night, he slept well through sheer exhaustion.

Next morning, he walked into Irene's office.

'I trust you sorted out the Mackenzie contract?' she asked, without even looking up.

'I did,' he said. He took a seat and sat in front of her. 'And I spoke to Ackroyd. Very helpful he was too.'

'I'm sure he was.'

'I'm sure he had reasons for being helpful too,' Murtybeg said.

She looked up, glaring.

'What business is it of yours?'

'How much did you pay him?'

'Fifty pounds. It's the going rate.'

'Does anyone else know about this? Does Mackenzie know?'

'Now what do you think? If Mackenzie found out, Ackroyd would be fired. Do you think he wants that? No, he wants to keep his job, and he wants to keep the money coming.'

'Who pays him?'

'No one. It's just posted to him. No name, no way anyone can be traced. He knows where it's coming from though. Now forget all this nonsense, we're going to have to find labour.'

'And we firing men only a little while back.'

'Never mind that. That was when Danny was in charge. It's different now.

'It is,' Murtybeg said.

'Now for labour – I hear the Famine's back in Mayo. Perhaps you should go over there, recruit more men – say five hundred – just the same way you did when Danny asked you. That way, you can do what you're good at, and I'll do what I'm good at.'

'There won't be any call for going to Mayo, there's plenty of cheap labour in Bradford.'

'After the riots?' she exclaimed.

'Even more, after the riots. The whole Broomfields area of Bradford, it's as poor as ditch-water. Kirkgate too.'

'But they're not Mayo.'

'And that is where you are wrong. There's more Mayo men in Bradford than any city in England. Excepting maybe Liverpool, and I'm not going there again. They put down one rebellion in Bradford, I don't want to be caught in another in Liverpool.'

'Fine so. Your choice.'

The days continued in a strange sort of way. They worked together, though the hostility simmered endlessly. He would have to defeat her, but in the meantime, be conceded to her ways of getting new contracts. He always met the contractor, sometimes meeting someone that she specified. He had no idea how she identified the key contact in the main contractor, nor how he was bribed, but he decided it was best to ask no questions for the present. That could come later. But for now, they were doing very well.

The one major problem was the Bank. Their cashflow was satisfactory, but the business was expanding, and more borrowings would be required. He wrote to the Manchester & Salford Bank, asking for an appointment. He was asked to present himself the next Tuesday, and ask for a Mr. James Winrow. He confirmed with Irene that Winrow was Danny's old contact. He guessed that Winrow might have been a factor in Danny's death, but he had no way of knowing for sure. He knew he was about to find out a lot more.

He was worried. If the pressures on Danny were sufficient for him to kill himself, how would he, as Danny's younger brother, carry on the business? How could Edwardes & Ryan survive? And if it didn't, what was his future? Soon though, another thought occurred to him. If Edwardes & Ryan really was in trouble, so was the Manchester & Salford Bank. He was beginning to think that only he knew how Edwardes & Ryan could avoid collapse. The question was – could he persuade this Winrow fellow? Suddenly, he had no doubt that he could. He would have to be tougher than Danny though. Far tougher.

When he entered the bank, the chandeliers startled him. It struck him at once why Danny would have had to create such a strong impression. For a moment, he was nervous, but when he considered it, he decided there was no need for fear. He was an owner of a large and growing labour contracting business. This Winrow fellow was only a senior clerk in a bank.

He sat down to wait.

'Mr. Ryan? Winrow's the name.'

Murtybeg stood. Winrow's face was long, and somewhat sallow. Murtybeg studied his eyes. Intelligent, no doubt, but was he a tough negotiator? He followed him up to his office.

One of the clerks brought tea. At first the conversation centred on the recent riots in Manchester, Bradford and Ireland. But Murtybeg was on his guard. Oddly, he felt more alive than he had ever done in his life.

Then Winrow came to the point.

'We hear your brother is dead?'

'Yes,' Murtybeg said. 'Killed by a train. A horrible accident.'

'Yes,' Winrow replied, 'most unfortunate. It leaves us in a very difficult situation though. You are aware of the financial situation of Edwardes & Ryan?'

Murtybeg was thinking fast.

'My brother kept a lot to himself.'

'Perhaps, then, you might be so good as to cast your eye down this.'

He passed a sheet over to Murtybeg.

'As you can see, on Edwardes & Ryan's last loan relating to the works on the North Staffordshire line, full repayment was to be made by May. I must tell you, Mr. Ryan, this repayment has not been made.'

'Nor will it be made,' Murtybeg said, 'unless Edwardes & Ryan stay trading.'

Winrow's eyebrows rose.

'Stay trading?'

'That is just what I said, Mr. Winrow. You cannot take my brother to court, and I owe you nothing.'

'That is debatable.'

'Perhaps, but it is at least uncertain, and your loss may be even larger than you think. If you want me to take on the debt, you must let us pay you over the next few months.'

'You mean you want to trade your way out of bankruptcy?'

'That won't be necessary,' Murtybeg answered, 'We are only bankrupt if you force a bankruptcy. Yes, we will have a cash bind. But the cash will come in, I can assure you of that.'

'In the present condition of the railway market, you say the cash will come in?'

'Most certainly. And whatever you might think, the market is getting better. Yes, we have had riots across the country, but the money markets have great faith in railways. Where else can they invest their money?'

Winrow shook his head.

'I wish I could have your confidence, Mr. Ryan. All these small contractors you are working for; they are hardly the most creditworthy.'

Murtybeg was feeling angry now, but he succeeded in not showing it.

'True enough,' he said. 'We do work for small contractors.'

'Including Andersons, I believe.'

'Yes.'

'You know the financial position of Andersons?'

'I do not. I would consider that to be a private matter between Andersons' and the bank.'

That quietened him, Murtybeg thought. He can't tell me about Roy's financial position, or he would be in breach of faith. Even what he said was a breach of faith. But it gives me a warning.

'Yes, yes of course,' Winrow answered. 'But even apart from Andersons you are working for some very small contractors.'

'Not very much anymore, Mr. Winrow. In fact, the most of our work will be with the greatest contractor of all. Brassey...'

'On the North Staffordshire line? That has ended.'

'Yes, our contract has ended, but there are other smaller Brassey excavations on the North Staffordshire to be bid for. We have a high standing with Brassey. And we have the Mackenzie contract too.'

'That too will finish soon.'

'Yes, but we have just signed another contract with Mackenzie over in Bradford.'

'Winrow looked at him in astonishment. 'You're working for Mackenzie again?'

'We are.'

'I hadn't heard that.'

'We've only just taken on the contract.'

Winrow looked more astonished than ever.

'And how are you going to finance this new contract, pray tell me?'

'Through the Manchester & Salford Bank, of course.'

'Through the Bank!'

'Yes. Like I said to you, Mr. Winrow, we have a little problem with our cash flow. You can allow us to trade out of it, but if you don't, and force us into bankruptcy, you will take a loss. And cause huge delays to Brassey and Mackenzie contracts, both clients of yours, I understand.'

Winrow stared at him. He had gone pale.

'You're asking us to give you more cash? You never asked us, and you have taken on a contract with Mackenzie.'

'Yes.'

'We'd only be throwing good money after bad.'

'By no means. Your only chance of getting your money back is by dealing with me. And indeed, going on lending to Edwardes & Ryan over the years to come.'

Winrow stared out the window. For some time, he said nothing.

'And you expect us to lend to you on a contract we never discussed?'

'I do. Because I know it will make money.'

'Can you prove all this?'

'Yes,' Murtybeg said. 'I can show you where the money is in the business, and show that Edwardes & Ryan need not be bankrupted. I can show you the Mackenzie contract, and the profits that will be made on it, both for Edwardes & Ryan – and the Manchester & Salford Bank. You may call it trading our way out of bankruptcy, and perhaps it is, but I can tell you Mr. Winrow, it will be to the gain of both parties.'

Winrow had a baffled look. Murtybeg knew that he wanted to believe what he had been telling him, but the question was – how convincing had he been?

At length, Winrow stood.

'All very interesting, Mr. Ryan,' he said. 'The only one thing we need now, is proof of your assertions. Could you be as good perhaps as to get some figures together to show the existing situation of Edwardes & Ryan, and the way in which you propose to lead the business forward – as you put it – to the gain of both parties.'

When Murtybeg left the building, he felt light-headed. He walked down Mosley Street and across to St. Peter's Square. He had not won, but he surely had not lost. He knew too that his discussions with Winrow would be reported to the board of directors of the bank. What then?

The next days were busy ones. He worked sixteen hour days, slogging his way through Balance Sheets, Profit & Loss accounts, Cash Flow projections, contract details and many other things. Irene worked alongside him, but still the hostility was there. After he had explained the details of his meeting with Winrow to her though, he suspected that she respected him more than she had done before.

They fought with each other constantly, agreeing and disagreeing on figures. Sometimes agreement only came through utter exhaustion.

When they were both satisfied with the figures, he sent a hand-delivered note to the Manchester & Salford Bank requesting a meeting.

He received a hand-delivered reply requesting his presence.

'And it's only me, they want,' he said to Irene.

He saw the hostility in her eyes, but she conceded, this time at least. He wondered what the Manchester & Salford would make of her, when they finally met her.

His second meeting with the Manchester & Salford was a rough one. Apart from Winrow, three directors quizzed him endlessly on his figures. After two of the toughest hours of his life, they finally agreed to extend Edwardes & Ryan a new loan against the Mackenzie contract for £10,000, and £5,000 against other contracts. The North Staffordshire loan was extended for six months against the new Brassey contracts.

When he returned, Irene went through the figures again. He sensed that she was impressed with his ability. Through it all though, he could not shake off the feeling that she was being evasive.

One morning, the maid handed him a letter. He did not recognise the handwriting. He slit it open. The letter heading gave the name of Rothwells, a firm of solicitors. It was a long letter, with much detailed legal terminology, but from what Murtybeg could deduce, it stated that, since Danny had died intestate, his property, in toto, passed to his common-law wife.

Irene owned Edwardes & Ryan.

Chapter 5

Evening Post, New York. July 1848:

Immigrants. There arrived at New York during the month of June, from abroad, 23,047 passengers, of which were from Ireland 11,524; Germany 7,829; England, 2,331; Scotland 642; France, 216; Holland 347; Switzerland 235; Spain 17; Wales 125; South America 4; Italy 66; West Indies 60; Denmark 7; Norway 163; Sweden 11; Poland 9. The total number of immigrants arrived since the first of January is 85,782.

Breaking coal.

Day after day, there was the never-ending sound of the breaking and shovelling of coal. There was coal dust deep in his lungs, the taste of it on his tongue and in his nose; the prickly feel of it on his face and the dirty feel of it in his hair.

July was blazing hot. Luke was well used to shovelling rock and clay from his work on the English railways. There, he and the rest of the Farrelly gang could shift more tonnage every day than any gang on the railways; and earn more money with it. The only difference in shifting the dirty black anthracite coal was the raging July heat that burned New Jersey and New York as if in a furnace.

Luke noticed that Jack Kilgallon found it impossible to keep up with the other men. He was not used to this kind of brutal labour, and he was paid less than the others. Slowly though, his muscles built up, as he became accustomed to the savage heat.

Every day the anthracite came in barges down the Morris Canal to the terminal at Jersey City. When the barges were cleared, it was time to break the anthracite. This was done in a half open shed. Luke was grateful at least to get away from the searing rays of the sun. Smashing anthracite with sledgehammers was hard work too. Every hour a break was called for water. Luke was surprised that, despite the amount he drank, he never needed to piss. He didn't think it was possible to sweat as much.

The older men were only paid half rate. Luke pitied them. They could pay very little rent. Perhaps there were shacks along the Morris Canal, in the same way as along the English railways. Not that Farrelly would ever have allowed that for his gang. He, Luke and the others had been the lords of English railway building.

The old men raked, using big rakes and small rakes, separating the smashed anthracite into two different grades. The smaller pieces were sacked, and carried to barges to cross the Hudson to Manhattan, or onto carts for distribution around Jersey City, Hoboken, Newark and other New Jersey cities. Larger pieces were sent by barge to ironworks further up the Hudson River.

The feebler old men crawled through the smashed anthracite, searching for 'slate' – rock mixed among the anthracite – which could explode with heat. Sometimes there would be none if the slate had been well picked out in the Pennsylvania mines.

Still, Luke knew that any of them were lucky to have a job. There were thousands out of work, right across New York, New Jersey and Pennsylvania. Every day, he heard stories of hundreds of barges laid up, right along the Hudson river and the Erie Canal. Still, anthracite came down along the Morris Canal. Wages were low, but there were hundreds of men willing to take his place.

Seán Óg worked with Luke. He was one of the Tourmakeady men. He was a gentle fellow, slow of speech, but with a powerful build and a hard weather-beaten face. He had almost no knowledge of English.

At water break one day he gulped back his water, and turned to Luke.

'*There's talk they're breaking the anthracite by steam.*'

Luke looked at him in surprise.

'*By steam?*'

'*Up in the mines around* Schuylkill. Lackan *too, I understand.*'

'*And you believe it?*'

'*I do, it's the God's honest truth.*'

'*Arra, will you stop being such an amadán. There's no such thing.*'

Jack came over.

'*Where did you hear this?*'

'*One of the Galway fellows in the barges, he was on about it.* Breakers, *they call them. They do the work of a hundred men.*'

When they went back to the anthracite breaking, Luke spoke to Jack about it.

'What do you think?'

'I don't know what to think,' Jack replied. 'But one thing's for certain, if they try breaking anthracite by steam, there'll be no jobs for us down here.'

'*Arra*, I wouldn't worry. They'll still be needing men to be shovelling it on and off the barges.'

'Not if they use steam for that too.'

A few hours later, they were unloading from one of the barges. The bargeman sat on a bollard beside them.

'One of our fellows was telling us something about breaking coal by steam,' Luke said to him.

'And so they do,' the bargeman said.

'It's not a joke then?'

'No joke. They've only got it running a year or two, but they do it alright.'

They walked back towards their lodgings that evening.

'Sounds as if it's real, this steam business' Jack said.

'Perhaps. We'll find out soon enough, as soon as we go up to Lackan to meet the other fellows. There's only one other thing that worries me though.'

'What's that?'

'If they can break coal by steam, they can dig it by steam too.'

Jack slapped his forehead.

'I never thought of that.'

On the Saturday, work stopped early.

'Only eight hours working!' Jack said, 'I'm not used to that.'

'And not used to Sundays neither, not swinging a sledgehammer at all. We'll be doing it in our sleep, I tell you.'

'Would you go on out of that. Now tell me this, are you going over to Costellos' this evening?'

'I am. Are you coming?' Luke asked.

'Try and stop me!'

'Well we better get a move on, that barge is going to be moving any minute.'

They raced to the dock, just as the barge was being cast off. Laughing, they jumped across the widening gap.

'Next time you do that, you'll be dead,' the bargeman said.

'*Arra*, what of it.'

They sat on top of the sacks of anthracite.

'We look like black men,' Jack said.

'I don't know about me, but you sure as hell do.'

They reached the Cortland Street Terminal.

'Come on, there' the bargeman shouted. 'You got a free ride; you can at least help me to tie up.'

They jumped off and tied the barge to the bollards. A lot easier than weighing anchor, coming up the St. Lawrence to Quebec on the Centaurus. Anchors were heavy beasts, even with many men on the capstan winch. That had been a fearsome voyage. Well over a hundred dead, before they even reached Quebec, and then the horrors of Grosse Île.

They left the terminal and walked across the city to Five Points and Orange Street.

'You know,' Jack said, 'getting the coal dust up your nose is one thing, the stink of this place is worse.'

'It's easy upset you are,' Luke said. 'Sure when you're out milking the cows, don't you get the same smell of shit?'

'And that's something I haven't smelt for a long time, and pray I never do. Sure they're only starving in Ireland.'

'Wouldn't you think of farming in America? Thousands of acres for farming.'

'No way,' Jack replied. 'I've had enough of farms for ten lifetimes. Let's just get up to Lackan when your wife arrives, and work out what the lie of the land is, once we meet your old gang. I'm damned sure of one thing, we'll earn better money there than we're earning across on the Morris Canal. It's one right hell hole of a place, it is.'

When they arrived in Costellos' bar, Costello was serving. The bar was hot, and humid. Costello was sweating, his shirt streaked and wet.

'Well, lads, come over to do a bit of work?'

'That, and to get a pint or two inside us as well,' Luke replied.

'Well, the first thing is to get ye looking respectable. Would you go out the back and get well cleaned. I'll get *Páidín* to drop each of ye a clean jacket.'

They went out to the shack at the back. They both stripped off, and Luke sat into the zinc bath. Jack poured the water over him.

'Damn it, that smells as bad as the streets.'

'Why wouldn't it? Isn't that where it came from?'

He took a scrubbing brush that was hanging beside them. 'Here, let me start scrubbing you down. Can you picture if your wife arrived over from Ireland today? What'd she be thinking of you? She'd run a mile.'

When Jack had finished scrubbing Luke, they changed around, and Luke scrubbed him until the skin glowed red. There was a knock on the door.

'*Mr. Costello said to drop these down to you.*'

'*That it was good of you, Páidín,*' Luke said, pulling his trousers on. He put on the jacket, and when they were both ready, they went back to the front bar. It wasn't yet busy. Costello put a beer in front of each of them.

'How are ye finding the work across the way?'

'Damned hard,' Luke said.

'Hard!' Jack echoed. 'Damn it. At least you were used to it on the railways. It was a lot harder for me.'

'Might be,' Luke said, 'but at least you're toughening up to it.'

'Slow enough, too,' Jack said.

But Luke was thinking of other things. *Conaire* – Costello's brother and Luke's companion and friend on the Atlantic crossing, in the mills of Quebec and the forests of Ontario.

'Forget all that,' he said, abruptly. 'There's only one other question I'd have for you, John.'

'I thought you might,' Costello said.

'Any word of him?'

'Not a whisper. I'm telling you, *Conaire* is dead. And isn't that a terrible thing to say about my own brother.'

'Sure you can't be certain of that.'

'As certain as anybody can be. He has my address. He'd have written by now, no matter where he was.'

'But he can't write.'

'He'd know people who could write for him. Sure wasn't that what you were doing for him, the time ye were up the forests in Ontario.'

Luke considered that. 'Well, there are other possibilities,' he said. 'He might be logging out in one of the Territories. Or working down Louisiana way as a cowboy.'

'God help him if he is,' Costello said. 'He won't last long in that line of work.'

They spent all Sunday working in the bar.

Sundays were always busy in Costellos'. It was a good opportunity to earn extra dollars, and not as brutally tough as working in the anthracite terminals.

Luke was serving two men when he heard them talking about the potato crop.

He interrupted them.

'*Have you heard anything about it?*' he asked. '*What's the news from Ireland?*'

'*A great crop, by all accounts. Leastwise in Kerry it is.*'

'*It's a great crop all over, I'd say,*' the other man said. '*If it's doing that well in Kerry, what would be wrong with the rest of the country, that it couldn't do the same. No, there's no sign of blight, that's for sure. From all we hear, even the pigs won't be able to finish all they're being fed.*'

Luke passed over their beers.

'*Well, that's great news.*'

One Saturday afternoon, Luke was back in Five Points without Jack, who had preferred to have a night out with the Tourmakeady men.

When he arrived in Costellos', Costello asked him into the back office.

'There's something I'd like to ask you, Luke. You're a true born Irishman, as I understand it.'

'Sure what else could I be?'

'I don't know. After all those years in England...'

'Well, I can tell you one thing for sure. I'm not an Englishman. How could I be that?'

'Oh, I don't know. From what we hear of your cousin Danny, he'll be an Englishman before much longer.'

Luke laughed. 'My cousin Danny can do what he likes. I'm damned if I want anything to do with him anymore. But yes, John, I can assure you I'm an Irishman, and, please God, I always will be.'

'And a good Catholic too?'

Luke hesitated. Other things flashed through his mind. Croghancoe. He remembered that day by mountain, and the vast power he had sensed behind it. He still could not understand what had happened to him. Was it some sort of madness? Or some vision of something or someone he would never understand.

'Yes John,' he said after some hesitation. 'I'm Catholic.'

'A Mass goer?'

'Not all the time, but I know I should. In fact, there's no excuse. There's a church in Jersey City.'

'There is. St. Peter's has been there this long time.'

'But what's this all about, John? You're not going to tell me I should become a priest, are you?'

Costello laughed.

'Far from that,' he answered. 'Something else entirely. You've heard of the Ancient Order of Hibernians?'

'Of course, I have. Why do you ask?'

'Never mind. We'll talk again. In the meantime, there's an immigrant boat in. I want you to help out.'

'Surely,' Luke said.

Costello gave him a police baton. 'Hide that under your coat. And you can take my sister with you.'

Luke was pleased to be accompanied by Catherine Costello. He had always found her to be an attractive woman, tall and elegant, but a strong woman too. Sometimes in his own mind he compared her to Winnie. Still, in Winnie's absence, he found himself enticed by Catherine. He should not, but she was in New York, and Winnie was not.

'I'm glad you're coming,' she said to him. 'John goes often enough, but I don't like him doing it.'

'Why not?'

'Because he's a saloon keeper.'

He did not press her about that.

When they arrived on the docks, a ship was already tied up.

'We must wait,' she said.

She sat on a bollard. Luke stood beside her.

'What now?' he asked.

'Once they come off, we must get in fast. Get them before the runners do. You know yourself – if they get them, they'll be jumped half way to some lodgings that doesn't even exist. And there's cutpurses here too that'd have your money, before you even knew it was gone.'

'Rough business,' Luke said.

He had been watching the waiting crowd. He picked out some groups of men in groups of two and three. Were they all meeting relatives? When the immigrants started coming through, the crowd pushed forward. Luke saw two of the men going forward, but they went in different directions as they got closer. At once, he was on the alert.

One accosted a woman with two children. The whole family were thin, with all the signs of hunger fixed on their faces. The woman's dress was ragged, and she had a bitter and defeated look in her eyes. The children were barefoot.

She stopped and put down her bag. The man had moved around slightly, so that she had her back to his accomplice moving in. She did not even notice when the bag was lifted.

Luke moved quickly. He followed the bag, grabbed the man by the collar, and jerked him back. He was a small man, hair well cropped to his skull. He looked up at Luke. Then he dropped the bag and ran. Luke thought of chasing him, but instead he took up the bag and carried it back.

The other man had disappeared and Catherine was talking to the woman, who looked upset. Luke set the bag down in front of her.

'Good work, Luke,' Catherine said. 'Now we've more to do.'

Another group had been accosted by a man, tall this time. She moved closer, listening from behind. Luke stood in beside her.

She turned to him whispering. 'He's saying he'll bring them to the cheapest boarding house in Manhattan.'

'What's wrong with that?'

'Doesn't exist. They'll be jumped and relieved of everything.'

Already the group was moving.

'Come on,' Catherine said. Luke followed.

'Now – those two over there. They're following.'

'But they're well back,' Luke said.

'They won't be in a while. Come on, we've no time.'

Luke ran. He stood in front of the first man.

'Where are you...?'

He got a head butt straight to the nose. He doubled up and tried not to scream.

A full minute later, he stood and looked around. 'Where are the runners?'

'Gone off with them.'

'God help them,' he said.

'God help them is right,' said Catherine, 'because no one else will. Now let's get you home. You've blood all over your shirt.'

Next morning, they were helping to clean up the bar.

'You might do some deliveries for me, while we finish the cleaning?' Costello said to Luke. 'A few bottles of gin and whiskey.'

'And how would I find the way?'

'I'll send Catherine with you. She knows the way, and she knows the prices. And mind you take good care of her.'

He gave Luke a sack of bottles and a baton. 'Just hold this inside your belt,' he said.

Luke hefted the sack over his shoulder.

'Damned heavy,' he said.

'You should be fine, a brawny fellow like you,' Costello said.

They left, and walked along Orange Street. The street was teeming with whites and blacks. Luke knew from the accents that many of the whites – most perhaps – were Irish.

They came to the first drop off.

'Hagerty's,' she said.

There were pigs in the courtyard, snuffling at a trough. They walked down into a tiny cellar. The stench was far worse than outside. Luke found it hard to breathe. There was little air, and what there was, was stifling and hot.

Six beds occupied the room. Chamber pots stood under the beds, some close to overflowing. Luke put his hand to his nose.

'You're not used to this, are you,' Catherine said. 'It's only slops for the pigs.'

A woman and two children were lying on one bed. She was drunk already. Her eyes lit up, when she saw Catherine. She stood, and reached out for the gin bottle that Catherine had taken out of the sack.

'Catherine, alanna…'

Catherine whipped the bottle away, and stood back.

'You'll pay first.'

The woman returned to the bed and took a silver half dime from under the mattress.

'You're hard enough. And coming along with a tough fellow too.'

'I'd need him, with the likes of you,' Catherine said.

They walked back up the steps, across the courtyard and back into the street. At least the stink was less.

They arrived at a tenement, and climbed five flights of stairs. The room they entered was tiny. Two men approached her, and paid without comment. Two far tinier rooms extended from the back. From one of them came the sound of snoring.

They made another delivery and left.

Over the following weeks, they visited more tenements, but the story was always the same. Some were cellars, some high up in attics, some in hovels.

Then, one morning, they came to what Catherine described as 'The Old Brewery'. This was an old building right in the centre of Five Points. He had seen it before. As he soon found out, it was no longer a brewery.

At first sight it appeared to be a well-built structure, with a ground floor, two upper floors and an attic above the 'Old Brewery' sign. There was a liquor store on the ground floor.

'Ah yes,' Catherine said, when he pointed it out to her. 'That's Brennans. They don't like us.'

'Damned sure they don't. How do we sell here so?'

'Simple. We undercut them. They have to pay rent for their big shop in this neighbourhood. We just take our gin from my brother's cellar. It costs nothing extra for rent.'

They made their way up through the building.

'There's two hundred people living here,' she said.

'Two hundred!'

'Wait till you see.'

The floors were divided and subdivided, many with lofts dividing the floors further to create extra levels. Many families lived in tiny rooms, eight and ten to a room. In some, it was impossible to stand erect.

Quickly, they sold out. When they came back to Costellos', she gave the money to her brother.

'She'll make a good businesswoman too,' Costello said.

'A rough business, I'd say,' Luke said.

'It is,' Costello said, 'and one that'll show you the reason you don't want to stay in the Five Points.'

'What about yourselves, so?'

'We've got a business, haven't we? Five years saving for it, I was, working the other bars, and always intending to have my own. By God, it's the only business I got to know living here, and it gives a good enough living too for Eileen, Catherine and myself. Why would I go anywhere else?'

The next week, he visited the docks again. He was more careful, and only once got into a squabble, which he terminated with one quick blow to the other man's jaw.

Working the quays, he noticed many of the immigrants now were from County Mayo. Through them, he heard of a massive eviction in the south of the County, carried out by Lord Lucan. He thought back to the Clanowen evictions at *Gort na Móna* the previous year. Hundreds of people on the road, women keening, children crying. From all he heard, the Lucan evictions were enormous compared to *Gort na Móna*.

There were reports too of another failure in the Irish potato crop. It seemed though, that this was partial, and given the early news of a bumper crop, Luke was not too concerned. There were always potato failures in Ireland. Mayo too. Sometimes they lost part of the crop, sometimes it affected one part of the country only.

They had heard enough of the excellent crop in July, and the thought of more hunger in August was too much to contemplate.

Another failure? Only a rumour. Ignore it.

When he returned to Orange Street that night, Costello was waiting for him. They found a quiet part of the bar and Costello placed a whiskey in front of him.

'What do you know of the Hibernians? Costello asked him.

'Not a lot, to be honest,' Luke said. 'They're a secret society, so how could I know much?'

'There's a lot for you to learn so,' Costello said.

'Isn't it oath-bound?'

'It is,' Costello replied, 'but only about certain matters that are restricted to those who have to know. For the rest, we are an open society, a fraternal organisation if you like, and sure what's wrong with that?'

They spoke for an hour. For the most part, Costello did the speaking, with Luke asking an occasional question.

As he walked back to the Cortland Street Terminal that night, his head was reeling. So much information. So many things to think about.

He did not know if there was a Hibernian Club in Jersey City, and somehow this did not interest him. He suspected the main power of the Hibernians would be concentrated in New York. The idea of an organisation of Irishmen seeking to control a major city, or even parts of it, fascinated him.

This would never have been possible in any of the major British cities such as Liverpool or Manchester, and even Dublin was more directly controlled from London, whether its City Council was Irish or not. He doubted too whether Quebec or Montreal could ever have Irish control against French opposition.

But New York?

Through Costello, Luke had found out much more about the workings of the organisation, and its increasing political work in the city. He also heard more of the social and charitable aspects of the organisation, and the assistance it provided to Irish immigrants pouring into New York. The Hibernians fought the runners targeting the immigrant ships; they provided food and cash for the most miserably poor of them, and they found jobs for them among their many contacts in the city. And when the immigrants were established, they were expected to assist the Hibernians, not only in its charitable work, but also in rounding up the Irish vote at elections, and finally in voting themselves.

What impressed Luke too was their Irish nationalism. Having experienced famine in Ireland, he was moving in this direction himself, but the strength of it in the United States surprised him. Ireland was colonised by Great Britain, not by America. Also, most Irishmen in New York were proud to become American and fought hard for citizenship. Many times, Luke heard the expression 'Irish American'. That meant pride; pride against the whole damned world. And political power? Irish power?

One evening, he returned to Mrs. Gleeson's boarding house, washed himself, and came downstairs. A man rose.

'Luke Ryan. It's been a long time.'

'Mick,' Luke said in surprise. 'Mick O'Brien, is it? How the devil did you get here?'

'Sure I sailed out of Liverpool, didn't I? No time to swim!'

Luke laughed, and slapped him on the shoulder.

'Always the joker, eh! Well, by God, it's good to see you, Mick.'

'And you too, Luke.'

They sat at the table as Mrs. Gleeson served.

'A hard crossing, was it?' he asked.

'A damned hard crossing,' Mick said. 'A fast one though.'

But why had Mick left? Luke knew the O'Brien family had taken the Grogan farm after the Grogans had emigrated. Clearly, it was not enough. The real mystery though was that Mick O'Brien was here in Jersey City.

'How the did you find me?' he asked.

'I met with your people before I left. There was some story of a friend of yours called Costello having a brother owned a bar in Five Points. Didn't take me long to find John Costello, and to run you to ground after that.'

He untied his laces, and kicked his boots off.

'One other thing,' he said. 'There were fellows in Costellos' talking about blight back home.'

'*Arra*, we've all been hearing about that this long time,' Luke said.

'They were pretty serious about it.'

'Sure you know the way it is. The slightest touch of blight – or mildew even – and they're saying it's all over the country. Sure we've blight every year.'

'I don't know that you're right there,' Mick said. 'Sure, the potatoes rot here and there every year, but that's because of the weather, not the blight.'

'Did you see any?'

'Not in England…'

'Well don't you be worrying about it. We'll wait and hear what everyone else has to say.'

More rumours, he thought. Am I so sure now?

Next day, Mick accompanied them to the anthracite dock. It was another roasting day, hot and humid. There were the usual lines of men, waiting hopelessly for work.

'Just stay with us,' Luke said. 'Them fellows won't know you.'

Inside, Luke took him across to the foreman.

'Who's he?'

'One of ours,' Luke replied.

'We've no places.'

'I know.'

'Can he work?'

'As well as any of us.'

'A dollar the start.'

'Fifty cents.'

'Seventy-five.'

Luke slipped him three quarters. The foreman took one coin and clicked it against the other two in turn. Then he pocketed them.

'And he'd better be good. He'll be first out if we need less men.'

They walked over to the others.

'That was pricy,' Mick said.

'I know. Only started it a few weeks back, the bastard. The rest of the fellows outside, they can't afford to buy work, and they'd be too weak anyhow. And forget what he said about first out. You're in, and there's an end to it.'

'I'll pay you back on Saturday.'

'Fine so.'

He gave Mick a shovel, and they began to work.

'Damn it, I'm not used to this,' Mick said at the break.

'Ah, you get used to it in time,' Luke said.'

'I don't know; I've never done work like this before.'

74

'Weren't you shovelling muck on the railways.'

'Not in this heat.'

'You'll be grand. Build up your muscles, and the sweating gets less.'

They worked on.

'Carrigard?' Luke asked him. 'How's Carrigard?'

'Bad enough,' Mick said. 'Your family and mine won't starve, whatever about the rest. But there's bitterness there too.'

'Why's that?' Luke asked.

'It's ever since they took the farms. We took Grogans', you knew about that?'

'Yes,' Luke said, 'and we took Bensons' too.'

'So there you have it. There's many will never forgive us for that.'

'But they were gone,' Luke said. 'Bensons and Grogans, they'd left the farms, gone to America. They didn't need the farms. Why would anyone whinge about it?'

'Don't ask me,' Mick said. 'Jealousy maybe, just jealous they didn't get the farms themselves. And bitterness that the Ryans and the O'Briens survived with no one dying.'

'That was near enough,' Luke said. 'Father had fever, he came close enough to it.'

'Yes, and two of ours got fever too, and lived. But we didn't starve, and why not? Because we were working and had enough cash. I was sending money back from the railways all through the worst of it. And you were a supervisor on the Famine Relief. You'll never be forgiven for that.'

'But damn it, I was doing the best I could,' Luke said. 'If it wasn't for Famine Relief, how many more would have starved? What did they expect me to do?'

'You're right,' Mick said, 'but still, you're the one who was choosing who would go on the Relief Works, and – even worse – who wouldn't. They'll never forget that. And there's many here in America won't forget it either.'

'So what do you think?'

'You don't have to worry about me,' Mick said. 'We're old friends, all those years working together on the railways, and I understand it all too. I know what you had to do. And the other lads who worked with us in England. They understand too. So long as you resist.'

Resist? Resist who? Or what? Luke decided not to ask.

That night he lay awake in his bunk, thinking.

1846 again?

Total failure? Famine following. Or there already?

To hell with it. Stop thinking like this. All we're hearing are stories. If there was a real blight – or famine – we'd know all about it soon enough.

Still? If there was a famine, he would have to send money, increase the amount he was sending. How much would he have left for rent or food or the cost of letters?

If there was a famine.

Now, he was more concerned about Winnie. When would she arrive?

Is she alive or dead?

He desperately wanted to travel to Lackan, and meet all his old friends who had experienced nothing of famine in Ireland. Working on the railways was tough, but there was no hunger. Shovelling anthracite was no tougher.

But he could not travel. He had to wait for Winnie. But when would she write again. He had written to her, and sent her the money for the ticket. There was still no answer.

What then? One thing was certain; he would never return to Ireland. Whether Winnie came this year or next year, his future – their future – was in America. Ireland meant nothing but hunger, even in the good years. And England? No, he certainly would not work with Danny.

At least in America he would have work, whether in New York, New Jersey or Pennsylvania. Tough work perhaps, but they had more freedom than they ever had in Ireland.

But where was Winnie? Why hadn't she written?

When should I give up and say she's not coming?

He soon got his answer.

Mrs. Gleeson gave him a letter.

'From Ireland,' she said.

Luke stared at the letter. It was Winnie's handwriting, but, for the first time, he was frightened to open it. He realised all the rumours of the past weeks had worried him, more than he realised. Did this letter contain the truth of it? Was it good news or bad?

He ripped it open and skimmed through the letter in seconds. There was no mention of blight.

Then he started reading it again more slowly.

'Oh Christ.'

'What is it?' Jack asked, alarm in his voice.

'She's leaving on a ship out of Westport. Late July, she says.'

'*Speak in Irish,*' Seán Óg asked.

'*My wife is leaving Mayo in late July.*'

'*She'll be here in September so. Early September.*'

There was a silence around the room.

'*Well?*' Seán Óg asked. '*What else does it say?*'

'I'm just reading it.'

'Well, read fast, you fool,' Jack said. 'What does it say about the blight?'

'Nothing. She says nothing of any blight.'

'Well, thank God for that,' one of the other Tourmakeady men said. 'I was getting worried before. All these fellows talking.'

'Sure they're only making things up to amuse themselves,' Jack said. 'Pay no mind to them.'

Luke lay back in his bed that night, thinking. He was deeply relieved. No blight. She would have said it if there was. But then, it all began to gnaw at him again. The ships on the Atlantic crossed at different speeds. There was talk of steam ships that could bring the crossing down to three weeks.

Could the blight have settled after Winnie had written her letter? He listened to all the snoring. There were fellows who weren't concerned, and he was only worrying about ghosts.

He had been a fool to listen to it all. Nothing but rumours, no truth to any of it.

Chapter 6

New York Sun. September 1848:
No Scarcity of Food. It is estimated that the harvest of the
United States this season is sufficient to feed half the people
on the globe, abundantly. With scarcely an exception, every
species of grain, fruit and vegetable is yielding throughout
the country, an extraordinary crop. Of beef, pork, butter,
cheese etc., the same plenty abounds and while our population
are secure of every comfort and luxury in the way of food, we
shall have a surplus sufficient to meet all the Famine that may
occur in the Old World.

The next time he visited Costellos', Catherine was serving behind the bar.

'I thought you might like to see this,' he said. He put Winnie's letter on the counter.

'Mayo?' she asked.

'Yes.'

She opened it and looked through it.

'Well, that's good news anyhow. She'll be here soon. And she says nothing of blight.'

'She doesn't, does she? But we keep hearing stories.'

'I know,' Catherine said. 'It never stops, does it? All these stories, I don't know the right of it.'

She's right, he thought. When will we ever know, what's happening in Mayo?

Luke took the letter back.

'The one other thing that's worrying me, she's taking a long time coming.'

'*Arra* no,' Catherine said. 'Sure when I crossed, it took seven weeks. No, she'll be here soon enough, and you're to stop worrying.'

He joined her in serving beer. The bar was busy again.

Costello tapped him on the shoulder.

'Come here with me,' he said, 'there's people I want you to meet.'

Luke was puzzled, but followed him through to the stairs and up to the first floor. Costello knocked on a door and entered, Luke following.

Three men sat at a candle-lit table observing him. *Páidín* was serving whiskey. He held the bottle up to Luke. He nodded. Two more whiskies were served.

'This is the fellow, John, is it?' one of the men asked.

'Yes,' Costello replied, 'Luke Ryan. Originally from the County Mayo.'

'Out John's part of the County, are you?' another asked.

'No,' Luke said, 'the opposite end. Kilduff, out the Dublin side of Castlebar.'

'You've heard of the Ancient Order of Hibernians?'

'I have,' said Luke, without commitment.

'What do you know of it?'

Luke hesitated. Was it a secret organisation or not? If he said too much it would compromise Costello.

'Very little,' he said. 'All I know is what I've heard on the street.'

'What's that?'

'That it helps new Irish immigrants, that's all.'

'That's all?'

'Isn't it enough?' said Luke.

There was a whispered consultation between the men.

'So from what you've heard, would you like to join the Ancient Order of Hibernians?'

'I would.'

'And what are your reasons for wishing to join?'

Luke thought, carefully.

'A number of reasons, but two main ones. The first is the simple one of wanting good company. God knows, this is a big city, and it's easy for any Irishman to get lost in it. When John told me the Hibernians were an Irish friendly society, I thought it a good way of meeting other Irishmen, and that was good enough for me.'

'There's other friendly societies...'

'Yes,' Luke said, 'and to be honest about it, if John had spoken about another one, I might well have joined it instead.'

One of the men wrote notes with a stubby pencil in a well-worn notebook.

'There was another reason?'

'A simple reason too,' Luke replied. 'It's just how I've been sick and tired these years past of having others direct our lives. From the time I was old enough to understand it, I was always against it. I knew what the other landlords were doing, not that we could complain about our own, but some of them were downright evil. And the Clanowen evictions at *Gort na Móna* last year; that angered me more than I can tell you. I've worked on the English railways too, and I know well how rough the contractors and their foremen can be. Again, we weren't so badly off, we had our own gang and our gang leader bargaining with the contractors. It was the other fellows who got it worse. And then, in Quebec and in Montreal, I saw what things were like, and I worked for the logging companies in the forests too. So when I found my way to New York, John told me about the Hibernians. One way or the other, it looked a good way of taking control of our own future.'

Had he gone too far? Shown too much knowledge?

'You're intending to stay in the city then?'

'For now, anyhow,' Luke said. 'I have to wait for my wife coming over from Ireland. I'm hoping she'll be here in few weeks.'

'And then?'

'Hard to say. I was intending travelling on to Harrisburg out in Pennsylvania. I'd friends there working on the railways. I'd worked with them long enough in England, and I reckoned that if the rails here were as good as England, there'd be good money in it.'

'You've changed your plans?'

'More a matter of having them changed for me. The rail building is slowing out that way, and they're all moving up to Lackan…'

'Lackan?' one of the men interrupted. 'That's up by Scranton?'

Luke looked puzzled.

'I don't know,' he said, 'I don't know the towns around yet.'

Costello put his hand on Luke's arm.

'You should know that's anthracite country. And the Order was founded in Cass Township. If you're moving up that way, you'll be staying close to the Hibernians, just as much as in Five Points.'

More whispering, then one of the men nodded at him. 'Fine,' he said, 'John here has spoken for you. You're in.'

Luke was surprised, but also relieved. He had not asked to join the Hibernians, but if he had not been interested, Costello would have sensed it from their earlier discussions.

'Come on, so,' Costello said. 'Let's join the meeting.'

Luke followed him to a back room off the bar.

He reckoned there were twenty or thirty men present.

He was asked to confirm that he was a true Irishman, and a true Catholic. Many other questions followed. At the end, he was requested to take the St. Patrick's Pledge, confirming his loyalty to the Order.

The rest of the evening passed in a confusing flurry of introductions and discussions. He tried hard to memorise the many names, but knew he could not.

The men were from all over Ireland, Belfast and Dublin included, but as he soon found out, most were from the west coast, all the way from the north of Donegal down to West Cork.

Apart from Costello, three were from County Mayo. One was from Erris, who Luke already knew was a friend of Costello's. Another was from Partry, close by Tourmakeady.

Costello introduced the third man as Matt Carroll, who owned another bar in Five Points.

'From the south end of Mayo', Carroll explained to him, 'close by Ballinrobe. There's bad news down that end too. Evictions, by the thousand.'

'I know. Lucan, wasn't it?'

'It was. Cleared out a dozen villages between Ballinrobe and Claremorris. Bringing in Scots fellows now, he is, to run his big farms for him. Tenant farmers with five hundred and a thousand acres. No room for the little man now.'

'And what about the people?' Luke asked.

'I don't know. But I'll tell you one thing, there'll be a good crowd of them coming through New York now.'

'Yes,' Costello said, 'and join the rest of us, forced out by the English. By famine and fever.'

'Not that New York made them very welcome though,' Carroll said. 'The coffin ships – they wouldn't let them land here at all, made sure they all went to Quebec. Turned them away from Boston and Philadelphia too. We didn't want any Irish, did we?'

'It wasn't us,' said Costello, 'it was the Know-nothings and their gangs. They've too much control, they have, and we must do something about it.'

'You're right, John,' Carroll said. 'We might be ashamed as New Yorkers, but as Irishmen, we can have pride in what we've done. Don't we do every damned thing we can for the poor immigrant? Protect them every way possible. Right from the time they get off the boat, guarding them against the damned runners and thieves who'd rob every penny from them and leave them with broken skulls in the process. That's the defence that the Catholic Irish provide for their own. And that's only the start. We find them work too so as the families won't starve. Feed the widows and orphans too. Yes, we stand up for our own like Christian men should.'

'I know what you're saying,' Luke said. 'As John here will tell you, I'd been on the boat runs myself. It's hard down the docks. I've had a few run-ins with the runners myself.'

'You know what we're talking about so,' Carroll said. 'But I'll tell you, there's more than that. Even when the poor immigrant gets settled, there's the protection rackets, you've no idea. There's gangs around who'd try to squeeze every penny from the immigrants, and beat hell out of them if they refuse.'

'And what about the Molly Maguires?' Luke asked. 'Do they sell protection?'

The bar went quiet.

'Who told you about that?' Carroll asked.

'I can't remember,' Luke said. 'There's so much talk goes on; you hear it everywhere.'

'Well, it's all talk. There's no such gang, New York or anywhere else. Every time there's murder committed, they blame it on the Molly Maguires.'

'They were there back in Ireland.'

'Maybe, maybe not,' Carroll said, 'though no-one could prove it there, and they can't here either. But I'll tell you this, if that gang is over here, I've never met one. And they sure as hell don't demand my hard-earned dollars for guarding us.'

'I'm pleased to hear that,' Luke said.

'It's not our way,' Carroll said. 'The Hibernians – we do it right. No protection rackets. No bribery, no street fighting, no beating or killing. We provide good company. You've seen that tonight now, Luke, haven't you?'

'I have,' Luke said.

'Don't you forget it either,' Costello said. 'Don't be paying no mind to any of the gangs or twisted politicians. That's not our way. You're sworn in to the Ancient Order of Hibernians. We're only for Catholic Irishmen, and no matter what the temptation, there'll be no violence.'

He was working at the terminal one morning. He rested for a moment, leaning on his shovel.

Then he saw her.

'Who's that over there, do you think?' he said.

Mick looked up. 'A woman! I wonder what she's doing here.'

She was wearing a long grey coat, a black dress and laced boots; and was holding a small bundle.

'God only knows,' Luke said, 'though I suppose it's a public street like any other. She's got a perfect right to be here.'

'She might,' Mick answered, 'but there's damned few women walk down here. What would she want doing in an anthracite terminal anyhow?'

She walked up to the watchman's hut. The watchman was inside but it was too late before he realised that a woman and baby had just gone past. He jumped up, ran out the door of the hut, and raced after her.

'Miss. Miss. You can't come here.'

A second later, he slipped on loose coal dust and fell on his back. There was the loud sound of a whistle, then the foreman was screaming.

'Back to work, you bastards.'

The men ignored him.

The woman came closer, walking along by the barges. All breaking and shovelling stopped.

Her shawl was tied around her neck, hanging down her back. Her long black hair hung down on one side, flung back over her shoulder on the other.

'Winnie,' Luke whispered. 'It's Winnie.'

'Winnie?' Mick asked.

Luke jumped off the anthracite.

'Winnie,' he shouted.

She looked up, not recognising him for a moment.

'Luke?' she said, her voice quavering. 'Luke.'

He ran over and they were embracing.

'Winnie, oh God, Winnie...'

There was a wailing sound.

'Careful, Luke. You don't know your own strength.'

'Sorry,' he said. He stepped back.

'God, would you look at the cut of you,' she said, wiping down the front of her coat. 'Do you never wash?'

'*Arra*, what, sure we wash every night. I'm working now.'

She held out the baby.

'Careful with him.'

Luke took him in his arms.

'That's Liam,' she said. 'Come on, Liam, smile at your daddy.'

The baby only frowned.

Luke said nothing. Liam, his own son. Their future in this rough world. He handed the baby back to her. 'Where's your bag?' he asked, concerned that it had already been stolen.

'Back at Steuben Street,' she said.

'Steuben Street! How in hell...?'

'I asked my way, after I got off the ship. They directed me to the ferry and from there to Steuben Street. I left my baggage with the landlady, and she directed me down here.'

He was looking puzzled. 'But...?'

'Did you think I wasn't able for it? Did you think I didn't have a tongue in my head to be asking my way?'

'I'll say this, Winnie, you're one tough lady.'

The rest of the men were back shovelling, the excitement over.

'Do you have work to be doing?' she asked.

'I do.'

'I'll just walk back to Steuben Street so,' she said. 'I'll see you tonight.'

Luke watched her go. His heart was still beating fast. All the long months worrying about Winnie and the baby had taken their toll on him. He had been praying that she could reach New York. It had never occurred to him that she might find him in New Jersey so easily. She was more of a woman than even he had thought.

He made his way back to Steuben Street that evening with Jack, refusing Mick's offer of a beer, as all the others went into the bar.

'Well, that was quite a surprise for you, Luke,' Jack said.

'Damned right it was.'

'And what class! As cool as you like, and all the walk of a queen! What on earth is a bog-trotter like you doing with a wife like that?'

'*Arra* what,' Luke said. He gave Jack a playful punch in the back. 'How would you know anything about it?'

'And you going on about a shipwreck.'

'I never said that.'

'You didn't have to. It was written all over your face.'

'The hell it was. And anyhow we haven't heard the full story yet.'

They reached the house. Winnie was with the baby, talking to Mrs. Gleeson in the sitting room.

'Well, here's the great hero,' Mrs. Gleeson said, 'ordering his wife across the Atlantic and all. God knows, it'll be great to have another woman around the house. Might put a civil tongue on the fellows here. But we'll only have one problem – where the devil are we going to put the three of you?'

'Well, I was thinking...' Luke said, uncertainly.

'Thinking what, you *amadán*. Sharing a room with ten men snoring. Don't be mad, can't you see from the look of this girl she's used to better than that.'

Winnie was just about to protest, but decided to agree instead.

'Yes, Luke,' she said, 'Liam and myself are used to a higher class of conduct.'

'So there,' Mrs. Gleeson said. 'Now you fellows just get yourself upstairs and washed.'

Winnie winked at Luke, as she was led into the dining room, and the door closed between them.

Luke and Jack went upstairs, where Jack scrubbed him down well.

'Got to be in good order for tonight,' Jack joked.

'Don't I know it,' Luke said.

''Higher class of conduct.' Where did she get the likes of that from?'

'God only knows. Sure as hell wasn't from Mayo.'

He got out of the tub and scrubbed Jack in turn. When he was finished, he dried himself and looked at his face in the broken mirror. Not so bad looking? Carefully, he combed his hair.

'Don't worry,' Jack said, 'you're gorgeous as you are.'

Luke flicked a wet towel at him and went downstairs. He was surprised that Winnie was already feeding the baby at the breast.

'Doesn't he look much better now?' Mrs. Gleeson said, looking at Luke. 'Amazing what a touch of soap will do. Believe me, my girl, if it wasn't for my insisting, they'd never wash from one end of the week to the other.'

Luke sat down.

'You've little enough opinion of us.'

'And sure why would I have more,' Mrs. Gleeson said. 'And I suppose it's your dinner you're expecting now, is it? Expects to be waited on hand and foot.'

'Well...yes,' Luke said.

'Well, you'll have to wait. Now to serious matters. Where are we going to keep the pair of you? We've no spare rooms you know. I'd been thinking we could throw eight or ten of the lads out for the night, it's not as if I haven't been tempted before. But sure they might stop paying me, and where would I be then?'

Winnie had taken the baby from the breast, and re-arranged her dress. She held him close, waiting for him to fall asleep.

'Mrs. Gleeson is suggesting we could take one of the storerooms,' she said.

'Storerooms?' Luke said. 'Sure you can't even stand up in them.'

'Don't you be minding him,' Mrs. Gleeson said. 'We've got three up in the top floor. I'm sure with a bit of rearranging, we could get everything into two. The one on the side has a window. We can open the window, freshen it up, get a bed in and warm it up again after. And if you'd given us enough warning, we'd have had it all ready. But seeing as you didn't, we'll have to wait until the lads get home. Stopped off in the saloon, no doubt. A bit of hard work before their dinner wouldn't hurt them. Might sober them up too.'

Winnie sat down to table that night with twenty coal heavers and anthracite smashers. Despite Mrs. Gleeson's protests, she would not accept anything except soup with bread. The baby was asleep in the kitchen.

Luke had been astonished at how quickly a storeroom could be cleared, but reflected that men who were used to shovelling coal and heaving coal sacks would hardly be put off by furniture and sacks of clothes. What was also unbelievable was the way in which all the furniture had been put into the other two rooms. At first, he had thought it impossible, and came to admire the ingenuity of the other men. And Mrs. Gleeson.

Now the room had been swept out and freshened up, with a large bed and a chest-of-drawers. A single mattress served as Liam's cot.

As Luke had said, the room was hardly high. Wearing her shoes, Winnie's head just touched the ceiling. Luke had to crouch all the time. Still, it was clean and private.

Winnie's presence had influenced the men, just as Mrs. Gleeson had predicted. They were still unruly, but far less than before. And when Winnie spoke, they were even civil.

When the plates were taken away, Winnie was asked to tell of her journey.

'Rough enough,' she said. 'The ship wasn't so bad. We all had some class of a cabin. Six of us to a cabin – seven including little Liam here. Still, it wasn't as bad as the steerage we hear about.'

'Many deaths?' Mick asked.

'Two.'

'Two in the cabin!'

'No. Two in the ship.'

'Two only? How was that?'

'I'm not sure,' Winnie said, 'but from all I heard on the ship, New York and Philadelphia won't let in the ships unless they're clean. Nothing like all we heard about Quebec from last year, that's for sure.'

'Then you were damned lucky,' Jack said. 'Did Luke never tell you about the ship he came out on? The Centaurus.'

'He never said a word,' Winnie said.

'Maybe he didn't want worrying you,' Jack said.

'And maybe we've had enough of this talk,' Mrs. Gleeson said.

'No,' Jack said, forcefully. 'She's damned lucky coming out on a ship where hardly a sinner has died. And Luke never told her about The Centaurus.'

'Why should I?' Luke said. 'It'd only be worrying them back home. And anyhow I'm here, aren't I?'

'You are,' Jack said, 'and how many of your shipmates are not? What was the number you said? A hundred dead? Over a hundred?'

'Something like that,' Luke said. He had no desire to go further. The horrors of the Centaurus were something he would prefer to forget.

'I should have guessed,' Winnie said. 'You went steerage, didn't you? That was a nice letter we got from you from Liverpool, but even then, you knew.'

'Yes, *alanna*, I knew. But I didn't want wasting money on a pricy ticket for me.'

'And waste it instead on a pricy ticket for me?' Winnie said.

'That's different,' Luke said. 'And anyhow, it was better that you got over on a higher class of a ship. It took long enough though, didn't it?'

'It did, right enough,' Jack said. 'And you should have seen your husband here. Terrified of a shipwreck he was.'

'I never said that,' Luke said.

Winnie raised her hand. 'Well, if you all want to know, we'd one bad storm. I thought we were going to sink. You should have heard the shrieking. Poor Liam, sick from the gut, and crying all night. So yes, we had our winter storm alright, only it was in the middle of summer. And the first port of call was Philadelphia. Between one thing and another, I reckon it added another week to the voyage.'

Mrs. Gleeson raised her hands.

'We'll have no more of that. We've heard that story a hundred times. Sure the poor girl has just arrived in from Ireland with her baby. Let's make her welcome and not be bothering her with misery.'

Seán Óg, not being able to understand what had just been said, raised his hand.

Tell us about the blight, and the hunger.'

'Terrible entirely,' she said. Silence. No-one spoke. '*Ye didn't know?*'

'*We've been hearing stories,*' said Luke, '*but your own letter said all was fine.*'

'*I know. The letter I sent you, sure it was true what I said. But then, a few days later, it all began, and I'd already posted the letter. I was going to send you another, but your mother said I'd only be wasting the postage, since you'd know soon enough. And anyhow, I'd be here soon after the letter.*'

'True enough,' Luke said. '*But what's happening in Mayo? What's the real story?*'

Winnie hesitated. Her eyes were wet.

'*It's terrible. The blight is back.*'

'*We thought it was only bits and pieces,*' Seán Óg said.

'*Bits and pieces is right,*' Winnie said. '*It's only the bits and pieces that are left green, and I'll tell you this, they're going to rot, I know that for a certainty. No, the potatoes are gone and there's famine coming. What with that and the evictions, Mayo is in a terrible way.*'

There was an agonised silence in the room. It might only have been seconds, but it felt as if it lasted forever. Then the questions started. Luke knew that Winnie was making a great effort to keep calm, answering everyone's questions and giving more information, not only of what she had seen around Kilduff and Carrigard, but what she had heard from the rest of the County.

'*Why didn't you tell us earlier?*' Seán Óg asked.

'*I was afraid to,*' Winnie answered. '*It's a hard thing to tell. I was hoping ye'd all have known already.*'

As the full story sank in, Luke felt a trembling sensation. He steadied himself on the table and brought himself back to normal. No one else had noticed. They were all too involved with the story of County Mayo.

No rumours now, he thought. Now we know the truth of it.

That night they made love for the first time. Liam slept through it all. Luke lay back afterwards, listening to the regular breathing of the baby.

He thought of asking Winnie more about Mayo, but she was distressed about it already. But what of her voyage?

'That was some journey you had,' he said.

'Ah sure, I didn't get half way through telling it. I'll tell you later. Times are hard at home. By God, your money was most welcome. But I'm thinking I might have to send money to my own people in Brockagh too. One way or another, I'll have to find work.'

Luke was uncertain.

'There's mills around,' he said, 'but you'd not be able to work there with a baby.'

'It's needlework I'm thinking of. They say there's enough work in making shirts, and that you may work in your own home.'

'Yes,' he said, 'and for damned little too. No, you'll not do that. We'll send the money to Brockagh out of my earnings. Anyhow, now that you're out here, we won't have any call for money for tickets. Which reminds me, you never did finish your story about the crossing. How did Liam take it?'

'Badly enough at first. The first week he was sick. I could hardly get him to suck, and when I did, he only threw it all up again. He went awful thin. To be honest, Luke, I thought he would die, but then after a week or so, the illness went, and he sucked and sucked, and put on all his weight again. After that, I'd take him up the deck, when we were seeing whales and the like. He's a happy child, curious too. The girls in my cabin, they just loved him.'

'What kind of girls were they?'

'Decent girls. Not starving, neither. One girl, I got to know well. Her mother and father died in the fever. She and her sister got the money sent to them by their brother in Schenectady. You weren't the only one bringing your family out you know. They were from out Erris...'

'Erris?'

'Sure they wouldn't have had two pennies to rub together. They wouldn't have got here without their brother's money.'

'What about the evictions though?'

'What evictions?' she asked.

'Torán.'

'Oh, Torán, we'd heard all about that. But it wasn't there they were from. Out half way between Bellacorick and Belmullet. More the east end of Erris.'

'They were lucky so.'

'They were. There were few enough chances for them in Mayo.'

'Nor in America,' Luke said. 'Thing's aren't great here, in spite of all ye may hear in Mayo. That's why Farrelly and the lads have left the rails and gone mining. The reason I'm in New York too. If I'd been going on to Harrisburg, I'd have waited for you in Philadelphia. Instead of that, I'm waiting for you here in Jersey, and, by God, Winnie, it's hard work. Not well paid, neither. Working with Irish lads makes it easier, though the foremen are damned tough. But if a man didn't have good friends, this country would break him.'

'Good friends?'

'Jack and Mick. You've met them. Jack's a lad from Turlough I met up in Quebec. We were together all through the winter in the forests along the Gatineau. Mick's from Carrigard. He came out to New York, not knowing where I was, and found me inside a day.'

'But how?'

'He'd heard a friend of mine called Costello had a brother with a bar in Five Points. He followed my trail from there.'

She hugged the baby closer to her.

'Are you saying we should have done the same?'

'Arra no,' Luke said, 'sure that'd be far too risky. Mick could take the chance; it'd be no harm if he never found me. But you and Liam, you couldn't do that. You know, Winnie, there's enough people lost in this country. The fellow I'm talking about whose brother has the bar, his name is *Conaire*. Or was *Conaire*, I should say. *Conaire Ó Coisteala*. Costello as they say it here. I'm sure I mentioned him in the letters I sent ye last year. I met him on the ship coming across, and we worked together in Quebec and in the forest. But they set us working in different parts, me in the forest and him on the river. When we came back down to the river, he wasn't there. No one knew where he'd gone. We haven't heard word of him since, never came to New York like he was intending, and never had anyone write a letter for him. His brother reckons he's dead. So in a way, it was lucky Mick found me. If he'd known I wasn't with *Conaire* any longer, he might never have gone to Costellos' to find me. Still…I'd still like to know what happened to *Conaire*.'

'But…?'

'There's many ways to die in this country Winnie. Many ways to get lost too for that matter.'

'You make it sound terrible, Luke.'

'Oh, I don't know,' he said, 'sure how's it any worse than Mayo? If *Conaire* had stayed there – his family were out in Erris – he'd have been evicted. They were all evicted out in *Torán*, and from all we can understand, there's damned few left alive. But just remember this, my love, we're going to live. We won't lose each other, and tough and all as it's going to be, we'll make a good living, send money home, educate Liam and however more babies we may have. And in the end, it'll be worth it. We'll have our own house, warm in the winter, any amount of food to eat and our children to play with and take care of us in our old age.'

The next morning, Luke went back to the terminal. He half expected to be teased, but he was not.

'A fine woman,' Jack said. 'With all your talk of whenever she'd be sailing, you never told us that.'

They walked across to the dock.

'I'm not surprised,' Mick said. 'I'd heard enough about her in Carrigard.'

'I'm sure you did,' Luke said.

'There was enough bad feeling against the Ryans, that's for sure. But even so, all said she was a decent woman, but tough with it. Very tough.'

Winnie tough? Yes, perhaps. Like everyone, she would have needed to be tough to live through the winter of 1846 and 1847, and the fever that had followed it. Here, they were away from all that. Yes, the winters were cold here, but people were well used to that. Still, Five Points and Jersey City were tough places to make a living.

He had little doubt that it would be even tougher raising children in a mining town.

One evening, they discussed it all.

'We're going to have to send money back to Mayo,' Luke said. 'You know that as well as I do.'

'I do,' Winnie said, 'and some for my own family too. It's not that we can afford it, but we have to do it. Isn't that the way of it?'

'It is,' Luke said.

'And the sooner the better. We'll have to arrange the money tomorrow.'

'But I'm working,' Luke said.

'Don't worry,' she said. 'I'll go over on my own.'

'I don't know that you should.'

'I came on my own.'

'Yes, but that was only from the docks.'

'Just give me directions to the bank, and stop all your worrying.'

Next morning, Winnie left Liam with Mrs. Gleeson, and took the ferry across to Manhattan. When she returned, she gave the draft to Luke.

'Well?' he asked.

'I found the Chemical Bank easy enough.'

'Anne Street and Broadway?'

'Yes.'

'And?'

Now she was silent. Then she spoke.

'Oh God, is it all like that?

'It is, my pet, and worse. If you think Anne Street is bad, wait till you go to Five Points. Or perhaps, you'd better not.'

That evening, Luke wrote a letter to Michael and Eleanor, enclosing the draft and requesting that cash also be sent on to Winnie's parents in Brockagh.

Chapter 7

Freeman's Journal, Dublin, August 1848:

State of Mayo. Castlebar. The idea that the half-starved population of Mayo were, or are, about to rise in rebellion, is laughed at by everyone here conversant with the state of the county. Yet still the preparations for war are going on. General Sir Michael Creagh arrived here on Friday, and assumed the command of the military stationed in this garrison and county. He immediately put himself in communication with the Earl of Lucan, Lieutenant of Mayo; and with the other authorities of the county. Subsequently there was an inspection of the powder magazine, the barracks, barrack stores, military depots and the Repeal loop holes of 1843.

The news of Danny's death had come as a shock in Carrigard, and the fact that Pat had given no cause was mysterious to Eleanor. Fever? Or some kind of accident? A rock-fall, perhaps? Who knows?

'We'll have to wait and see,' Michael told her.

'Or should we write to him?'

'I don't know. I'll think about it. Was there any money with it?'

'None.'

'Strange.'

'Yes, we could certainly do with it.'

She was surprised when another letter arrived from Stockport three days later. Surely, nothing could have happened to anyone else. Pat even? No, the handwriting on the envelope was clearly his. She ripped it open and the two money notes fluttered out.

'Well, that's one good thing,' Michael commented.

'So what does he say about Danny?' Eleanor asked.

'Still nothing. Nothing at all. Just says he thinks the two pounds might be of use to us.'

'Maybe he forgot the money last time. Or maybe he's heard about the blight. He'll know that we need it now more than before.'

'Yes,' Michael said. 'They'll have blight all over England by now.'

But Eleanor's morbid curiosity was even more than before.

'You'll have to write now, Michael. Find out what's happened to Danny.'

'Yes, yes. I will.'

But he did not.

Two days later, yet another letter arrived from Pat.

'No money this time,' Michael commented.

'What does he tell us about Danny?'

'Nothing. Good news for a change, though. He's coming home.'

Eleanor was startled.

'Coming home? Pat?'

'He's coming home to Mayo.'

'Has he lost his job? Is that it?'

'No,' Michael said. 'He's been offered some position with the County in Castlebar. This Gaffney fellow, he wants him back.'

'Must be some kind of clerking so.'

'Yes, I think it must.'

Eleanor could not sleep that night. Pat was coming home. Many thoughts swirled around her head. A position with the County. How long would that last though? And what would he do when it finished? Go back to England? Or stay on the farm? Who knew? And what of Sarah?

She was more impatient than ever now. She had no idea when Pat would be returning. Tomorrow? Next week? Next month?

Kingstown was a revelation for Pat. Kingstown port was nothing compared to Liverpool in extent, but the single dock was enormous. He tried counting the number of ships inside, but gave up. He watched the long harbour walls as they came in, until they disembarked at a dock at the end of the harbour.

'All rock?' he asked an officer at the end of the gangway.

'Granite. Every bit of it.'

Pat thought of the railway embankments Danny's men worked on. Nothing like this, and all rock! He had expected it in Liverpool but not in Ireland.

'Where did they get the rock?' he asked.

'Up there,' the officer answered, pointing to a quarry. 'Top of Dalkey Hill. They used to just push the wagons over the edge and let them roll down the rails on their own. They'd get up to one hell of a speed.'

Pat wondered whether he should believe it.

He walked towards Dublin. At first the coast was rocky, the breakers sending spume high into the air. Later, it became calmer and flatter, and, as the tide ebbed, a wide beach opened beside him. Children were splashing in the water, an impossible distance out from the shore.

When he reached Sandymount, he spotted a bar. The sun was half way across the sky. He went in and ordered a pie and a beer. He joined three young men at a table, and listened to their accounts of famine in Ireland. Then they spoke of the rebellion. They too had heard that half the country was in rebellion, and the government overthrown, but it turned out these stories had been over-blown. The real rebellion in Ballingarry in County Tipperary had only lasted for a day or so. One or two men had been killed, but in the end, it had all fizzled out. What kind of rebellion was that?

When he reached the city, he turned west on the Liffey, past the Guinness Brewery and the front of Kingsbridge Station.

He crossed the Liffey by the King's Bridge, and turned west on the same route as he had used going to England, only four or five months before. It all seemed so long ago.

The poverty on the west side of Dublin was not as extreme as he had expected, from all he had heard of the famine in Ireland.

Lucan, Maynooth, Kinnegad, Mullingar.

Crowds outside all the workhouses though. And the potato fields were blackened.

Three days later he arrived in Longford. There were hundreds of people outside Longford Workhouse. He was surrounded by a dozen wasted women begging for food. He pushed through and went on.

He left Longford and walked towards the Shannon. For the first hour, he met gaunt people walking towards him.

'To the Poor House,' one woman told him. 'Where else?'

He passed one body in the ditch, two dogs tearing at it, growling at each other. He crossed the Shannon. As he came closer to Strokestown, more wasted figures were on the road. On one occasion, he was threatened by three young men, who mocked his clothes. He was afraid they might try to steal the corn in his pack, but then they backed off.

Crossing through the rest of Roscommon and into County Mayo was a real shock. Again and again, he passed by tumbled mud cabins. Ballaghaderreen Workhouse was the first in County Mayo. It was far worse than any of the midlands workhouses. But Knockanure Workhouse was worst of all. There was a vast crowd outside the gates. Hundreds? Thousands? There was no way to count. There was a keening sound from the women. The crowd stretched over the whole road. He pushed his way along the wall of the workhouse, as far as the gate. He peered through it, to where inmates wheeled rough-made barrows with corpses. He remembered the nightmare of the death pit – the naked white bodies and the squeaking of the rats.

He had thought of visiting Voisey. A decent fellow, Voisey, who had always done his best for the inmates, and for Pat. A deeply religious man.

But the sight of the barrows had put him off, and he suspected he would have chances to meet Voisey again over the next few weeks. He pushed on, past two corpses at the edge of the wall. How many had fever? Dead or alive? Too late for that now.

At last he broke free of the crowd, and walked out the road towards Kilduff. He had been six days travelling from Kingstown.

It was late when he arrived in Carrigard.

It had just begun to rain. He drew himself under the shelter of the slates, and knocked.

Michael answered. He took a step back in surprise, and then he shook Pat's hand.

'Good to see you, my lad.'

Pat entered. Eleanor was seated. A single candle was burning on the table. She came over and hugged him.

'Pat, thank God you're home.'

He thought she looked thinner in the face than she had been, but perhaps it was just that the faint light made her look older.

He placed five sovereigns on the table.

'And look what I have for ye.'

The queen's head glinted amber in the candlelight. *Victoria Dei Gratia.* Eleanor grasped the coins. 'Oh Pat!'

'That'll help us all get through till Luke gets settled,' Pat said.

'It will,' said Eleanor, 'and we're thankful for it.'

He sat down at the table as Eleanor poured three cups of *poitín*. He had noticed the animals at the end of the house. The smell of manure was strong. Michael followed his gaze.

'Not what you're used to, I'd say.'

'I wasn't expecting it,' Pat said.

'They'd all be gone for eating if we left them outside.'

Pat sniffed at the *poitín*. The pungent aroma helped to kill the stink of animals.

'You'll have a good job with Gaffney in Castlebar,' Eleanor said.

'I will,' Pat replied, 'but I must say, crossing the country I had my doubts. It's in a terrible way, and Mayo the worst.'

'Isn't that the more reason you should be helping your own people rather than building railways in England.'

There was a silence, only interrupted by the quiet breathing of the animals.

'You're right,' Pat said at last. 'And I don't think railways are the thing for me anymore. Not with Danny gone.'

Silence again. The horse snorted.

'So…what happened to Danny?' Michael asked.

'He was run over by a train.'

He saw the immediate reaction in Eleanor's eyes. Her face went pale.

'By a train?' she gasped.

'How could that have happened?' Michael asked.

'It was on purpose,' Pat replied. 'Danny killed himself.'

'Killed himself?' Michael echoed.

'Yes.'

'But…but…how could they know?' Eleanor asked. 'Who saw it?'

'Only the engine driver, and I must confess, I never spoke to him. It was the fellow in the morgue told me, but I reckon he wasn't lying. Danny stood by the side waiting, and only stood on the track a second or two before. No way could the driver stop.'

'It's hard to believe,' Eleanor said.

'I'd find it so,' said Pat, 'except for one other thing. Danny had no reason to be out on the Manchester & Birmingham railway. He had no contracts there. His main contract was on the North Staffordshire, and smaller ones around Manchester, and up north, but nothing in the direction of Birmingham. No, Danny killed himself right enough.'

'But why?' Michael asked.

'Hard to be sure, but he'd been in a bad way. There's been a terrible crash in the money markets in England. The banks are near bankrupt, and the railway companies – they're cutting back on contracts all over.'

'So is Edwardes & Ryan going under?'

'I doubt that,' Pat said. 'This Irene woman, she's a tough lady. She'll see it through right enough. How Murteen will end up, God only knows, but he'll have to be tougher than Danny ever was to be dealing with the likes of that bitch. We had all reckoned Danny as a tough fellow, until we met her, and I'd never have expected the likes of that in a woman. How long Murteen will last, I haven't the slightest idea, but if he's still there this time next year, I'd be surprised. All I know is that she was a desperate burden on Danny, and that surely didn't help.'

He sipped at his *poitín*.

He was getting used to the smell of the animals. The rain of a few minutes ago, was heavier now, drumming against the windows on a rising wind. Lucky to get back before that, he thought.

'There was something else too,' he went on. 'When Uncle Murty and Aunty Aileen left Danny, that was a terrible blow to him, and even I could see that. It's a strange business, when you think about it. The son leaving his father and mother, that's only natural, but the other way around, you'd have to question that.'

'So why…? Why did they leave?' Eleanor asked.

'Well, working with Danny, that was a great surprise for Uncle Murty. Or more in the line of a shock. He had expected an easy clerical job in Stockport, and so it was, except for having to deal with Irene every day. But worse than that, it was when he found out how Danny – and Irene – were running the business.'

'But we heard good reports of that,' Michael said. 'Roughneen, Lavan and the rest. They were all earning good money.'

'Yes,' Pat said, 'and keeping their mouths shut too. No, it wasn't the fellows around here that were doing badly at all. It was the fellows out west – Erris, Achill, Partry, and around – they'd have a different story to tell. At first, Danny would meet them off the boats in Liverpool, and when he got too busy, Murteen would do it instead. Always looking for desperate fellows, straight off the cattle boats from Dublin or Westport. Starving they were. And what did they find when they got to Liverpool? Either they weren't let off the boats if anyone on the boat had fever, or the workhouses wouldn't have them, so they starved. And the English hated them.'

'But why?' Eleanor asked.

'They reckoned they were taking their jobs from them, and I suppose they were right too. But worse than that, the Irish navvies were driving wages down all along the railways. Look at the wages that Danny was paying them. Ten pence, eleven pence a day.'

'But Roughneen…?' Eleanor asked.

'Yes, I know. Four shillings a day. Good money. But the fellows from the west of Mayo, they never got that kind of wage. They were starving and desperate, having to send money back to their families, or bring them over when they could. And with only being able to speak Irish, what else could they do? I'll say one thing though, Danny fed them well; well enough to build up their strength, though with the cheapest cuts of meat. Vile stuff, I wouldn't touch it myself, but healthy. And the places they were living in along the railways, shacks only – *sceilps* we'd call them – and they were deadly places. The fever killed them at an awful rate.'

The candle flickered. Eleanor stood, and found another in the cupboard, a rough one, made of dirty tallow. She held the wick over the lighted candle until it flared. She licked her thumb and forefinger and extinguished the spent candle, then pressed the new one into the liquid tallow beneath.

'But what had all this to do with Murty?' Michael asked.

'It was his conscience,' Pat said. 'Once he saw their conditions, he reckoned Danny was no better than the worst of the landlords back here in Mayo, and he himself was all part of the scheme. But he knew Gilligan and the lads were working over on the Leeds & Thirsk railway, and they were working under far better conditions. They have their own gang, as you well know, and they worked direct with the big contractors. Worked damned hard too, and earned damned good wages.'

'But sure Murty wouldn't be able for that kind of work.'

'That's not what they wanted him for. They wanted someone to look after the money side of things, and deal with the contractors' bosses, so as to make sure everything was done right. It wasn't a hard job. No, Murty was happy enough with it.'

'And what about Aileen?' Eleanor asked.

'Well, the time I met her over in Leeds, she was the same as usual. Quiet as she always was.'

'And what about now?'

'Hard to say. I didn't meet her for long, the time of the funeral. But you know what she thought about Danny. It was a desperate shock for her and my own guess is that she'd be worse now. Don't take that as gospel though, I don't know for sure.'

Eleanor's lip was quivering. Pat looked away.

'And Murteen?' Michael asked. 'What was he doing all this time?'

'Like I say, going down to Liverpool Docks – Liverpool Workhouse too – and recruiting the poor beggars off the boats. Not that he liked it, I can tell you. He forced himself to do it though, and that's a hard thing for any man. And it's another reason why I don't think Murteen will last the course.'

'And what about Jamesy McManus?' Eleanor asked.

'You'd heard about that?'

'Sure it was all around Mayo. They're saying he got shot.'

'I didn't think you'd have heard about it. But yes, he got shot right enough. It was on one of Danny's contracts where Jamesy was foreman. There were differences between his men and the English navvies on the next part of the line. Some English fellow got beaten on Jamesy's site. He'd been running some class of shebeen, and when he died, Jamesy got shot in return. I've no idea who started it all. Something to do with the Molly Maguire gang, that's what they're saying.'

'But sure they're not in England,' Michael said.

'They are, and that's for a certainty. Liverpool, perhaps even Manchester, I don't know. But sure wherever there's Irish, there's Irish gangs. The Repealers too, though they're not killers like the Molly Maguire gang are. And Liverpool – the government fears what might happen there. The army is crawling all over the place.'

'Good God,' Michael said, 'I thought it bad us having rebellions over here. From all you're saying, it's as bad over there.'

'I don't know,' Pat said. 'It's bad, that's for sure. What happens next, I don't know.'

Eleanor put a bowl of corn on the table in front of him.

'Would you hold your whisht now, and just eat up.'

He took a spoonful of the corn. Hard perhaps, and a bit gritty. Imported corn from America. Who knew? There were other things on his mind.

'So how about Winnie,' he asked. 'Gone to America? She'll be near there now.'

'She will,' Michael answered. 'She left back at the end of July. Luke wrote around that time. He had some kind of settled address in a place called Jersey City, right beside New York, I understand. So he sent the money, and there was a ship going from Westport to New York a few days later, so we booked the passage. A good class of ship. We saw it ourselves, when we brought Winnie over to Westport.'

'You brought her over?'

'Sure it'd be too far for her to go on her own with her bags and the little baby.'

'That was kind of ye.'

'There's another thing,' Eleanor said, interrupting. 'We thought we'd go and visit Sarah, but they told us the workhouse was in a desperate way with the fever, and they wouldn't let us in, and they said she wouldn't come out neither. Whether she got our message or not, I couldn't tell you.'

'Not surprising,' Pat said.

'Was there some falling out between ye?'

'Not a falling out. At least not with Sarah. More with her mother. I don't know, she was never all in favour, and when I went off working with Danny, I think she was reckoning I'd only be some class of a navvy in England for the rest of my life. At least that's the way I understand it. Sarah wrote me, and let me know, but sure what could she do about it?'

Yes. Eleanor thought. *So that's it. But now he's back and a clerking with the County too. Will it last though? If it does, they'll have a chance, but if it doesn't...*

That evening, Sabina arrived from Kilduff, and Pat had to repeat much of what he had said earlier. When he was finished, Eleanor turned to Sabina.

'So tell me,' she said, 'you never told us any more about the revolution.'

'Oh that,' Sabina said. 'All these armies they were raising; sure they weren't there at all. Only a few hundred men when it came to it. Killed a few fellows, and then surrendered. They're all to be transported. The Battle of the Widow McCormack's Cabbage Patch – that's what the dealers are calling it. They think it's funny.'

After Sabina left, Pat retired early. Eleanor stayed up making the brown

99

bread, hoping she wasn't disturbing him. When she went to bed, Michael was sitting at the small table beside the wash-hand basin.

'What are you doing, Michael?'

'Just writing to Luke and Winnie. They'll be wanting to know about the hunger and what happened to Danny.'

'Well, you can tell them the better news too. Pat is home.'

'Yes,' Michael said, 'I'll tell them that too.'

Pat left for Castlebar. Eleanor gave him half a loaf of bread and kissed him on the cheek.

'Now you make sure to mind yourself, and don't be catching any of them fevers around Mayo.'

'I won't, mother.'

'And let us know what this Gaffney fellow wants with you. It's strange that he should have asked for you only.'

'I don't know the answer to that either, mother, but I think the fact that I was Luke's brother had something to do with it.'

He left and walked through Kilduff, and out the Castlebar road. As he came closer to Castlebar, he saw the evidence of an eviction. A gaunt woman stood at the side of the road. Her blouse was ragged. One shrivelled breast drooped inside.

'*Cloonteebawnan*' she said in answer to his question. '*They threw us out and levelled the houses*. Lord Lucan. The Exterminator.'

As he continued towards Castlebar, he walked past straggled lines of families with donkeys and carts, dead bodies in many of them. Starving children with protruding ribs, bald heads and hair on the face, sat on the carts and the donkeys. He heard more and more about the Lucan evictions and wrecked villages all around Castlebar.

Aughadrina, Ballure, Ballinabul, Ardvarny, Sarnaught, Aghaleska, Antagua, Curnamara, New Antrim, Stabal, Knockthomas, and Ballymacragh.

And Gallows Hill.

As he approached the centre of the town, he saw a thin straggling line of ragged people along the edge of the Mall. He walked over to see what was happening.

A group of mounted soldiers were riding in formation down the Mall. Fifty or so, Pat thought. Their magnificent appearance caught his eye at once. They wore red uniforms topped with high black bearskins. All the horses were grey. He remembered what the soldier in Liverpool had told him of the Scots Greys being sent to Castlebar.

The officer carried a large axe, glinting in the sunlight.

On an order the group turned, maintaining perfect formation. Then they stopped. The officer roared a command and the soldiers whipped out sabres, holding them level towards the front. Pat was alarmed now.

'*What's happening,*' he whispered to an old woman standing beside him. She turned a thin face towards him.

'*Arra, pay them no mind*' she said, '*They're only playing at soldiers. They think they're still at* Waterloo.'

Another command was shouted, and the entire formation charged the length of the green, coming to a rapid halt just before the link chain at the end. A baby was crying.

'*Sure it's only a game,*' the old woman said. '*They do it every day. Trying to frighten us. Showing what great lads they are.*'

'*Aye*' Pat said, '*and I'll tell you, they frightened me too.*'

'*It's easy frightened you are.*'

'*Maybe I am.*'

'*And wouldn't you think they'd have enough starving people to frighten in their own country, not to be coming here to frighten the babies in Mayo.*'

He went on to the workhouse. Hundreds of people were milling around the front gate, many standing, more sitting or lying. A group of soldiers looked threateningly at the starving mass, but there was little danger from these people. Closer in, a woman lay on the ground, but whether she was alive or dead, he could not tell.

He pushed his way through the crowd, who parted without a word. As he got through, a soldier pointed a bayonet at his stomach.

'I'm here for George Gaffney' he said. The man looked at him.

'George Gaffney,' Pat repeated. He held out Gaffney's letter. The man snatched the letter from Pat, and held it as if to read it, though, as Pat noticed, he was holding it upside down.

'Hold on here,' he said to Pat. He went back and handed the letter through the gate to a bored looking corporal, who walked back towards the administration block with the letter. Pat stayed standing, the bayonet still pointing towards him.

A full ten minutes later, Gaffney appeared at the gate.

'Pat. At last. All this time I've been waiting for you.'

'I'm sure you have' said Pat, 'and you'll be waiting a lot longer if this fellow doesn't get out of my way.'

The corporal shouted at the soldier, and the bayonet was lowered. Pat went to the gate.

'We can't risk opening it,' Gaffney said. 'You'll have to climb.'

'I know. Amn't I well used to that.'

He pulled himself up, balancing above the spiked bars at the top, and dropped down the other side.

Gaffney led him towards the administration block.

'Over in England, eh?'

'I had to. Wasn't much point in staying here, once Knockanure let me go.'

'So how's England?'

'Well, they've more food than here. But the way some of them are treating the Irish, you wouldn't believe it. And not just the English gangers, the Welsh too. The Mayo fellows are worst of all, and leading the lot, was my own cousin.'

'Your own cousin?'

'Danny. Murtybeg's brother.'

'Ah yes. I remember Murtybeg. Daniel Ryan too. He has a savage reputation all along the west of Mayo.'

He opened the door to his office. They entered the room. Papers, files and crates were lined along the wall. One wall consisted of a bookcase, floor to ceiling. Every shelf was stuffed full of paper. There was a desk, a chair and a rough-cut table.

'Like you say, he was a tough fellow, our Danny,' Pat said. 'He worked with Luke on the Railways before the hunger started. Too damned cute to come home with Luke though. Reckoned there were great chances in contracting on the Railways – what with giving work to all the Mayo fellows coming over at wages that were near starvation. They didn't know any better, coming from Ireland. That's why he wanted men from the Mayo Workhouses. But you know all that, I'm sure.'

'And you were working with him this past while?'

'Yes, to my eternal shame. I worked with Danny and Murtybeg and Danny's wife-to-be. Herself and Danny, a more vicious pair you never met. They had me working on accounts. Being family, I was paid well, and I had enough money to send a good amount back over to Kilduff. But I knew I couldn't keep working like that. It turned out then that the real reason they wanted me was to give out the sackings when contracts were being cancelled.'

'Sackings?'

'Yes,' Pat said, 'the number of contracts were down, so Danny didn't want the men. It was either them or the business.'

'And what happened after the sackings? What did the men do?'

'Damned if I know. And damned if Danny would care. I guess the most of them would have gone to Manchester Workhouse, though how many'd get in, God only knows. The Workhouses are snowed under with Irish beggars.'

'What about Liverpool?' Gaffney asked.

'Liverpool is worse. They say there's tens of thousands of Irish coming through every month, and the workhouse doesn't want them. They're sending them back too.'

'I know,' Gaffney said. 'We hear of shiploads of them coming back into Westport. Killala and Ballina too. But sure the workhouses there are all full, so there's crowds of them end up back here in Castlebar, looking for admission.'

'I can understand all that,' Pat said. 'It's not just our fellows, there's sackings right across the railways, thousands and tens of thousands of fellows on the tramp. They're starving, up and down the length and breadth of England. The government is terrified of them. I've seen what it's like in Liverpool. They've got the army all over the place, and everyone's talking of revolution. All these sackings have England in a terrible way.'

Gaffney picked up his pen from the desk.

'So that was why you came home, was it? Prefer to be working here with us than sacking men in England.'

'That was part of it, right enough, but not the only thing. I'd decided to stay on for Danny's wedding. And then, a few days before he was to be wed, Danny went and killed himself.'

'He did what!'

'Killed himself. Thought he was smarter than the rest of us but in the end, he wasn't. The Railway Panic, he never saw that coming.'

'Yes, I'd heard about that.'

'Terrible time, it was, on the railways. Still is. Danny lost contracts, and the ones he kept, they had to drop their prices. In the end, he couldn't take it, tough and all as he was. Stood in front of a train – it tore him to pieces.'

The expression on Gaffney's face was one of disbelief.

'Whatever Danny was; it must have been one hell of a kick in the teeth for you.'

'It was,' Pat said, 'and it wasn't the last one either. Once Danny was gone, that damned woman of his reckoned she could run Edwardes & Ryan on her own, and that was the day after the funeral. Not one for weeping, I'll tell you. I worked out bloody fast that I couldn't work for a woman like that. So when your letter arrived, by Christ, it was most welcome. I left Murtybeg behind though. God only knows how he'll deal with that bitch. We'll see.'

'Poor fellow,' Gaffney said. 'But anyhow, this is my office. I'm sure you're used to better offices in England. Better wages too.'

'*Arra*, pay no mind to that,' Pat said. 'I'm happier back here doing the little I can, and God knows, it looks as if you'll need it. But tell me this. What are the dragoons doing in Castlebar?'

'Oh, the Greys. That's nothing but foolishness. The Crown have got this idea that the starving men of Mayo are about to rise in rebellion.'

'Rebellion? Are they serious?'

'They are. It's utterly daft, of course, but still they go on preparing for war. General Creagh arrived here and assumed the command of the military. There's talk the Earl of Lucan is coming too.'

'Lucan!'

'Why not? He's Lieutenant of Mayo and represents the civil power, as they put it. He'll be advising Creagh. Can you imagine it, Pat, the Exterminator himself advising the army on war? He won't even pay his poor rates to feed the people. Well versed in evictions he is, though, so you can guess the kind of war the dragoons will be waging against Mayo.'

'That's terrible.'

'It is, but there's damned little you and I can do about it.'

'So what can I do then?'

'Plenty. But it's not just sorting out paper I'll be wanting you for,' Gaffney said. 'There's a lot more than that in what I'm expecting from you. You can see from the papers around you, the County and the Unions are in a state of utter chaos. But no, there's worse than that.'

He went over to the shelves and took down a folder of papers.

'Here,' he said, 'look at this. Letters begging for help. They come from all sorts of people – masters of workhouses, justices of the peace, local committees of all sorts, landlords even. And worst of all, priests. And that might shock you, why I say 'worst of all'. I'll tell you why, it's because they're closest to their flocks, and they can describe the suffering of the people. They'd wring tears from any man. Yes, we know – you know as well as I do – that Mayo is in a terrible condition. No matter what we do, it can never be enough. We need money – tens of thousands – no, more like hundreds of thousands – to make the slightest impression on it all. And what do we have? Less than ever before. Half the landlords are bankrupt, and can't pay a penny of the County Rates. As for the other half – Lucan and the like – it's like getting blood from a stone. The Rates Proctors are going up and down the county trying to get money from them, bankrupt or otherwise. They send them letters, they take them to court, and what do they do? They get judgements against them, but judgements aren't money, they won't feed anyone.'

'So what can we do?' Pat asked.

'Ensure that whatever little money we have is spent in the best possible way. And that is impossible to assess. Everyone who writes in to us, the priests especially, their parish, their village, whatever, is the worst of all. I don't blame them for that. They've no idea what's happening in the next parish, how could they? The same with all the rest of them. So sitting here in Castlebar is no use at all. We have to decide which parishes and which baronies need the money the most. And for that we need someone who's willing to travel the County and decide…'

Pat looked up in shock.

'Decide!'

Now he understood the full reality of what he was being asked to do. Not just observe. Decide too.

'I know,' Gaffney said, before Pat could say anything more. 'Giving out sackings in England was an awful job, I'm sure, and I'm not saying this is any better. In fact, it might be a great deal worse, but at least you'll know that the work you're doing is beneficial to humanity.'

'But you want me to decide where the food goes.'

'If not you, your reports will decide it for us. Not that there's much money for food anyhow.'

He threw a notebook on the desk.

'Here, you'll need this.'

He put a pencil on top.

'You might as well take notes of what I'm saying, Pat, and get well used to taking notes. The way I reckon it is this. There's starvation right across the county, but the centre is best, or least bad, should I say. The Plains of Mayo – that's the better land. Lucan's gangs are still evicting people for sheep runs there, but we have some knowledge of that. And we know all about his evictions around Castlebar. And in spite of the dreadfulness of that, I still reckon the real starvation is around the edge of the County.'

'I'd say you're right.'

'Four places are worst. The Ox Mountains, and you'll know them well enough from your work in Knockanure. Father Nugent is the priest in the mountains. Then there's Erris, and God knows it's savage there, and damned near unreachable. And Partry – we're getting fierce reports from there. Father Ward particularly. And the seacoast from Leenane to Louisburgh, close up to Mweelrea Mountain, there's many dying there.'

'And Achill?' Pat asked. 'What about Achill?'

'Don't think we haven't thought about that.' Gaffney replied. 'No, for the moment, we have to leave it to Nangle and his gang of damned missionaries and proselytisers. It's not what we'd want to do, but he has his friends in Dublin and back in England, and he can get the money and food supplies from there. Our task for now is to feed their bodies, and Nangle can do that for us in Achill. Their immortal souls can wait till after.'

'So then, it's the Ox, Erris, Partry and Mweelrea?'

'That's right. So what I want you to do is to travel these areas for us. I want you to meet everyone you can. We'll give you names of the people who have written us letters, and anyone else we know, but like I said, they'll all tell you their area is worst. Have them take you to the villages and farms around? Note down everything about evictions, and find out in each village how many survivors there might have been from starvation and disease thus far. You should go into the cabins too to witness the truth of what you're being told, but be careful you don't get fever. And everywhere you go, sit down in the evenings or whenever you can, and scribble notes as best you can. Always remember, whatever you say, we must assess the worst need and want from what you tell us. People will live and die on foot of your notes.'

Pat stayed two days in the County offices with Gaffney. He read all the desperate petitions, requests, demands and pleas from all around the County. What he read was a picture of Hell. And his job was to find the truth of it.

He found the County maps and studied them too. Many of them were Ordnance Survey Maps, mostly from the 1838 survey, though some were many years older, and, he suspected, far out of date.

There were villages, hundreds of them, most of whose names he had not known. Mountains, lakes and bogs. He wondered how easy it would be to find any of them.

Then it was time to go.

Gaffney organised a pack for him with a single change of clothes and a package of food. He also gave him an introductory letter and a general provisions requisition for use in the Unions around the county, so that he would not starve.

'There's no point in sacrificing yourself,' he told him. 'You have to be able to think clearly.'

Then Pat took a horse from the stables, forced his way out through the gates, and set off in the direction of Carrigard and the Ox Mountains.

Chapter 8

Dublin Evening Post. September 1848:
The Earl and Countess of Lucan, the Ladies Bingham, and
suite, arrived at Castlebar House on Friday last, on their usual
autumnal visit to his lordship's estates in the county Mayo.
The noble Earl and Countess are in excellent health.

As he rode out of Castlebar. It was cold, but not raining. The cartloads of
starving children and dead bodies no longer upset him.

Eleanor was surprised when he arrived with a horse.

'Best bring it inside,' she said. 'We don't want losing it.'

He led the horse through the door, and settled it down on straw at the far
end of the kitchen. Eleanor sat him down with a cup of buttermilk.

'Now tell me, what's this job Gaffney has for you?'

'The worst possible, mother. He wants me to travel the County and
make reports back on the condition of every part of it.'

'Don't they have reports enough?'

'They do, and that's the problem. Everyone who reports, priests and all,
they make it sound as if their parish is the worst. Since the County doesn't
have enough money, they have to decide which parishes are really the worst,
and where the money might go.'

'So how do you choose?' Eleanor asked. 'How do you choose where to
start?'

'Well, we've a good idea of that already. Erris, Partry and Mweelrea for
sure, but seeing as Luke and myself were working in Knockanure and up the
Ox Mountains, Gaffney reckoned it was best to start with the Ox, so I'm
heading over to Knockanure now.'

He rode on to Knockanure. The usual crowd of men, women and
children were outside the gates, most thin, some skeletal. With difficulty,
he fought his way through, and, using Gaffney's introductory letter, he was
admitted with his horse.

The next morning, he walked to the Union building. To the side, two
inmates were working beside a heap of clay. The edge of the death pit.

Voisey met him.

'Pat! What brings you here?'

Pat explained Gaffney's plan.

'Yes, yes,' Voisey said quickly. 'Come on in.'

Pat gave his horse to an inmate, and followed Voisey into the administration block. Voisey sat him in front of his desk, as Pat explained the plan in more detail.

'I can see the sense of it,' Voisey said. 'You know what, I'm only hoping you see us as the worst, because, by God, we need the money. Where could be worse in Mayo?'

'There might be one or two places,' Pat said, without revealing more.

'So what's your plan?'

'I'm thinking of going on up to Brockagh and meeting with Father Nugent, find out what he thinks.'

'Yes,' said Voisey, 'that'd be an excellent idea. In fact, best of all might be to do that, and then visit me on the way back.'

'I'll do that so,' Pat said, 'but tell me this, how's Knockanure, how's the workhouse?'

Voisey made an arch of his fingers, as if thinking.

'Frightful. We can't feed the whole countryside, and you see the results of that at the gate. We're always near bankrupt. So for those we do admit, we have food, very little, but enough to keep body and soul together for a few weeks at least. So long as we can keep the grain merchants paid, the corn will keep coming.'

'And the fever?'

'Not as bad as it was last year, but it's always there. There's times I wonder what good we're doing, any of us. If the hunger doesn't get them, the fever will, and it just goes on and on.'

An hour later, Pat left Knockanure, and rode in the direction of Brockagh.

That evening he found a ruined cabin, the straw-thatched roof half collapsed. He took some of the thatch from the ground and brought it in to what was left standing of the cabin. He brought the horse inside too and slept on the straw.

When he left, it was raining and still dark. He rode on, his hat pulled down to his nose.

Slowly, the rain cleared, as the sun rose behind grey cloud. By the time he reached Brockagh, the sky was clear. The town was quiet. There was no answer to his knock at either the church or the priest-house. Two men stood leaning against the corner of a cabin, watching him closely, but saying nothing.

From memory, he found his way to Gallagher's. Winnie's mother answered his knock.

'I know that face,' she said.

'Of course, you do,' Pat answered. 'Pat Ryan.'

'Luke's brother, is it? Come on in out of that. Better bring the horse in too.'

She sat him at the table, as two children came shyly out of the back room, and stared at him.

'I've met these young fellows before,' Pat said.

'You have,' Mrs. Gallagher said. 'These are our twins. Up to devilment the pair of them are, all the time.'

'No, we're not,' one of the boys said.

'They think they can get away with anything when their father's not around. That's right, you little devil you.'

There was no answer from the boys.

'Is John out working?' Pat asked.

'Out working is right,' Mrs. Gallagher said. 'Over in England he is, himself and young John, building railways.'

'But – young John?'

'I know, ten years old he is now, and a sharp lad. I don't know what kind of work they'll have him doing, but I'm hoping it's a bit lighter than the men. It's hard work building railways, I understand.'

'It is,' said Pat. 'But we never heard of them going to England.'

'John didn't want saying to anyone.'

'But why? Why did he go?'

'He couldn't take it any longer, what with friends and the like not knowing him anymore.'

So Gallagher had left. Like Luke, he could not take the hatred? Had he been blamed for working as a foreman? Perhaps.

'I understand,' Pat said.

'So what about Winnie?' she asked him. 'She's gone now too?'

'She is,' Pat said.

'To a better place, I hope,' she said; tears in her eyes.

'Jersey City. It's right by New York. A much better place, by all accounts.'

'I'm sure it is,' she said. 'It was a pity she couldn't come over. She wrote me, but said the ship was going too soon for to visit me.'

'It was,' said Pat.

Mrs. Gallagher wiped at a tear running down her cheek.

'Ach, I'm sorry, 'tisn't crying I should be when my daughter is off to a new world. The little lad too. But even so, 'tis sad he had to go, and I not even having seen him. Sure it would have been impossible for any of us to travel with the way the County is. I'd have tried to make it down your country myself, but with John gone and two little ones, sure what could I do.'

Again, she wiped at her cheek.

'And what about yourselves,' Pat asked. 'Are you intending to join John in England?'

'Not as long as I don't have to,' she said. 'So long as John can send us enough money to buy corn, we'll stay here. He still believes in Mayo, believes there's a living to be made here, when the times come together again. God knows when that will be though. And it'll take longer for people to forget the Relief Works – they're already saying they were worse than the workhouse. So yes, we're eating, but that's only because of the money John sends back. There's thousands around here dying from hunger and fever. How long it can go on, I just do not know. All I know is this, we're planning on waiting until the early harvest next year. If the potatoes are gone at that time, then it's off to England with all of us.'

It was late in the afternoon when he returned to the church. A priest was standing on the steps outside, and Pat recognised him as Father Nugent.

A donkey and cart had drawn up alongside. An old man knelt by the cart. It was only as Pat got closer he realised what was in the cart. Corpses. All were desperately emaciated; yellow and purple in colour. Father Nugent raised his hand in blessing. When the blessing was finished, the old man stood and wordlessly took the donkey's bridle. Slowly the cart turned and trundled past Pat. Neither he nor the old man said a word.

Father Nugent glanced at him as he came up the steps.

'Do you think all these blessings are worth anything?' he asked.

'What?'

'All these blessings, and we can't even bury them in consecrated ground. There's no one with the strength to dig graves anymore. Do you think there's a God at all? Do you think he listens to us?'

'Well, I don't know...but sure there must be. If there's not, what's the point of living?'

'Indeed,' Father Nugent said, 'and what's the point of dying neither. So who are you?'

'Pat Ryan. We met at my brother's wedding, right in this church.'

'Luke! Luke Ryan and Winnie Gallagher, wasn't it?'

'It was.'

'And how is he? What's he doing now?'

'Gone to America,' Pat replied. 'He left last year at the end of the summer. She's followed him now.'

'Yes. I'd heard stories of that, but I didn't believe them.'

'It's true, right enough.'

Father Nugent shook his head.

'What's wrong with this country, Pat? We can't even keep our best. It's men and women like that we need for Ireland. If there ever is to be an Ireland.'

He ushered Pat inside to a pew and sat beside him.

'Tell me of Luke's dear wife. What of young Winnie? How is she finding America?'

'I don't know that she'd be there yet,' Pat said. 'She's gone out of Westport, herself and her baby son.'

'They've a son?'

'They have.'

'It's sad they're all leaving. I knew Luke well, you know. For a young man like him, he was able beyond his years. Tough too, but God knows, that came with the task he had to do. And all he wanted to do was help, get money into the people's pockets so they wouldn't starve. But they were working for seven pence a day – Castlebar would have it no other way – and then they dropped to tuppence ha'penny with the piecework. Oh God, they hated him for that, though it wasn't him that decided it. And the winter, it was almost as if they blamed him for the snow and ice too. But the County people, they'd never let up, insisted they had to work, right through the snow, wouldn't pay them otherwise. No, I never wondered at him leaving the country. What else could he do? And poor Winnie too. Not the only ones either. John Gallagher – he left too.'

'I know. I met with Mrs. Gallagher.'

'You did?'

'I did,' Pat said. 'She told me much.'

'Yes. He had to go. Himself and the son. Old John had worked as a foreman with Luke, and they hated him for it. Young John was only a child, but he had to go too.'

Pat thought of Danny and the horrific conditions of the navvy shacks.

'Do you know where he went in England?' he asked.

'Somewhere around Manchester. Martin Davitt and his family had already gone over, and Gallagher knew him. And there you have it, the Gallaghers, a family scattered over three countries. And the ones leaving Ireland are the lucky ones.'

'I know,' Pat said. 'God knows, we saw it all in Knockanure Union; what with the death pit and the rest of it. The fever killed them at a terrible rate last year. And worse in the mountains, from all I hear. It was hard on ye all here.'

'You're right there,' Father Nugent said, 'but in many ways, Luke had it the hardest of any of us who were trying to help. He was lucky he didn't die, there were times I thought he came near it. One time he was in the mountains with me, he saw something that terrified him, something I couldn't see.'

'And you saw nothing?'

'Nothing at all.'

'He must have been feverish so. Wasn't that it?'

'Maybe it was,' Father Nugent replied, 'or maybe it was something else. I don't know, and now I'll never know. But enough of that. I'm sure it's not for such talk you came here.'

Again, Pat explained Gaffney's plans.

'It's quite a task you've got,' Father Nugent said when he had finished.

'It is, and I'm hoping you can help.'

'What would you want to know?'

Pat took out his notebook and pencil. 'Well,' he said, 'I've been through Brockagh and the lowlands, but it's the mountains Gaffney wants to know about. 'Where would you suggest? Where's the best to go?'

'Or the worst, you mean. I'd suggest you follow where your brother's been, then you'll understand Luke, and you'll understand what happened in the mountains, and what's still happening there. Follow the lines of the Famine Roadworks. Go from here to Ardnagrena, then up to Lisnadee. You could go over to Knocklenagh too. Ask for Timothy Durcan; he worked with Luke the same way as John Gallagher did. He'll show you where to go – up the mountains above Knocklenagh – Benstreeva, Teenashilla, Burrenabawn, and Croghancoe. All the mud villages right across those mountains, that's where the dying was done. In the villages, and on the Roadworks.'

'So what happened the roads after?' Pat asked.

'We had to leave off any that were not complete. Lisnadee – we finished that, and even the road to Ardnagrena, they got the base of the road down so it can be finished easy enough when Castlebar has money again. But it's the roads up the mountains – the ones going over to Teenashilla and Burrenabawn, we never got a chance of finishing those. Some of the roads got as far as the lower villages in the mountains, but sure what use was that? There's no one living in them anymore, so the roads ended up going nowhere. Another few years, and the cabins will have melted into the ground with no sign that anyone ever lived there at all.'

'And the people?'

'The most of them died. The fever was terrible in those parts. The snows too, some of the villages on Croghancoe were cut off for weeks and buried under snow. In most of them, not one person lived. But even where some were left, when they heard of free passage on ships leaving from Sligo, they all walked over – men, women and children.'

'I know,' Pat said. 'I'd heard of that. Lord Palmerston, wasn't it?'

'It was. Some kind of government fellow in London, I believe. He was trying to clear his Sligo estate, all around Cliffony and Mullaghmore. No money in tenants now. The story was that the families from Croghancoe and Teenashilla and Burrenabawn mixed in with the Palmerston tenants in Sligo Dock, and nobody noticed them. Not that there were many of them left by the time they got to Sligo. And the voyage to Quebec was terrible.'

'Yes,' Pat said. 'I'd heard tell of that too. The Ashburton...'

'A hundred dead on that bloody ship, they say. It was just as bad on all the others. And the Carrick of Whitehaven sank.'

'Oh God.'

'Oh God is right. As if there were a God.'

'I don't know,' Pat said, not wishing to talk about it. If a priest did not believe, could he?

'And this Palmerston fellow,' Father Nugent went on, 'what a great fellow he is too. I was reading it in the Tyrawly Herald the other day, how he believes in freedom for all the nations of Europe. They can have their revolutions, but Ireland can't, and the only freedom his tenants have is the freedom to die. A godly man, no doubt.'

Pat closed his notebook.

'I'll have to go where you're telling me so,' he said. 'Lisnadee and the rest.'

'I suppose you'd better,' Father Nugent said, 'but 'tis getting late, and you'd best wait for morning. I'd go with you tomorrow, but I've too many visits to be making around here. They're all looking for Extreme Unction and even here, I can't get to every one of them. But before you sleep...'

He took a bottle and two cups from the cupboard.

'...have some of this.'

Pat tasted it.

'*Poitín.*'

'Yes, it'll warm you a bit. Now I don't know how long you'll be travelling, I'll be travelling the lowlands myself over the next day or two, and then up to Knocklenagh. So what we should do is this – if the both of us ask after one another, we'll be sure to meet, somewhere around Knocklenagh perhaps. No matter where we go, either of us, there'll be people will see us.'

'Fair enough,' said Pat.

He slept in the priest's house that night. The next morning, he attended mass in the tiny church. Even for a weekday, there were very few people, most of them women wearing ragged shawls and shifts.

He left Brockagh. Sometimes people came walking against him. He asked one family where they were going, and was told they were to meet Father Nugent in Brockagh in the hope that he might give them money to emigrate. Pat knew there was no chance of that.

Some of the houses on the road were still occupied, smoke from turf fires spiralling out from their chimneys, or from the front doors of the tiny cabins with no chimneys.

He stopped by a cabin with no smoke. Curious, he knocked on the door. There was no answer. He stepped inside, sniffing. He knew from the smell that it was only decomposition. The sweet smell of fever gangrene was absent. He stepped into what might have been a bedroom. Four corpses lay on the bed, two adults and two children. They were advanced in decay, but there was no sign of any animals having found them. He felt his stomach rising to vomit, but he fought the urge, holding his hand over his mouth. He would have to stop this. He had seen enough dead bodies already, their flesh rotting or eaten. If he could not take these sights, he could not 'observe' Mayo.

He left the cabin, carefully shutting the door and pushing the latch home. Then he leaned against the window, took his notebook out and wrote a description. He re-mounted his horse.

Ardnagrena. He walked along the new road, leading the horse at the edge. The base of the road had been laid, but these were large stones. From time to time, there were heaps of smaller stones on the side, but he knew that there would not be enough to give a proper top surface. He passed two quarries with more heaps of stone. Later, he met another donkey and cart, hauling more bodies towards Brockagh.

Lisnadee. Even though Father Nugent had told him it was finished, he was still surprised at the quality of the new line. It was solid, and very well surfaced. He thought back to all the years he and Luke had helped Michael in the quarry, and in repairing the public roads after winter. Yes, Luke had known how to do it, and to do it well.

Knocklenagh. This was a larger village, with perhaps as many inhabitants as Brockagh. He knocked on a door, but there was no answer. At the second door, a lean woman pointed him in the direction of Durcans' house. He knocked. A woman answered the door, two children grasping her skirt.

He asked for Timothy Durcan.

'He's dead,' she said.

Pat started.

'Oh, I'm sorry, I didn't know.'

'The fever took him. Only a few weeks back. But what brings you looking for him anyhow?'

'Father Nugent sent me,' Pat said. 'I'd have thought he'd have known.'

'Ah, sure the poor man, he's fully distracted. He couldn't even make it across to Knocklenagh the time Timothy was dying. Too many dead around Brockagh and up the mountains that time. Sure he wouldn't know who was dead and who was yet living.'

Pat left Knocklenagh, and followed Mrs. Durcan's instructions towards the mountains. As she had told him, there was no road towards Benstreeva, only a half-trodden track, part overgrown. He passed by the track, leaving Benstreeva behind. He reckoned he would see enough further up.

At Teenashilla, he followed a well-built road up the mountain. There were no quarries here, but glancing behind him he saw them far back, on the other side of the main road. How had the stones been brought up the mountain? Donkey and cart? Or creels on men's backs?

The first village was mud cabins only. A few doors were hanging on their hinges. The first was empty, the next had the remains of two bodies. The third and fourth were empty.

Further on, there were two cabins with smoking chimneys. Up here there was no problem in digging turf, as the cabins were built into the bogs around them. He knocked on the door of one cabin, but there was no answer.

At the next, an old man came out. The first word he said was 'Food.'

Pat took out a slice of brown bread and gave it to him. He munched it quietly, observing Pat.

Pat waited until he was finished.

'What has happened around here?' he asked.

The man looked at him as if he was mad. Then he spoke.

'Hunger. Snow. Fever, then hunger again. What else is there to say?'

'I'm sorry,' Pat said, 'I'm sorry to trouble you.'

He mounted his horse and rode back down towards the main road. Half way down he stopped and sat on a turf bank. It was getting colder in the mountains.

He took out his notebook, and started to write.

What had he seen? People who did not exist? Even the living were only ghosts. There were no tenant farmers here, only desperate people clinging to an existence on a bog on the side of a mountain. Who knew they were here? Had any of them paid rent? All they grew were potatoes for survival. What rent could they pay? What landlord would care about them, or even know that they were on his land? Who owned it anyway?

When he reached the main road, he turned again and travelled up towards Burrenabawn Mountain. The road was good, but stopped abruptly. Since he was a short distance from the next village, he rode up the beaten track, noting that it had not been over-grown. Another tiny mud village, seven houses only. The story was much the same as at Teenashilla. Only two houses inhabited, the rest housing only bones.

He returned to the main road and rode towards Croghancoe. He came to another mud village some distance on, but no road had been built that far. There was a single cabin beside him, no smoke issuing. It was empty. He brought the horse inside, took his blanket from one of the panniers, and wrapped it around himself and the coat. He slept.

Croghancoe. As he reached the mountain, the day was bright but very cold.

A road had been built up to the first village on the mountain. Again, conditions were the same as the lower mountains. The road went on to another mud village, but even before he reached it, Pat could see it was empty. The doors to all the cabins were open, but there was no one inside. At one of them, he found a femur, blackened gristle still attached to one end. He left. The road went on, but after a few hundred yards the top surface came to an end, and the road base ended a hundred yards further.

Twenty yards to the side, there were three small trees. He dismounted, led the horse across, and tied it to one of the trees. He sat down and began to write.

He was startled as a shadow fell across the notebook. He looked around, drawing himself up quickly. A tall, old man stood behind him. His trousers were shredded at the ends, patched socks showing above broken shoes. He wore a rope as a belt, a thin shirt and jacket showing under his patched coat. His wispy hair was white, a grey beard covering most of his emaciated face. He was far taller than anyone Pat had seen in the mountains. Or anywhere else?

He leaned on a blackthorn stick, observing Pat.

'*Let you not be frightened,*' he said. '*There is no call for fear.*'

'*Who are you?*'

'*Cairbre Mór is the name to me.*'

Pat regarded him doubtfully, watching the expression on the man's face.

'*Pat Ryan is how they call me,*' he said, hesitantly.

'*I know who you are.*'

Pat stepped back. He was frightened now, though he could not think why.

'*But how...?*

'*How would I not know? Now let you be seated.*'

Pat sat again. The old man sat alongside.

'*So what more do you know about me,*' Pat said.

'*More than you know about yourself. Your eyes tell much.*'

Pat turned away.

'*So you've been travelling here, and writing what you've seen,*' the old man said. '*And now you must make your report, but to who? The Workhouse? The Union? Or perhaps the County?*'

Pat was surprised again at how much this stranger knew of him. He was less fearful now.

'*The County, since you say it,*' he said. '*They want to know what happened here. And what's still happening, for that matter.*'

'*Sure why bother a young fellow like yourself. There's thousands in the workhouses can make reports. Or would, if they could write.*'

'*Are you saying I'm not needed?*' Pat asked.

'*No, my young friend, not that at all. You're most welcome.*'

He put his hand on top of Pat's head and turned it towards him.

'*Look straight at me,*' he said.

Pat looked at him, and felt the power of the pale grey eyes running right through him. He was frightened again.

'*By God, you're most like him,*' the old man said.

'*Like who?*'

'*Luke.*'

'*Luke?*'

'*Your brother, or did you think I was talking of the Evangelist. Maybe I should, but it's your brother was better known in these parts. He held the power of life and death over us, he did, though it was a power he never wanted. And the ones who wanted it, sure they never had it. The priests, they thought they had power, but what could they do? Pray the Mass? Give out the Last Rites? And what difference did it ever make? The people cried to heaven for food, but they died anyhow. And last year they thought the priests' prayers were answered, but now they see they were not. No, the priests have no power, but your report will have power. On your word, people will live or die.*'

Who was the last one who had said that to him? Gaffney. Voisey and Father Nugent knew it well too, though neither had said it. But the old man was right, it was a power Luke had never wanted. Nor did he. But now he had it, and could not be rid of it.

'*On my word, you think?*'

'*I do,*' the old man said. '*Here, for certain. But where else?*'

'*Where else? But what…?*'

'*Is this the only place they need to know about?*'

'*It is not,*' Pat said.

'*Where else, then? The County? All of it?*'

'*Perhaps. In time…yes.*'

'*So many reports! You are a man of vast power. Much of Mayo depends on your words.*'

He pointed to the far west.

'*Look there, the mountain. You know it?*'

Far in the distance, a high, rocky peak stood out against the horizon. It was bathed in bright sunshine, grey clouds racing down from the north.

'*Croagh Patrick?*'

'*So you may call it. Cruachán Aille is the real name to it.*'

117

'Yes,' Pat said, '*just by Westport, where the ships go for America.*'

'*But not your brother.*'

'*No. He left from* Liverpool.'

'*I know.*'

'*You know?*' Pat said, half questioning.

'*I do. We'd all heard of his leaving in these parts. He's trying to escape what happened here, but his story will follow him wherever he goes.*'

Pat thought about that. Would his own story follow him too? Working with Danny? A dangerous thing to have done.

'Yes,' he said, '*it probably will.*'

The old man nodded. '*So where will you go when you leave here?*'

'*Erris, I'd say. They say things are very bad out there.*'

'*Ah yes, I know it. It's one of the places you must visit if you wish to understand Mayo.*'

'*You've been there?*'

'*I have.*'

'*What was the business that took you there?*'

'*I'm from there.*'

Pat was surprised again. '*You're from Erris?*'

'*I am.*'

'*So why did you leave there?*'

'*It was all to do with a woman. There's some very powerful ones, you know.*'

Powerful, Pat thought. Irene? Yes, there were some very powerful women. Troublemakers too.

'*I know,*' he said.

'*Yes,*' the old man said. '*I knew of a most beautiful woman who was living at Dún Flidhais, at the south end of Carrowmore Lake in Erris.*'

'*She was trouble to you?*'

'*She was. I met her at the cattle fair in Crossmolina. Her husband was a breeder of cattle, and said to be a rustler too. The fact that she was married meant nothing to me, and the pair of us were carrying on together. But when the husband found what we were about, there was one almighty fight, and I fought him like a savage. He would have killed me, but I hit him between the eyes with a rock, and he dropped to the ground. Then his family came after me, and I ran like hell, all the way from Dún Flidhais to Dún Chiortáin. I reckoned even Dún Chiortáin had become too hot for me, and anyways, I had lost the woman. So I went across to Glenamoy and Glencalry, then Sheskin and Eskeragh.*'

'*Glenamoy to Eskeragh!*' Pat said. '*That's a hell of a long way walking. The most of it bog too.*'

'You know Mayo well then?'

'I've studied the maps,' Pat said. 'They are remote, the Sheskin bogs.'

'So they are, and it's another area where there are many people living no one even knows of. People out living in mud cabins, or cabins of turf. They were hungry then, they're hungry now. 'Tis another part you must travel if you wish to understand County Mayo. Anyone who doesn't know Glencalry nor Sheskin nor Eskeragh, doesn't know Mayo. And those other places, all the way up the tongue of land to Dún Chiortáin, they're all places you must visit too if you are to understand Erris.'

'I'll go there if I'm asked,' Pat said.

The sky overhead was darkening. Pat pulled his coat over his head. The old man stayed bare headed.

'But now,' he said, 'we are here in the Mountains of the Ox.'

'Yes,' Pat said, 'though you never said how you got here from Eskeragh.'

'It's easy said. From Eskeragh I went across the lands of Tyrawly, out to Ballycastle and down to Ballina. By then I was starving. When I was in Ballina, I met a girl selling eggs, and she fed me. She was from the lands of Tireragh, up here by the Ox Mountains. So I went with her, out by Brockagh till we came to her home in Ardnagrena, and there we settled. She's long dead now, poor woman.'

In the distance, curtains of rain were crossing Nephin.

'So what happened here?' Pat asked. 'What were the terrible things that Luke could not even tell me? Will you tell me?'

'I will.'

Pat took his pencil and notebook out.

'It was the time of the great dying,' the old man said. 'Yes, I know you saw it in Knockanure Workhouse, but what happened here was terrible. Disgusting too. Ardnagrena, Croghancoe and more. They forced them to work on the roads when they were already too weak to lift a spade. Then, when the roads weren't built fast enough, they brought in piecework so they would have to work to death to feed their families. Then when the snows came, the men still had to work. Women and children too. They died on the Works, they died walking to them and walking home. The bodies of those who died working – your brother and his gangers carried them home on their donkeys and horses. The others who died on their way to the Works and on their way home, we buried them where they dropped, sometimes digging a hole in the bogs, sometimes just throwing them into the ditches with a few scraws of heather over them, hoping the foxes wouldn't find them, but knowing full well they would.'

The narrative went on and on. Much of it concerned Luke and the Roadworks. This fascinated and horrified Pat. More horrifying though were the old man's descriptions of the people dying in their cabins from starvation and fever. Again and again, the old man named names. Pat was writing very fast, but even so he found it difficult to keep up. People, roads, fields, mountains, houses and villages. And always death. Death, death, death.

The old man paused. Pat stopped his scribbling, and looked around.

'*Go on,*' he said.

The pause was only momentary before the narrative went on.

'*When the snow covered the land, all these villages here disappeared. Sure how could they not? They're only little tigíns and the snow was ten, twelve and fifteen feet deep. When we dug them out in the spring, all of two months later, there were none left living. In most, the foxes had found them first as the thaw began, and there was little left. You can't blame the foxes; they were starving too. You've seen the village below, no one alive. We tumbled the houses on them, or buried them in the bogs. The same with the bodies that appeared from the drifts when the snows thawed – they'd been buried in ice by their people, or died in the snow trying to find their way back from the Relief Works. The foxes got many of them too. Foxes and rats. And that was the story right across the mountains.*'

For a moment, Pat thought the old man had said enough, but then he went on again. Pat was concerned he might not get back to Knocklenagh. But the story had to be told, and the old man was telling it.

'*So how many died?' you'll ask,*' Cairbre Mór said to him. '*You'll have to have that for your report, won't you? The officers want figures, it's what they love in the way a man loves a woman.*'

'*It is so,*' Pat said.

'*I'll tell you then. Over on Benstreeva there were well over seventy families scattered across the mountain. Teenashilla, forty families in two villages and more in the farms around. Burrenabawn, over sixty in three villages, the same again on the mountain, Croghancoe, sixty in two villages, God knows how many on the mountain. You do the sums. Well over three hundred families I can tell you of, and I'm only a half-schooled man. How many in each tigín then? How many in each family? Six? Seven? Eight? Work it out yourself. How many are left? You can count them from those few with smoke still streaming out the doors or the roofs, and there's damned few of those. But I know you know that, and you've counted them all already. You're that kind of lad, so you can do the sums. A few dozen families made it out by Sligo, though from what we hear of the Sligo ships, many of those are dead. So there's your report for you. The report we all depend on. No one ever came up here to count them, when they were counting people everywhere else in their census. When they die, no one will ever know, and their little cabins will fall and melt into the ground, leaving not a trace behind. And in years to come, your report will be the only proof that men ever lived on these mountains. Remember this. Few of these people can write…'*

'*But you can? Read and do numbers too?'*

'*I can,*' the old man said. '*No mystery there. There was a young fellow used to come around the mountains, teaching, carrying a blackboard on his back. But that was many years ago. Most of the men of my age are dead, and few are left to read or add. For the rest, there's many would hold letters and numbers to be some class of magic.'*

'*They'd be right,*' Pat said, wryly, still surprised at the old man's facility with arithmetic.

Cairbre Mór stood. '*Now I've said enough, young man. If you don't leave soon, you'll be lost.'*

So saying, he shook Pat's hand and walked back up the mountain.

Pat watched, until he disappeared. Then, concerned that he would not find his way, he made his way down slowly, leading the horse with him until he came to the edge of the road. He mounted and rode down to Knocklenagh without stopping. As he rode, it began to rain. The horse stumbled, and he dismounted and walked along the edge of the road, leading the horse. Whenever the rain was heaviest, he would shelter, sometimes under trees or rocks; sometimes in cabins, sharing them with the dead. At times, he doubted he would reach Knocklenagh at all.

He thought of the old man's story. His tale of leaving Erris was a silly one, but still, he had a good knowledge of the north of Erris, and the boglands to the east of it. That at least was solid information, whatever about his story of chasing a woman.

His story of what had happened in the Ox Mountains was horrific, but Pat had expected that. He had seen just as bad, even in the lowlands around Castlebar. He had been surprised by the old man's ability with arithmetic, but he had heard stories of itinerant schoolteachers before. Even so, the fellow's easy facility with figures was unreal. It had been as if figures were sacred to him, as they had once been to wise men in the mountains of ancient lands. Magic indeed.

Enough of that. What now? He would have to meet with Father Nugent again. That might not be easy.

When he reached the village, it was still raining heavily. His coat and clothes were wet through. He was hesitant about going to Durcans' as there was no man present, and people might talk, but the cold overcame any concern he might have had about that.

Mrs. Durcan answered his knock.

'*I was looking for Father* Nugent,' Pat said.

'*He's just been,*' she replied. '*He said you'd come back this way. He's staying up at Tommy Gill's, and said you should join him there. They'll have a bed ready for you.*'

She gave him directions, and Pat went out into the rain again.

He found Gills'. The woman of the house welcomed him in. Father Nugent was sitting by the fire with Gill and two children.

'Come in, come in, Pat,' Father Nugent said. 'I knew we'd meet soon. Let's hear your story.'

'He'll dry off first,' the woman said.

She led him into a room and gave him a short length of rope and a blanket.

'Here, wrap this around yourself and bring your clothes out.'

Soon after, Pat was sitting beside the fire, his clothes drying on a wooden rack, and a cup of *poitín* in his hand. He sipped at the *poitín,* and told them of what he had seen in the mountains.

'Worse than here so?' the woman of the house asked.

'Much worse, I'd say.'

'It is,' Father Nugent said.

'I met a fellow told me about the time of the snow. *Cairbre Mór* was his name.'

He had no doubt that the priest would know who he was talking about.

'That old rogue,' Father Nugent said. 'You mustn't mind him. He's all *piseógs* and fairy tales.'

'That's as might be,' Pat said, 'but he knew who I was at once.'

'That's easy enough,' Father Nugent said. 'He'd have heard of someone coming from Castlebar and Knockanure. Sure we all knew of that, these past days; the world and his wife knew it. He'd have heard of you too from the workhouse last year. And if he'd seen you taking notes, he'd have guessed from that too. No, there was no magic. All a matter of common sense, taking a few facts and filling the spaces in between.'

'You might be right,' Pat said.

'So what did he tell you?' Gill asked.

'A lot about Luke, to start with. A lot too about what happened here in the mountains through the winter, the kind of thing Luke would never talk about.'

Pat told them all that *Cairbre Mór* had told him about what had happened in the villages of the Ox. He told too of what he had seen himself. When he was finished, he thought of the old man's story about chasing a woman. Should he mention it? Or it might only be a fairy-tale, and telling the story might make him look a fool. He decided not to mention it. The story of the misery of the Ox Mountains was enough.

When Pat was finished, Father Nugent began to speak, telling more of what had happened around Brockagh, Lisnadee, Knocklenagh, and further up the mountains. Again, Pat took his notebook out, and scribbled as fast as he was able. He was desperately tired, and his whole body was aching for sleep, but this could not be missed. Father Nugent's knowledge was unending. Village by village, road by road, boreen by boreen; naming families; detailing hunger and fever; evictions and death. From time to time, Gill or his wife would add detail, but for the most part they left it to the priest. Sometimes Pat would interrupt with a question, but it was hardly necessary. By the time Father Nugent finally stopped, the family had gone to bed. Pat was far beyond exhaustion when he finally retired. He slept till the sun was high in the sky.

For the rest of the day, he accompanied Father Nugent around the lower end of the mountains, as he sought out families needing the last rites. Pat's mind was numb, but still he took notes, while fighting the urge to throw up. Again, they spent the night in Gills'.

When he left Knocklenagh, he rode direct to Knockanure Workhouse and asked for Voisey. He gave a full report of the places he had visited and all that he had heard from Father Nugent. He spoke too of the horrific stories *Cairbre Mór* had told of Lisnadee, Ardnagrena, Teenashilla, Burrenabawn, Benstreeva and Croghancoe.

Again, Voisey gave more detail, corroborating and adding to the information Pat already had.

Riding back towards Castlebar, Pat decided to divert by Carrigard. He saw Michael in the distance, repairing stone walls around the rath. He waved at him.

When he arrived at the house, Eleanor hugged him close.

'*Pat, my son… How are you?*'

'*I'm fine, mother.*'

'*Sit down there, and hold till I put the porridge on.*'

Then Michael came in.

'Well, Pat. What have you seen?'

'What I've seen, you don't want to know.'

Eleanor was surprised. She silenced Michael with a finger to her lips.

'We had a letter from Luke yesterday,' she said.

'How's he doing?'

'Not so bad. Winnie has arrived safely, little Liam too. They sent some money.'

'Yes,' Michael said. 'I sent a pound to the Gallaghers this morning.'

'It'll certainly be valued,' Pat said. 'John Gallagher has gone over to England working. It's only Mrs. Gallagher and two of the young fellows who are still there.'

Eleanor handed him another letter.

'What's this?' Pat asked.

'I wouldn't know. It's for you, so I didn't open it.'

He saw the Westport postmark and he ripped it open.

'Well?' she asked. 'What is it?'

'It's from Sarah. She says her mother is dead.'

Chapter 9

Leeds Intelligencer, England. September 1848:
Two contracts upon the original line remain to be completed, namely the Bramhope & Leeds contracts, situated between Weeton Lane and Leeds. These contracts include the heaviest work to the line; they have made considerable progress during the last six months and are expected to be opened early in the course of next year. All the arches of the Wharfe and the Aire Viaducts are keyed in, except one arch of the latter erection over the canal at Armely. The works of the tunnel are fast advancing towards completion.

Murtybeg's initial reaction to the solicitor's letter was one of shock. He had known he would have to be tough with Irene, but through all this, he had never even considered the ownership of Edwardes & Ryan. In a vague sort of way perhaps, he had thought it might be owned by himself and his parents, but further than that, he had not gone. He had never heard of common-law marriage, and never thought that Irene might be the true owner.

Many times, he woke up in the middle of the night, trying to work out what to do next, but his thinking went around in circles, until he would fell asleep again through sheer fatigue.

For some time, neither he nor Irene commented on the letter. He tried to minimise his contact with her, and said little when they met, beyond discussion of bids and contracts.

He said nothing either to any of the gangers about the ownership of Edwardes & Ryan. It appeared to him that Irene had not either. Perhaps she too wanted to keep it quiet, for now anyhow. She was clearly playing a long game, and if she could, so could he.

He had reckoned that anything he said might be used against him, and the other clerks would back up Irene. So he said nothing, and this did not seem to concern her. Perhaps she wanted him to stay working with Edwardes & Ryan, so long as he knew his place.

One evening, he decided to bring up the issue over dinner. He waited until the maid had brought out the tureen, and ladled soup out for both.

'So you wish to own Edwardes & Ryan.'

'I do own it,' she said, her face icy cold.

'I don't think Danny ever intended it that way.'

'What Danny intended, is of no consequence. The law is the law.'

Murtybeg was very tempted to walk out at once. He held himself back. He had negotiated the Manchester & Salford Bank into a corner. Could he do the same with Irene? It would take much longer, that was for sure.

'So what now?' he asked.

'You just do as you're doing. Negotiate with the banks, you're excellent at that. Deal with the big contractors and source our labour.'

'Yes,' he said, 'the business does need me.'

'You can be replaced fast enough.'

'You expect me to believe that.'

'Try me,' she said.

He hesitated.

'Fine,' he said. 'I'll stay on. There is, of course, the question of my salary.'

'I'm not going to reduce it.'

'No, you're not' he said. 'We're going to increase it. Another two shillings a day.'

He stared straight into her eyes, challenging her.

'Fine,' she said, 'two shillings extra, and, by God, you're going to work for it.'

A small win for me, he thought that night. But where the devil do I go from here?

The next morning, she threw a copy of the Manchester Times onto his desk.

'The East Lancashire Line are requesting bids.'

He looked where she was pointing. 'That'll be a big one.'

'It will. And we'd better get it. You're going to have to prove you're as good as what I'm paying you.'

Again, Murtybeg held back on saying anything abrupt. How long would this continue though?

'Fine,' he said, 'but this time, I think we better talk to the Manchester & Salford first.'

'And have them wreck all our prospects?'

'Not so long as we have proper projections.'

Murtybeg wrote to the East Lancashire offices, requesting a copy of the proposed works. When he received it, he went through distances and depths, estimating cubic yards of soil and rock to be removed, horses and carts required and many other items.

That evening, and well into the night, he and Irene worked on the figures until they were both content that they had everything right.

Through the long hours, Murtybeg observed her closely. A most attractive woman, no doubt about it. He could understand what had attracted Danny to her. Still, he hated her for the woman she was, and considered her approach to business to be pure evil. How to break her grip? That was the problem.

He arranged a meeting with the Manchester & Salford Bank. The morning of the meeting, he met with Irene for breakfast.

'I want to warn you of one thing,' she told him. 'You had better get the Bank on side.'

'I'll try,' he said.

'Trying isn't good enough,' she said. 'I've already submitted our bid to the East Lancashire.'

She placed a copy of the contract on the table.

'Wasn't that a bit hasty,' he said.

'Why? Aren't the estimates accurate?'

'They are, but if we don't get the bank lending, we'll look like fools to the East Lancashire.'

'So?'

'So we can always go back and withdraw our bid. They'll have plenty of other bids.'

'It won't be so easy to do that,' she said, as she threw a letter on the table.

'What?'

'They've already accepted it.'

He looked at the letter in horror. Who had been bribed this time? And what would the Manchester & Salford do?

Murtybeg found his negotiations with the Bank surprisingly easy. An eight-thousand-pound loan was granted, with few questions. Winrow barely glanced through the projections.

Had he been bribed? No, not possible.

Or maybe someone at a higher level – one of the directors? Not possible, either. Perhaps he was just becoming too suspicious of everyone.

There were other matters to consider. Most vital was the Mackenzie contract in Bradford. On this occasion, he took Roughneen with him. They took the train from Stockport Station into Manchester Piccadilly Station, where he bought two newspapers.

'I don't have to tell you Johnny, that this is a vital contract for us now. The North Staffordshire is well under control. Our original contract is finished, but I'm hoping we'll have more. Brassey is certainly happy with all we've done. Now we have to prove to Mackenzie that we can operate at this level. I'll want you to run the contract.'

A whistle sounded, and the train began to move. They ran and pulled themselves into a carriage, laughing. Murtybeg threw a paper to Roughneen.

'Might as well keep up with the news, Johnny.'

Murtybeg was reading the Stock Market reports, when Roughneen exclaimed, 'see this, Murteen!'

'What's that?'

'Something about the Leeds & Thirsk line. I wonder how the lads are doing over there. The Thirsk to Ripon part is done. The Bramhope to Leeds part is to open by the end of the year.'

'That's where Gilligan and the lads are?'

'Dead right, it is,' Roughneen said. 'Your father too.'

'I know.'

'How they'll get by when the contracts are over?'

'There'll be work enough for them. There's plenty of work in Bradford, and that's only a few miles from Leeds.'

'But what kind of work?' Roughneen asked. 'They'll be reckoning on four shillings a day, and who in the name of God will give them that?'

'Not us, for sure,' Murtybeg said.

The train stopped at Ashton.

'This is where the riots were a few weeks back,' Murtybeg said.

'Pretty rough too, I understand,' Roughneen said.

When they reached Bradford, Roughneen stared at the forest of chimneys around them, as they spewed tall columns of smoke into the sky, forming an umbrella of black and yellow clouds, which nearly obliterated the sun. An acrid stench of smoke and sewage, tore at their nostrils.

'Damn it,' Roughneen said, 'even Manchester isn't like this.'

'No. Quite something, isn't it? There's hundreds of mills here. More woollen mills than anywhere in the world. That's what they say.'

Roughneen coughed. 'By Christ, they stink.'

'Oh, you'll get used to it.'

As they walked towards the Mackenzie works, there were torrents of raw sewage pouring into the River Beck.

'I don't know, Murteen, but I think this is worse than Little Ireland.'

'Could be.'

They had come to the Mackenzie office on the Colne Extension. Murtybeg entered and asked for Ackroyd. A minute later, they were sitting at a desk in Ackroyd's office.

'Delighted to meet you again, Mr. Ryan.'

'You too, Mr. Ackroyd. I know you want to get started on this contract as soon as possible. I thought therefore I'd introduce you to my foreman,

Mr. Roughneen. He's our top man. I know Mr. Mackenzie would expect nothing less.'

'Of course.'

For some time, they discussed the contract with Ackroyd.

When they left the office, they found a small bar. A wooden sign swung outside – The Grenadier Inn painted over a red-coated grenadier leaning on a long-barrelled gun.

They each ordered a pie and a beer.

'So now there's the question of workers, Murteen,' Roughneen said. 'Where's the workhouse?'

'I don't know yet, Johnny, and I'm not even sure it'll be needed.'

'But sure what else can we do? Go back to the Liverpool Docks, find Mayo men there? That's sixty miles away.'

'No, Johnny. We'll find them right here. Look all around you. Whether you know it or not, this is County Mayo.'

'County Mayo!'

'Just listen to the accents and the language. Not even English, the most of it. Now before we go any further, let's have a word with mine host.'

Murtybeg went to the bar and ordered two more beers. He asked for the head barman.

'Gentlemen.'

'We're looking for workers for the Colne Extension.' Murtybeg explained. 'We thought you might help us.'

The man was startled.

'Why should I help you?'

'To sell more beer,' Murtybeg answered.

'More beer? Just how would you do that?'

'What I'm wanting is this. We should put out the word that we're looking for new workers. We can use the table just inside the door here. That way, we'll find workers, and you'll sell beer.'

The man returned to pulling beer. He said nothing.

'And when we pay them, they'll be drinking ale by the keg,' Murtybeg added.

'How many are you looking for?' the man asked at length.

'Hard to say,' Murtybeg answered. 'Two hundred to start. What do you think Johnny?'

Roughneen nodded his head.

'Oh, and one other thing,' Murtybeg added. 'Mayo men only. That's all we'd be wanting.'

'I understand,' the barman said. 'And, by George, there's enough of them around.'

Murtybeg thought he detected a hint of contempt in his voice.

'I know,' he said. 'Most from the west of the county. And that's most important too. We're only looking for fellows from the far west. Erris, Achill, the Killaries and Partry. Nowhere else. Here, I'll write them out...'

'No need. We've heard enough talk of Erris and the rest of them. Dirt poor too.'

'You know what we're talking about, so,' Roughneen said. 'You're well-informed...'

'For an Englishman, you mean.'

'Well...yes.'

'We have to know our customers. And near half of them are Irish, Mayo or Sligo, as they never cease telling me. They drink our beer, so I listen. But enough of that. What next?'

'What we need now,' Murtybeg said, 'is one clean table, two chairs, two pens and a bottle of ink.'

'Fair enough, but first, how much are you offering to pay them?'

'A shilling a day.'

'A shilling!'

'Do you think we should offer less,' Murtybeg said.

'No, no,' the barman said. 'It's just...'

'It's just nothing,' Murtybeg answered. 'We're offering full board and lodgings too. Now if you just start telling some of the fellows around the bar, we'll see what happens. Tell them they can tell their friends too.'

The tables and chairs were set up, as Murtybeg and Roughneen spoke to the drinking men at the bar.

Response was rapid.

Soon there was a long line of men winding out the door and along the street. Progress was painfully slow, though. For each man, Murtybeg or Roughneen wrote down a name and address, and then gave each a docket with a name on it.

Soon the bar was crowded. Murtybeg called the barman over.

'I know you're busy selling beer, but do you know anyone here can read and write? We're getting behind on this.'

'My sons. They're well able.'

He brought over two young men, fifteen or sixteen years old, Murtybeg guessed. They sat down beside Murtybeg and Roughneen, and began to write out dockets for those who could speak some English. When questions were asked of them in Irish, they referred to Murtybeg or Roughneen, but most of the time the signing-on proceeded without any break.

Murtybeg was startled when three women joined the line. '*I'm sorry*,' he said in Irish, '*no women*.'

'*They always take women on the roadworks,*' one of them said. '*Back in Mayo...*'

'*This isn't Mayo.*'

The women left.

'I thought you said it was Mayo,' Roughneen whispered. 'Sure you were only joking at me.'

'*Arra* what,' Murtybeg replied. 'We might be paying little, but it's not famine relief. Now just keep working.'

After some time, he stopped. 'How many left to two hundred, do you think, Johnny?'

Roughneen did a quick count. 'About fifty.'

Murtybeg walked along the line from the desk, and out to the street, counting. When he came to fifty, he stopped.

'*No more needed,*' he said.

There were protests, but Murtybeg stood his ground. '*Two hundred is all we need. There's no point in staying here.*'

Afterwards, Murtybeg and Roughneen found an inn close to the Colne extension, and stayed there for the night. Next morning, he left Roughneen with a draft for fifty pounds, drawn on the Manchester & Salford Bank.

'I'm leaving you in control now, Johnny,' he said. 'God knows; you'll have lots of work to do now. In the meantime, I'll just be heading over to Leeds to see how mother and father are getting on. The rest of Gilligan's gang too.'

'That mightn't be a bad idea,' Roughneen said. 'We might get some notion of the kind of fellows we'll be up against back here in Bradford when the Leeds & Thirsk closes.

Murtybeg walked to the Leeds & Bradford Railway Station. Roughneen had been right, the sheer stink of Bradford was disgusting. Everywhere he went, sullen people watched him. Once he heard a woman point him out.

'*That's the man. That's Ryan.*'

But he knew he was safe. He would not be attacked. Bradford was under military occupation, with soldiers everywhere.

He reached the station and took a train for the short journey to Leeds. Once again, he walked out the Leeds & Thirsk line to Bramhope, and found the Gilligan gang.

Doyle put his pick down, as he spotted him.

'It's Murtybeg!' he said.

Gilligan walked across.

'By God, you're becoming a common enough caller.'

'Why not. I was just over in Bradford; thought I'd come across and say hello.'

'How's it with Bradford, then?' Doyle asked.

'Going well.'

'When will you be enlisting men?' Gilligan asked.

'We already have. But don't worry, lads, the work isn't for the likes of you. We're only paying a shilling a day.'

'A shilling a day!' Gilligan echoed.

'The same as always. But there'll be plenty enough contracts around Bradford. You know that as well as I do.'

'Won't be none worthwhile,' Doyle said. 'Not if Edwardes & Ryan are undercutting all the navvy contractors around.'

'I wouldn't worry about that, neither. You're ten times stronger than any of our fellows, the whole lot of you. Like I said, there's plenty of other contracts, and the Mackenzie one is the only one we have. Or are likely to have, for that matter.'

'And are you using Mayo men, as before?' Gilligan asked.

'We are.'

'Straight off the boat at Liverpool?'

'No need. There's thousands of Mayo men in Bradford. Tens of thousands of them.'

'Yes,' said Gilligan, after a pause. 'I'd heard of that right enough. Kirkgate, Broomfields and around, isn't that it? None of us fellows would ever go in there. Rough places, I believe.'

'Rough enough,' Murtybeg said. 'I wouldn't worry though; you'd be safe enough. The military have it under martial law after the riots last month. Now if you don't mind, I'd like to have a word with my father. Any idea where he is?'

'Back in the boarding house, working. You know the way?'

'I do.'

Murtybeg continued down the line towards Bramhope. He could see, as the newspapers had said, that the Bramhope Leeds section was coming to an end. Bright, parallel rails snaked over parallel wooden sleepers for most of the distance. Navvies were still working on one siding, though even here the sleepers were already bedded in, and rails were being carried to finish the works.

He knocked on the door of the boarding house, and was brought into the parlour where Murty was working at the table. He looked up, astonished.

'Murteen. Here again, so soon?'

'I was over in Bradford. Sure it's no distance. But before anything else, tell me, how's ma?'

'Oh, you know, the same as ever. She's up in the bedroom for now. Danny's death shocked her something terrible.'

'Yes, I can understand that. But what can we do?'

'There's only the one thing for it. I'll have to get her out working.'

'Working! But sure there wouldn't be much around here.'

'No, over in Bradford, I'm thinking. The lads are talking of contracts there when our work on the Leeds & Thirsk ends. I know there's many a mill in Bradford, and from all we hear, they're taking on workers.'

'Yes,' Murtybeg said. 'They had a bad crash last year, the mills did, but I understand they're doing very well now.'

Murty put down his pen and rubbed his eyes.

'So tell me, Murteen, how's business with you fellows?'

'Well,' Murtybeg said, 'the business is going well, there's no doubt about that.'

'Still working the same way, paying the workers nothing?'

'Not quite nothing, Pa, but little enough you might say. Still, we're keeping those fellows alive. We feed them well.'

'That's the way you might think of it Murteen, but no matter how much you feed them, the fever kills them at a terrible rate. But enough about that. How do you find working with this Irene woman? Or have you sacked her already?'

'I'm afraid not, Pa. In fact, if there is any question of sacking, it's me that might be sacked.'

'Sacked! You! But how...? Who sacked you?'

'Irene.'

'But she couldn't. She doesn't own the business.'

'Oh yes, she does. She's the one that owns Edwardes & Ryan.'

Murty stared at him, wide-eyed.

'But how can that be?'

'Simple. There's this notion they have here of a common-law wife. She maintains that because she lived with Danny, she was his wife under common-law, whether they were married or not, and so she inherits the lot.'

'But that's nonsense. She's still not his wife.'

'She's not, but she has the same rights.'

'But that's mad.'

'Oh, it's common enough over here,' Murtybeg said. 'And sure didn't we have it in Mayo for long enough. How many people in Mayo were married proper in your grandfather's time, do you think? And they took over their farms, no problem. It was only the landlords and the like had to get married, and that was all because they had so much money and land. No, I can see the point. And you know, the worst about it is this. If she hadn't been living with Danny as husband and wife, the family would have gotten Edwardes & Ryan direct.'

'The family!'

'You, me and ma,' Murtybeg said. 'Yes, pa, we're the ones who would have owned the business. We'd be wealthy now. No need for you or ma to work either way.'

Murty looked at him, half in horror.

'And make money out of the sweat of poor starving Mayomen? Damn it to hell, Murteen, how could I do that.'

Before leaving, Murty brought Murtybeg up to the bedroom. They opened the door.

'She's still asleep,' Murty said.

Murtybeg crossed the room and kissed Aileen on the forehead.

Then he left Bramhope and travelled back through Leeds, Bradford and Manchester to Stockport.

Next day, he and Irene spoke for hours about the contracts with the East Lancashire, the Colne Extension and the smaller contracts they held. She was even courteous, but still treated Murtybeg as an employee, even if a senior one.

In many ways, it was a bizarre situation, as if both sides were held in check by the other, and neither could move.

Still he mulled the matter. He began to think that he was accepting the Rothwell opinion on common-law marriage. Was he afraid, perhaps, of the legal profession? One way or another, he would have to seek professional assistance. But could he afford it?

If the expenses were handled through Edwardes & Ryan, there would have been no problem. But as the family no longer owned Edwardes & Ryan, there was no way he could do that. Irene certainly would not permit it. And his own cash at bank would not stretch to legal fees.

One morning, he read through the Manchester Times. There were references to various legal cases, and names of solicitors in Manchester. These he discounted – a firm of solicitors in the centre of the city could be quite expensive and, in any case, that was where Rothwells were based, and they might talk. Another problem was that he had no idea of what other legal arrangements Irene might have had. Did she have other contacts in Manchester? Or Stockport? He began to look further afield.

At last, he found what he wanted, when he saw a reference to a solicitor in Oldham. His name was Abraham Sternberg. He took a note of the address and the following day, he took the train to Oldham.

He found the address easily enough and knocked. An elderly woman answered the door.

'I'm looking for Abraham Sternberg,' he said.

She ushered him into a room with a table and six chairs. 'A moment please.'

A minute later, the door opened.

'Abraham Sternberg's the name. I'm told there's someone looking for me.'

'Murtybeg Ryan is my name. I don't know if you can help me, but I have a legal problem, and I'm looking for some kind of lawyer.'

'Fair enough, let's be seated.'

Murtybeg sat and began to outline the situation with Edwardes & Ryan. He noticed that Sternberg had heard of the business, though, with Danny's reputation, he was not sure if that was a good point or a bad one. When he was finished with the explanations, he passed the letter from Rothwells over to Sternberg.

'In confidence,' he said.

'Of course,' Sternberg replied. He glanced through the letter, and returned it to Murtybeg.

'I might be able to help you,' he said, 'but not in the way you might expect. First of all, I and my partner, Mr. Wolfson, are conveyancing solicitors. We specialise in the legal aspects of property transfers.'

'I see,' Murtybeg said. 'So there is no way you can help me?'

'Can I ask you, Mr. Ryan, if a case were to be taken against Miss Miller and you lost, what would be your financial circumstances personally?'

'Not very good.'

Murtybeg was becoming more depressed as the meeting went on.

'Yes,' Sternberg said, 'that's exactly what I thought. And the other point is, what you need is a barrister. Solicitors cannot take actions in the higher courts. Even we must be represented by a barrister at this level. But I can tell you, barristers do not come cheap. Solicitors are cheaper, but even so, anyone on Rothwells' level would be expensive. Miss Miller is hardly stinting on expense.'

Murtybeg drummed his fingers on the table. 'Somehow, I thought they would be pricy, right enough.'

Tea had arrived. Murtybeg waited until it was poured. Then he stood.

'It's kind of you to bring the tea, but I don't think I'll be needing it.'

Sternberg waved him back to his seat.

'No, no, Mr. Ryan. Before you go, can I make another suggestion?'

Murtybeg sat. 'Any suggestion would be most helpful.'

'I hope so,' Sternberg said. 'We might in fact be able to help each other. My nephew – my brother's son, Louis – he's a barrister. Not long qualified, mind you, and the poor fellow's not doing too well. He spends all his time in the Law Library, but he's not getting much in the line of briefs.'

'So what do you suggest? That we might give him a brief, is that it?'

'Indeed. If he's such a sharp young fellow as his pa says, he could be well worth having. And given that he's so little coming in, he'll hardly be charging as much as a firm of top barristers. Will he?'

Murtybeg considered that.

'Yes, yes,' he said, 'it seems like an excellent idea. For all I know, he might still be too expensive, but at least it's worth trying.'

'Fair enough,' Sternberg said. 'I must tell you though, that even for a junior barrister, a referral from a solicitor is essential. Now, if you hold on a minute.'

He went out into the back office, and Murtybeg could hear him dictating a letter. He came back in and handed it to Murtybeg.

'Here you are, this should suffice.'

Murtybeg stood. 'And how much do I owe you?'

'Oh no. I couldn't charge you for this service. And in any case, I might just be giving my young nephew a helping hand. Who knows?'

Next day, Murtybeg took the train into Manchester Piccadilly and walked to the Manchester Law Library.

There was a man at a table, just inside the entrance.

'I'm looking for Mr. Louis Sternberg,' Murtybeg said.

'Referral?'

'What?' Murtybeg asked.

'I need the referral from your solicitor.'

'Oh yes,' Murtybeg said, 'hold on a moment.' He passed it across. The porter glanced through it and gave it back.

'Louis Sternberg. Down the corridor, the double doors straight in front of you. You'll easily find him there.'

Murtybeg followed the instructions and found himself in an extensive library, volumes on both sides and up to the ceiling. After asking for Louis Sternberg three times, he ended up in a small room to the side. Asking again, he was directed to a table under the window.

'Louis Sternberg?'

'Yes?'

Blue eyes looked up over a pair of spectacles, questioning.

'Your uncle referred me to you. He said I'd find you here right enough. We might have work for you.'

'Work?' There was a rapid smile. 'Why don't you sit down?'

Murtybeg sank into an old chair, tooled with green leather.

'Murtybeg Ryan is the name.'

'Murtybeg? An Irish name?'

'It is.'

He passed across the letter from Abraham Sternberg.

'This looks fine. So what can I do for you?'

Rapidly, Murtybeg explained the situation about Danny's death and Irene's takeover of Edwardes & Ryan. Then he showed him the letter from Rothwells. Sternberg glanced through it.

'As it happens, there was hardly any need to show me this. What you've said is sufficient. There's one very important point of law that Rothwells are doing their best to ignore.'

'What's that?'

'The concept of common-law marriage was abolished in England and Wales in 1753.'

Murtybeg was stunned.

'You mean...?'

'Just that. Miss Miller has no rights in law. She is merely an employee of Edwardes & Ryan, no more.'

'So what do we do now?'

'Send a letter to Rothwells. They know damned little of the law, they're no more than a firm of conveyancing solicitors.'

'No, no,' Murtybeg said, 'I'd far prefer you to do it.'

'I'd be delighted to,' Sternberg said, 'but I think it's better not at this stage. Rothwells are not aware that you are using legal counsel, and if they knew you were talking to me, they might recommend their client to brief counsel too, and you most certainly don't want that. No, I think it's better if you drop them a note in your own name, just indicating that you are aware of the fact that common-law marriage was abolished. Don't even mention the 1753 Act. Even that would imply that you are too knowledgeable.'

'Fair enough,' said Murtybeg. 'That would sound most sensible.'

'Yes,' Sternberg said, 'it's by far the most direct way to handle the situation, and the cheapest too.'

'Now what about your charges.'

'My charges? Oh, there's no charges for this. Any barrister could have told you this. I'd be embarrassed to charge.'

'Well, that's very decent of you,' Murtybeg said, 'and now I'm the one to be embarrassed.'

'There's no need. Edwardes & Ryan are an expanding firm. I am sure we will have reason to meet again.'

'Most surely.'

When he returned to Stockport, Murtybeg wrote a letter to Rothwells.

He wrote another letter to Louis Sternberg, enclosing a copy of the letter he had sent to Rothwells, and expressing his thanks. A few days later, he received a letter from Sternberg with six words:

'Excellent, that should do the job.'

Murtybeg could not believe his luck. He had been worried about costs, but had been given the best legal advice for nothing at all.

Chapter 10

Manchester Times. October 1848:

Manchester Trade Reports. Our home trade demand has also, we regret to say, undergone a change for the worse, owing in a great measure, we think, to the great and rapid fall which has taken place in railway property, and which is exercising a fearful influence on traders of almost every class; this it will continue to do as long as 'calls' are made to an extent from £3,000,000 to £4,000,000 monthly. The amount now required to complete existing engagements is estimated at about £30 millions, at the rate of payment which has been going on for the last three years, will cover a space of three months; after this period has elapsed, we may look for a return of capital into its legitimate channels and with it a more prosperous state of things in commercial matters.

Over the following weeks, life continued much as usual in Edwardes & Ryan. Murtybeg had thought about Irene's position in the business. She had tried to take it over, but now the Ryan family owned it, and she would have known that by now. Rothwells would have told her.

He could have attempted to fire her, but saw no reason for this. Danny had never dared to, because she knew the business better than any of them.

He did notice though that Irene's salary was higher than his own. Only by a shilling a day, but even so, it annoyed him. When he suggested reducing it, she refused to accept any reduction and in the end, he gave in. She had allowed him a two-shilling increase, and it was not worth arguing about a shilling a day reduction. Also, it gave her a small victory, and that might serve to ease any disappointment she may have felt from her failure in taking over Edwardes & Ryan.

But even so, there was one subtle change.

No ten percent amounts were added to contract quotes anymore. Murtybeg expected that the volume of new contracts might drop, but they did not. Could cash be leaving the business in other ways, though? He checked all payments, including cash transactions, very carefully, but still there was no sign of any malfeasance.

All this time, Irene worked quietly. In some ways, this worried him even more. Irene was not a woman to take defeat easily.

As the business expanded, the borrowing requirement grew. Murtybeg arranged another meeting with the Manchester & Salford. This time, Irene came too. This was on her own suggestion. At first, Murtybeg was doubtful, but then thought it might be a reasonable idea to have two top negotiators rather than one.

He noted that Winrow greeted Irene as if he already knew her. Perhaps he had been bribed after all. But now, there was little chance of that being done. Winrow went through their latest projections.

'These look to be eminently satisfactory,' he told them. 'There is one little problem now though.'

Neither Irene nor Murtybeg said anything.

After a pause, Winrow went on.

'If we grant this latest application, your borrowings from the Manchester & Salford will be approaching thirty thousand pounds.'

'And aren't we worth it?' Murtybeg said, facetiously.

'I've no doubt your business is an excellent one,' Winrow said. 'There are, however, two main concerns. The first is that you have few assets on which we can take security. The second is that, in spite of your high profits, your share capital is still very low.'

'That will increase,' Murtybeg said.

'I've no doubt it will, Mr. Ryan. Still, it is low at present.'

Murtybeg made to speak but Irene stopped him.

'I would make two points to you, Mr. Winrow. The first is this. Your very best security is the quality of contractors for whom we work. I don't have to tell you, Mackenzie and Brassey are the top contractors in England, or all of Europe for that matter.'

'I don't know,' Winrow said. 'There's Peto & Betts.'

'Ah yes,' Irene said, 'And the only one reason we have no contracts with them is that they themselves have no Works in the north of England at present. We could, of course, bid on contracts around London, but it is not our policy to do so at present. I still maintain that the quality of our contracts is the best guarantee you will ever have.'

Winrow nodded. 'And what was your second point?'

'If you cannot lend to us, we will have to find a bank that will.'

A few days later, they received the confirmation of the lending facility from the Manchester & Salford.

'By God, I'd hardly believe it,' Murtybeg said. 'You really gave it to Winrow that time.'

'Yes,' she said, 'and I know what you're thinking. You're wondering if there is a backhander to him too.'

'Did I say that?'

'You didn't have to. But in answer to the question, no there was not. You have to deal with these bankers the hard way. And one other thing you must remember, the banks only make money out of lending. We are top flight borrowers, and they know that. Our credit is up there with both Brassey and Mackenzie, and the problem that the bank have is that there are insufficient other businesses of our quality they can lend to.'

Murtybeg recalled all the references to problems on the railway works that he had read in the Manchester Times, the Bradford Observer, the London Times and many other newspapers.

'Yes,' he said, 'I'd guess you're right.'

'And that's where Danny was too soft,' she said. 'He was all bravado. He could never see that when a business gets to a certain level of borrowing, they have the bank over a barrel. Certainly, he had problems with the fact that he had been borrowing in advance on the North Staffordshire line, and when the bank found out the section he was working on had been terminated, they came after him. All he had to do was threaten bankruptcy – then the bank would have had to take an enormous loss, and questions would have been asked. Directors would have lost their jobs. Winrow too. No, when a business is in a tight corner like that, the only option the bank have is to allow their debtor to trade out of it.'

'But they'll hardly do that unless they believe such a business can trade out of it.'

'Exactly. And we convinced Winrow that we could.'

'Correction,' Murtybeg said, 'I did it. If I hadn't convinced Winrow on that point at my very first meeting with him, there would have been no further meetings. Still, he's trying to protect the bank's position, and I think he's accepted your point that the quality of our customers is far more important than the capital we have in the business.'

He was still concerned about Irene. She had her ways of working, and even if he was unsure whether bribery had stopped, she had other ways of doing it. He had been amazed at her treatment of the bank. Very few women dealt with banks, and none would dare to treat them like that. He had to acknowledge, though, that her approach had worked. She no longer had any stake in Edwardes & Ryan, she was only an employee, even if a highly paid one. How long could that last though?

Her ruthlessness became even more apparent. One day, she was going through Roughneen's wage sheets from the Colne Extension.

'These wages are too high,' she said.

'Too high?' Murtybeg echoed. 'What do you call too high?'

'A shilling a day.'

'Damn it, we can't push them any lower.'

'Have we tried? I think we can get them far lower.'

'Like what?'

'Pay them nothing at all.'

This time, Murtybeg was almost speechless. Was the woman mad?

'So how would you propose to do that?' he asked.

'We pay them in scrip.'

'Scrip! You're really saying...'

'Think about it. We set up a truck shop on site. Give them their dockets for the amount owing, cashable only at the store. They'd have no choice.'

'Irene, in the name of God...'

'And we could set up a truck bar too. Saturdays only.'

'I've never even heard of one of those.'

'Well look around you. On all the other Works, where do the men go on a Saturday? They don't even get paid on site. The foremen insist on paying them in the nearest bar or shebeen, and that's where half their money goes by the time the weekend is over.'

'And the other half?' he asked.

'Don't forget, we're feeding them already. What else do they need? Anything they want, they can buy at the truck store. And for both the store and the bar, we can buy in bulk, push our own costs down, and make an excellent profit.'

'But much of that money is needed for starving people back home. You know that as well as I do.'

'You're beginning to get like Danny. Becoming too soft.'

'That's not soft, God damn it. It's reality.'

'Fair enough,' she said. 'Two shillings a week cash for their families, the rest in scrip.'

'Fine,' Murtybeg said, 'but only on our new contracts.'

'Yes,' she said, 'and that includes the Colne Extension.'

Roughneen was astonished when Murtybeg explained the truck system to him. He had seen it operate in other parts of England and understood it well.

'It's just that I never thought I'd see it working here,' he said.

'Or maybe didn't want to, Johnny. Is that it?'

'I don't know, I'm not sure it would work quite so easy. We've said we're paying a shilling a day cash. We never said anything about truck.'

They discussed it in detail for the rest of the afternoon. Still, Murtybeg could see that Roughneen was dubious.

'Fair enough,' Irene said, when Murtybeg got home. 'Let's cut him in for ten per cent of the truck store profits, over and above cost. He'll find ways of doing it then.'

The next day, Murtybeg received requests from Brasseys regarding the final, smaller contracts on the North Staffordshire.

He went to discuss it with Irene, but she was not there. Puzzled, he began the work on them himself. He noted that he had some weeks to return the documents, and was thankful for this, not only because he wanted to discuss it with her, but also because he wanted to walk the territory and assess the work involved.

His clerk handed him a letter. It was marked 'hand delivery'.

In it, Mr. Rothwell of Rothwells explained in very few words that they did not recognise Murtybeg's interpretation of the 1753 Act. They requested Murtybeg's attendance at the Manchester Probate Court the following week. Little wonder that Irene had disappeared.

He went into Manchester.

'She doesn't give in easily,' Sternberg said.

'Did you think she would?'

'Well, I've never met the woman. But I'll tell you this, Mr. Rothwell must have been thinking about this for quite some time. I wonder what little scheme he's come up with.'

'How do we find out?'

'It's like he says. We'll have to attend the Probate Court.'

'Fine,' Murtybeg said. 'But tell me one thing...'

'My stipends?'

'Well...yes.'

'Normally, I work for one shilling an hour.'

'Yes, yes,' Murtybeg said uncertainly. 'But how much do you think a case like this might cost overall?'

'Impossible to say,' Sternberg said, 'and that's the problem. It could be five, ten or even fifteen pounds.'

'It's just, if we lose...'

'I understand your concerns. Your own means, in cash terms, would be limited, as compared to Edwardes & Ryan. So what I would suggest instead, let's work on a contingency basis.'

'A contingency...?'

'Very simple. If we win the case, I'll charge. If we don't, no charge whatsoever.'

Murtybeg felt his interest quickening.

'So...if we lose, there is no charge.'

'Exactly. And then there would be no change in your personal circumstances whatsoever. On the other hand, if we win, I would charge twenty-five pounds flat. This can then be paid directly out of Edwardes & Ryan, rather than your own pocket.'

Murtybeg was bewildered, and thinking fast.

'I must say, I'd never have thought of that,' he said. 'I didn't know the law could work that way. That would be excellent.'

They stood outside the Court, waiting.

'I'd never even heard of a Probate Court,' Murtybeg said.

'Why would you?' Sternberg said. 'It's very new. They only started in Manchester last year.'

Murtybeg spotted Irene on a corner at the far side of the street. Beside her was a tall man, wearing a gown and a collarette.

'That's Michael Pritchard over there,' Sternberg said. 'He's one of the top barristers in Manchester. She must be worried.'

'She's not the only one,' Murtybeg said.

'I'll bet he'll be surprised to see me.'

'He might,' Murtybeg said. 'And that's Irene Miller beside him. But, sure as hell, she won't be surprised to see me.'

As they waited, another carriage arrived. The passenger paid the cabbie, and walked across to Irene and Pritchard.

'That's Rothwell,' Sternberg said.

'What's he doing here?' Murtybeg asked.

'He's only here as an observer, I'd say,' Sternberg said. 'As a solicitor, he can't plead her case. But since he's instructed Pritchard as Miss Miller's counsel, he has an obvious interest.'

An hour later, the Registrar read down Murtybeg's letter regarding the 1753 Act.

'Mr. Ryan has described the situation most succinctly for one not accustomed to such matters,' he said. 'What do you have to say, Mr. Pritchard?'

'Succinct indeed,' Pritchard said, 'but there are several vital points to remember. Daniel Ryan and Irene Miller already had a very close relationship, as evidenced by the time they were living together, and the fact that they were already affianced. Their wedding had already been booked, and the Reverend Southwood, will confirm that if required. There is no doubt that if it had not been for Mr. Ryan's unfortunate accident, they would be man and wife by now.'

'Fine,' the Registrar said 'but we still must face the fact that they were not actually married.'

'There is another point though,' Pritchard went on. 'The Act of 1753 only applied to England and Wales.'

Murtybeg started. Sternberg put a hand on his arm.

'Don't worry,' he whispered, 'let's hear what else he has to say.'

Pritchard glanced at them angrily.

'Mr. Daniel Ryan was born and brought up in Ireland, and the concept of common-law marriage still prevails in Ireland.'

Sternberg only smiled, listening attentively and making occasional notes as Pritchard spoke.

Then he stood.

'My learned friend has made a most interesting point. I regret to inform him though, that his argument is inapplicable. We must indeed accept that Mr. Daniel Ryan was born and reared in Ireland, and thus must be seen as having been an original native of that country. Mr. Pritchard might argue therefore that this leaves us with half a common-law marriage.'

The Registrar smiled.

'But there is another more important point,' Sternberg went on. 'The 1753 Act most definitely does apply to Ireland. As Mr. Pritchard should be aware, the Act of Union between Great Britain and Ireland, which came into effect on the first of January, 1801, prorogued the Irish Parliament in Dublin, which means that, as of that date, Ireland was ruled directly from Westminster, and – most important – the laws of England and Wales over-rode any prior legislation of the Irish Parliament. Furthermore, Mr. Daniel Ryan was most definitely born after 1801.'

The Registrar had been scribbling notes in a large volume.

'Go on.'

'I would point out one other item too. This case is being heard in England, and one way or another the 1753 Act is most definitely applicable here.'

The registrar had put down his pen.

'You'll have to do better than this, Mr. Pritchard,' he said. 'I don't like to say it, but I think you are wasting our time.'

Sternberg tapped Murtybeg on the knee. 'I told you not to worry.'

They left the court.

'Did you see the look on Pritchard's face,' Murtybeg said.

'I did,' Sternberg said, 'and I never expected that. Pritchard was unaware of the Act of Union.'

'But you'd done your research.'

'That's what you are paying me for.'

Murtybeg clapped his hand on Sternberg's shoulder. 'Well, by God, you've done good work today and I'll tell you something else. After all these years, I never thought I'd be glad of the Act of Union.'

The next morning, Murtybeg received Sternberg's invoice, in an envelope marked personal. He had a cheque sent at once.

That afternoon, he sacked Irene. Lavan was in the room at the time and looked around in surprise.

She stood up from her desk, eyes blazing.

'You'll regret this,' she said. 'You think you know how to run a business like this. Let me tell you, you most definitely do not. You can manage it your own way, but you'll find very soon that the contracts aren't coming in.'

Saying that, she left.

'By God, you're a brave man, Murteen,' Lavan said.

'What choice did I have? Either we run the business, or she does.'

'Still, she had her ways of bringing in business.'

'Bribery, you mean,' Murtybeg said. 'Well, we've stopped all that. That isn't the way we run the business.'

'It mightn't, but it worked.'

'Worked? Look at the past month. No backhanders to anyone, and we're still running the business.'

'Ah yes,' Lavan said, 'but there's a reason for that. Anderson and the other contractors, they reckoned all they had to do was wait. Irene had them all convinced that she would end up controlling Edwardes & Ryan. They reckoned that when she did, the payments would start again.'

Murtybeg looked at him in surprise.

'You didn't believe that, did you?'

'I did,' Lavan replied, 'but one way or the other, it'll be up to you now. There's one sure way of getting contracts, and it's for you to make use of it, whether you like it or not.

Chapter 11

New York Daily Tribune, October 1848:
The calamitous condition of the Irish People may be justly ascribed far more to the monopoly of her soil by a few capitalists than to the other oppressions of the British Government. And yet it is a monopoly many times worse, that we are asked voluntarily to create in a region sixteen times as large as all Ireland, and which seems to form almost the sole refuge which Providence has left her unhappy exiles. For my part, until I forget the history of my native country, written in the sufferings of her People, I can never contribute, by my vote or any act of mine, to the infliction of a kindred curse upon any portion of the land of our adoption; still less upon our vast Western Territory, which is capable of containing a population of an hundred millions, and in which the children of the Emigrant and the native born citizens are to mingle and to share the blessings which, in the decision of this great question, we secure to them, or the degradation and wrong which we shall inflict upon them. US politician, Robert Addis Emmet, attacks the extension of slavery into the Western States.

Michael's letter arrived at Steuben Street.

'*Any great news?*' one of the Tourmakeady men asked.

'*Nothing great about the hunger, anyhow,*' Luke replied. '*The same as we knew already. Says there had been patches of potatoes left across the County, but they're all gone now. Any that were dug have rotted. The rest is family news.*'

'*Bad news?*' Winnie asked.

'*It's Danny. He's dead.*'

'*Dead!*'

'*Killed himself,*' he said, flatly.

'*Killed himself! Danny? You're telling me Danny killed himself? But how...?*'

'*Stood out in front of a train.*'

'A train?' Mick echoed. 'Ah no, not Daniel Ryan. He was far too tough a fellow for that. It was an accident, surely? What would he want with killing himself?'

'Daniel Ryan?' Seán Óg asked. 'The railway boss, was it?'

'The same,' Luke said. 'He's dead. Killed himself.'

'But…what was he to you?'

'A cousin.'

Seán Óg stared at him in disbelief.

'He was a tough man right enough,' he said. 'There was many a man from around Tourmakeady and the Partry Mountains knew that very well.'

'There's many a man would have wished him dead, too,' one of the other Tourmakeady men said.

'And starve at home in Partry?' Seán Óg said. 'What would be the good of that? The lads worked for Ryan, not out of choice, but need. What will happen now, and Ryan gone?'

He shook his head in bewilderment.

'And you're a cousin of his?'

'I am,' Luke said, 'but sure what fault is that of mine. When I knew him, he was a decent enough fellow, but he changed. By God, he changed, as you all have cause to know.'

They spoke about it in bed that night.

'But if Danny killed himself,' Winnie asked, 'what reason would he have for that?'

'From all we can gather from what father wrote, there were two reasons. Pat reckoned that Danny was running out of money.'

'Sure that can't be true. All Danny would do was fire workers. That would stop the money going out quick enough.'

'I'm not sure it was that easy, Father reckons it was to do with that woman of his. Pat had said that was the real problem. A woman that Danny couldn't stand up to. She must be some lady.'

'They're hearing a lot from Pat.'

'And there, at least, is the good news,' Luke said. 'Pat's home in Mayo. He's got a job with the County and, by God, am I glad of that. They'll have more money coming into the farm and more to eat.'

Winnie kissed him. 'That's the thing about you Ryans. Hidden depths. Hard to get to know you.'

'There were hidden depths to Danny, right enough.'

'And what about you? Isn't it time you told me more about the forests and New York?'

The question surprised him. Over the next few nights though, he told her much of what had happened in the quarantine sheds in Grosse Île, in the saw mills of Quebec, the fever hospitals of Montreal and in the forests along the Gatineau.

He told too of the journey to New York and of conditions in Five Points. He was surprised when she asked to visit it.

'But there's other parts of New York...' he said.

'Maybe there are,' she said, 'but that's not where the Irish go, is it?'

'Well some of them do.'

'Stop putting me off. I want to see Five Points, and that's an end to it.'

One morning, they left Liam in the care of Mrs. Gleeson again.

Winnie was weaning Liam by now, though the baby kept trying to return to the breast. He almost regarded Mrs. Gleeson as a second mother, though, and accepted Winnie's absences without protest. Luke felt the life of a boarding house keeper was hard enough for any woman, and little Liam certainly lifted Mrs. Gleeson's spirits. As for Winnie, a day or two away from the baby was a relief, and she was determined to understand New York and the life of the Irish in the city.

They took the Jersey City ferry to the Cortland Street terminal. Luke paid for the tickets. He had no desire to bring Winnie across the Hudson on a coal barge.

She was fascinated by the skyline. 'Manhattan!' she exclaimed.

'Yes,' said Luke, 'and Governor's Island just over there. That's Castle Garden.'

'And over there? Where's that?'

'Staten Island. That's where they have the quarantine hospital.'

'Quarantine?'

'For the people who had fever coming in. Not half as bad as Quebec, from all we hear. Grosse Île was a living hell. Staten was bad enough but nothing compared to that.'

'And where's that behind Castle Garden?'

That's the Battery. On up there, all those piers there, that's where the boats from Boston come in. Up further, that's for the boats from France. On up again, that's where the ones leave going up river to Albany, top of New York State. And the boat going across up the river there, that's the Hoboken Ferry. There's more piers beyond, but I don't know them.'

'You know enough.'

They landed. Luke led her along Fulton Street, across Broadway and up William Street to Five Points. As they left Broadway behind, he could see the shock in Winnie's eyes.

'You were right,' she said. 'It's much worse than I'd thought. Is it all like this?'

149

'Pretty well. The stink isn't as bad in the winter, when the shit is frozen. Worse after though, when it all melts again.'

They passed two children begging on the street. Winnie gave them a cent. 'They must be cold like that.'

'I'm sure of it,' Luke said. 'Not that their mother or father would give a damn.'

They had arrived at Costellos'. Winnie coughed as the fug of cigar smoke and whiskey hit her.

'This is Costellos'?'

'Indeed,' Luke said, 'one of the better bars around here.'

He saw Costello at the end of the bar.

'Come on,' he said to Winnie.

Costello looked up from the beer he was serving.

'Luke...'

He glanced at Winnie. 'I thought you had a wife back in Ireland?'

'Sure what of that,' Luke said. 'A man can't be without a woman for that length of time.'

A look of shock came across Costello's face, then Winnie broke out laughing. Costello looked at her puzzled.

'Well, it's nice to know someone has been keeping an eye on him, keep him out of trouble,' she said. 'How do you do, Mr. Costello. I'm Mrs. Ryan. The same Mrs. Ryan you're so concerned to defend.'

Costello's expression changed, as he realised he had been fooled. He laughed and held out his hand. 'Well, by God, Mrs. Ryan, you're most welcome.'

Two whiskies were poured out. 'Your health,' Costello said. 'I'm happy Luke brought you over, though I didn't think he'd have brought you this way.'

'Why's that?' Winnie asked.

'There's few who've got out of Five Points would ever admit they knew it, nor bring anyone to visit.'

'He didn't want me to see it,' Winnie said, 'and that's the reason I wanted to. That, and understanding my own country.'

'Your own country?'

'Look, Mr. Costello,' she said, 'we all came from County Mayo. Another word for Hell. Sure we love Mayo, we love Ireland. All our families are there. Those that are living anyhow.'

'I understand what it is you're saying.' Costello said. 'But what has it to do with Five Points? Is it that you want to understand a second Irish Hell?'

'Something like that,' she answered. 'And that's something my husband would never understand. He wants we should make our way up in life, but while I'm inclined to agree with that, I also reckon we should understand where we've come from. Am I making sense?'

'You are,' Costello said. 'A lot. You really want to see Five Points?'

'I do.'

He opened the door behind the bar.

'Catherine.'

Catherine came out. Yes, an attractive woman, no doubting it. It amused him to think what Costello might have thought if he had tried walking out with Catherine. Not just delivering gin or food either. To hell with all that. Winnie was here now.

Costello had introduced the two women.

'What deliveries are you doing today?' he asked Catherine.

'Three bottles of gin down to Cow Bay.'

'That's a damned dangerous place,' Luke said.

'It's alright if they have the money,' Catherine said. 'After that it's a rice drop-off to Mrs. Fordyce up the Old Brewery, then fifty cents to the McGifford family behind Transfiguration.'

'The McGiffords. They're from the Palmerston evictions, aren't they?' Costello asked.

'Yes,' Catherine answered. 'Mrs. Fordyce is too. Somewhere around Cliffony.'

'Be damned careful so. Now, the reason I'm telling you that is I want you to take Mrs. Ryan here along. She might not be used to that kind of thing.'

Luke went to protest.

'No,' Costello said, 'she wants to see Five Points, and I say, let her see it. She won't find a better guide than Catherine here neither. Be wary with bringing her to Cow Bay now.'

'Dead right,' Luke said. 'The rest of them there, they're sure as hell not Irish evictions. Not even Irish.'

'No,' Catherine said. 'Not our people.'

After the two women had left, Costello poured a second whiskey.

'She's a sharp lady, your wife,' Costello said. 'You'll go far with her.'

'Not much further, I won't, if you go on sending her down places like Cow Bay.'

'It's what she wanted. Anyhow, they're safe enough. Catherine's been down many times; it's done her no harm.'

'Not yet,' Luke said.

'But forget that a moment,' Costello said. 'Since your wife is in New York now, how long more are you intending on staying?'

'Not long,' Luke said.

'So what about the Hibernians?'

'I was going to ask you about that,' Luke said. 'You mentioned a branch in Cass Township, the headquarters, I think. The only problem is that Cass is a good distance from Lackan, and I doubt I'd be travelling too much if that was my branch.'

'I wouldn't be worrying about that,' Costello said. 'There's another branch in Lackan. I'll give you a contact.'

He took a notebook from behind the bar, and wrote a name and address.

'This is all you'll want. Just call on Eddie, and say John Costello sent you.'

On the ferry back to Jersey City that night, Winnie was quiet. At last, Luke nudged her.

'Well, what did you think?'

'What should I think? I'll tell you this though, I never expected to see anything like that. Is this the America we all dreamed of?'

'Didn't I tell you, you shouldn't go to Five Points?'

'Oh no, that's not what I'm saying. I wanted to, and now I have. I reckon too there's many places like it in towns up and down this country. Still though, there's good and bad. Sure, I saw hunger today, but no outright starvation, and that's something.'

'It is. When you're hungry, it's all that matters.'

'I blame the landlords,' Mick said one night.

'I'd agree with you,' Luke said. 'All the evictions, people out on the roads dying. Lucan, Palmer, Gore-Knox and the rest of them, they're right bastards. But there's one thing you can't blame them for.'

'What's that?' Jack asked, intrigued.

'The blight.'

'The blight!' Mick exclaimed. 'Sure we don't even know what brings the blight. Maybe the landlords are poisoning the crops.'

'Why in the name of God would they do that?' said Luke. 'It would only hurt themselves. No, I agree with you as far as the evictions go, and right savage bastards they are there too, killing people like that. But the blight, that's only silly. Everyone knows what causes the blight. The rain and the lightning, that's what.'

'You don't know that,' Mick said.

'Open your eyes,' Luke said. 'Any time we've had blight; it's been wet weather. A long dry summer, you never get it. That's what you said yourself.'

'That's still doesn't let the landlords off the hook,' Mick said.

'And I wouldn't do that in a month of Sundays,' Luke said. 'If Lucan and Palmer and Clanowen were hung, drawn and quartered, I'd think it wouldn't be enough for them. Lucan – the biggest landlord in Mayo – he was worse than any. And didn't I see evictions myself at *Gort na Móna*, just beside Kilduff? A Clanowen eviction, that was. Easy on Lucan and the County fellows to ignore that, the bastards, and they sitting in Castlebar, not even caring what was going on over our side of the county. And where did the starving people all end up? Over in Castlebar Workhouse, with Lord Lucan doing the paying? Not a chance of that. No, it was Knockanure Workhouse had to take them in, those that would be taken. And do you think my good Lord Lucan would give a damn about the workhouse in Knockanure, and he not paying for it?'

'I'm not too sure he'd give much of a damn about the workhouse in Castlebar neither,' Jack said. 'I can't see him paying for that neither.'

Every weekend now, Luke and Winnie visited Five Points. On occasion, Luke accompanied Catherine and Winnie, selling gin around Cow Bay and The Brewery. Sometimes too, he went on other Hibernian missions distributing food and money around Five Points. He found these just as disturbing.

The Hibernians limited these to those families in direst need. Once again, he visited the cellars, tenements and rookeries, but no matter how much he saw the grinding poverty, it always sickened him.

He felt there was a conflict in Costello's activities. While the food would all be eaten, some of the cash at least would go on drink. On another 'gin run' with Catherine, he recognised families who had received money and food. Whether Costello knew of this type of conflict, or whether he cared, Luke did not know.

One afternoon, Luke stayed working with Costello and did not accompany Winnie and Catherine.

'What were you doing yourself all the time I was out?' she asked him, as they crossed back to Jersey City.

'Oh, a few things. Spoke with Costello and one or two of the fellows at the bar for a while. Then I went up to the Chemical Bank. Got five pounds out to send back to Mayo. I wrote them a long letter too to go with it; telling them how well you and Liam were looking and all about Jersey City and our plans for meeting all the fellows up in Lackan. I told them too to take thirty shillings out of the five pounds and send it up to your mother in Brockagh.'

'It's well you did,' she said. 'It's a lot of money.'

It is, Winnie, but by God, even with Pat back, they'll need it. The hunger in Mayo is only getting worse.'

At a Hibernians' meeting in Costellos' one night, there were heated arguments about the Young Ireland movement and the failed rebellion. Luke had only heard confusing stories of this across the summer.

'It was a disgrace.' Carroll said. 'Thinking they could rise the whole country, and what did we get? A brawl in Tipperary.'

Costello stood, furious.

'We'll have none of that kind of talk,' he said. 'That's playing into the hands of the British. Mitchell and Smith-O'Brien – they did what they could.'

'Yes,' Carroll said, 'and let the British papers make propaganda out of it. The Cabbage Patch Rebellion! They want to make fools of us all, and we let them. And what did the rest of the country do, for all their grand talk? Burnt a railway station. Did they even do that? Great heroes, aren't they?'

'Well, they tried, at least,' Costello said, 'and now they're paying the price.'

'What price? Tell me that.'

'The prison ships to Van Diemen's Land,' Costello said. 'Eaglehawk Neck most like, that's where they keep the worst. No one's ever escaped from Eaglehawk.'

'They will though,' another man said. 'We'll get them out, bring them to America. You'll see.'

One of the younger men brought up the subject of the Molly Maguire gang. At once, Luke was on his guard. He was gratified though when he heard Costello condemning it.

'The Church is against all kinds of oath bound societies. You should know that.'

One of the others made to protest but Costello silenced him.

'Any such organisation has no need to take an oath of silence, unless they have something to hide. And that gang sure have a lot to hide. Including murder.'

'But no one can prove that,' Carroll said.

'It'll be proven in time,' Costello said, 'and in the meantime, none of us will have anything to do with it.'

After the meeting had broken up, Luke assisted Costello in cleaning the bar.

'I was troubled to hear talk of the Mollys again,' he said to Costello.

'Yes, and it's a troubling problem to us too. The police, they find it hard to distinguish between the various Irish societies. There's many of them convinced that there's gangs in the Hibernians. But I can tell you, here and now, that is not the case. If we thought any man was in the Maguires, they'd be thrown out straight away.'

'Yes,' Luke said, 'and I'd agree with you on that. But tell me this, John, if they're oath bound, as we say, then there's no way of knowing whether a man is a member or not. He could join the Hibernians, and no one would know.'

Costello stopped wiping the table he was working on.

'I suppose you're right, Luke, and there's damned little we can do about that. All we can do is keep our eyes open. Think of it this way. If a man is a murderer, he's not going to tell anyone about it, oath-bound or not. That's the reason you have to be recommended when you join the Order. Vouched for, if you like. The only reason you're a Hibernian is because I vouched for you, and I know damned well, you're not a member of the Molly Maguires, nor a murderer either.'

Luke hesitated. He remembered the battle of Lord Sligo's wall back in Mayo, when they had to defend their own corn supplies against starving men and women who wanted it for themselves. He remembered too how he himself had saved Michael's life by hitting an assailant with a rock. That man had died; he was sure of it. Was he, Luke Ryan, a murderer? Perhaps not. He had only been defending his own father's life. Still, he was a killer, he was sure of that.

'You're right John,' he said, 'I'm surely not a murderer. There's just one other thing though. We describe the Mollys as oath-bound. Don't we take an oath ourselves when we join the Order?'

'Ah yes, but that's a different matter. It's more in the line of a pledge. We pledge our loyalty to our fellow members, and while we may have our secrets, they are not criminal secrets. The Mollys are oath-bound killers.'

'There's some who'd think them patriots,' Luke said.

'Well, I sure as hell wouldn't. And anyone who might, is only deluded.'

Next morning, they took the ferry back to Jersey City.

'Did Costello say anything about cholera?' Winnie asked.

'Cholera? Where did you hear that?'

'Catherine just said it to me. There's some question it's come to New York. All kinds of wild stories, you wouldn't know the truth of it. But still...'

'*Arra* no. We'd have heard of it if it had come to New York. Where would she have heard it anyhow?'

'The Dutch and the Germans. She says they're all talking about it. The ships coming in from Hamburg – they're carrying it. There's terrible stories from over there. Thousands – tens of thousands – dead, that's what they're saying.'

'I just hope to God they're only stories,' Luke said. 'Or that it stays in Hamburg.'

Luke's membership of the Hibernians was something that Mick deduced very rapidly.

One afternoon in the terminal, they sat on a bollard for the break. On the passenger docks across the Hudson, one ship was discharging, two waiting behind. Where were they from? Ireland? Liverpool? Or anywhere else in Europe? He had seen ships from Bremen and Hamburg; Bordeaux and Le Havre. But most were from Liverpool, carrying Irish men and women fleeing Ireland through England's biggest port.

Mick was nudging him.

'I don't know why you're in with those Hibernian fools,' he said. 'Hot air, that's all they're good for. Hot lead is what we need.'

'I might half agree with you,' Luke said. 'Hot lead is what some of those Know-nothing gangs might need. We can't do things that way though, can we?'

'Why not? There's others that would.'

'And I suppose you're part of these others, are you?' Luke asked.

'I'm not saying I am,' Mick said.

'And you're not saying you're not.'

'Never mind me,' Mick said. 'Isn't it about time you thought of doing something serious.'

'Like what, working harder?'

'Resisting.'

'Resisting?'

'Resisting like we've always done. Stand up for our rights. Ireland or America, it doesn't matter. We fought the landlords, we shot enough of them, didn't we. Their agents too. And now we're carrying on the fight in a new land. Have you ever thought of where you're going?'

Luke looked across to another dock where another train was coming, drawing many wagons of anthracite.

'Going to join Farrelly,' he said. 'Digging anthracite instead of shovelling it.'

'Yes, you are,' Mick said, 'and what kind of foremen will we have when we get there? God knows, these ones are bad enough, but once we get up to the anthracite belt, then you'll know what foremen are. Then you'll know what resistance is.'

Realisation was slowly coming to Luke. It was as he had always suspected. A terrorist group in Ireland and America. There was only one group that fitted that description.

'You're talking about the Molly Maguires, aren't you?' he said to Mick.

'I never said I was,' Mick answered. 'Whatever I'm talking about, you're going to be one, whether you know it or not. Whether you join in Jersey City or up by Lackan, you'll join. You're not the kind of man to bow down and take defeat.'

A barge had stopped, and had been tied up. A whistle blew.

'Yes,' said Mick, as they walked towards the barge, 'you'll join, and so you should, since you know so many already.'

'Around here?' said Luke, surprised. 'In the terminal?'

'How would I know,' Mick replied, cagily. 'Maybe there are, and maybe there's not. And maybe there's more in Five Points, and you don't even know it. Inside the Hibernians too.'

'I can assure you of one thing,' Luke said. 'The Hibernians don't even allow it.'

'You can believe what you want on that one,' Mick said. 'But how would they know who is and who isn't a resister. One way or another, the Hibernians aren't resisting...'

'Violence isn't their way,' Luke said.

'Sure, it isn't. And what do the Hibernians go for instead? Going all weepy about the old country. Is that resistance? The Young Irelanders showed us what that was all about, with their little rebellion. I'll tell you this Luke, the next time there's a rebellion in Ireland, it'll be a real rebellion led by real men.'

They climbed up on the wagon and started shovelling.

So what was Mick? A man who might or might not be a member of an organisation that might or might not be violent, and might not even exist. An organisation with no name. Was Mick only trying to inflate his own importance? Maybe, maybe not.

As the weather became colder, more and more Irishmen appeared in Jersey City. They stood forlornly outside the terminal, shivering.

'And there's just no jobs for them,' Jack said.

'Sure how could there be?' Mick said. 'They're just pouring into New York. And it's not that I wouldn't like to give my fellow Irishman a start, but not at the expense of losing my own job.'

'You're right,' Jack said. 'Still, I find it hard to take. Look at them there, hardly an ounce of meat on their bones, nor a thread of clothing neither,'

'Damn it to hell,' Mick said, 'what choice do we have. It's either them or us. They starve or we starve.'

Luke concentrated on shovelling. He had found over the years that hard physical labour was one way to work out his own fears. Still, it gnawed at him. Irishmen, hungry and freezing, come all the way to America, and what did they find waiting for them? Hunger and death in the land of plenty.

They were working beside a group of English coal heavers one morning.

'These fellows,' Mick said. 'They've got far too many of them here.'

'The English, is it?'

'Them and the rest. The Taffs and the Jocks too.

'Damn it, there's a lot of people you don't like,' Jack said.

'And rightly so,' Mick said. 'Look at the Polack and the Dutchman. We've got to keep wages up here. Can't do that with all these fellows pouring in, and them not even able to speak English. You mark my words, the New York docks will be Irish, from one end to the other. But by God, we're going to have to fight for it.'

Irish from end to end, Luke thought. Doubt we'll see that.

'How could we make that work?' he asked.

'The Union. An Irish Union. Once we have our own Union, we'd have our own wages. Strike for it if need be. But first we've got to make sure and keep the other fellows out.'

'And what of the black fellows?' Jack asked.

'Keep them out too,' Mick said. 'Sure what are they only slaves? Used to working for nothing at all. What do you think that'll do for wages in New York City? No, they're only good as cotton pickers or cowboys.'

'Sure look at the work we're doing?' Luke said. 'Shovelling anthracite – any *amadán* could do that. There's more skill in cotton picking. So who's the slave in New York? The black man or the white man?'

'Yes,' Mick said, 'but we get paid.'

'And damned little too,' Luke said, angry now. 'And the slaves – they get fed and sheltered. We have to pay for our board and lodging, and there's damned little left after that. How can we stay sending money back to Mayo, when our savings run out? These wages are damnable.'

'And that's the reason we have to send the escaped slaves back down south,' Mick said. 'We sure as hell don't want them here in New York. Whatever chance we have of getting higher wages, we won't have a hope in hell once those fellows start coming here by the thousand. And it's not just New York, I'll tell you. If they're ever to free the slaves – which they won't – they'd spread everywhere. Can you see Liverpool and Manchester, overrun by the black man?'

'There wouldn't be much cotton picking over there,' Luke said.

'Maybe not, but you'd find them working all the low paid jobs on the railways. Your cousin – Danny – he would have been glad of them, I'm damned sure. He'd would have had them in his gangs fast enough.'

'And what about Mayo?' Luke asked.

'*Arra*, sure they're starving there.' Mick said. 'Even the black man knows that.'

Luke went back to shovelling anthracite. Mick's comments had disturbed and angered him. He felt that he had been right in one way though. Freed slaves could always undercut Irish wages. And Irish wages were low enough already.

*

One evening, a letter was awaiting as they returned from the terminal. Mick flicked it across to Luke. 'It's addressed to you.'

Luke opened it.

'It's from Farrelly, up in Lackan. Says if we're interested in working as miners, now would be the time to go.'

'It would,' Mick said. 'except we'll need more money for travelling. We'll be a while here yet.'

That evening, Luke replied to Farrelly's letter, saying they would travel to Lackan as soon as they had the money.

Chapter 12

Dublin Evening Post, November 1848:
Judging from the intercourse kept up by Mr. McMurray of
New York with this city, and the continual presentation of his
cheques, and the cheques and orders of bankers and agents
in the States on the Provincial Bank, Royal Bank, the Bank
of Ireland and others, we do not exaggerate the sum received
from emigrants in the States by their friends in this country
in setting it down at about a million during the year 1848.

They both went to deposit Luke's wages at the Chemical Bank. On the
way back, in the ferry, Winnie fed Liam at the breast. There were only two
women beside them.

'A wise precaution,' one of them said, observing her.

'Don't I know it,' Winnie said. 'I'd been trying to wean him, but breast
feeding is the one way of protecting against cholera, and God knows, we'll
need protection, the times that are in it.'

'Is it any wonder the cholera spreads though?' the woman said. 'Have
you seen the kind of water they're drinking? We can't be protecting children
by breastfeeding them all the time.'

'I've heard there's one sure way of stopping that,' the second woman
said. 'Boil the water.'

'I'm not so sure about that,' the first woman said. 'It's only superstition.'

When they arrived in Steuben Street, the other men were sitting in easy
chairs, smoking.

'Seen any sign of the cholera yet?' Jack asked him.

'No.'

'They're saying there's cholera in Manhattan.'

'Not at all. It's only more stories.'

'It's more than stories. Some French ship came in a few days back; they
were riddled with it. There's cases in New York today. Leastwise, that's what
we're hearing.'

Luke thought of all that Winnie had said of what she had seen at Five
Points over the weeks. She would have known cholera. Catherine too. He
knew just how fast-spreading cholera was, and still remembered the outbreak

of 1832, as Winnie would have. At that time, cholera was more a disease of towns and cities than countryside, but they were living in a city now. He decided that Winnie and Liam should stay in Steuben Street. Manhattan might be too dangerous.

Every time he visited Five Points, there were Irish men and women begging in the streets – more than before. There were stories of more evictions back in Ireland. Whenever he passed the Cortland Street Terminal, he saw the long lines of thin, ragged men waiting for work, though he knew full well they had no chance. There was no work to be had in New York or Jersey City.

He no longer travelled on the ferry now, preferring to use the coal barges, which cost nothing for the crossing. Here, he heard the bitterness among the bargemen.

'Damned Irish,' one of them said. 'Pouring into New York, they are. Rabid with every damned disease too. Fever and cholera. They have to be kept out.'

'But how?' another asked.

'Send them straight back to Ireland when they arrive. And it's not just the sickness; they're taking our jobs too. They'll work for damned near nothing. Starvation wages, that's what they're used to in Ireland, they're worse than slaves. I'll tell you this, there'll be nothing but Irishmen in the coal terminals if this goes on.'

Luke realised that they had not recognised him as Irish, and said nothing.

That evening, he went to the bedroom and checked through their money and their bank account.

'It might be enough to get us to Lackan,' he said to Winnie. 'It'll be a close call though.'

The days passed. Now there were fewer barges tying up at the terminal. As they were emptying one barge, he asked the bargeman about it.

'It'd be freezing higher up by now,' he told him. 'The barges back at the mines won't be able to get through. Another few days and there'll be none here at all. You'll be able to go skating on the canal by then.'

'So when do they open again?'

'Springtime.'

When Luke arrived back at Steuben Street, Winnie was not in the dining room. He went up to the bedroom. Liam was asleep at the top end of the bed. The rest of the bed was covered with cut-outs of cotton. Winnie was in the corner, stitching under the light of a candle.

'Winnie!' Luke exclaimed, 'what are you doing?'

'Stitching shirts,' Winnie replied.

'But…?'

'Mrs. Gleeson. She does it too. She signed me up for it. Ten cents a shirt.'

'Ten cents?'

'I reckon on a dozen shirts a week, if I work at it. A dollar twenty, if I keep at it. And I'm well used to outworking from the time we still had linen weaving back in Mayo.'

'But a dollar… That's terrible.'

'It's all we can get, *a grá*, and at least I don't have to go out to work.'

'But we'll be going to Lackan soon enough,' he said.

'Well, this'll help us when we get there. We don't know how long it will be till you get work, and even then, how long it'll be till they pay you. And I'm not sure that there's any outworking of shirts in Lackan neither, so I might as well do it while we're close to New York.'

Luke lay awake that night. The turn of events had shaken him. Now, there was no obvious source of earnings for himself, once the canal froze. And his own wife was earning pennies, stitching shirts.

Next day, he took the coal barge to Cortland Street, and then went to the Chemical Bank, withdrew all his dollars and closed the account.

It was more urgent than ever to go to Lackan. He had enough dollars for a train journey. At least the anthracite mines would be open across the winter.

As it turned out, it was not to be that easy.

The barges stopped. Then the canal froze, all the way to the Hudson River. Now they had hours standing around, doing nothing. And it was bitterly cold.

Luke stood at the edge of the dock, looking at the ice on the frozen canal.

'Damned hard too,' he said.

'Frozen solid,' Jack said. 'It's like up in the forests. You could walk across that.'

The terminal closed, and the men were paid off.

'And little enough too,' Luke said, looking at the few coins in his hand. 'There won't be much to send back to Mayo, that's for sure.'

'No,' Jack said, 'they'll have to wait till we're well established in Lackan. They'll be hungry back home, but there's not much we can do about that.'

There was a bar close by, but no one wanted to spend money on beer. They stood around outside, stamping their feet and blowing into their hands.

'We've got to get to Lackan damned fast,' Mick said.

'I know,' Luke said, 'but how are we travelling? Have ye found that out yet?'

'By train,' Mick said. 'Sure how else would we get up that far?'

'I know that, but which way? And how much?'

They walked to the terminal of the New Jersey Railroad, found a booking clerk, and asked about trains.

'NJRR down to Philadelphia' the clerk told them, 'then the Philadelphia & Reading to Schuylkill.'

'And how far is it to Lackan from Schuylkill?' Luke asked.

'Damned if I know,' the clerk answered. 'There's no rails though. Some kind of a stagecoach connection, I understand.'

'Well now we know,' Jack said afterwards. 'So when do we go?'

'Right away,' Luke said. 'If there's no work here, we'll have to move damned fast. Next few days, I'm reckoning.'

As he came home, he heard the baby crying before he even reached their room.

'What's wrong with him?' he asked Winnie.

'I don't know, I don't know,' Winnie said. 'He's been like this for hours, won't stop. He was vomiting a while but that stopped. I think he's nothing left inside him. I've tried him on the breast, but he won't take it.'

'Not surprising, if he's vomiting.'

He felt the baby's forehead.

'I've done that,' Winnie said, 'it's not fever.'

'Sure he's only sick in the stomach so,' Luke said, 'he'll be better in a few days.'

No, it definitely wasn't fever. He knew the sweetness of that. This was different.

Winnie stayed sitting beside the child all night. Luke tried to sleep, but could not.

There was a knock on the door.

'Can you not get it to shut up,' one of the men said.

'What do you want me to do?' Luke asked, 'strangle him?'

It was near dawn when Luke finally slept. When he woke, Winnie was sitting beside the baby.

'Did you sleep at all?' he asked her.

'How could I?' she answered. 'He's going to die.'

He looked closely at Liam. 'There's no way we know that, *alanna*. Is he hungry yet?'

'No, but if he isn't hungry, he's surely thirsty. I tried giving him a bit of water, to see if that was what's wrong with him. He took it all, and then more and more, almost as much as I could give him.'

'I wonder why he'd do that if he was vomiting. Does he throw that back up?'

'No,' Winnie said, 'and he doesn't piss it either. He's got terrible diarrhoea, doesn't stop. That's where all the water is going.'

'We should get a doctor so,' he said.

He asked Mrs. Gleeson for directions, then walked, half running, to the doctor's house, through a fine drizzle and the slush of mud and coal dust.

'He's not here,' the housekeeper told him. 'He's down at the infirmary.'

He went to the infirmary.

'He's up in the cholera ward,' one of the nurses told him.

'Cholera?'

He found the ward, and found the doctor. The stink was overwhelming, and he recognised it at once. The very same as Liam.

'My baby's very sick,' he said.

The doctor looked up at him.

'I can't come now,' he said. 'Not a hope in hell. Look at what's around you. We've a hundred here, hundreds more we can't even admit.'

'Cholera?' Luke asked.

'Cholera, and deadly. Is your baby drinking much?'

'Never stops drinking.'

'It's cholera so. There's not much you can do. Rehydration only.'

'What?'

'Water, just keep giving him water. Try putting a little salt in it, not too much. It might cure him.'

'What's the chances?' Luke asked.

'There's about half of them dying. Now I'm busy…'

He went home.

'Cholera!' Winnie gasped.

'No doubt about it now. And there's no way the doctor can make it here. He says the only thing we can do is keep feeding him water with a little salt.'

'That won't be hard,' Winnie said, 'he's drinking gallons.'

Luke sat, watching. After a while, Winnie turned to him.

'No point in sitting around,' she said, 'Go and see what the fellows are doing.'

He went downstairs. The men were silent.

'It's cholera for sure?' Jack asked.

'It is.'

Jack whipped his hand to his mouth. 'Oh God, I'm sorry. Not much you can do about it, is there?'

'There's not.'

'But…but you can't keep him in the house,' Mick said. 'He'll infect everyone. It'll have to be the infirmary, won't it?'

'They're full,' Luke said, 'they're not taking in anyone.'

'I'm sorry, Luke,' Jack said. 'I'm desperate sorry.'

Not that it made any difference to Luke, either way. The doctors could do nothing for Liam, and the infirmary was only a quarantine. A place to die? Liam would have to stay in Steuben Street.

'This wrecks everything,' Mick said. 'What will you do about Lackan?'

'Well, I can't go with ye.'

'I know,' Jack said. 'Do you want one of us to stay behind?'

'Sure there'd be no point in that. You fellows go up to Lackan. We'll come up whenever we can.'

'I don't feel right about that,' Jack said. 'Leaving you in the lurch like that. Surely there's something...'

'Not a lot you can do,' Luke said. 'Just go up there, and get yourselves set up. I'm sure Lackan isn't a big place. I'll find ye soon enough.'

Next morning, Luke went with them across to the New Jersey Railroad, and watched in misery as they bought their tickets. Then they all walked back to Steuben Street.

At times, Winnie rocked the child in her arms, but it had little effect. Luke knew she was terrified of losing Liam. So was he, for that matter, but even more, he was terrified of losing Winnie. Cholera was highly infectious. Had she had it before, though? 1832 perhaps. If she had, she might be strong enough to resist it. He told himself that he had to stop thinking like that. Winnie would survive. She was too strong to die. But what about Liam?

The diarrhoea was nothing but water now, and the thirst went on.

Winnie took Luke's hand and placed it on the baby's chest.

'Feel how fast his heart is beating.'

'It is, isn't it,' Luke said. 'I felt my own heart going as fast as that, but only after a hard hour's work shovelling.'

'It shouldn't be like this, and he only lying down,' Winnie said. 'And look here.'

She pinched the baby's skin and when she took her fingers away, the ridge on his skin remained where she had pinched him.

'It doesn't go back,' she said, 'and that's not right.'

'It isn't. It's part of the disease, I'd reckon.'

She was weeping.

'He's going to die, Luke. You know that.'

'Let's wait and see.'

'There'll be little waiting. Cholera kills fast.'

At last, they slept.

There was a knock on the door.

'We're going now, Luke.'

He opened the door. Winnie called out from behind him.

'You go on, sure there's no point in staying here. Go and say goodbye to your friends.'

He walked with the other men to the NJRR Terminal. Jack, Mick, *Seán Óg* and two of the other Tourmakeady men were travelling.

The train came in. The five men found a carriage. Luke stayed standing in the corridor.

'We'll see you there soon enough,' Jack said, 'and at least we might be able to advise you as to how best to get there. If ye haven't left first.'

'Aye,' Luke said, 'that'd be useful. Even when the cholera is gone, I'd say the little fellow will be weak enough, and we wouldn't want to be travelling too soon.'

They heard the whistle.

'You'd better be going now,' Jack said.

Luke was surprised when all five men stood to shake his hand. He returned to the platform, and the train disappeared in the distance.

He went back to the coal wharf. There was no anthracite now, and the wharf was covered in snow. He stared in frustration at the Morris Canal. Of course, it was frozen. Why hadn't he thought of that? Up in the Ontario forests, even the St. Lawrence had frozen. He picked up a sliver of stone, and flung it at the canal. Frozen solid. He picked up another and spun it at the canal, watching as it skimmed all the way across. Then he walked home to Steuben Street.

Again, he counted their money. Still enough to get to Lackan, he reckoned. But how sure was he of that? The other men had only bought their tickets as far as Philadelphia. How much would it cost from Philadelphia to Schuylkill? And how much more for the coach to Lackan. And even if he had enough now, how long would the cholera continue? How long would he have to stay in Jersey City without any wages, except what could be earned from making shirts?

Whenever Liam slept, Winnie returned to stitching shirts. She could do it faster now. Mrs. Gleeson gathered them for the contractor, and brought the money back up to Winnie. On one occasion, Luke tried stitching, but he found the work far too intricate.

'I'll never have you do this again,' he said. 'I promise.'

'It mightn't be within your power,' Winnie said. 'Either way, I'm not sure they'd have this class of outworking in Lackan. It'd be far too dirty a town. God knows, it's hard enough keeping this house clean, and it's not even beside a coalmine. In a coal town, you'd need real washing to keep the clothes clean, and have the shirts ready for when the fellow comes around.'

'I don't know the rights or wrongs of that,' he said, 'but I promise you one thing Winnie, when we get to Lackan, I'll make the money, we'll have enough to live on, and we'll never see hunger or cholera again.'

Having nothing to do, he walked back to the doctor's surgery. As he had expected, there was still no chance of getting a doctor to see Liam. In any case, it would be useless.

When he returned, he saw Winnie had begun feeding Liam beef tea, a sort of light soup which provided some amount of food. This was on the advice of a nurse who had come to the house unasked.

Next morning, the nurse returned. 'He's improving,' she said to Winnie.

'I know,' Winnie said, 'I think he'll make it.'

'He will,' the nurse said. 'He's a lucky lad too. There's thousands dead in the big cities. It's been one terrible epidemic.'

When the nurse had left, Luke hugged Winnie.

'We'll make it, Winnie, girl. We'll live, and so will Liam.'

He still felt badly shaken, and he knew Winnie did too.

Leaving Mayo, he had thought he was leaving hunger and disease behind. Would Liam have gotten cholera in Mayo? Maybe, maybe not. But now it was nearly over, and neither he nor Winnie had gotten it either. The family was still together.

He walked to the New Jersey Railroad Terminal to buy his tickets. There was a line at the ticket clerk's desk. As he waited, he saw two Irish men from the coal terminal ahead of him in the line.

A man behind him growled.

'Damned Irish. Crawling all over the place. And what do they do? Steal our jobs, and bring us cholera. They're the most accursed bastards. If they stayed in their own country, we wouldn't have cholera here. Thousands of dead, and what do we do? Just let them pour in.'

'I know,' his friend said. 'We should keep them all out, and the rest of the Irish, kick them out too. They're a worthless gang of lazy scum. Don't know how to work, all they know is how to beg, live off charity and kill us with fever.'

Luke said nothing, until he reached the clerk's table.

'Two for Lackan.'

'I can only give you a ticket to Philadelphia.'

'Fine so.'

'Two only?'

'And one baby.'

'He'll be free,' the clerk told him.

Luke paid. As he turned away, one of the men behind him grasped his sleeve.

'Hey, Paddy, isn't it time you went back to your own country?'

Luke pulled his arm away.

'If you're not careful, it's Kingdom Come, you'll be going to.'

The man stared at him, but said nothing.

'Step outside,' Luke said. 'You can fight me there.'

The line had gone silent. Luke walked away. There was a scream from behind him.

'Bloody Irish. Cholera laden scum, that's all you are. Why don't you get out of this country? We don't want your filthy diseases here.'

But no one followed him out.

'It's a story we'd heard before,' Mrs. Gleeson told him that evening. 'There were stories of the cholera in 1832. That time they blamed the Irish fellows working on the railway gangs for bringing cholera to Pennsylvania, and then to New York. There was a big gang of Irish lads, most from Derry and Donegal, working at a place called Malvern. Damned near sixty of them. All died of cholera, almost every one of them. Or that's the story, if you want to believe it. There were two lads lived; said it was murder.'

'Murder!' Luke exclaimed.

'Just like I said. The story was the Philadelphia people reckoned if they killed the Irish fast enough, the cholera would go away. Now, mark you, I'm only telling you what I heard. What the truth of it is, I just don't know. But let's just hope they don't get any ideas like that around here.'

'But we're the ones who are suffering,' Luke said.

'Aye,' Mrs. Gleeson said, 'and a good excuse for the bastards to attack us. The cholera has made them frightened. But it's not your fault Luke, nor little Liam's either.'

At last, it was time to go. Luke paid Mrs. Gleeson the rest of his rent. After they had breakfast, Luke packed their bags, and slung them over his shoulders. Then Winnie took the baby in her arms, and they walked along the street to the New Jersey Railroad.

Chapter 13

Telegraph & Connaught Ranger, Mayo. December 1848:
In short, wherever men have erected their miserable hut in
our county, starvation and death have ferreted them out.
The declining sun beholds the mourning orphans weeping
on the high roads over the inanimate bodies of their starved
parents. The stars of night keep vigil over the dead; the broad
canopy of heaven their shrouding sheet; the loud howling night
blast wailing over the dead, until the sun again and again
makes his journey around the earth. Mayo! Mayo! To mourn thy
dismal fate is indeed poor consolation. Throughout the length
and breadth of the county, it is one vast howling wilderness.

In December, another letter arrived from Luke, enclosing money for the
family and for Mrs. Gallagher, and telling of their plans for Lackan. His
letters brought great relief to the family. It was clear to them that he was well
settled in America with Winnie and Liam, and could afford to send money
back to Carrigard as long as the hunger lasted.

Next day, Pat left Carrigard to travel to Castlebar. Two dead bodies this
time. And again, the carts with miserable families in them, creaking their
way towards Castlebar.

When he arrived at the Union buildings in Castlebar, it was bitterly cold.
Despite this, there was a large crowd in front of the workhouse gates, six
soldiers in greatcoats standing guard in front of them. The crowd was very
quiet though, no keening and only one baby wailing. Four fires burned along
the edge of the wall.

He pushed his way through, identified himself. This time, the gate was
opened a little, and he pulled the horse through. There was the same crowd
of men, women and children in the Stonebreakers Yard. Some were wearing
rough coats to protect against the bitter cold, but many were not. Some had
rags wrapped around their hands, but many others had not. Their hands
showing white and blue as they grasped the sledgehammers, rising and falling on the rock they were breaking.

He walked around the side of the yard, left his horse with a stable-
hand and entered the administration block.

'Pat!' Gaffney exclaimed, standing up from his desk. 'You're looking cold.'

'And so are the people outside, I'd say,' Pat said.

'I know, I know. And I wish there was more we could do for them. I'd turn heaven into hell, but we just don't have the money. Now what have you got to tell me?'

Pat took a chair and sat close to the fire in the corner. For some time, he spoke in a low monotone; Gaffney straining to hear but saying nothing. When Pat had spoken himself out, Gaffney stood up.

'It's as bad as all that?' he asked.

'Worse. Words aren't enough...'

'Have you got your notebooks?'

Pat opened his pack, and brought them out. Gaffney sat again and began to flick through them.

'You met Father Nugent, did you?'

'I did. He told me much, but sure I didn't need the telling; I could see it with my own eyes.'

Gaffney read on. At last he put the notebooks down.

'Yes,' he said, 'it's worse than even I had thought. And that's just the Ox. The workhouses can't even feed the people inside, but, from all you're saying, it's even worse in the mountains, and I'm beginning to think it's there we'll have to concentrate whatever funds we have. Now what I want you to do is this. I want a proper report put together out of all your notes here. Your best copperplate too. We want it so as the Grand Jury and the rest of the fellows will read it. Make it as detailed as you like, but make sure it's accurate. And when you're finished, I'd like you to copy it out three times more.'

Pat spent that day and the next in the Union building, writing. Many times, he had to stop and think, so as to marshal his thoughts. Sometimes, he choked on what he had written. Even the memories were enough to sicken him. He would have to control his mind and stop reacting like this. How did Father Nugent put up with it? And Voisey? And what of the people themselves? Perhaps they were numbed by how much they had seen.

Gaffney came in and took up what had already been written, glancing through it quickly.

'Very good, Pat,' he said, 'you've certainly a way with words.'

'Thank you, Mr. Gaffney.'

'There's one thing from all you say that causes me great concern though. It's all this you say about the underclass...'

'The underclass?' Pat asked.

'Just a word I use for it. The landless men – the people in the mud cabins – the ones who are never on any rent rolls, never enumerated...'

'No one even knows they exist,' Pat said. 'Isn't that what I'm telling you?'

'I know it is,' Gaffney replied. 'It's just what I've always known myself. You know, I was reading in Dublin once that there were half a million cabins in this country at the time of the last census. 1841 that was. I'd have said the number would have been higher by the time all this began. It would have been higher again with all the people the census missed. Can you imagine it, Pat? Five hundred thousand *tigíns*. More? How many people would live in each of them?'

'I've no idea, Mr. Gaffney. Three? Four? Five?'

'So there you have it. Two million people, give or take. A quarter of the whole country, and the half of them we don't even know about. How much money do you think these people have?'

'Sure they wouldn't have any money at all. They've nothing to sell.'

'And there's the point again. These people will never emigrate. They don't have the strength to get to Dublin, or the chance to get across to Liverpool even if they got that far. And they sure as hell don't have the money to get to America. The landlords won't pay their way either – they don't even know they're there. Or don't want to know perhaps. So these people have to stay here, isn't that it? No money for leaving, no money for corn neither, so what do they do when the potato runs out?'

'They starve,' Pat said.

'Yes, Pat,' Gaffney said, 'starve is right. The tenant farmers, they can still buy corn, even if it's damned little. They've got enough money to make it to Liverpool, and most have family in America who can send them money to cross the Atlantic. But the underclass, they're not tenants. Their people never went anywhere, because they never had the money, and people who never went will never send back remittances. This is what the fools in Dublin Castle can never understand. This famine is going to wipe these people out, the whole famished brood of them. By the time this is over, there'll be damned few mud cabins left.'

When he handed over his completed reports, Gaffney took one copy, and locked it in his cabinet. 'For posterity, you might say,' he said. 'No one's ever going to destroy that one.'

Then he and Pat went through the remaining copies, paragraph by paragraph, for the rest of the morning. At last, Gaffney took three large envelopes. Carefully, he inserted a copy of the report in each.

'This one is for the Grand Jury here in Castlebar,' he said to Pat. 'And this one is for those damned fools in Dublin Castle. And this – this is for the Connaught Telegraph. Mr. Cavendish will know what to do. He'll be selective, mind you. We wouldn't want people to know he was copying a County report, would we?'

The weather continued cold. Pat worked on correspondence and accounts under Gaffney's instructions. In many ways, he found it relaxing. Had Gaffney known how worn out he had been. Perhaps. But his rest was not to last.

One morning, Gaffney came into Pat's office with an inmate. He was young, Pat guessed. Twelve or fourteen, perhaps.

'Pat, I'd like you to meet Thady McLaughlin,' Gaffney said. 'I know how much you are overworked, and I thought you might need someone to help.'

'Indeed,' Pat said. 'All help would be appreciated.'

'Thady here can read and write. Best of all though, he's fast at arithmetic. Very fast.'

'That could be useful,' Pat said.

After Gaffney had left, Pat fetched a chair from the other side of the room and sat Thady down. He was dressed in the striped workhouse garb. The stench was overwhelming.

'So you can add?' he asked.

'I can.'

'Let's try you so. Try adding this column.'

Pat went back to the letter he was writing and was surprised when Thady told him he was finished, less than a minute later.

'My God, that's fast,' he said. 'They taught you well. Where did you learn adding like that?'

'Croghancoe.'

'Croghancoe!'

'Séamus Doherty would come around every second week, stay two days. Blackboard on his back, and a leather strap in his pocket. He beat the hell out of us. We learnt fast enough.'

Thady could do his numbers! What of *Cairbre Mór*, another man from Croghancoe who could do his numbers. Might Thady know him? He decided not to ask.

'I didn't think many could read and write on Croghancoe, let alone do arithmetic,' he said.

'There weren't many in the class,' Thady said. 'Only a dozen or so. The rest had no use for book learning.'

'But how did you get here?'

'Walking. They wouldn't let us on the Works at Croghancoe, so we walked all the way over. My mother and father died on the journey.'

'Died?'

'My father and myself, we buried my mother in a bog. Then he died, and I had to do the same for him.'

'*Oh God!*' Pat said.

'*Oh God! What call is there for that? Blessings won't bring them back. Whinging neither. Here, give me another.*'

Pat slipped him another page and pointed.

'*Here. This one. Do it at your own pace.*'

Pat watched as Thady worked on the column. As he did so, Pat checked the first column he had added, but Thady was ready before Pat was. Without being told, he went on to adding another column. By now, Pat had finished the first, and found Thady was precisely right.

He was very quiet. Pat sensed some sort of resentment there, though whether it was directed against the workhouse, or against him personally, was hard to say.

A female inmate entered, and put a bowl of oatmeal in front of Thady. She left without a word. Pat realised it was lunchtime. Thady started to eat the oatmeal, and between mouthfuls, continued with his work. He looked at Pat.

'*There's no need for you to stay. I don't need overseeing.*'

Pat was a little surprised. He locked his letters away.

'*Do you not trust me?*' Thady asked.

'*I trust no-one with these letters.*'

'*Must be dangerous.*'

'*Dangerous enough.*'

He left to go to lunch in the administration canteen. Better eating here than living on workhouse fare. Afterwards he took part of his steak and brought it back up to the office. He held it out to Thady.

'*I've no need of your charity,*' Thady responded. '*You may eat it yourself.*'

Pat munched on the steak, still watching Thady working. He had completed a lot over lunchtime.

'*You're fast,*' he said.

'*I know.*'

At dinner time Thady left the office and returned to the main workhouse canteen.

Work continued the same way over the next few days. By now, Thady was doing almost all the arithmetic, while Pat concentrated on letters. Sometimes, after working hours, he checked Thady's calculations, and found they were always correct. But very few words passed between them.

'*You're a strange fellow,*' Pat said one morning.

'*No stranger than yourself.*'

'*You talk very little.*'

'*I don't talk to the Ryans.*'

Pat looked up in amazement.

173

'You don't? Why on earth not?'

'You lived through the Hunger.'

'So did you, Thady. Aren't you alive now?'

'I am, but damned near wasn't. Your brother was a right bastard.'

'My brother!'

'Luke Ryan. He was the one wouldn't let my father or my mother on the Relief Works. And now they're dead.'

Pat was speechless. He knew there was little he could say that would change Thady's thinking.

'And you,' he said at last. 'Did Luke take you on the Works?'

'He did not.'

'Sure he couldn't take everyone.'

'That's what they all say. And before you say it again, yes, I'm still alive and no thanks to ye, nor your breed neither. Ye crucified our family, but I'm the one that feels guilty. Can you explain that?'

'You've nothing to feel guilty about,' Pat said.

'Oh, but I do. I lived through it all, I saw it all and I'm still living. But if I feel guilty, so should you. Your brother more so.'

And there the conversation stopped.

Any further attempts at discussion were met with – 'I've work to do.'

One day, Gaffney called him to his office.

'Time to go, Pat.'

'I know.'

'Now let me tell you about Erris.'

He took out a map.

'You should take this with you. There are three areas that concern us. The first is this part north of Nephin and Nephin Beg, running all the way up by Sheskin to Slieve Fyagh and Ben Mór. The Ballina Belmullet coach road runs through it, but there's little else. That's why the map is blank.'

'I'd noticed,' Pat said. 'And I've heard of Sheskin.'

'Nothing but bog, the most of it. Some of it is very difficult to cross, and our problem is that we know very little about it. We have no idea how many people are in there or even what they're living on. You can approach it from Newport, from Castlebar or from Foxford, I'll leave that choice to you.'

'Fine,' Pat said.

'Now the second area is this strip running up to Dooncarton and Pollatomish. Stories we're getting from there have been dreadful and I'd like to know what you think. You can read them before you go.'

'I will,' Pat said.

'Good. Now, there's just one area out here we categorically need information

174

on. That's the Mullet Peninsula and we've heard terrible things about that place since the Walshe evictions. A savage business. Just before Christmas too.'

'I'll find it and see what's there,' Pat said.

'I knew I could depend on you. There's just one little problem though. I'm afraid on this occasion we can't let you have a horse. There's been too much piracy out Erris and all down the Mullet, and the County reckons that if we gave you one, it'd only be stolen for eating.'

'I understand.'

'But I must stress, on this occasion, your report will be of the highest importance.'

He handed Pat a newspaper.

'This is *The Times*,' he said. '*The Times* of London no less. Look here.'

Pat took the paper.

'Erris! They're writing about Erris.'

'They are. And isn't it about time they did.'

For a minute, Pat read through it, while Gaffney remained silent. Then Pat folded the paper.

'This is…this is horrible.'

'Yes,' Gaffney said. 'Appalling, isn't it? Even *The Times* is beginning to understand what's happening in Mayo. This will really shock the nice gentlemen in London, and make them throw up their breakfasts with the fright of it.'

'Lucan can't ignore this then,' Pat said.

'He can try. And it's not as if we'll be able to shout louder than *The Times* can. *The Times* hates Ireland and the Irish. They've been calling this famine a blessing. We've got to shame the bastards. And Lucan.'

'But how…?'

'Through your reports, Pat. If we do it right, Mr. Cavendish will select whatever extracts he wants and have them re-written in the Connaught Telegraph. Some will find their way into the English papers, and counter *The Times* and their vicious bigotry. They might even force *The Times* itself to print more of the truth about Mayo. So that's why you're going to Erris, Pat. We can't have a London paper knowing more about it than we do. Especially the bloody Times.'

Chapter 14

The Times, London. January 1849:
At Doona, a village in Erris, two families, Lennane and Quin, nine in number, occupied a small mud cabin, Lennane, the father, was in prison for sheep stealing. His wife and children were therefore compelled to enter the work-house, but lately left it that they might eat a small quantity of potatoes that were growing on a patch of ground attached to the cabin. The Quins were allowed a stone and a half of meal a week, but, one of them catching fever, went to the hospital, whereupon the allowance of meal was reduced half a stone. The children of Lennane also caught the fever. The eldest died in a few days, and was buried in the potato garden. Seven others died, but the survivors were too weak to remove their bodies, which lay putrefying amid the living until the neighbours burst in the cabin door, when they found one of the bodies devoured by rats, and the stench from both intolerable. As the survivors crept from their hovel, their appearance horrified the spectators.

Pat spent the rest of the day reading frantically through letters, reports, maps and accounts – anything he could find relating to the far-flung barony of Erris. Once again, he wrote in his notebook, trying to form a picture of what he was going to see. He felt a deep dread, but comforted himself with the thought that he had already been through the Ox Mountains, and he knew what he was looking for.

On looking at the map again, it struck him that if he approached from Newport, a small diversion would bring him to Westport.

Why not?

The next morning, he was let out the gate; the soldiers guarding it, as it was opened and shut quickly. He forced his way along the workhouse wall. There was a woman lying on the ground, thick frost on her clothes. Her shins were bare, the same frost covering her purple ankles and feet. Her eyes too were covered with frost. Was she dead or alive? He walked on.

The frost thawed, and by the time he reached Westport it was raining, and there were very few outside the workhouse gates. He was quickly admitted.

He found her office. The Clerk of Union was working on a high desk in the corner.

'Someone for you, Sarah.'

She spun around from her desk. 'Pat! We hadn't been expecting you.'

'Well, isn't it a nice surprise for you then?' he said.

She ran, and embraced him. 'What are you doing in Westport?'

'I'm just heading from Castlebar up to Erris.'

'Erris! Why Erris?'

'Oh, it's simple enough. Gaffney – the fellow I'm working for – he wants reports on the districts around Mayo to judge which needs help the most. Not that they have much cash to be helping them with.'

'But Pat – you've got to be awful careful. There's disease everywhere.'

'I know,' Pat said, 'and before we go further, I wanted to ask you about your mother. What happened?'

'Fever. It was just she was going in and out of the infirmary sheds, and you know how dangerous that is with them all crushed so close together. She knew the risk she was running.'

'But you were working in the sheds too, weren't you?

She hesitated before answering. 'Oh, the devil take it. That was different.'

'No, it wasn't, Sarah.'

The Clerk stood.

'I'm delighted to meet you Pat,' he said, 'but I'm sure you two have much more to be talking about. I might go for an early lunch.'

When he had left, Sarah embraced Pat again.

'And it's not that I'm not sorry about my mother,' she said. 'Please understand that. But one way or another, she was the barrier between us. I know too the way she was thinking, and she wanted a better match for me. She reckoned you'd end up working as a navvy in England again.'

'She might have been right,' Pat said.

'Fair enough, if she was,' Sarah said, 'I'll take that risk. But I'm thinking you'll most likely stay in Mayo.'

'I think you're right too,' Pat said, 'but the question is – as what? Working for the County, or working for my father back in Carrigard?'

'Does it matter? One thing's for certain. Staying in Mayo is better than going to Australia.'

'I wasn't thinking of going that far.'

'You mightn't have been. But the Union were thinking of sending me there.'

'To Australia! Were they intending on transporting you?'

'They were thinking about it. There's this new idea they've got – the Earl Grey Scheme, they call it here. They're looking for older girls who are orphans – and I'm an orphan now. They reckon there are too few women in the Australian colonies so they're sending them out of Ballina, over to England and down to Port Phillip. And I'll tell you one thing Pat, it's lucky I wasn't among them. They reckoned with mother out of the way that I'd be an easy victim, but I'm damned if I'm going to go out to Port Phillip just because they're short of women for making babies.'

'Were they going to force you?'

'They wanted to. The Master here, he's a dreadful man. Wants to get rid of me, I know that, and I've no longer got mother to protect me. Right at the moment, I'm earning nothing. Board and keep only. I can't go on like that; you know that as well as I do. I'm sick of it all. Sick of the workhouse and the fever sheds. All these years, living in workhouses. I usen't mind it when I was a child. It's only as you get older you can see the suffering. Carrigard – it's our only chance.'

'I don't know,' Pat said. 'You'd find it tough settling into Carrigard. You've never worked on a farm in your life.'

'But a workhouse is worse. And your farm is better than any other in Carrigard, I know that for a certainty. Ye've the quarry too. Ye're strong farmers.'

'I wouldn't say that.'

'Ask the inmates here, so. They'll tell you. And your mother, she's a strong woman. Could we get on, your mother and me? I know we could. And we wouldn't have to rear our children in a workhouse. So let's not beat about the bush, Pat. We're getting married.'

'And isn't that what both of us want?'

'It is,' she said.

He considered her words.

'So what's our future going to be?' he asked at length. 'At least people get fed in England and America, but this country can't even feed its own. We'll be depending on my earnings, and depending on Gaffney to keep employing me. He wants me travelling the County, reporting back on famine. What if there's no famine? He'd have no reason to. Which puts us to a straight decision – England, Ireland or America? Isn't that it?'

'No, it's not. There's no choice. You can't leave Carrigard, Pat. God knows, your father has too much already with two quarries and two farms. He's not a young man either. I'd guess already it's getting too much for him. And anyhow, if there's no famine, there won't be such a call for your earnings. Would there?'

'So what are you thinking?' he asked.

'I'm thinking it all comes back to Carrigard. If not this year, then next year. God knows, we love each other, not like many who are forced to marry. We'll stand by each other, no matter what. And your mother, she's a loving woman, and a very powerful one too, something you men might never have noticed.'

'Oh, I'd noticed right enough,' Pat said.

He slept that night on a floor in the Administration building, his greatcoat and blanket wrapped around him. The room was still warm enough from the fire in the grate. After a few hours, he put more turf on the fire, and slept well for the rest of the night.

As he began his journey to Erris. Sarah walked out with him. Men and women were at work in the yard, smashing stones.

They reached the outer gate, and he turned to hug her.

'Your horse?' Sarah said.

'What about it?'

'Where is it?'

'Safely in its stable, back in Castlebar, and I'm afraid it's staying there. This is a walking journey.'

'Walking!'

'Of course,' Pat said. 'I can't take the horse; it'd never return if I did. You've heard yourself the stories of piracy out by the Mullet. People are desperate there, more desperate than they've ever been. And what do you think a horse is? Food, that's what it is. Just like a cow except more meat.'

She screwed up her face. 'Oh God! They wouldn't...'

'Of course, they would. When horsemeat is all that's between yourself and death – what would you do?'

'But then,' she said, 'if they're that desperate, what will happen to you? Does it frighten you?'

'Oh, I'm frightened right enough,' Pat said, 'but it's not desperate people that frightens me. They won't eat me! It's what I might see, that's what really frightens me. In fact, it's what I know I'm going to see. I'll tell you Sarah, I never wanted this job, but you know yourself, it's the only thing that keeps me in Mayo. Otherwise I'd just have to swallow my pride, travel back over to Stockport, and work with Irene.'

'So there's worse things than Erris?'

'*Ach*, I don't know. In many ways, it'd be easier in England, but a woman like that is enough to break any man's pride. She broke Danny's.'

The rain had stopped, and there were many more outside the gate than there had been. The inmate guarding it nodded at Pat, but did not open it.

Rapidly, he pulled himself up, over the spikes at the top and dropped down the outside.

'Now, you take care of yourself,' he said through the bars to Sarah. Then he walked through the military and out along the road towards Newport.

When he reached Newport, he found it a little odd, but no odder, he reflected, than Castlebar or Westport. There were many comfortable houses in the town, and, despite famine, many people who were not starving. As he left the centre, the houses were poorer. Then, he came to an auction – beds, tables, pots and anything else movable. The result of evictions, he guessed. When a family had no house, what use were tables?

Thankfully, he left the town behind.

One woman walked towards him, a baby on her back.

She stopped to rest, and he came up alongside her. She looked up in alarm.

'Rest easy,' Pat said. '*I mean you no harm.*'

She smiled weakly.

'*I'm sorry,*' she said. '*For a long time now, strangers have meant nothing but pain.*'

'What has happened here?' he asked.

'*These are the lands of Sir Richard McDonnell. We could not pay rent. His driver took our things, pots, pans and even our clothes, and sold them at auction. Then when that was not enough they destroyed our cabin, and we are starving.*'

'How long...?'

'*Last summer. We have sheltered with friends while my husband worked in England, and sent us money. But now the money has stopped. Where he is, or whether he is alive or dead, I do not know. And with the failure last year, my friends cannot feed themselves, and I cannot buy corn.*'

'Is it so bad around here?' he asked.

'*Bad enough for those who are evicted. But for those who remain, they have the comfort of knowing that it could have been worse. Sir Richard's evictions in Keel – they were worse.*'

'Keel! On the island of Achill?'

'*It is. All of Keel was evicted by Sir Richard.*'

Pat thought of giving her some of the bread in his pack, but then thought better of it. He had a job to do, and it was important for the County. If he started giving his bread away to everyone he met, he would never complete his task.

'Where are ye headed?' he asked.

'*Westport. That the workhouse might take us.*'

This put Pat in a difficult situation. It was most unlikely the workhouse was taking anyone in, so what to do? But was he certain? Let her walk on to Ballinrobe in her condition? Her last hope?

He stood. *'I'd best be going,'* he said. He gave her a halfpenny. *'They might have corn in Newport. Westport even. 'Tis a big town.'*

She took the money. *'God bless you, sir,'* she said.

She went to stand, but sat again. Pat offered his hand, and pulled her up. Then he turned, and walked on. He would have to stop giving money away.

Where now? Gaffney's first request had been the areas in the north of Nephin and Nephin Beg. He sat and spread a map out beside him.

He had already gone west to Westport and Newport, rather than taking the shorter road up from Castlebar. Not that that mattered much.

He spotted Eskeragh on the map. It was on the coach road running across the centre of the bogs. *Cairbre Mór* had mentioned Eskeragh. Why not head that way first? But where was Glenamoy on the map?

He found it at last. Eskeragh to Glenamoy – ten miles? But what was in between? On the other side of the coach road the map was blank. Sheskin was not even marked.

He stood and followed the road through Glenhest. When, at last, he found the road going north from Castlebar he was exhausted. He found a deserted cabin, gathered straw and reeds from around it, and formed a rough bed. He took his blanket out of his pack, wrapped it around himself and slept.

Before dawn, he continued, passing Nephin and Glen Nephin. Now he was following a rough tangle of boreens, always taking direction from the sun. Small settlements and isolated homes, none on the map. Some houses were stone, some mud. Some were occupied, some deserted.

When he reached the coach road, he was worn out. He entered a cowshed. An old woman was milking a cow. She looked up in alarm.

'I was only looking for a place to sleep,' he said.

'Well, come inside so,' she said, relaxing her face.

She had little more than buttermilk to give him, and he gave her two slices of bread in return. That night he slept in a bed under a heavy blanket. The cow had been taken inside the house.

He followed the coach road to Eskeragh. It was only a tiny village, a mere scattering of houses. They were all empty. He turned onto a rough boreen running north into the bogs.

There was a small settlement, a few cabins standing. An old man was sitting at the side of the road. His cheeks were drawn in. Pat asked directions. The man pointed with his stick.

'*You may keep to the high ground. Go straight west, or you will not cross the bog alive.*'

No boreens now. He walked across the higher part of the open bog, firmer than the to the side. He met two women coming against him, pulling a rough sled of turf, balanced on two stripped branches. He nodded at them, but they did not respond.

The old man was right, there would be no way through the lower part of the bog. He trudged between potato ridges, though he knew well there would be no potatoes left. He saw some rough huts and made his way to them. They were built of turf, no more. All were empty, a gnawed ribcage in one.

After more walking, he was surprised to see a monkey-puzzle tree in the distance. At first, he thought his sight was deceiving him, but as he came closer there was no doubt. He had seen these on a few occasions in England, on the driveways or in the gardens of stately homes. There was no way on earth a monkey-puzzle could be growing in a Mayo bog. Yet, there it was.

As he climbed higher up the ridge he saw a large two-storey house with a slated roof behind the monkey-puzzle. He made his way to a wrought iron gate on the other side of a rough gravel boreen. Curious, he opened the gate, and walked in.

'What do you want?' A shotgun was pointing directly at him.

'Nothing at all,' Pat said.

'Get to hell out, so.'

He continued along the boreen. It had begun to rain, a fine drizzling rain that he had been approaching for miles, crossing the mountains and moving out across the bog. He came to another small village. Some houses were made of stone, though most were mud. Four of the cabins had collapsed. He heard voices. He went to one of the stone houses and knocked. A woman answered and looked at him in alarm. Her cheeks were hollow and her clothes were ragged, but what else had he expected.

'*I was looking for shelter from the rain,*' Pat said.

Her face relaxed a little.

'*Shelter we can give you, but food we have none.*'

'*Fine so.*'

A man, and a very old woman sat on stools by a fire. The man waved him across, and he sat on a ledge beside the fire.

'*Ye have come from far?*' the man asked.

'*Down by Kilduff,*' Pat said.

'*What brings you to these parts?*'

'*I was walking to Belmullet, but thought to take a shortcut across this way. I got lost.*'

'*You won't be lost now,*' the woman said. '*All you have to do is follow this road to Glencalry.*'

'*I had not known of this road,*' Pat said.

'*The people from here, all the way to Erris, know of it. They call it the Bealach Garbh.*' The Rough Road.

'*A Famine Relief road?*'

'*Never. This road has been here for a thousand years. More even.*'

Should he believe that. Why worry?

'*What of the house back the way?*' he asked. '*I was surprised to see that here.*'

'Sheskin Lodge. *It's the hunting lodge of the* McDonnells.'

'*Hunting?*' Pat asked.

'*They come here for the hunting season in the month of August.*'

'*For a month?*'

'*Yes,*' the woman said, '*and isn't it well for some. A big house like that, they built for their enjoyment only. Eleven months empty but no one else is let use it.*'

'*And this village?*'

'*Sheskin. The best-known stopping point on the Bealach Garbh. The only one in these parts.*'

'*And what of the people in the bog?*'

'*Who knows?*' the man answered. '*And who wants to know? No one knows they're there, no one has ever counted them. There's many parts of the bog no one can pass through, unless they know the paths. They're there free of rent, and even the* Census *men don't know of them.*'

The rain had stopped.

He left the village, continuing roughly north, through Glencalry, until he came to a gravelled road. He asked directions to Glenamoy and was directed to the village. He sat on a wall, and wrote his notes.

Later he found a well-built stone house. He knocked on the door. A man answered it.

'*I'm looking for lodgings,*' Pat said.

'*Tuppence a night.*'

'*A penny.*'

'*Penny three farthings.*'

'*Fair enough.*'

That evening, the woman of the house fed him with cabbage soup and a little brown bread.

He slept under sheets, grateful for the luxury of it.

Next morning, he left Glenamoy, and, following the man's instructions, found his way to the coach road at Bangor Erris.

He saw a house, with a rough notice outside reading 'Ales, Wines & Spirits'. He sat outside and asked for a beer, but there was none. A chipped cup was put in front of him, and part filled with *poitín*. He passed over the ha'penny demanded. The day was warm for the season. There were no other customers. For some time, he wrote in his notebook.

The barman joined him.

'Are you travelling far?'

'I am,' Pat said, 'out towards Belmullet and beyond. Just looking around.'

'Why on earth would anyone want to look around this godforsaken place?'

'I have my reasons,' Pat said without further explanation. He mixed water in with the *poitín*, and drank it slowly.

The barman was suspicious, but Pat decided to ignore it.

'I'd heard things were bad in '47,' he said.

'The worst in Mayo, I'd say,' the barman answered. 'The fever did awful damage in Belmullet in that year. Bangor was no better.'

'But you lived.'

'I did, and my wife too, but we lost three children.'

'I'm sorry,' Pat said. He sipped at his *poitín*.

'Here's the Bianconi,' the barman said suddenly. A carriage was approaching, four men sitting on each side.

'What on earth...?'

'The Bianconi. Comes through from Ballina every Wednesday, headed to Belmullet.'

'Of course.'

The carriage drew up outside the bar. The driver jumped down, and handed a bundle of letters to the barman, who signed for them.

Four passengers alighted from the carriage, and sat at a table. Three were served with water and *poitín*, except for an army captain, who produced a hip flask and drank directly from it.

'Who are you?' he asked Pat.

Pat flinched, expecting trouble.

'Pat Ryan,' he answered.

'Captain Aldridge of the Forty Ninth Regiment of Foot. Won't you join us?'

This was unexpected. He hesitated. The man was clearly drunk. Then Pat realised there might be information to be gleaned here.

'Why not?' he said.

The captain pulled a chair from the next table.

Pat discovered that, apart from the captain, there was a doctor, a lawyer and a local land owner.

'So what are you doing here?' the land owner asked him.

'Travelling for my employer,' Pat said.

'And who might that be?'

'The County.'

'The County?'

'The County Grand Jury. They sent me here to make some kind of report on Erris.'

'A report? I could give them a report. I could tell them all about Erris, and the way the gentry are being destroyed.'

'How so?' Pat asked. This was certainly information.

'Look, I've seventy cabins in this area. Mud cabins the most of them. They paid little enough rent anyhow and whatever they paid was in corn, not cash. Duty labour too. Now with the potatoes gone, they've eaten the corn, and they're too weak for any labour. There's hardly any of them paying rent, but I still must pay the County Rates. I've been over to see the Rates Proctor in Ballina, but they're not interested, all they want is for the rates to be collected.'

'That's tough,' Pat said, startled that he should hear a landlord talk like this. He was relieved the captain was asleep, and snoring.

'And it's not that I'm expecting you to feel sorry for me,' the man went on. 'Sure, we've had our good times, myself and the wife, Dublin, Bath, Newmarket, London. Paris even, just the once. There were years that weren't so good neither, but no one on earth thought this was going to happen. No, they'll bankrupt me, those damned proctors, and I'll tell you this, young man, I won't be the only one.'

He took a deep draught from the *poitín*, and laughed nervously. 'So that's Erris for you. I'm going back home to Belmullet. God only knows why.'

'And God knows why we're going to Belmullet either,' the lawyer said. 'They've no laws. All anyone is interested in is registering the ownership of land, but nobody knows for sure who owns the most of it.'

'Does no one do anything?' Pat asked.

'They tried. They've given up. A year or two back they opened a fishing station in Belmullet for the washing and curing of fish. Worked well for a few months, but then there was that piracy off the peninsula. The locals, they raided a boat, stole tons of grain and flour off it.'

'Yes,' Pat said, 'I'd heard about that.'

'So after that, they just closed the fishing station.'

'But what did that have to do with it?'

'Nothing. A kind of revenge, if you like. But that's Belmullet for you. They're still talking of building a workhouse there. That might be some progress. But I'll tell you this, Belmullet is hell on earth.'

'I don't know if that's the worst,' the doctor said. 'Dooncarton is in a terrible condition; from all we hear. Were you planning on heading up that way at all?'

'I am.'

'All on past Barnatra there – Gortmeille, Inver, Dooncarton itself. Pollatomish, Kilcommon and Faulagh too.'

Dooncarton? Pat thought back to the old man in the Ox Mountains. *Cairbre Mór*. He had said *Dún Chiortáin*. The sound of it would have been different in Irish, but it was close enough.

But it was not only *Cairbre Mór*. Gaffney had asked him to travel to Dooncarton.

The lawyer woke the captain. As the passengers climbed back into the carriage, the driver offered Pat a seat to Belmullet for sixpence. Pat was tempted, but Dooncarton came first.

He crossed the river flowing out from Carrowmore Lake, and turned right to follow the west side of the *loch*. He slept on hay inside a rough built stone shack. It was icy cold.

At dawn, he spread out his map, and memorised the villages and roads, before he left. As the sun slowly rose, he saw a mountain ahead of him, a smaller one to the left. He came to a boreen. A woman was standing at the doorway of a cabin, a baby in her arms. The baby had a bloated belly.

'*A farthing sir?*'

Pat walked over and gave her a farthing. He thought of the food in his pack, but he was uncertain he could get back to Westport or Castlebar if he gave more away.

'*What's up this road?*'

'*The village of Ráth Muireagáin. A mile or so.*'

'*Ráth Muireagáin?*' Pat asked.

'Rathmorgan, *they call it in the stranger's tongue.*'

'*Ah, yes.*'

He walked on to Rathmorgan. There was no one about. Some of the doors were locked, and he did not stay. Carrowmore Lake sparkled below him to the east, and he followed a rough boreen by Knocknascollop Mountain back to the road north along the lake.

He crossed another paved road, and walked by the long inlet of Broadhaven Bay.

He sat by the edge of the water. The tide was out, and in the inlet, seals were drawn up and lounging on the rocks. Twenty, thirty, forty? He had no idea how many. Beyond them, was the outline of the Erris Peninsula.

A man walked up from the waterside. His hair was thin and grey, blowing in the light wind. His face was wizened, near brown from long years in sun and rain. The suit he wore showed all the signs of many years of wear, though Pat reckoned it could once have been one that any man might have been proud of. He was sure it had not been made from the local homespun wool. More surprising was the coat he wore, which was clearly an old army greatcoat, long faded to grey. One single brass button remained.

'*Tá an ocras orm.*' The hunger is on me.

Pat was undecided. He could give him bread, but if he did, would he have enough to get back to Westport. In the end, he opened his pack and gave the man a small slice. The man sat beside him.

'*The seals. The old women say they're the spirits of the dead. Only fantasy of course. But I'll tell you this, they're better fed than we are. They go out to the ocean and feed on fish till they're bloated. Then they come back to rest and sleep at Trá Chinn Chiortáin. Isn't it a terrible thing we cannot do the same. We go out with our little boats, but what we take from the ocean is pitiful. You can be sure of one thing; it will never make up for the loss of the potato.*'

'*I suppose you're right,*' Pat said.

The man told him much of fever and famine in the area.

At last, Pat stood to go.

'*Are you travelling far?*' the old man asked.

'*Far enough,*' Pat said. '*As far as Dún Chiortáin.*

'*What brings you there?*'

Pat hesitated.

'*Would you take it amiss, if I did not answer that question?*'

'*Suit yourself,*' the old man said. '*And that God may go with you.*'

'*And also with you,*' Pat said.

He travelled on.

Gortmeille, Greamhchoill.

The scenes were no different to before. Mud cabins, most with smoke issuing through the front door, some collapsed. He saw one with a rough-made door, closed against the rain and the wind. The roof had rotted and buckled. He pushed against the door, but he could see through the gap between the door and the wall that it had been knotted from the inside. He pushed harder, and the twine gave way.

Inside were three dead bodies, well advanced in decomposition. He gagged, went out again and tried to tie the door from the outside, using a nail that had been hammered into the hardened mud, but it was impossible.

As he travelled, he met and passed people walking, or some just sitting at the roadside. No one begged now.

At one point, the road had disappeared under an avalanche of mud. He reckoned it a hundred yards across and tried to walk it, but he kept slipping. At last he went back, and climbed high up the mountain until he was above the slide, and then made his way back down to the road on the other side.

Dún Chiortáin. Dooncarton.

Most of the village was above him on a higher road to the right, just below the steep side of the mountain. He turned and walked upwards. After a few minutes, he stopped, and sat on a wall.

Out on the ocean he spotted a fountain of water. Thinking he might have imagined it, he watched the whole ocean. Another fountain erupted, and soon afterwards a large whale breached the surface from further out, jumping high. From his vantage point he could now see the creatures moving, hard to pick out against the water, but they were there.

More cabins, many collapsed; some deliberately, he reckoned. As he walked back towards the main road, he saw a stone circle to the side, but could not work out why it was there. Curious, he walked across to it. The wind was blowing from the ocean, but behind one of the stones he found a rough-made hut built into it. There was no one around. He crept inside and lay down on the rough straw he found there. Could this strange place be the *Dún Chiortáin* that *Cairbre Mór* had mentioned?

The harsh cold woke him early, and he started out before dawn.

Poll a'tSómais, Cill Chomáinn, Fálach. Many more cabins. More dead bodies.

He came back to the Killala Belmullet road again, where he turned right and came to Barnatra again. He stopped and scribbled more notes. Then he walked on towards the Mullet.

It was evening when he reached Belmullet, and it was raining.

He crossed a bridge and was surprised to see that it was open at both ends, and clearly man-made. A canal in Belmullet! Unlike any other canal, this one had no locks. To the east and west, there was open water.

Some of the blocks were freshly chiselled. Famine Relief? Perhaps it was. Building canals could be just as useful as building roads. More so.

As he entered the town, he was surprised to see an inn which was of a better character than he would have expected in Erris. He was more surprised to note a line of twenty or thirty people out the back, all showing clear signs of starvation. Curious, he entered the hotel.

'Out the back if you want to be fed.'

'What?'

'Beggars out the back.'

'I'm not one of the starving,' Pat said. 'There's no hunger on me.'

'So what's your business?' the man asked angrily.

'I was looking for a beer,' Pat answered.

'You can pay?'

Pat flipped a penny on the desk.

'Guinness,' he said.

The doctor and lawyer were sitting at a table, drinking in the light of two candles. On an instinct, he went over.

'May I join you?'

One of the men nodded to an empty seat. 'You might as well. We've exhausted whatever conversation we had between the pair of us. Are you staying over?'

'I don't know,' Pat said. 'I haven't asked about the room rate, but I doubt I'll be spending money on that.'

'You took a good soaking. You'll need to dry off before you go anywhere.'

'Sure what of that. Maybe the innkeeper will let me stay in the stables.'

'I wouldn't do that if I were you. It will be full enough tonight, with the class of people you might get fleas from. Still, there might be other stables around.'

'I hope so,' said Pat. 'I'm not sure I should be spending too much on a bed. My employer's money, you understand.'

'Of course. The County.'

'Yes,' Pat said, 'the County.'

'So where have you been since we met you last?'

'Up around *Poll a'tSómais* and *Inbhear*. Desperate conditions, just like you said. So I see what I see, then stop for a while and scribble a few notes in my notebook.'

'A notebook?' the doctor asked. 'If it's not asking too much...'

Pat reached into his pack, pulled out the notebook and placed it on the table. The doctor started to leaf through it. Pat and the lawyer said nothing. Then the doctor spoke.

'Mother of God, is it really like this?'

'Could be worse,' Pat said. 'Sometimes I feel if I put in all I see no one would ever believe me.'

'Did you see any evictions there?'

'Not that I could say for certain. No cleared villages anyhow. Quite a number of abandoned houses, many fallen in. Some might have been levelled on purpose, I don't know.'

'Not like down the Mullet,' the lawyer said. 'Captain Aldridge could tell you all about that. He was in on the Walshe evictions last Christmas – *Torán* and the rest. Upset him no end, the poor fellow. Thought he'd be off fighting

189

for his country in Afghanistan. Never thought he'd be throwing people out of their homes in County Mayo. Now he can't even show his face in public, neither in Bangor nor Belmullet.'

'Is that why he's not here?' Pat asked.

'Gets his dinner sent up to his room, he does. Doesn't want anyone to see him eating. He'd always thought of himself as a good Christian fellow, but what he saw and did that night destroyed him.'

Pat was surprised at how normal everything was in the inn. The innkeeper had come from behind the bar and started collecting the empties.

'You do good business here,' Pat said to him.

'You wouldn't call it that,' the innkeeper answered. 'It's better than last year though. Or '47. That was the worst.'

'Yes,' the doctor said, 'The very worst.'

'There was no business at all that time,' the innkeeper went on. 'From the beginning of the year right up to the autumn, damned little. Sure the fever here near wiped the town out. Everyone knew about it too, the Connaught Telegraph made sure to tell it to the world. And what the fever didn't finish, the hunger did. No, I'll tell you this, there's thousands died around here. And the worst of it is, no one will ever know how many. There's people living and dead in Erris who were never acknowledged by any landlord and never saw any soup kitchen, let alone got fed by them.'

Yes, Pat thought, the landless men again. Gaffney's underclass. Gaffney had been right.

'I know,' Pat said, 'I'd heard terrible things about Erris.'

'I'm sure you have. Now if you'll be excusing me, I've work to do.'

He wiped down the table, threw the cloth over his wrist, picked up the empties and left.

'A tough fellow, I'd say,' Pat said.

'Ah now, he's a decent enough man,' the doctor said. 'Every evening he gives ha'pennies out the back for anyone wanting to buy corn.'

'And food?'

'No food, unless they use their money to buy it. Sure if he gave out food all the time, he'd have a thousand out there and no food for the hotel.'

After two more drinks, Pat left the bar. The doctor and lawyer were still talking, more argumentative now.

He walked past the waiting line of people at the back door of the hotel. It was near impossible to see in the dark, but most were hungry, that was obvious. Their clothes were drenched through. Whatever clothes they had – even the women's shifts – were thin, with no other covering. Two of the children were close to naked. The back door opened, and the line started to shuffle forward.

He walked out from the town in the direction of the Mullet. On the outskirts of the town he found a stable. There were no horses, only a cart. On the side was a deep stack of hay. He lay into it, and fell asleep in seconds.

He was woken by the distant sound of music. He took his pack over his shoulder and slipped out of the stable, listening. The music was coming from the town. He walked back into the town again. What he saw astonished him. A hundred or more soldiers marching, led by a brass band. He recognised the uniform as that of the Forty Ninth Regiment. Incredibly, the soldiers began to sing. He listened carefully and recognised the words of 'The Girl I Left Behind Me'. An Irish song. Or was it English? Was this the same army that carried out evictions right across Mayo?

The line by the hotel was longer now. The people were in the same condition as the previous night. He suspected many of them might have been there all night. The same ragged clothes, the same half-nakedness, but at least it was no longer raining.

How weird it was to hear such music in Belmullet, one of the most miserable places on God's earth. And the army? Did they really think that starving people were in any condition to attack a corn store? Or that singing songs would stop them trying?

He walked back out, heading south into the Mullet Peninsula. To the left, the oatmeal coloured sands stretched across the inlet towards the mainland.

Geata Mór. Currach Buí. Droim Riabhach.

Mullach Rua.

He passed through what had once been a village. All the cabins had been demolished, mere heaps of stone, with rotting straw and reeds. He thought of what Sarah had told him about the evicted people who had turned up at Westport Workhouse rather than Ballina. But how many had died? He scrambled up the ruins of the cabins. In many, the Atlantic winds had blown the roofing away. On one, there was a skull, and the remains of a skeleton protruding from beneath the rocks. No rats here. They had already finished their business.

Torán.

Many of the houses still stood, and he knew from the smoke issuing from the cabins, that some were inhabited. Many more had been demolished.

The village was quiet, but one man was leaning against the side of a cabin, observing him.

'*Are you planning more destruction?*' the man asked.

'*Not I. I'm no landlord's man. I'm only here to see for myself what has happened in this town.*'

The man walked to another cabin, and beckoned Pat to follow. He opened the door, and ushered Pat inside. There was a family group in one corner, all dead. The father's body was far gone in putrefaction. The corpse of the mother was fresher. Pat was relieved that he did not gag. He would have hated for this man to see his weakness.

'*It's the custom here,*' the man told him. '*The last to die closes the door rather than having the shame of their dying be seen by everybody.*'

They went out into the fresh breeze.

'*Ye've had an eviction here?*' Pat asked.

'*Mr. Walshe, the bastard. Half of Torán, all of Clochar, Mullach Rua, and more besides. The army and the peelers threw them all out. May God damn them all to hell.*'

'*And where are they all gone?*'

'*Many left, walking for Belmullet. Others made holes in the sand dunes, but they're all dead now.*'

'*Over there?*' Pat said, pointing at the dunes.

'*You want to go?*'

'*I do.*'

'*You may go on your own so. I've seen enough pain to last a dozen lifetimes.*'

There was a raw wind blowing off the Atlantic, though the sky was clear. Pat drew his greatcoat around his neck and ears, and walked into the wind. There were sand dunes ahead of him, and he walked half blinded, trying to keep the sand out of his eyes.

He came to a *sceilp* in the lee of a dune. It had been well dug into the sand. There was no sign of a spade being used. The hole had been hand-scrabbled, or dug out with flat stones. The roof consisted of sods of marram grass torn off the dunes.

He scrambled inside through a hole on the side. Inside, the height might have been two feet, where the sand had not already blown back in. Inside were three skeletons, two of small children, interspersed with seaweed and a heap of seashells. The last food of the family!

He made his way out of the *sceilp,* and struggled up one of the dunes. He felt fear, though he knew he was in no danger. He sat on a bank of grass and rushes looking out over the Atlantic breakers. The sand was dazzling white in the sun. To the south, the high mountains of Achill showed brown and purple against the blue sky. To the west, green islands were set into the dark blue of the ocean, white clouds scudding above. To the north and east, the broken villages of the Lower Mullet.

He took his notebook out of his pack, and began to scribble. After an hour, he slammed it shut, and placed it in his pack.

He stood and walked along the ridge of the dunes. As he dropped into the hollow between two of them, he saw something yellow, waving. He knew it could not be reeds from the way it was moving. Curious, he went over. Human hair! Long, like a girl's. He wiped the sand back and saw the white of a small skull.

Another flat piece of white showed just above the sand. It looked like a stone or a large seashell, but he knew it was not. No hair protruded. Again, he wiped the sand away, and found himself looking into the sockets of two eyes. Only the bones remained. His fear returned.

He stood again and ran down the slope of the dune, stumbling and falling at the bottom. He eased himself up again, and walked quickly away. He scrambled over the ruins of *Torán* and continued down towards the end of the Mullet.

Clochar. Eachléim. Fód Dubh.

More devastated villages. More ruins. He found one cabin where the roof had only partly collapsed and the door had shattered. Inside, was a heap of straw. Grateful, he dropped down on it. There were bones in the corner, but whether human or animal, he no longer cared. He slept for longer than he had thought possible.

He rose for his journey back to Belmullet. As he started walking, he saw a primitive *currach* in the water, one man paddling it.

He dropped down to the water's edge. The man had seen him. Pat waved. The man pulled a fish from the bottom of the boat, and held it up. Pat waved again. The man paddled the *currach* towards him. He held the fish up again.

'*A penny.*'

Pat thought of bargaining, but realised that this man was very poor.

'*Fine,*' he said. The County could pay.

As he was taking the penny out of his pocket, a thought struck him.

'*What is that land over there?*'

'*Kinrovar.*'

'*Is it part of the mainland?*'

'*It is.*'

Another way home? He had already seen Belmullet, and the long neck of the Mullet. No need to double back.

'*Is it far from there to Bangor?*'

'*Near a day walking. Less for a fit young man. You wish to cross?*'

'*I do,*' Pat said.

'*Tuppence more. Thruppence with the fish.*'

Pat paused. Expensive perhaps, but worth it to see a part of the country that no one knew?

'*Tuppence*' he said.

'*Thruppence.*'

Three pennies were exchanged. Pat took the fish, wrapped it in a shirt and put it in his pack. Then he found himself in the *currach,* holding a paddle.

'So *what happened here?*' he called out against the wind.

'Evictions.'

'*Yes, I'd heard that much.*'

'*It was that* Mr. Walshe *decided to rid himself of his tenants. A coward of a man, he could not do it himself so he had the* Forty Ninth Regiment *to protect the drivers. The people were all turned out of their houses, and the roofs pulled down. That night the people made shelters of wood and straw, but the drivers destroyed them too. It would have pitied the sun to look at them, but there was no sun, and they had to go under hail and storm. It was a night of high wind, and their wailing could be heard at a great distance.*'

'What happened to them after?'

'*Sure what chance did they have? After the eviction, some walked away, some stayed. Half-naked they were. Some managed to crowd into some kind of cabin for a few nights before they died. Others lived in sandbanks, eating seaweed, trying to last it out. But none of them did, sure they're all dead now, any of them that remained behind.*'

'None *left?*'

'*A few made off towards Belmullet, hoping to reach the workhouse in Ballina or Westport. God only knows what happened to them. I don't. None returned.*'

By the time they drew up on land across the sound, Pat's arms were aching more than they ever had before. Even working in the quarry in Carrigard had never been like that. They beached the craft and he stood. The man disembarked, and helped Pat out into the surf. Then he shook his hand, gravely, and climbed back into the *currach.*

Pat struggled up from the beach, and took out his notebook again. When he finished writing, he found a primitive track, and headed east.

Many of the cabins here were no more than holes in the bog, covered with a layer of turf sods, and hardly obvious from the surrounding bog until nearly upon them. Here too, many had collapsed.

The door spaces had no doors, and the tops were darkened by smoke. Some that were higher than the bog had entrances at both ends. Perhaps it was to let the wind clear the air of smoke. But what of heat then?

Where the cabins were occupied, he could see within some of them as he passed. None had any furniture. No tables, no chairs, no benches, no beds. In some, flagstones served as benches. A few had some kind of chest for whatever possessions the family might have had. Some had clearly been forced open.

Many cabins he entered were empty. In others, there were the remains of what had once been men, women or children. Once, he saw movement in a heap of rags and realised that this was a human person, though whether a man or a woman, he could not tell. No one else was in the cabin. He took some of his remaining bread out, but it was clear that he or she was beyond the ability to eat. He left and walked on.

He passed people inside and outside cabins, many too weak to stand, their limbs thinned down to the bone, or sometimes frightfully swollen. Some children had bloated stomachs too, with bald heads and a down-like covering of hair on their cheeks. How often he had seen that before, in the workhouses and on the roads.

At Trawnanaskil, a group of people had gathered on the beach. The tide was well out. An enormous black object lay along the beach in front of them. As he came closer, the people looked at him in alarm. He made an appeasing gesture.

''Tis fine, I mean you no harm.'

'Are you from the landlord?'

'Not I.'

Most of the people turned away from him and went back to the whale, slashing at it with knives. One man stayed with Pat.

'Is it here long?' Pat asked.

'Since yesterday. It often happens when the tide is high that they swim in too far.'

''Tis a big one.'

'You might think so,' the man said, 'but it's young yet. And 'tis terrible stuff to eat, but what else do we have. It was sent from the Almighty surely, to lessen our hunger.'

He walked back to the road. Scrawny people walked towards him.

'Is there any left?' a woman asked him. Her face was shrunken, and heavily wrinkled.

'Plenty enough,' he said.

Tulachán Dubh. Gaoth Sáile.

Images of Torán and Clochar flashed through his mind, intermingling with pictures of a slashed and bloodied whale. He fancied he was on the edge of madness, but walked on.

Hours later he reached Bangor. He went through the town without stopping, and turned towards Westport. It was near dark.

He glimpsed a movement, then a man leapt over a stone wall, knocking the top stones as he did so. He ran towards Pat. Alarmed, Pat started to run down the road, but two other men appeared in front of him. He looked to the side, but there was another man there. Within seconds, they had closed in on him. Two grabbed his arms and forced him to the ground. One held his face into the mud, and his pack was nearly jerked from his back.

He resisted, clasping his hands so as to hold the straps and pack on his shoulder. He was clubbed from behind, and blackness descended.

Chapter 15

Morning Chronicle, London. November 1848:

We say therefore that we grudge the immense sum which
it appears likely that we are to pay this year to Irish Unions
very much indeed, because we know that it will be thrown
into a bottomless pit, and because we feel the money, thus
wasted, might be better spent in removing them than
feeding in idleness the people of Mayo – in getting rid of
the burden, than in perpetuating it. The district where this
unmanageable surplus of labour exists is not very large;
we are subsidizing 22 Unions only; and it is quite certain,
either that we must go on subsidizing them, or that a large
proportion of their inhabitants must die of hunger, and
a large proportion of the remainder find their way as beggars
into Great Britain. Under such circumstances, we submit
that there cannot be a better opportunity for the experiment,
of which so much has been said – of national colonization.
At any rate, we can see no other plan which affords ground
for the slightest hope as respects the districts to which we
referred.

Murty too was concerned about contracts, but his concerns were different
to Murtybeg's. For months past, he had been anxious, and his anxiety was
turning into fear. Fear for his own future, and that of Aileen.

The contract with Brassey was coming to an end, but what would follow
it? Working as an independent gang with Brassey had meant high standards
and, with the gang's capacity for hard work, they were paid very well. So
well in fact that they could afford to have Murty working most of the time
on the paperwork, with little work on building rails. For a man of 63, this
was vital. He could never keep up with the rate of work that the rest of the
gang took as normal.

Every week, he bought the newspapers and checked which of the main
contractors were working locally. Brassey had no new contracts in the area
at all. One day, he and Jim Doyle walked down to the Weeton Lane section
of the Leeds & Thirsk, to check if there were any prospects there. One

glance told the story. It was clear that that section was nearing completion. What was even clearer were the dozens of navvies standing around, waiting, hopelessly, for any prospect of work.

'It'll have to be Bradford, won't it?' Doyle said.

'Yes,' Murty replied, 'and at least there's work there. How much, I don't know, and with who is another question. Mackenzie has contracts there. This fellow McCormack too...'

'McCormack?'

'He's a contractor to Mackenzie. That's what I've heard, though I'm not sure of the truth of it. Either way, he's got works in Bradford. Anyhow, whether it's him or Mackenzie, I don't think we'd be able to work as a single gang.'

'We won't,' Doyle replied. 'And even if we could, what size of a gang would we be? Roughneen, Lavan, McManus and the rest of them. All gone off working with Edwardes & Ryan.'

'Yes,' Murty said, 'and I thought when Danny died, they might not have stayed on with Murtybeg. But they seem to like it well enough. He's still paying their foremen well. Same as Danny – that was always his way – pay his foremen well, and grind the workers into the dirt. And what's worse, I fear young Murtybeg is doing just the same. My two sons, one after another, and all they can think of is how to make the most money out of poor suffering humanity.'

'I know,' Doyle said. 'But the real question is piecework. We're well able for it, that's why we make so much money. But we'll have to work like common navvies in Bradford. There's no piecework there, and we'd be paid damned little. That's what it all comes down to, isn't it? The way they pay us.'

They walked back towards Bramhope.

'You know, Jim,' Murty said, 'there's one other issue here, and that's the question of the ownership of Edwardes & Ryan. I'd been assuming that Murtybeg, having taken it over, was the actual owner. But this Irene woman, who lived with Danny, might claim that she owned it as Danny's common-law wife. And, strangely enough, there's another thing that has occurred to me over the past few days.'

'What's that?'

'The thought that the first claim on a dead man's estate might be through his parents. It's even possible that I'm the owner of Edwardes & Ryan, in common with Aileen.'

Doyle stopped, and grabbed Murty by the arm.

'But...but do you know?'

'I don't, and I'd have to talk to some lawman to find out for certain. And somehow, I'm not sure that I really want to find out. If it is true, I could fire not only Murtybeg but Irene too. Then the question is, would there be an Edwardes & Ryan at all? It might be argued that the world would be a better place without Danny's damned business. But I'll tell you one thing for certain, I wouldn't run it the way Danny did, and the way that Murtybeg is doing. I just wouldn't be able for it.'

Another shock awaited Murty when he and Doyle returned. Gilligan – their own gang master – announced that he was leaving the gang.

'Going to work with Murtybeg,' he explained. 'He's written me a letter, offering me a job as a supervisor out on the Colne Extension. Six shillings a day! I couldn't possibly refuse.'

'I don't suppose you could,' Murty said, 'though at least Judas held out for his thirty shekels!'

Gilligan swung around, eyes blazing.

'There's no call for that. If it wasn't for your damned pride, you could be working with your own son right now.'

'I could, couldn't I' Murty said. 'Help him abuse his starving workers.'

'You should at least think about it,' Gilligan said, trying to sound more reasonable.

'Fine,' Murty said, not wishing to provoke Gilligan further. 'I'll think about it.'

But there was no thinking to be done. If Murtybeg had turned as vicious as Danny, then there was no point in working with him. But was Murtybeg that bad? His earlier discussions with Murtybeg had convinced him that the same approach was being used. The only difference was that this time it would be abusing the Mayo slum-dwellers of Bradford. Not the poor emigrants straight off the boat, but the poor emigrants who had made it out of Ireland and were starving in an English city instead.

The fact that Gilligan was leaving destroyed any future they might have had anywhere on the Leeds & Thirsk, though that might have been unlikely anyhow. But if there was work to be had in Bradford, no matter what kind of work it was, it would give him the chance of judging Murtybeg's work methods in that city. There were two problems though. The first was his own age, which would certainly tell against him. The second was Aileen. Her mental condition was fragile following Danny's death, and taking her to Bradford would be a problem in itself. Finding somewhere to live, while he himself might only be earning half a navvy's wage, would be far more difficult.

On Gilligan's last day, Murty paid him his remaining wages, bitter at having to do it. For some time, he stayed in the boarding house, trying to think it all through. Then he walked out along the railway tracks to where Higgins and Doyle were working. He nodded to them, then took a shovel and began to work. By the time of the first break, he was sweating heavily.

'You shouldn't be doing this,' Doyle said.

'I know, Jim, and what you're going to say is that I'm too old for it. And maybe you'd be right. Even so, I'd better get used to it. There won't be any paperwork for me in Bradford. Isn't that it?'

Doyle leaned on his shovel.

'So is it Bradford then? Is that what you're thinking?'

'I don't see any way around it,' Murty replied. 'It's where the work is. Perhaps I'll only get half pay, with the age of me. If that's the way it has to be, so be it. But one other thing about Bradford. It'll give us a chance to gauge Murtybeg's methods of working. Is he going to be the same kind of savage gang boss that Danny was, before he killed himself?'

Higgins had been listening to the conversation. 'You're reckoning Danny killed himself? He really did?'

'No doubting it,' Murty responded. 'And it goes to show that even great wealth can't protect you from yourself. And now we've Murtybeg taking over. Will he be able for it? That's the first thing I'm thinking. And if he is, would he be the kind of man we'd wish to work for? Already, I'm sure I won't work with him. Still, being in Bradford would tell us a lot more.'

Murty worked the rest of that day, shovelling dirt and clay. He tried working faster, but after some time he heard the sound of his pulse in his ears, and the speed of it frightened him. He stopped and leaned on his shovel, gasping. There was no point in killing himself. He would be lucky to even get half wages in Bradford.

That evening, they discussed it all again.

'The talk is the work here is finishing on Saturday week,' Doyle told them.

'So that's it?' Higgins said.' Bradford, it is.'

When Murty told Aileen that night, he saw the fear in her eyes. He could hardly blame her; he was nearly as fearful himself. But already he was forming a plan.

First, he discussed it with their landlady. It was arranged that he would leave Aileen with her, while he accompanied Doyle and Higgins to Bradford to see what was possible. He still had sufficient cash to pay her for two weeks, and perhaps even to live for a few weeks in Bradford.

Mrs. Price was a Welsh woman, but despite the regular rancour between the Irish and Welsh, she was a practical woman and understood the situation at once. That evening, Murty explained it all to Aileen, and while he could see that she did not like it, he felt better that he was leaving her in capable hands. The promise of returning within two weeks served to calm any further concerns she might have had.

*

On the Sunday, after they had been paid off, Murty travelled together with Doyle and Higgins to Bradford. Walking down the track from Bramhope to Leeds, they saw the speed at which the Leeds & Thirsk was being completed. The stink of Leeds was just as Murty had remembered it when he left Danny to work on Gilligan's gang.

Then they took the Leeds & Bradford Railway for the short journey to Bradford. He wondered where Murtybeg's contract was. More to the point, where were McCormack's contracts in Bradford.

The town was nauseating, as always. Still, it came as a shock. Manchester's mills had been filthy, their chimneys pouring dirty black smoke into the sky day and night. Leeds was not much different, but Bradford had to be the worst. The unending stink of raw sewage disgusted Murty even more. Gilligan had often described the Broomfields ghettoes of Bradford to Murty and the others. Inwardly, he prayed that the railway works would not be in Broomfields.

Then there were the dragoons.

'Hardly surprising when you think about it,' Doyle commented. 'How else would they keep people in this hellhole of a city?'

'It's not a matter of keeping them here,' Higgins said, 'it's a matter of keeping them working, and keeping them from rioting when they are here. The riots they had here were something dreadful, and I'll tell you this, the city is terrified of what would happen if they had an English rebellion. I'm damned sure an Irish rebellion is quite enough for them.'

'Yes,' Murty said, 'and an Irish Famine too.'

'We're well away from that,' Doyle said.

'I'm not so sure of that,' Murty said. 'I think a lot of what we're seeing here is the Irish Famine following us all the way to Bradford, just like it did in Liverpool and Manchester. And that's the other reason they have the army here. The famine people, they must be kept quiet too.'

They passed a group of men on a street corner. Murty recognised the accent and went back.

'*Mayo, are ye?*'

'*We are,*' one of them replied. '*You too, I'd say. More towards Castlebar, I'd guess though.*'

'*Close enough,*' Murty said. '*Kilduff, a little east. And ye?*'

'*The very top end of Erris. Dún Chiortáin. You might have heard of it.*'

'*I have,*' Murty said. '*But tell me this, are ye working?*'

The man stayed silent. One of the others stepped forward.

'*I'm working. Myself, the wife and daughters in the mills up on Caledonia Road.*'

'*Not like us,*' one of the others said. '*They won't take us into the mills.*

We're more used to harder labour than that anyhow.'

'Railway building, is it?' Doyle asked.

'That's what we're trying to do. It's a matter of getting work when and where you can.'

'Up the Colne Extension?' Higgins asked.

'There's some work going there, right enough. A disgusting place though. A Ryan contract; what would you expect?'

Taking directions from the men, Murty went with Higgins and Doyle towards the new line of rail, snaking out in the direction of Colne. Very quickly, they reached the earthworks. Murty saw the rough shacks; water and sewage running behind them to a stream. As he walked towards one of them, there was an angry shout.

'Who in hell are you?'

Murty turned around to answer. It was Roughneen.

He stared at Murty in surprise.

'Sorry, Master,' he said, 'If I'd known it was you…'

'Don't worry yourself, Johnny,' Murty replied, 'I was just here with Jim and Ed looking for work.'

'Yes,' Roughneen said, 'I'd known you'd been looking for work.'

'Gilligan told you, did he?' Doyle asked.

'He did. He said the three of you would be into Bradford. I didn't think you'd want to be coming here though.'

'And so we wouldn't,' Murty said, 'excepting we were walking out this way, and your shacks were the first we came to. But don't let that worry you. We wouldn't be looking for work with the likes of Edwardes & Ryan anyhow.'

Roughneen looked as if he had been hit in the face. Murty was not concerned, and said nothing more. They left the Colne works.

'Where now?' Higgins asked.

'There's other works in Bradford,' Murty said. 'Let's see if we can find them.'

Higgins asked a woman for directions.

'That's the McCormack Cutting you're looking for,' she said. 'That's where the work is. It's over in Broomfields.'

She gave them directions.

'Broomfields!' Doyle exclaimed as they left. 'Just where we didn't want to go.'

They soon found the cutting in Broomfields. There was certainly more activity here than on the Leeds & Thirsk. There were lines of men hacking at the side, and clay being shovelled into the waiting carts. Murty could see that the work had only started. The cutting was not deep, and only ran for fifty yards.

At the front of the cutting, where the digging had not yet commenced, houses were being demolished. A crowd of ragged people watched in silence. Beyond them, were five or six police, accompanied by a few dragoons, their horses tethered to a doorframe propped up with bricks.

There were shacks to the sides. Just the same kind as Danny had been using around Manchester. And the same as Murtybeg was now using on the Colne Extension.

They found a foreman, who directed them to a site office.

'Two shillings a day,' the clerk told them, 'and you can start right away. Do you have picks or shovels?'

'Not with us,' Higgins replied.

'You'd better buy some so. You can talk to the foreman about that.'

'Two shillings a day!' Doyle exclaimed as they left the office. 'God, we'd be earning four shillings on the Leeds & Thirsk any day.'

'Yes,' Higgins answered, 'but that was for piecework. Here we don't have to work so fast.'

'Which might be no bad thing,' Murty said.

They returned to the foreman, and bought their implements.

'Pricy enough too,' Doyle said.

'What did you expect? They're out to make money, these fellows.'

'Don't I know it?' Murty said, 'and I having two of the most grasping sons on the face of the earth.'

'Still,' Doyle said, 'two shillings a day.'

'Consider yourself lucky you're not with Murtybeg,' Murty said. 'A shilling a day would give you cause to be moaning.'

They were put to work on the cutting, Doyle with a pick, Higgins and Murty, shovelling the dirt away. Murty was grateful to be working at all. He thought of the evictions they had all seen back in Mayo, and those being carried out by Danny's men in Ancoats, in the centre of Manchester. Little Ireland as they had called it. And now, here in Bradford, he could have been working on an eviction himself, flattening houses in the centre of an English city. He wondered who the people were. Were they Irish? And the men destroying the houses, Irish too?

He noticed the accent of the men beside him. Mayo perhaps?

'*These fellows by the house,*' he asked, '*where are they from do you think.*'

'*Mayo, where else?*'

'*Like yourselves, I'd say.*'

'*Like all of us, my friend. The most of them were from out near Castlebar. The* Lucan *evictions – Ballure, Knockthomas, Ballymacragh and the rest of them. There's some talk of evictions down by Ballinrobe too. More of* Lucan's, *the bastard.*'

'*There must have been many of them,*' Murty said.

'Thousands, I'd say. The way they live here is terrible. Those houses, forty or fifty in each of them.'

'No,' Murty said, 'that's not possible. Sure they're hardly more than tigíns.'

'Sure look at the crowd there. That's just from that single house. How many do you think are there?'

Murty shook his head.

They worked on.

'What do you think of what he was saying?' Murty asked.

'I'd reckon it's true right enough,' Doyle answered.

'But I wonder where that crowd are going to go?'

'God only knows,' Higgins said. 'Somewhere else in Bradford, most like. Otherwise Leeds, Manchester, who knows. Sure you know what it was like in Liverpool yourself.'

Murty was deeply shocked. Even worse was the thought of what he might have done if he were given a sledgehammer, and told to work on the demolition. A Mayo eviction! He went back to shovelling clay.

He found it to be brutally hard work, though as he observed, Higgins was not working as fast as he normally would, keeping only to the rate of work of the men beside them.

'Don't worry, Master,' he said to Murty, 'they're nothing like as fast here. You'll strengthen up to it soon enough.'

'Maybe you're right,' Murty said, 'I just hope to God you are.'

That evening, they were directed to one of the shacks at the end of the cutting. They knocked on the door and entered.

It was already occupied by one woman, and eight men, most sitting around the table, but two were lying asleep on the floor at the back of the shack. There was a stink of piss and tobacco, but not of fever.

'We were told ye had lodgings,' Higgins said.

'Lodgings *we have*,' the woman answered in Irish. '*Mayo men, are ye?*'

'We are,' Doyle said.

You're most welcome.' She was cutting a large slab of cheese. '*Ye have been working, have ye?*'

'We have,' Murty replied. '*On the digging, not on the house-breaking.*'

She did not respond to the comment on house-breaking. Perhaps she was used to it, Murty thought. Perhaps she no longer thought about it.

'*Ye'll be hungry after your working,*' she said.

'We *will*,' Murty said. '*Hungrier than I ever thought possible.*'

'*Well, we're glad to see ye. We'd more here up to last week, but three of the lads went on the tramp. They're reckoning there's better chances down south.*'

'*I don't know that there are,*' one of the other men said. '*Still, it's their decision. I doubt we'll ever hear from them again, though.'*

The table was rough. It had been crafted from timber off-cuts; cutaway sleepers acting as legs. A single candle stood on it. The men were sitting on beer kegs, all damaged in some way or another.

'*Cheap seats,*' one of the men explained. '*The brewery don't want them.*' He pulled more out from under the table. They sat while the woman served bread and cheese.

As they soon discovered, some of the men were from near Tourmakeady; the rest from the island of Achill. Murty knew Achill had suffered cruelly in the Famine. On questioning, it turned out that they were from Keel, towards the west side of the island.

'*That's out where the* Nangle Mission *is?*' Murty asked.

'*No, not* Nangle,' one of them answered. '*We're much further out than that.*'

'*Hungry times?*' Higgins asked.

'*Worse than hungry. It was the evictions threw us out.* Sir Richard McDonnell *and his drivers.*'

'*I hadn't heard of that,*' Doyle said.

'*Not many have.* Lucan *had the real name of the* Exterminator, *but there's others catching up fast.*'

'*And what about the* Nangle Mission?' Murty asked.

'*It's not for us, though tempting enough I'd say,*' one of the other men answered. '*He's feeding his own, the ones in the* Mission, *but sure they converted long since. They were turncoats long before they were soupers.*'

'*Enough of that kind of talk,*' the woman said. '*It wasn't to talk of* McDonnell *or* Lucan *you came here for. It's lodgings ye're after?*'

'*It is,*' Higgins said, '*but what might it cost us?*'

'*It's cheap here,*' the woman said. '*Very cheap. 'Six shillings a week…*'

'*Six shillings!*' Doyle exclaimed. '*That's pricy.*'

'*Hold your horses. It's six shillings for all twelve of us. Sixpence a man for the week.*'

'*Sixpence!*' Murty said. '*But sure that's nothing at all.*'

'*Isn't that what I'm telling you? McCormack's aren't charging rent, not like that bastard Ryan does, up on the* Colne. *He even charges for sleeping on the floor. With us, the money all goes for food, and a bottle of whiskey for Sundays. Now it's time to eat.*'

Murty was hungry enough and ate well.

That night, rough blankets were strewn on the floor. Murty slept with Doyle and Higgins under the table, lying on his back. He listened to the snoring of the men around him. It soon became clear that the woman and one of the men were living as man and wife. What of it?

*

The next few days were tough for Murty. He was building his strength. At first, other men stared at him in surprise, but this soon ceased. He no longer felt out of place. While some of the men were well fed, many of the newer workers were thin, and Murty knew that in time he would be able to work faster than them.

'*You're well able to work,*' one of the Achill men said one night. '*I thought at first you were slow, but you're catching up.*'

'*And I'd have caught up further, if I was more used to it,*' Murty said. '*Back home all I'd be doing was sowing and digging the potatoes.*'

'*And what of the rest of the time? I'd say a man like you wasn't working at digging all your life.*'

'*I was a master.*'

'*A master! A school master! Truly?*'

'*Aye. A little school of my own, teaching the children all around. But then the government brought in the new schools and I wasn't good enough for them, so here I am, working on the rails in England.*'

'*And your family?*' the woman asked. '*Did you leave them in Mayo?*'

'*I didn't,*' Murty said. '*It's only my wife I have with me. She's staying in the lodgings we had over the far side of Leeds until such time as I get well settled here.*'

'*Ye'd need a room for yourselves, that's for sure.*'

'*We will,*' Murty said.

They sat at the table as the woman served food.

'*I know a place like this will be tough for any married woman. A teacher's wife would be used to better things, and God knows it isn't shacks she'd be used to.*'

'*What other choice is there?*' Murty asked.

'*Éamonn here has a cousin down in Adelaide Street. They're renting a house, but have room for lodgers. Now, I must warn you, it's not much, but it's better than this. It'll be more than six pence a week, I'd say. Whatever she charges though, it'll be better for ye than here; and with your wife in the mills, you'll be well able to pay.*'

Murty looked at her in surprise. Aileen working?

'*Would they have us though?*' he asked.

'*Don't worry,*' the man called Éamonn said. '*I was talking to her last week. Her last lodgers left. She'd be pleased to have more.*'

'*And where's Adelaide Street?*'

'*Not far. I'll show you in the morning.*'

The next morning, they crossed to the other part of Broomfields. When they reached Adelaide Street, Murty saw the house was small, but well built. The woman of the house opened the door.

'*Éamonn,*' she said, greeting her cousin. '*What brings you…*'

'*Lodgers,*' Éamonn said. '*Murty Ryan. A master from Mayo. He's looking for a room for two.*'

'*A master?*' she asked.

'*Was a master,*' Murty corrected. '*I'm a navvy now.*'

'*That's a change for you.*' Her eyes were sharp, but welcoming.

'*It is,*' Murty replied, '*but sure what of it? I'm looking for a room for myself and my woman.*'

'*Well, we can offer you a separate bedroom and a bed to sleep on. Small, but better than the shacks Éamonn and the lads are used to.*'

'*I know,*' Murty said. '*The shacks were a tight squeeze, right enough.*'

She brought them in and led Murty upstairs, while Éamonn waited at the bottom. The room she showed him was small. The bed was solid enough, an old striped horsehair mattress on top, cotton sheets folded alongside. There was a single trunk by the wall.

'*Not what a master might be used to,*' she said.

'*It's grand. And it's a year or two since I was teaching.*'

'*So what happened? Did they evict ye?*'

'*In a way. The new schools came to Mayo, and the girls and boys had to go to them, whether they liked it or not. So I was left with no school, and no choice but to come to England.*'

She shook her head in sympathy.

'*I'm sorry, but you're here now, so we must all do the best we can. Now you'll be wanting to know how much all this will cost.*'

'*Most important, as you might guess,*' Murty said.

'*Three shillings the week for the room. But your wife, when will she be here?*'

'*A day or so. She's still over near Leeds, where we were last working.*'

'*She'll be working soon enough so. The mills have a call for workers.*'

'*But she has not worked for years. She might not be up to it. And anyhow, I'd heard they aren't taking on any workers.*'

'*That was earlier in the year. They're desperate for workers now. Spinners, sorters, washers, they're taking people in from all over.*'

She took Murty's hand.

'*Bríd Ó'Ciaragáin is the name to me, or Kerrigan, as the English say it. Bríd ye may call me. We're Mayo. Like yourselves, I'd say.*'

'*Indeed. Kilduff and around. And ye – Keel too? Same as Éamonn?*'

'*We are, though we left well before the evictions.*'

Murty took the train to Leeds and walked out to the new rails towards Bramhope and brought Aileen back to Bradford. On the journey, she said very little, and nothing at all as they walked through Broomfields.

Bríd greeted her warmly, when she entered.

'*Come on in out of that and we'll get you settled.*'

Murty was grateful for it. Aileen would be in shock already from what she had seen.

Bríd brought them inside, and they sat around a table, more solidly built than those in the shacks. She took out four cups and splashed some whiskey into each.

'*Ye'll be tired after all your travelling,*' she said.

'*We are indeed,*' Murty replied, '*and Aileen tires easily with travel. Isn't that right, my pet?*'

Aileen nodded, but said nothing. *Bríd* was looking at her. Murty knew she had noted her silence.

'*You'll sleep well tonight then,*' *Bríd* said to her. '*A day or two, and you'll be up and working with Máire and Sinéad in the mills.*'

Aileen looked up from the table. '*Máire and Sinéad?*'

'*My daughters. And you mustn't worry about it all. As long as you're in this house, you're with us. And Máire and Sinéad will be with you in the mill.*'

'*It's very kind of you,*' Aileen said.

They moved their baggage to the bedroom. Aileen took her clothes out of her bag and sorted them carefully on the floor.

When they returned to the downstairs room, a man and two young women were there.

'*This is my husband Tomás. And these are Máire and Sinéad, like I was telling you. Tomás works as a woolcomber in the mill. Máire is on the spinning, Sinéad on the weaving and for myself, I stay at home and do nothing.*'

'*Would you listen to her?*' Tomás said. '*I go out in the morning and there's all this linen in a heap in our room. Come back in the evening and what do I find? Three shirts.*'

'*Hard work making shirts,*' Murty said.

'*But sure what else would I be doing,*' *Bríd* said. '*It's not that it pays much, though there's families that live on it, God knows how. It's just that I have to keep the house and stay at home, so I might as well be doing something. It earns enough to pay for the whiskey!*'

Next morning, Murty left Adelaide Street and walked to the Broomfields Cutting. In many ways, Adelaide Street was no different to the rest of Broomfields. The hard, gritty dirt and the unending stench of smoke was enough to remind him that they were living in a mill town.

What surprised him though, was how easily Aileen had accepted the offer of working in a mill. He was grateful that the two young women were friendly, helpful and delighted to look after Aileen. They too had noticed how quiet Aileen was. He wondered what working in a mill would be like. He had never even been inside one. How would Aileen find it? He would find out tonight.

It was raining when he reached the cutting. But first, he fetched his shovel from the shack.

'*Well, how was it?*' the woman asked.

'*Just as you said,*' Murty replied, '*but we have our own room. And better than that, my wife will be working in the mill.*'

'*That might be hard on her.*'

'*It might,*' Murty said.

For the rest of the morning, he considered the matter. If Aileen could stay working, it would solve their money worries. He would not have to beg for a clerical position with Murtybeg, and he did not want that. The only question now was – what had happened to Aileen today?

When he returned that evening, *Sinéad* was cooking, with the rest of the family sitting around the table.

'*You never told us she could spin,*' *Máire* said, as soon as he walked in.

'*Spin? But I…*'

'*Yes, spinning.*'

'*But…but that was linen. Years ago. That was before the machines came.*'

'*And so it was. But what of that. I've got her working with me on one of the spinning machines. She knows what it's all about. Another few days, and she'll be working her own machine. She'll be up to half a crown a day without any bother.*'

Murty was stunned. Half a crown! Two shillings and sixpence. Soon Aileen would be earning more than he did. That would most certainly be a change.

They sat down to dinner.

'*You keep a good house here,*' Murty said.

'*We do,*' Tomás said. '*Not like the rest of the houses around here.*'

'*I'd guessed as much. Not that I've been inside any others.*'

'*Nor would you want to,*' Sinéad said. '*Right hellholes they are. Twenty to a house…*'

'*Twenty! But…*'

'*Twenty is right. And I know what you're thinking. How do you fit twenty into a house with only three rooms? It's one hell of a crush, that's how. And some of them sleep in shifts. Some of the miners work that way. They come home with the sun, straight to bed and sleep half the day.*'

'*A hard life. How do they put up with it?*'

'*They don't*' Bríd said. '*The anger is always there. You heard of the riots here before Christmas?*'

'I did,' Murty said. 'I wasn't there, but I saw enough of what followed. Dragoons in the streets.'

'Not just in any streets either,' Tomás said. 'Right here where we live. The Battle of Adelaide Street, they call it. In the worst of the riots, they came right here, smashing in doors. Bríd saw it all.'

Murty looked to Bríd.

'You did?'

'I did,' she said, 'and I'll never forget it. It was that one of the ring leaders lived two doors down. But there were hundreds of us to resist. The police came in with cutlasses, and all the special constables, they had their sticks, slashing at the people.'

'That's terrible.'

'Terrible enough. But even then, they were unable to force their way forward, as we drove them back with stones and pikes. In the end, they ran. They ran from Adelaide Street; can you believe that? But we lost the next battle when they sent in the dragoons, a whole squadron of them, fully armed. That's what it took to break Adelaide Street. And Bradford.'

'It sounds like war,' Murty said.

'It's war, right enough, outright, bloody war,' she said. 'How else could they keep us down?'

'So who's fighting this war?'

'We are,' she said, sharply.

'And that's the right answer too,' Tomás said. 'The newspapers, the police and the politicians will give you other answers. Some will say it's the Charter lads are behind it, fighting for Parliamentary Reform. Others say it's the Unions fighting for Union Recognition. More will say it's the Repealers fighting for Irish Independence. The government are terrified of them all. But what they can't see is the real reason for the riots.'

'Which is...?'

'Hunger.'

'Hunger!'

'Look, Murty, what the people want is food on their tables. Parliamentary Reform and the rest of it, they're big words, but they don't mean nothing to anyone with an empty belly. All the beggar women you see around, with their scrawny brats on their laps, they're the real threat to the government. And if you don't believe me, look what happened right here in Adelaide Street.'

'We're not all beggar women, mind you,' Bríd said.

Tomás laughed.

'Ye're not. Still, if they paid us right, there'd be no riots. We're fine with three in the family working. But think of those trying to live on one wage. The mills and the mines pay damned little. And look at what they're paying *on* the Colne Extension – *who could live on that? And the poor devils who're being evicted for the railway works. They're starving.'*

'*I know,*' Murty said, impassively.

'*They're terrified of us, the government are. And even if you see less of the soldiers now, we all know they're there, hiding away in their barracks. The army works in the mill owners' interest. Never forget that.'*

After dinner, Murty sat by the fire with *Tomás*, talking quietly, now in English.

'What you were saying about hunger is surely true,' he said. 'But tell me *Tomás*, this Charter business. Is it really so weak? They frighten the hell out of the army.'

'Damn the lot of them,' *Tomás* replied. 'They were supposed to do great things for us, but now they're finished. Feargus O'Connor, he's Irish, and having him as a Chartist leader was a big mistake.'

'A mistake?'

'Most surely. You might find it strange to hear me saying that, but mixing Irish Repeal with Chartism was mad, and something they would never have considered if O'Connor hadn't been with them. If the Repealers want to repeal the Union of Great Britain and Ireland, that should be done in their own way, though for my part, I reckon it's a waste of time anyhow. Ireland would starve without the Union.'

'They're starving, anyhow,' Murty said.

'True enough, but we're in England now. And it isn't the Union of Britain and Ireland should concern us. Trade unions to take on the mill owners, that's what we need. And that's what the Charter once promised.'

'It did?'

'It did, but that was before Feargus O'Connor and his gang of Repealers joined in, and started to turn to violent ways. Thousands of pikes they had in Bradford then, the long ones, enough to skewer the dragoons and drive them off their horses. The Irish in Bradford, they weren't thinking of easy protest, more of revolution. Not just the trawneen of a revolution we had in Ireland last year. 1798, that was what was driving them, that and the slaughter of '98. The Repealers of Bradford wanted revenge for that.'

'They've long memories,' Murty said.

'They have, right enough, but little good it did us. They gave the government a fright, but they gave them an excuse too. Once the Repealers were mixed up with the Chartists, they could call the whole movement a revolutionary organisation, and bring in the dragoons to put down the terror in Bradford. No, no, they should have gotten rid of O'Connor and had nothing to do with Irish Repeal.'

'But what had any of this to do with Trade Unions?' Murty asked.

'Not a lot,' *Tomás* replied. 'In some ways, you might say that the Charter started out as a Trade Union movement. The other general strike back in '42; it was understood to be a Charter thing, but afterwards they got into this talk of Parliamentary Reform. Great talk, but nothing to do with Trade Unions. Then the Repealers killed it. I was a Chartist myself, believed in it all, but what did we end up with? The army in Bradford, nothing more.'

Next evening, Murty wrote a letter to Carrigard, giving his new address in Bradford. He felt it was best not to say anything about the conditions in which he found himself, and simply mentioned that Aileen was well. He did not wish to tell them about her new job, in case she could not keep it. And if she did, then there would be good news.

He walked down to dinner. There was a heated discussion going on.

'Wakefield. *I tell you it's in* Wakefield,' *Sinéad* said.

'*I'd heard it's in* Liverpool, *right enough,*' *Tomás* said. '*No question of it coming over the mountains yet. They haven't even got it in* Manchester.'

'*What's all this?*' Murty interrupted.

'*Arra, nothing,*' *Tomás* said, '*There's stories about cholera in* Wakefield. *Sure there couldn't be. It's all stuff and nonsense.*'

'*But* Wakefield…?' Murty asked.

'*It's twenty miles away.*'

'*And isn't that what I'm telling you,*' *Sinéad* said. '*Twenty miles is nothing. If it's in* Wakefield, *it'll be in* Bradford *soon enough. You just wait and see.*'

Chapter 16

Manchester Times. February 1849:
The people of South Lancashire and the West Riding have lately been called upon to support a whole army of Irish paupers, who have been driven from their home by the oppression of the landed aristocracy, many of whom are seeking to escape from bearing their fair share of the national burden, by hunting the peasantry off their estates and stocking them with black cattle. In the Union of Kenmare, it is stated, that one thousand dwellings have been levelled to the ground within the last 12 months. The starving inmates were turned adrift, the feebler proportion of them to die by the wayside, the hardier ones to beg their way to England, and swell the amount of poor rates in Liverpool, Manchester and the surrounding districts.

Murtybeg found it a relief to be running the business without Irene. Over the previous weeks, her sullen presence had irked him. Also, the question of bribery was always in his mind. He had ordered it stopped, but he was not certain that it had been. Now Irene was gone, how many smaller contracts might he no longer get? He would have to wait and see. In the meantime, he was certain that the larger contractors were not involved in bribery. Brassey was certainly not, and he was sure that Mackenzie himself would not do so either. Mackenzie would not have known of Ackroyd accepting bribes.

His parents would be relieved to hear that he was rid of Irene. He would have to write them a letter, but there were other things on his mind.

The Mackenzie contracts were running well, and he was confident he would get more, even without Irene. But now it was time to bid for more Brassey contracts. It was essential to get back in on the North Staffordshire. Over the next few days, he visited the proposed new works, and walked where the new cuttings and embankments would be. He also discussed it in detail with Brassey's managers there. They knew of Edwardes & Ryan from the previous works that had been carried out, when Danny was still alive.

Then he returned to Stockport and spent long hours costing the work. He was confident he could under-bid any of the other excavators, since his labour was far cheaper than any of them. His one concern here though was that he might be bidding far too little. It would be useful to know how much the competition was bidding.

When he was confident of his costings, he visited the Manchester & Salford Bank again. Winrow was far friendlier than in the previous negotiations. He quickly agreed a further £2,000 lending against the new North Staffordshire contracts, on the understanding that there would be part payments from Brassey over the short period of each contract.

Murtybeg sent his bids to Brassey's, requesting a meeting. Two days later, Mr. Simon Johnson of Thomas Brassey & Co., wrote, requesting his presence in Birkenhead.

He travelled from Stockport into Manchester and took the Liverpool train. He had had no time to book a hotel, but decided to stay at Buckleys'. Couldn't he have gone to Brown's again? It would have been the safer thing to do. Danny would have stayed at Brown's. Or better again, the Adelphi. Whether or not he could afford it, Danny always kept up appearances.

But Danny was dead, and Murtybeg knew he was responsible for Edwardes & Ryan now, and there was no point in wasting money. He had no one to impress. Buckleys' was cheap, but what of it?

He found a porter, who got him a cab just outside the station. He threw his pack in on the seat.

'Where to, gov?'

'Scotland Road.' The cab stopped.

'Sorry, gov, don't go near it.'

Murtybeg swore. 'Double fare.'

'Treble.'

Murtybeg took his pack out of the cab, and walked away.

'Fine so, double fare,' the cabbie shouted after him.

Murtybeg mounted the cab again. He gave the street number.

'Buckleys'?' the cabbie asked.

'That's it.'

'Not many stay there these days. Dangerous place.'

'Fine,' Murtybeg said, annoyed.

He looked out at Liverpool. England's greatest port? The cab passed lines of marching troops. Then cavalry.

As they neared Scotland Road, the city began to change. Yes, he remembered the tenements and crowded courtyards from the first time he had come over in 1846, when he was working on the English harvest. Could it have been so little time? And even since then, Scotland Road had worsened. Hundreds of people in the streets and yards.

A soldier was standing at a door. The door had a white cross painted on it. Then more soldiers, more crosses. This time, he did not recognize the insignia. They were regular infantry.

They arrived at Buckleys' and Murtybeg paid off the cabbie, twice fare, and no tips. He put his pack on his shoulder and walked to the door.

'Be careful, gov,' the cabbie shouted after him, 'there's cholera there.'

Murtybeg froze. He looked back at the cab, uncertain what to do. Cholera!

He walked back, and gave the cabbie a farthing.

'Just hold on here a few minutes' he said. 'If I can't get a room, you'll have another fare. If I'm not out soon, just go on.'

The cabbie tipped his hat to him.

He walked into Buckleys'. A stench of urine hit him. He ignored it and went to the desk where Mrs. Buckley was sitting.

'Tuppence a room, sharing,' she said, before he even asked for anything.

'Is there disease here?'

'Sixpence for a room of your own,' she said, without even answering his question.

He thought of that. Perhaps it was safe enough.

'Fine.'

'Payment up front.'

He put the sixpence on the desk.

A scruffy boy grasped his pack, without asking. Murtybeg followed up four flights of stairs. The room was on the top, under the eaves.

'Is there cholera here in the hotel?' he asked the boy.

'There is.'

'Was there any in this room?'

'No.'

Murtybeg thanked him, and flipped him a farthing.

He looked at the bed. Despite the boy's assurance, he decided not to risk it, and slept in his clothes on top of the blankets.

He rose early. As he descended the stairs, he saw a soldier standing at one of the corridors. He stopped in puzzlement. The soldier raised his hand.

'Cholera.'

'The whole corridor?'

'Only three rooms,' the soldier said. 'Twenty people maybe. But they're saying it's a new kind, kills in days, no one lives. Worse than '32.'

He left Buckleys'. The condition of Scotland Road no longer disturbed him. The soldiers and white crosses did. He cut down towards the docks. More soldiers. More crosses.

Cholera in Liverpool.

He took the Mersey Ferry, and on the Wirral side of the river, he took a cab to Birkenhead.

'Brassey's offices,' he said to the cabbie. No need to give the address.

When he arrived, Johnson was waiting for him. He was friendly, and they quickly completed the business. Johnson stood up to walk him to the door.

'Which way did you come?'

'Through Liverpool. I hadn't known about the cholera.'

'Yes,' Johnson said, 'it was a dangerous way to come. I'd advise you to go back by the Birkenhead & Cheshire. Then you can connect across to Manchester or Stockport.'

'That's exactly what I'm intending,' Murtybeg said.

After the meeting, he spent much of that day travelling. It did not matter. He had no desire to visit Liverpool again, at least not until the cholera was gone. But if he didn't, where could he source workers? Strangely, he felt it would not be an impossible hurdle. There were enough starving men in Manchester, in the slums of Ancoats – Little Ireland. And there was no question of cholera in Manchester. Or perhaps he had just not heard of it yet.

It was late one evening when an unexpected visitor called by, carrying a folder. The young clerk showed him in.

'That's fine,' Murtybeg told the clerk. 'You can go now.'

The visitor sat in front of his desk.

'I don't think we've met?' he said. 'James Crawford is the name. Inspector Crawford. I'm from the Detective Police of Manchester City.'

'You're right that we haven't met,' Murtybeg said, 'I've heard your name though. I understand you've had some meetings with my late brother.'

'I have indeed,' Crawford said, 'and might I say, here and now, how sorry I was to hear of your brother's demise.'

Murtybeg was on his guard now. What did Crawford want?

'Indeed, Inspector,' he replied. 'I don't have to tell you; it was a terrible shock to all of us.'

Crawford took a pad and a pen from his folder. 'Would you have some ink, Mr. Ryan?'

Murtybeg fetched ink from the cupboard and set it beside him. 'You seem to have an interest in my brother's death,' he said.

'Indeed, we do,' Crawford said. 'We had at first assumed it to be murder, and we carried out a detailed inquiry.'

'Murder? Whatever gave you that idea?'

'It appeared likely at the time,' Crawford said, ignoring the question. 'But tell me Mr. Ryan, what was your opinion?'

Murtybeg stared out the window, not saying anything. A train was crossing the Edgeley viaduct, the Birmingham to Manchester line. An image of Danny's mangled corpse flashed through his mind.

'At first, we thought it was an accident,' he said, 'but from all I heard afterwards, I'm more inclined to think that Danny killed himself. Or if you prefer, if it was murder, he only murdered himself.'

Crawford was scribbling fast.

'Yes,' he said, 'I'm inclined to agree with you. Our investigations brought us to the engine driver, and from all we can deduce, Mr. Ryan stood out on the tracks intentionally. We were of the opinion that the man was telling the truth. He would have no reason to do otherwise. So in the end, we dropped it as a murder investigation.'

Murtybeg was more on his guard than ever. He knew that Crawford's meetings with Danny related to other matters, including the Molly Maguire gang. He was certain of Danny's involvement, and he guessed that Crawford was too.

'I'm a little confused here,' he said to Crawford. 'If you have concluded it wasn't murder, then why are we talking?'

Crawford put his pen down.

'We are still investigating an earlier killing,' he said. 'Mr. James McManus. He was one of your brother's foremen, I believe.'

'He was,' Murtybeg replied. 'Do you know anything about his murder yet?'

Crawford shook his head. 'I'm afraid not, Mr. Ryan. We've tried many leads, but all of them have come to a dead end. I do know one thing for certain though. Mr. McManus was a member of the Molly Maguire gang.'

Now Murtybeg knew for certain that he was on dangerous ground.

'I didn't know that,' he said, thankful that at least was truthful.

'No, I suppose you wouldn't,' Crawford said. 'Our reckoning though is that he was killed in revenge for an earlier killing. A Mr. Eckersley.'

'Yes,' Murtybeg said,' I know the name. That was the fellow who ran a shebeen once. He was beaten up, I understand.'

'And died afterwards.'

'Died? Do you know who might have been guilty?'

'Again, I cannot say for certain. I suspect strongly though that it was a Molly Maguire killing.'

'I see.'

'In any case, it was after that, that Mr. McManus was shot. And that in turn was followed by another murder. A Mr. Worsley, a foreman on the Baxendales' contract next to your brother's. So you can see the pattern, Mr. Ryan. First, Eckersley was beaten and died. James McManus was killed in revenge. Then Mr. Worsley was killed in revenge again. I have no doubt that Eckersley and Worsley were killed by the Molly Maguires. What's more, Mr. Ryan, I suspect they were acting on your brother's orders.'

Murtybeg was speechless.

'But…but…'

Crawford held up his hand. 'Don't worry, Mr. Ryan, I can see I've shocked you, and in fact, from your reaction, I see too you were totally unaware of this. If you weren't, you would be an accessory to murder, and that would certainly be a criminal charge, twice over. Whether it would be a hanging charge is debatable.'

Murtybeg recovered his composure.

'But if what you're saying…a hanging charge?'

'Yes, Mr. Ryan. Your brother knew that we knew of his involvement. We had insufficient evidence, as yet, to convict him. But it was only a matter of time.'

'I see,' said Murtybeg. 'And you're saying that's the reason he killed himself?'

'One of them anyhow. Now I'll just say one thing further, Mr. Ryan. Like I say, I don't think that you were an accessory to the murders. It is possible though, that you knew of your brother's involvement, post facto, so to speak. If you did, and you had not reported that to the police, that would be a criminal offence in itself. A lesser charge again than being an actual accessory, but serious none the less.'

Murtybeg was thinking fast, but still confused.

'I don't know what to say, Inspector.'

'Don't say anything. We'll assume you did not know about the murder, but you may well have known about your brother's involvement with the Molly Maguires.'

'Well, I…'

Crawford waved his hand again. 'No, don't worry. You will not be the subject of a prosecution. I promise you that. But can I ask you this, and I would advise you to answer truthfully. Have you yourself any association with the gang?'

Murtybeg was relieved. 'I can promise you, absolutely, I have never been involved with them.'

'And I believe you. Your name has never come up in our investigations.'

Nervously, Murtybeg twisted his own pen. Was Crawford aware of how he and Danny brought workers through the Port of Liverpool, and who had organised the payoffs to the police and port authorities? It seemed Crawford knew nothing of this.

'Nor should it come up,' Murtybeg said.

'No. But there is one other possible reason for your brother's death.

We believe he was trading fraudulently. He was not in a position to repay his bank debts. So at the very least, he might have been facing the Debtors Prison. That is, if the Manchester & Salford Bank decided to prosecute him.'

'But how do you know all this?'

'Our Fraud Department. Now I must admit I am not an expert in that area, so I leave it to my commercial colleagues to deal with it. Once again though, can I ask you were you aware of this?'

'Not while my brother was alive.'

Crawford held his pen in anticipation.

'But afterwards?'

'At my very first meeting with the bank after my brother's death, they made me aware of the situation. They could have bankrupted us there and then, but they did not. I proved to them that we had enough new contracts which would be profitable enough to pay off our debts within a reasonable time. It was all a matter of timing. The bank knew that, and that was why they were prepared to deal with me.'

Crawford looked satisfied.

'Very well, Mr. Ryan, 'but I must ask you one further question. Since your brother's death, have the Molly Maguires tried to contact you?'

'No. I can assure you of that.'

'I'm happy to hear that,' Crawford said. 'I had been very concerned that they might have tried to restart the contact with Edwardes & Ryan.'

'I wonder why they haven't,' Murtybeg said.

'Most likely, because of your brother's death, following so close on his foreman's murder. They may have felt it was too dangerous to continue dealing with Edwardes & Ryan. Or it might just be a matter of time. I must ask you one thing though. If any of them make contact with you, could you let me know at once.'

He took a page from his pad.

'Here's my address.'

Murtybeg took it, as Crawford went on.

'There are two men in particular you should watch for – Gene Brady in Liverpool and Aidan Sheridan, right here in Manchester. They're the gang leaders, top men. If either of them approach you, just drop me a line, and be very careful. They are most dangerous.'

'Dangerous?'

'Very dangerous, Mr. Ryan. We intend to hang both of them. When we have enough evidence, of course.'

When Crawford had left, Murtybeg spent quite some time staring out of the window. He was relieved at what Crawford had said, and he believed he himself would not be prosecuted. Still, his parting remarks had disturbed him. If any of the gang were to contact him, what could he do? Inform the police? Give evidence to hang men? He knew well the fate of informers, especially Irish informers. Even Crawford would not be able to protect him from that.

And McManus? Crawford had appeared certain of his ground when he stated McManus was in the Molly Maguire gang. But if McManus was, who else might be? Lavan, Gilligan or Roughneen? No way of knowing. The Molly Maguire gang were bound to silence, and there was no way any of them would have told him. Or would they? Would they have wanted to enrol him? He decided he was becoming too suspicious. They were his key men, and he could not afford to lose them. As it was, he was short of top level foremen. In fact, he was short of all sorts of men. He had thought again of his father, but dismissed it from his mind.

Over the following weeks, he employed two more clerks and a bookkeeper. Since he had sacked Irene, much of the burden fell on himself. At least the bookkeeper could assist him in carrying out costings for bids, and preparing projections for the Manchester & Salford Bank.

He visited all his sites. He felt better being out of the office. Travelling the rails still fascinated him. He realised he had a pride in the railway system, even on tracks where Edwardes & Ryan had no contracts. He was part of an enterprise that was changing the face of England, and in time, would change the world.

He was more relaxed tramping the sites with his foremen. Roughneen and the rest, these were men he had known since childhood, men he understood, and could rely on in any situation. The sites too, with their endless activity, energised him. He saw it all as an enormous challenge. This was what he was born for.

Back in Stockport, one of the big gaps he had, related to dealing with his suppliers for carts, horses, shovels, timber and many other items. He was no longer holding weekly meetings of the foremen in Stockport because of distances, but he ensured they all met every second or third Saturday. Long discussions were held at these meetings regarding suppliers, and Murtybeg encouraged them to deal with the suppliers in the same ruthless fashion as Irene had. Did they have it in them? Did he?

Roughneen's truck shop was running well, and, as Irene had anticipated, it increased profits for the business considerably. Murtybeg was surprised and gratified to find it was being run in conjunction with the Grenadier Inn.

'Geldart is a sharp fellow,' Roughneen told him. 'He knows enough of Mayo, and all about the bar trade. We split our ten percent half and half, and we're all happy.'

Roughneen had been a little more reluctant about the idea of paying in scrip, and taking the scrip in their own truck bar. But in the end, the profits involved were too tempting. At times, Murtybeg wondered what his workers were living on, but decided to put it out of his mind.

One other irony struck him. Eckersley, the man whose killing had started Danny's problems with the Molly Maguires, had been running his own shebeen on Danny's works. If all of what Inspector Crawford had said was true, then Danny must have been using the Mollys to force the shebeens off the sites. Perhaps he knew all this already, but preferred to ignore it, and let Danny run things his own way. But murder?

Now he was bringing the shebeens back. But that was different. Truck bars were managed by Edwardes & Ryan. Could they really control them though? Roughneen pointed out to him that previous riots and randies had arisen from Irish works that were alongside other works employing English, Welsh or Scottish labour. So long as the bars and the shacks were not close to other works, there would be no problem. Local people would object, but that was of little concern to him.

He was becoming more confident. For the first time since Danny's death, he felt he could make Edwardes & Ryan succeed, without having to pay the price that Danny had paid, and without Irene too.

But glad as he was to be rid of her, she had been Danny's woman, and that brought him to think of other matters. There was no woman in his own life. Perhaps he should do as Danny had done, and hire a female assistant. Idly, he fantasised about this. There were few Irish girls who would be as able as Irene with figures and negotiation. Perhaps look for an English assistant so? No, better to wait until he was better established, and Edwardes & Ryan was a top-level business, working for only the top contractors. Then he would have his choice of women. But work came first.

One evening, he noted the maid had left a letter on his bed. It was addressed to him and marked 'Eyes Addressee only.'

He slit it open. It was from Louis Sternberg.

Irene was appealing the decision of the Probate Court.

Chapter 17

Brooklyn Eagle, New York. December 1848:

The Cholera. In 1832, when we were visited by the Cholera, it made its entrance by way of Canada. It has now approached us at a more southerly point. It is said that it has made its appearance simultaneously in New York and New Orleans. The weather appears to be favourable for the propagation of the disease, and our city is in just the condition to be inoculated with it at an early day. We suppose no place was ever so outrageously filthy. We hear it said that the streets have not been relieved of their filth thoroughly since just before the last election and that heaps of muck and mush are standing in them, from month to month.

When Luke took Winnie and Liam to Lackan, it was bitterly cold. As they walked across to the terminal of the New Jersey Railroad, Luke wondered what their lodgings in Lackan might be like. He suspected the company-operated lodgings would not be of the same standard, nor have a landlady with the same concern for her lodgers. Mrs. Gleeson had been concerned about the baby travelling in such cold, but Winnie assured her Liam would be held close and warm.

At every stop, Winnie walked up and down the platform, carrying Liam, Luke following. She compared the engines at the front of each train, commenting on the size of their boilers. Luke was amazed at her interest.

'How can they pull so many carriages?' she asked.

'That's what boiling water does,' Luke said, 'and anthracite to heat it too. But they start slow, only slowly building up speed.'

'And the tracks here? That was the class of thing you were working on in England?'

'It was. Much of it too, hundreds of miles. But for the most part, we weren't laying the tracks, we were digging the cuttings and building the embankments with the clay and rock we'd dug out. Hard work, I can tell you.'

At Philadelphia, they changed for the train to Schuylkill. Luke bought the tickets, and they barely made the train in time.

From time to time, Winnie breastfed Liam, not concerned about anyone else in the carriage. She had given up trying to wean him for now. What surprised Luke though was her silence for most of the journey. For hours, she sat looking out the window, taking in the landscape. Even the frozen swamps of New Jersey fascinated her. She compared the trestle bridges with the iron bridges, and when the train began to climb, she stared ceaselessly at the snow-covered hills and forests, while Luke played endless games of penny pontoon with other passengers.

Sometimes, when she was more talkative, they spoke of Carrigard. Brockagh too. She was concerned about her own parents, whom she had not seen since she had married Luke. In the end, there had been no time.

Luke wanted to get Winnie and Liam settled, and ensure his own employment. He was still nervous of coal mines, having little idea of what it was like to work in one. He was used to working in the open air. In England, he had heard many stories of coal mines – dramatic ones too of firedamp and collapses killing men. How much he should believe?

The forests of Pennsylvania amazed Winnie. She had never seen woodlands so extensive before. The snow and ice were frozen to the hemlock, showing white and green against a blue sky.

The hills all around her excited her too, though she exclaimed joyfully when the train ran across flat farmland. Every time she saw anything of interest, she pointed it out to Liam, though Luke doubted whether the child could make anything of the scenes outside.

Once again, Winnie alighted at every station, hugging Liam closely to her with her shawl wrapped tightly around him. Plainly, neither mother nor child were concerned about the future.

'You should make sure he's warm enough,' he said.

'Don't you be worrying,' Winnie answered. 'I'm a mother now, you don't think I'd let him freeze, do you?'

At Schuylkill, it was bitterly cold. Winnie stayed inside the station with Liam, while Luke hunted out the coach to Lackan.

An hour later, they started the journey. There was little room inside the coach.

'I'll go out on top,' Luke said.

'No, I will,' one of the men said. 'You stay here with your wife and child.'

'But I couldn't ask...'

'My coat is thick enough. I'm well used to it.'

Within minutes, both Winnie and Liam were asleep. Luke stared out the window. It was snowing heavily.

They came to Lackan. It was clearly an anthracite town, grey and dirty in the way of all coal patch towns. Even this did not distress Winnie, and she exclaimed at the steep white sides of the culm banks streaked with black. Luke could only think what they might look like when the real thaw came.

The snow had stopped, but it was drizzling sleet. Luke took the packs out. They were heavy enough after the time they had spent in Jersey City. He looked for a cab. There were four waiting but they were quickly taken up by other passengers.

Winnie sat on one of the packs, holding her shawl over Liam.

'What now?'

'Let's get the packs over there and get under shelter anyhow. Then we wait.'

Soon after, another cab arrived. Luke and the cabbie manhandled the packs into it, as Winnie and Liam got in. Luke gave the address.

'Rough place, that,' the cabbie commented. 'Too many Irish, don't go there often.'

'I know what you mean,' Luke said. No point arguing.

They reached the address. The street was deep in frozen mud. At the end of the street was a wooden building, a continuous growling noise coming from it.

'I wonder what that is.' Winnie said.

'God knows,' Luke said.

Two women stood outside a door, one of them breastfeeding. A pig snuffled at her feet. She spotted Liam, and waved at Winnie. She waved back.

'Friendly enough, anyhow,' Winnie said.

Most of the houses were small, but well built. The cab went past them all until they came to a building made from rough-cut timber.

'This is the address.'

Across the road there was a row of small houses. There was a line of women outside one. From the smell, Luke knew at once that it was a butcher's.

A frozen stream ran along from where they had stopped. It went under a stone bridge and out by the side of the butcher's shop. A man wearing a bloodied apron carried out a tray of offal, and threw it in the stream. A pig ran onto the ice, then another, and both started fighting for the offal.

Luke helped Winnie down as the bags were taken off. He paid the cabbie and tried the door of the building. It was open. They went inside. Two blackened men sat at a table.

'*Who are you?*' one of them asked, speaking in Irish.

'*Since you ask, Luke Ryan is my name. We're over looking for the Farrelly gang.*'

'*All out working. Are you coming to stay?*'

'*I hope so,*' Luke said. '*We're joining Farrelly.*'

'*Him and the rest of the gang are staying up on the second floor. There's a few bunks to spare I know. Come on, let's show it to you.*'

One of them took two of the packs, and brought them upstairs. He opened a door.

'*This is where them lads bunk down*' he said.

The room was a long one, bunks three high running each side along the walls and even across the windows. Forty or fifty Luke reckoned without even counting. The floor was covered with coal dust, wet in places. There were packs under the lower bunks, covered in coal dust too. The blankets on the bunks were black. Blackened shirts, jackets and trousers hung off nails hammered into the ends of the bunks.

'*I know these ones down here are empty. Come on.*'

They followed him to three bunks at the far end, one above the other. There were no blankets, and the mattresses were black with coal dust. Luke put his packs in underneath.

'Well, this is it, my love.'

'*Are there many women here?*' Winnie asked the other man.

'*Sure there's none at all. This is only for the lads on their own. There's another building for the women and children, but you'll have to talk to Farrelly about that. Crowded, I understand, and they don't allow us men in neither. It's the next street over.*'

Luke looked out the window.

'*What's that building down there?*'

'*That's the* breaker.'

The man left.

Winnie was close to tears.

'Don't worry, my love,' Luke said, 'we'll work it out somehow. I'm sure there's a way of getting into the better houses along the street. And anyhow, Farrelly says there's many Kilduff people around, so we'll feel at home soon enough. This is a mining town, remember. I've seen many of them around England, though I must say this is a pretty rough looking one.'

It was late when Farrelly and the rest of the gang arrived back. Luke had found a candle, and some matches.

'By God, there's a woman down the end!' one of the men said.

Farrelly walked down. 'Who the devil…? By God, it's Luke.'

He clapped his hand on Luke's shoulder. 'You're most welcome, boy. And this must be your wife?'

'Winnie,' Luke said, 'and little Liam over there.'

Mick and Jack shook Luke's hand, and greeted Winnie. Then Luke recognised Mikey Jordan and Bernie McDonnell from his days on the English railways.

Mikey greeted him warmly. 'Luke. A friend from the past. 'Tis great to see you again.'

Bernie thrust out his hand, and grasped Winnie's. 'By God, I haven't seen as decent looking a woman this long time!' he exclaimed, hugging Winnie tightly. 'Begging your pardon girl, but 'tis a long time since I had a chance to do that.'

Winnie glanced at the wet coal dust on her dress. 'I'm glad you'd think me a decent woman, but maybe you should talk to Luke first about that.'

'*Arra*, what.'

There were a few other men whom Luke had not met since he had left working the railways in England. Dover? How long ago was that? Damned near three years, just as the hunger was getting brutal at home in Ireland.

'How many of you are here now?' Luke asked.

'A round dozen,' Farrelly said. 'All Kilduff men. Matt here only came out six months back.'

Matt? Matt McGlinn. Luke recognised him at once. He went to greet him, but McGlinn had turned away. Luke remembered the time he had had to refuse McGlinn on the Famine Relief Works in Carrigard. All according to regulations – they had only been taking on men with four children or more. Still, McGlinn had never forgiven him, nor ever would.

Could he never escape from it?

A bottle of whiskey was produced and cups were taken out from a wooden chest beneath one of the bunks, all well chipped. Winnie was handed one, and sipped slowly.

'Now the next question is – where are Winnie and the child going to go? You know they won't be allowed to sleep here.'

'I know,' Luke said, 'we'd heard. But we'll manage something for the night.'

A line of blankets was hung on a rope running from one window to another.

'That'll protect your modesty for the night at least, girl,' Farrelly said. 'And sure no one need know you're here tonight. We'll have you in the Women's House tomorrow night.'

'The Women's House?' Winnie asked, uncertainly.

'Women and children only. But don't worry, we'll organise something more for you soon.'

Farrelly left them. Luke saw Winnie examining her blackened dress. It might be difficult to wash that in a room full of men. There was no sign of clean sheets, nor blankets either.

Winnie sat on the dirty mattress. 'It'll have to do,' she said, 'isn't that the way of it?'

'It is, my love.'

*

Next morning, Farrelly took Luke to the store, while the other men went to the mine. Luke was in his roughest clothes.

'I hope this wasn't all too much of a shock to you,' Farrelly said. 'I must confess, I never even thought of the question of bringing your wife and baby along. We'll have them in the Women's House tonight. It's a hell of a lot cleaner, I can tell you. We'll see then what we can do about getting you a house, though it won't be easy, I warn you.'

'Like where?' Luke asked.

'There's family lodgings. We can arrange that when you get paid. Operator owned houses, of course, and the rent deducted from your wages. You'll be moved in with another family, mind you, but there's no harm in that.'

'I'd never thought of a Women's House,' Luke said. 'Are there so many single women?'

'Single is right,' Farrelly responded. 'Widows more like. That's what black lung does. Once a man goes down the mines, his days are numbered. Ten years, fifteen years, who knows? So the women spend half their lives as widows, bringing up starving children.'

'God, it's tough on them. How do they even live?'

'The lucky ones might marry again, but that's rare. No, they just have to get work as best they can. Some do stitching for the shirt-man when he comes through, but that's difficult enough with the dirt of the coal dust everywhere. So many of them take in laundry for the single miners, do cooking and suchlike, and provide other services.'

'I won't ask about that,' Luke said.

'Better not.'

'It's tough.'

'Very tough, I'd say,' Farrelly said. 'When the rail building ended at Harrisburg, we'd heard stories about good wages in the mines, what with working on loading wagons, and sure isn't that what we were well used to from all the English railways. Remember those times Luke?'

'By God, I do. We were one of the highest paid gangs on the rails then.'

'We were. Hard work, but we could do it. What never dawned on us coming here though was that the wagon loading is the best job in the mines, for us at least. We're used to it. The only trouble is trying to get onto the wagon-loading.'

'Not easy?'

'Not yet. We've had to start out as the lowest of the low, working down the mine. They'll all tell you the mining is a skilled job, and so it is for the Kilkenny fellows. The Welsh too. They've been working in mines, long before they come to America. They reckon the rest of us Irish have no skills, and are paid less. But it's worse than that too. The Welsh take the best drifts, where they can work standing. The Kilkenny lads get to work standing too, but the tunnels are longer, and it takes more walking to reach the coalface. But us, we get the worst of all. Our drifts are low, and it's impossible to swing a pick standing. Not like what you'd be used to on the railways. It's harder work for less coal, so less pay.'

'So how do we get the better drifts?'

'We don't. Or at least it's not my intention that we should. It's like I told you earlier. Working the mines is a fool's game. Ten, fifteen years is the most they'll last. The anthracosis gets them in the end.'

'Anthra…what?'

'Anthracosis. A big word for black lung. The more of the dust you breathe in, the less you're able to breathe. When you die, your son takes over.'

'My…son?'

How else can your widow live if she doesn't have someone working? By God, I pity them too. The Operator sure as hell doesn't. But I'll tell you this, Luke, it's not down the mines we'll be staying. One way or another, we're going to get on to wagon loading. They say it's the lowest paid job on the mines, but we're all fit, the whole lot of us. We're well able to work fast. No, I reckon we don't have to worry about the wages, we'll make as much as the best of them, and we'll live three times longer.'

They had arrived at the store, a long wooden shed, with walls constructed from thick wood, rough sawn from long timber trunks.

'Have you cash with ye?' Farrelly asked.

'Left it all with Winnie,' Luke said.

'What kind of fool are you? Here you are so, ten cents for a cap, fifty cents for the lamp and candles. That's sixty cents you owe me at the end of the week.'

He handed over the amount, and Luke took his cap and lamp.

They walked towards the mine.

'You've got to understand one thing, Luke. We're running our own gang, on contract to the Operators. Stanley Cantwell, he's the supervisor, a Kilkenny fellow. But we work our own way, don't have to meet him until we get paid. It's not like the railways though, we don't get paid by the wagon, only by the ton. They've their own ways of weighing it, mind. Got to watch them all the time. Three tons per miner is what they expect, not that we can make that much yet, but still it's good for eighty to ninety cents a day.'

They were walking across a bridge over a small stream. Farrelly grasped Luke by the arm.

'There's one other thing I must tell ye, and it's most important. That store up there, we just came out of, that's a truck store, run by the Operator. We've got to go there to buy our supplies. Not just caps and lamps, but all the other supplies we use – kerosene, copper, oil and the like. Blasting powder for when we've the chance to use it. We could buy them far cheaper elsewhere, but if we did, we'd be fired at once. When we first came here though, we were paid in scrip. That's Operator dockets, not cash, only to be used in the truck store. They weren't paying us real money at all.'

'No money?'

'No dollars. Only scrip. All our supplies – food, clothes and everything – had to be bought in the truck store, since nowhere else accepted their scrip. When we griped about it, we were told we weren't able enough and lucky to be getting what we did. We objected again though, said we were more skilled, and the Operators gave in half-ways – half our wages in scrip and half in cash. There was some question some of the Operators had been threatened, though I'm damned if I know about that. Anyhow, they paid us half in dollars from then on but still insisted we buy in the truck store. It's another of the tricks they use, you see. The truck store is half as expensive again as any store in Lackan. Funny enough, that stopped after a few weeks too, though they kept paying half in scrip. They told us we could shop wherever we liked with the rest of our wages. There were reports again about threats...'

'Threats from who?' Luke asked.

'The Molly Maguires, they say, though everyone keeps saying there's no such group. Still...'

'Yes,' Luke said, 'I'd heard about them in Ireland.'

They went on again.

'So that's the truck store,' Farrelly said, 'and there's one other thing about it. Don't ever, ever, ever, take credit from them. Make sure Winnie knows that too. If you ever see hear of her taking credit, just beat her within an inch of her life.'

'That's a bit strong.'

'Not when you see what goes on around here. There's many families are in hock to the Operator, and they'll never get out of it. It's a class of debt slavery. Once they give you credit, you'll be charged interest like you've never expected. They deduct the interest every pay day, and leave you with less and less wages. That way, you need more and more credit, and you can never get out of it. Would you believe, they even pass the credit on to the son as soon as the father is invalided out by black lung? Once they've got their claws into you that way, they've got you forever.'

They reached the mine. Farrelly checked himself in, and did the same for Luke. He brought him to the cage by the windlass, where men were already waiting. They entered, and the cage dropped down the shaft at speed.

'Don't be alarmed,' Farrelly said in the darkness.

They walked along a tunnel. It looked endless to Luke. At length, they came out into an area with wider tunnels, still with long sections of black coal wall dividing them, with occasional gaps.

'They're the pillars,' Farrelly said. 'They're what have to be left behind for holding up the roof. They always try to dig in as far as they can. 'Robbing the pillar' it's called. Damned dangerous too.'

Luke heard the sound of picks digging at coal.

'Now this area is the best for working,' Farrelly told him. 'Most of it is over five feet high. A man can work standing, or near it. Not as cramped, and the fellows can get a good tonnage out. The Welsh fellows keep it all to themselves.'

Luke followed him between the pillars, and then down another tunnel.

'And this is where we work,' Farrelly said. 'Less than four feet high, the most of it. Some of it only three.'

He gave Luke a pick.

'Just go in there on the left. If you don't know them from the colour of their faces, that's Mikey over there, and Bernie lying beside him.'

For the rest of the morning, Luke hacked away at the anthracite. Sometimes he was kneeling, sometimes lying. When they broke for food, his knees hurt and his arms and shoulders ached.

'I'm well use to swinging a pick, I just never thought I'd be doing it lying down,' he said.

'You'll get used to it,' Mikey said.

They returned to the coal face. Luke found he was sweating heavily. He had to lie sideways on the floor of the mine, jagged pieces of anthracite cutting into his arm as he swung. The effort of keeping his head up from the floor gave him excruciating pains in his neck. Inhaling the dust caused him to cough and splutter, even as he gasped for breath.

When they returned to the Miners' House, Luke was told Winnie and Liam had gone.

'*Don't worry,*' one of the other men shouted to him, '*they're just gone over to the Women's House, that's all. It'll be cleaner there, that's for sure and certain.*'

'*Thanks,*' Luke said.

He lay down on his mattress and pulled the blankets over him. His arms still ached.

Jack roused him.

'Time to eat.'

Luke followed him. He sat with the gang in the canteen. A large tureen of stew sat in the middle of the table. Kidney and liver floated on top, but there were many more meats he could not identify. He ladled the stew onto his bowl.

Mick nudged him.

'Dreadful slop, isn't it?'

'I've eaten better,' Luke said.

'But at least there's plenty of it,' Bernie said, 'more than we'd have been getting in County Mayo these years past. And sure why wouldn't they? They have to build us up to be able to swing a pick.'

Luke ate.

'And to really cheer you up,' Jack said, 'three cents a plate is what it's costing you off your wages.'

'That's right,' said Farrelly, 'remember what I said about the truck store. If they can't get you one way, they have to get you another.'

'What other ways are there?' Luke asked.

'They could reduce the wages more. Or get you working on robbing the pillars, and bring the roof down. There's always ways. But one way or another, you should be happy to have a job, any job. The railways are all closing down, thousands of men out of work. There's men starving in this country, Luke, don't you forget that.'

After dinner, he left the canteen and walked down to the Women's House. It was intensely cold. Farrelly's last comments had depressed him. Men starving in this country. What kind of place was America?

He knocked at the door of the Women's House. He was not allowed to enter, but asked for Winnie. She came to the door, Liam wrapped tightly in her shawl. She stepped out. It was a starry night.

'So how is it with you?' she asked.

'Tough. It isn't easy working in mines.'

'I can see that. You could do with a good scrubbing down too.'

'I know. But what of ye? Are ye getting fed?'

'Well enough. They'll be wanting payment at the end of the week though. But God, Luke, this is one terrible place. Most of them are widows, living on very little.'

'I know,' Luke said, 'Farrelly told me all about it.'

'The men die young.'

'I know that too. And we don't want leaving you a widow, do we?'

'So what can we do?'

'Damned if I know,' Luke answered. 'Don't think I'm not thinking about it. But for now, we'll have to put up with it. Get some better kind of work in the spring.'

'Like what? The railways?'

'There's not much work there,' Luke said. 'No, it won't be the railways. Not for now anyhow. But the one thing we can do, is get you out of this

231

place. There's family lodgings around, and once I have my first wages, we'll be looking for them.'

'I'll be pleased when you do,' Winnie said. 'This place is so damned miserable. Do you know, they have me doing the cooking for our part of the house? Twelve women and fifteen children. Unpaid too. Cooking for that crowd wasn't what I expected when we came to Lackan.'

'I don't know what any of us expected,' Luke answered, 'but one way or another it means you don't have to go out to work, and you can mind the baby while you work.'

'Yes,' she said. 'It's not that I mind it, but the women all demand it of me as a matter of right. We can't go on like this, Luke.'

'I agree with you, but there's very little other work that we can look for right now. Jersey City was rough, I can tell you, and we don't want to go back to that. Sure, I'd far prefer not to have you working, and to be just watching over a house of our own, and taking care of the baby, but that's not possible yet, my love.'

'Will it ever be?' Winnie asked.

'In a place like Lackan? I'm not sure. But let's wait and see.'

Back to hard labour. When they had filled a wagon, it had to be dragged back to the main tunnel, where it was linked up to a mule. It was impossible for mules to work in the low drifts though, and for much of that distance, two of the men had to drag the wagon by means of crawling on hands and knees. They used kneepads and gloves, but still it was brutally hard.

That evening, as they walked back along the tunnel, a young boy emerged from one of the other drifts. At first, Luke was unsure of what he had seen because of the poor light from his lamp, but looked back to make sure.

'Good God, Martin, they're using children for the wagons,' he said.

'I know,' Farrelly replied, 'sure they've been doing that for generations.'

'But he was only a child.'

'Twelve years old. If you want to believe that.'

'Twelve years!' Luke exclaimed. 'No bloody way. How do you work that out?'

'Simple. The laws of Pennsylvania say he's twelve. They bar children from working in the mines. The mother says he's twelve, and so does he, so who are we to argue with it?'

'But...but can't they check it out?'

They had arrived at the cage.

'Not a hope in hell. If you check it, you'll find he was born in Ireland, and who's going to write to Ireland to find out how old he is. It's the same old story. His father's most likely dead, and his mother needs the money. And by the time he really gets to twelve, he'll have been given as much older, and he'll be a miner. And he sure as hell won't make thirty.'

On Saturday, they finished early. At the Miner's House, Farrelly divided up the wages. He held Luke's until last, and waited until Luke had counted it.

'I'm just thinking,' he said, 'you and Danny used to be the best on sums when we worked the railways in England.'

'Hardly surprising,' Luke said. 'Most of the fellows can't add at all.'

'No, but I can, and by God ye were both far faster than I ever was. Now I want you to have a quick look at this. This is our contract account. Is it correct, do you think?'

Luke took the page. He went through the figures – tons, rates per ton, totals, deductions for oil at rates per gallon, and many more. He multiplied in his head, adding and then making the deductions.

'It's correct,' he said to Farrelly at last.

'Fine, but it mightn't have been. What I'd like you to do for us now is the same as you and Danny used to do in England, at least when Danny was still with our gang. Whenever we need supplies, I'd like you to go to the truck store and get them, and make sure the amounts are correct before you sign for them. It's not that I mightn't be able to do the same, but when there's a long line of men behind you, it's not easy to do all the sums. I sure as hell can't, and they won't have any arguments after I've signed.'

'Fine so,' Luke said.

'I'd also like you to come with me every Saturday when I go to the office for payment. Same thing, make sure the figures are correct before I sign for them.'

Mick had come in.

'*Arra* sure what good would that do?' he said. 'All your reckonings might be correct, but if they're giving you short measure at the weigh station, it doesn't mean a damned thing.'

'Short measure!' Luke exclaimed.

Farrelly waved his hand.

'It's what they're all on about all the time, Luke. There might be short measure, or there might not, it's just they won't allow us to see it, and we've no way of knowing.'

'It's wrong,' Mick said, 'and don't you believe otherwise, Luke.'

'There's plenty of time for worrying about that,' Farrelly said, irritably. 'In the meantime, we've got to get you and Winnie into a house. I wanted to let you know that I spoke to Cantwell about it. Ned Moran and his wife, they've an Operator house, not too far from here. A hundred yards or so. He's a Mayo-man, mind you, Ballina born and reared.'

*

233

A card game had begun. 'I'd best go and see Winnie,' Luke said.

'*Arra*, you'll see her soon enough,' Mikey said. 'Sure isn't the dancing on tonight? And what chance do you have of talking to your comrades? There'll be little enough when you have a *tigín* of your own.'

Luke sat and played pontoon. He made nine and a half cents on the game.

That evening, *Seán Óg* handed him two buckets. '*You'll need to be well washed tonight,*' he said. He led him to a hand pump at the rear of the house. Around the pumps, the ground was thick with ice. Gritty coal dust had been stamped into it.

All four buckets were filled and taken up the stairs to another room with three zinc baths. There was a queue of men at each.

'*Now, the deal is this,*' *Seán Óg* said. '*I'll scrub you down, then you do me. You go first.*'

They reached the top of a queue. Luke sat in and got half a bucket of cold water poured over him.

'*Christ, that's freezing.*'

'*Arra, would you stop complaining. Hold on till I scrub you.*'

'*That's some scrubbing brush.*'

'*Still complaining? We have to get half your skin off to make you half decent.*'

After Luke had dried down, he repeated the procedure with *Seán Óg*.

He took his good clothes out of the chest. As they walked down past the Women's House, two girls came out.

'Is there a Winnie Ryan still there?' Jack shouted.

'There is.'

'Would you be a good girl now, and tell her that her husband is waiting for to go dancing.'

At length, Winnie appeared.

'You're lucky seeing me,' she said. 'I'd to bribe one of the girls to take care of Liam.'

They arrived at the bar where there was a loud sound of conversation, and a thick cloud of pipe smoke. Luke bought a beer and a gin, and brought Winnie to join the gang.

'So how are you getting on?' he asked her.

'Not so bad,' she said. Earning a bit for a change.'

'Earning?'

'Sewing and stitching all day, making shirts. That's what we're doing when I'm not cooking. Only making a dime a shirt, same as in Jersey, but sure it's something to add to what you're earning.'

'Which isn't very much,' Luke said. He wanted to protest at Winnie stitching again, but he was already concerned about how much he could send back to Carrigard. And if the blight had hit again, what then? Maybe Winnie was right. Every dime would be needed.

A fiddle started to play.

'What's this?'

'A reel,' Winnie said. 'And you should know.'

Within seconds, tables had been cleared back, and the centre of the room was taken up with dancers.

'Come on you *amadán*,' Winnie said, taking Luke's hand. 'Let's dance.'

'But sure you know I can't...'

'Let's be having none of your excuses.'

A few minutes later the music stopped. Luke was sweating.

'Not used to this, are you,' Winnie said.

'Not used to the heat anyhow.'

Suddenly the hall went quiet. A passage cleared as a man strode across the room and came to Farrelly. He threw a page on the table.

'I want to know who the man was that sent me this.'

Luke looked at it. It was no more than a rough drawing of a coffin, with a cross on top. Under the cross, 'Dai Lloyd' was written in rough drawn letters.

Farrelly picked it up.

'Damned if I know,' he said, 'but I can tell you one thing, it surely wasn't one of our men.'

'Well, whoever it was, will pay the price. We'll not have death threats around here.'

He stalked out of the room.

Luke glanced over to Mick, who looked away.

'Who was that?' Luke asked.

That's Lloyd,' Farrelly replied. 'He's the Boss at the Number One Breaker. Rough bastard.'

'Why would he come over to us?'

'Suspects Molly activities around here. Mistaken, of course, but we can't convince him. He reckons we're part of the gang, or at least know who they are, even if we didn't do it ourselves.'

They were laughing as they made their way home that evening. Winnie was flushed from the dancing and excitement. Luke, Jack and Farrelly walked her back to the Women's House.

'You're lucky getting babysitting so easy,' Jack said.

'Edna? Sure she has no interest in dancing. A grand girl I'd say though.'

Luke was happy to see Winnie enjoying the night so much. Tough work was one thing, but Saturday nights might make it all worthwhile.

He embraced her. 'See you tomorrow, *a ghrá*.

Farrelly shook her hand gravely. 'And don't be ruining your eyes with all that sewing and stitching,' he said. 'It's not worth it for what they pay you.'

As they returned to the Miner's House, a voice came from behind.

'Luke Ryan?'

'What of it?' He was instantly on his guard.

'Remember Croghancoe?'

'Croghancoe?'

'You'd better watch your back.'

Luke swung around and grabbed the man by the lapels.

'I'll not have that kind of threat from anyone. Who are you?'

'A Mayo man, and before you think it, there's no point in hitting me, it'll only make it worse for yourself. There's many more from where I came from.'

Farrelly picked up a stick.

'Enough of that. We'll have no threats here.'

Luke released the man, and he was gone.

He was silent as they returned to the House. Croghancoe? He remembered all the starving people, working on road-building in the snow, driven to it by a Poor Law that could never understand human suffering. And he had been the supervisor.

Next morning, Luke and Winnie accompanied the rest of the gang to Mass.

'I wasn't expecting to be going to Mass in a place like this,' Luke said.

'Wait till you see,' Farrelly said.

They arrived.

'But it's only got half a roof,' Winnie said.

'Don't expect miracles,' Farrelly said, 'Lackan never had a Catholic Church before. It's taken us long enough to get this far, but don't be worrying now, we'll finish it out in the next few months, you wait and see. Whatever about your husband's doubts, this is a Catholic Church, consecrated and all, by the Bishop no less, only six weeks ago.'

Luke was surprised to see a large congregation, hundreds he guessed. The women were crowded at the front where the roof had already been completed over the altar. The men stood at the back, out in the open, as Mass began.

Afterwards, Luke and Winnie walked along the banks of the Lackawanna.

'I'd never have believed that,' Winnie said.

'You've got to remember one thing, my pet,' Luke said, 'this is a new country. It's not like Kilduff and the rest with churches standing for hundreds of years.'

Yes, he was thinking. The church in Kilduff after the '39 storm. It had no roof on it then either. The Ryans had heard Mass in a roofless church before.

'What was that business with Farrelly and that Welsh fellow last night?' Winnie asked.

'Couldn't you guess? The Molly Maguires.'

'But sure they're in Mayo.'

'And everywhere else. New York for sure. Lackan too. Don't let it surprise you. They're everywhere Irishmen are.'

That evening, Luke called down to the Women's House and, following Farrelly's directions, took Winnie, Liam and their baggage to the Moran house. As Farrelly had promised, they were welcoming. The rooms were clean, the floors well-scrubbed, though still showing the grey residue of coal dust. The once white lace curtains were grey too.

Mrs. Moran showed them to a room. 'Small enough, I know,' she said, 'but the Operator will only be taking a dollar seventy-five a week, I understand.'

'That's right,' Luke said. 'High enough a price too.'

'Nothing much we can do about it. We're paying two dollars fifty, though as you'll see, our room is larger, and we all share the kitchen.'

She turned to Winnie. 'Now call me Ellen. The cooking we'll have to share. Scrubbing the floors and washing the dust out of the clothes and the curtains too. A woman's work is never done. But don't worry, girl, we'll work it all out between us.'

Chapter 18

Jeffersonian Republican, Pennsylvania. February 1849:
The total amount of coal sent to market from Pennsylvania, during the last season, was 3,069,473 tons, being an increase of 93,880 tons over the amount exported the year before. This mass of coal, at $4 per ton, produced the sum of $12,277,892. Who does not perceive at half a glance that there is infinitely more wealth in the coal fields of this state, than there is in the gold mines of California?

Ellen Moran and Winnie got on well together, sharing shopping, cooking, scrubbing and child minding. Winnie had soon gotten used to the scrip system, and the necessity of shopping at the truck store. Still, the Morans resented the system as much as they did.

'The system is designed to screw us,' Ned Moran told them. 'Scrip and truck, they'll get you every way.'

'I'd heard it was worse before,' Luke said.

'It was,' Ned replied, 'and not so long back either.'

'But the Molly Maguires...?'

Ned looked uncomfortable.

'You shouldn't mention their name here. There's a lot of bitterness.'

'But wasn't it them that forced them to drop the scrip to half?'

'Might well have been, Luke, but there's no one can prove it either way. But if ever we want to get rid of the accursed scrip, it's not the Mollys we should be using.'

'Who then?'

'The Union.'

'The Union?'

Ned laughed. 'No Luke, not the Poor Law Union. The Trades Union.'

'A Trades Union? I don't know about that. Not around here, anyways.'

'Not many do. The Bates Union, they call it. John Bates, he started a Union down in St. Clair. An English fellow, but never mind that. Some kind of Chartist, I understand.'

'A Chartist! Weren't they the fellows that had a revolution in England? Didn't go far, from all accounts.'

'What would you expect? Sure the English aren't into revolutions at all.'

'They're not,' Luke said. 'Not their line of country.'

'Wait till you hear Bates, though. He'll tell you what a revolution is. They're holding a meeting in Pottsville, Wednesday next, and I'm going. A dozen of the other lads too. Will you come?'

Luke was thinking quickly, but could not decide.

'I don't know,' he said. 'I'm not sure I could get away on a Wednesday.'

'It's our only chance of getting rid of scrip, Luke. Push up the tonnage rates too. We have to organise. It's the only way forward.'

Luke found it hard to sleep that night.

A Trades Union? What would Winnie think of that? Or Farrelly, for that matter.

Next morning, he discussed it with Farrelly. They both put down their picks and lay on the hard anthracite.

'Yes, I'd heard of it,' Farrelly said. 'Didn't want mentioning any of it to you though. We'd need a day off to get down to Pottsville, and Cantwell, sure as hell, wouldn't like that. You say there's others are going?'

'There are.'

'Perhaps they're in a stronger position. It'd be risky for us though. I'll tell you what we'll do, Luke. You go on down with Moran, the rest of us will work an hour longer, make up for your tonnage, and Cantwell won't see you're missing.'

'Fair enough,' Luke said.

They left Lackan in the middle of the night. Winnie and Ellen had made up sandwiches – brown bread and butter with ham.

They found the coach. It was crowded.

'*Mayo men!*' one of the other men exclaimed as they tried to squeeze in.

'*Kilduff and Ballina. And yourselves?*'

'*Belmullet.*'

'*Belmullet!*' Ned exclaimed. '*Ye had a hard time there.*'

'*Hard enough.*'

'*Ye'll travel top side so?*'

'*Topside!*' Luke exclaimed.

'*Why not?*'

'*We'll have none of that now,*' one of the others said. '*We can share the top. And sure if ye wrap up well enough, you won't feel the cold. Come on Séamus. Yourself and Peadar for the first stage.*'

After the first halt, Luke and Ned went topside. It was well past dawn when they arrived in Pottsville. Already, a large crowd had gathered. Luke was astonished.

'There's fellows from all over,' Ned told him. 'Not so many from Lackan, it's a fair distance, as you can see. Pottsville, Cass, Port Carbon, St. Clair, Norwegian Township, Minersville, they're the ones you'll find. Some down from Schuylkill too, it's not so far as Lackan.'

'I never heard of the most of them.'

'Why would you? You'll know all about them when you're a few years here.'

The crowd had gathered in front of a platform. Six men came out and sat behind a table on the platform. All were dressed in thick coats and gloves.

It was still cold. Luke stamped his boots on the ground and blew on his fingers.

'By Christ, this had better be good.'

He stood with the other men, munching their sandwiches.

'And thank God for this,' Ned said. 'I was getting hungry.'

A St. Clair miner was introducing the main speaker.

'I wish to God he'd hurry up,' Ned said.

At length, he sat, and John Bates stood. There was a roar from the gathered miners.

For some time, he spoke of Chartism, and the failure of the Charter revolution in England. Then the Ballingarry Rebellion in Ireland. Then he was talking of the main Union demands. Scrip to be abolished. There was a roar from the crowd.

'We'll be lucky if he'll get that,' Ned whispered to him.

'Not a hope in hell, I'd say,' Luke answered.

The next demand was higher wages and tonnage rates. Another roar of approval.

'Not a hope of that, neither,' Ned said. 'The Operators, they're already complaining about the low price of coal, and how they're going to have to reduce wages. There's no chance of them being raised.'

And then – a demand for lien. That too was approved.

'What in hell is that?' Luke asked.

'Damned if I know,' Ned answered. 'All I know is that we're all lean enough. I wouldn't be demanding any more of it though.'

Bates was still speaking.

'And how do we achieve all these demands, my friends? There is only one way. We must force the Operators to give us what is ours by right. They don't understand anything else. We've seen all the failures of the revolutions and rebellions in England and Ireland. That is not the way to go. There is only one way to make these fools listen. We must organise. Organise and create a Union that is stronger than the Operators. That is the only way to make them understand. But believe me, we have already come a long way. You men are the future of the anthracite business. Here today, we will create a Union, and the Operators will tremble in their boots. Higher wages, lien, an end to scrip, we will achieve them all.'

He paused.

'Who here will join our Union?'

Hundreds of hands were raised.

'We might as well,' Ned said, raising his hand. Luke did the same.

'Thank you, thank you, my friends,' Bates said. 'Now we have power. Union power. And now we will use it. How do we use it you might ask? We use the most powerful sword in our armoury. The Strike. Bring the mine owners to their knees. All those in favour…?'

Again, many hands were raised, and slowly everyone followed, Luke and Ned included.

'I don't know about this,' Ned said.

'You voted for it,' Luke observed.

'So did you. And one way or another, we can't un-vote now.'

'We can't,' Luke said. 'It's like he says, though. We'll break the Operators.'

Bates was speaking again.

'And now, my friends, one final thing. The Union must be financed. It must pay its way, and it must provide a strike fund. Every one of us will pay ten cents per week and provide for those in hardship. Starting now.'

'Damn it, we'll all be in hardship,' Ned said.

'I know,' Luke said.

As they streamed out of the field, each dropped a dime into the buckets provided.

They made their way to the coaches.

'*What sort of fools are we?*' Ned asked on the journey back.

'*I wouldn't worry about it,*' one of the other men said. '*The Operators will give in soon enough. You just wait and see.*'

'*I wish I could believe that,*' said Luke.

When they returned to the house, Luke and Ned quickly explained the outcome of the meeting. Winnie turned pale.

Over dinner Ellen asked the occasional question, Ned replying as best he could, then they lapsed into silence. After the dishes were washed, they retired to the bedroom. Luke was grateful. He was desperately tired from the travel.

Winnie was in tears. 'For God's sake, Luke, we've no money.'

'Little enough, my pet, but sure we'll survive a week yet.'

'And your wages this week so far. Will they be paid?'

'Not a chance. But at least we won't have to pay the rent out of them neither.'

'We'll starve.'

'I doubt it will come to that. It can't last long. Not if everyone is like us, and I doubt there's many with money for food. No, the men will back down, and do it soon enough.'

'Then what is it all about?' she asked.

'God only knows,' he said.

He could not sleep that night, as his thoughts raced around and around, trying to work out a future. He thought of the hundreds of men voting for strike. Did they all have money he didn't know about? Very few, he reckoned. Were they such fools that they had just gone along with the passions of the moment? Very likely. How many now were facing a tongue-lashing from their wives for bringing their families to the edge of starvation?

Starvation, he thought. They had left Ireland to get away from it. So had the most of those other fools. And now they were facing a famine of their own making. And the night of the dance. The sketch of the coffin. They were desperate men who would do desperate things. Down in the mine, he knew why. Terror? Was that an answer? He remembered what Costello had said about all the gangs of New York, the Molly Maguires too. Violent men. Violence against the Operators. Not like a strike, violence against themselves too, and only brought on by themselves. No answer either way.

But the Hibernians. They were different.

Next day, as the strike began, he opened his trunk and ruffled through until he found the address from Costello.

'What are you doing Luke?' Winnie asked.

'I'm going to see the Hibernians tonight.'

'The Hibernians?'

'John Costello, he said I should join as soon as I got to Lackan, so I'm going to join.'

'What good will that do?'

'Self-help. Isn't that what the Hibernians are all about? Sure you know it yourself from all the food deliveries you've done in New York.'

'But what use would that be here? We're a long way from New York. And the Lackan Hibernians, sure the most of them will be on strike.'

'I don't know. But I've got to find out.'

They spent an idle day, sitting around the table with the Morans, mostly silent. That evening, Luke left the house. Ned did not come. He asked his way to the address Costello had given him. It was in a bar in a part of Lackan he did not know. It was not crowded. A barman came to him.

'I'm looking for Eddie McDonagh,' Luke said.

'Who wants him?'

'Luke Ryan is the name. John Costello from New York, he sent me.'

'Hold on here a moment.'

Within minutes, he was sitting in the snug off the back of the bar.

'Luke Ryan, is it?' a man said.

'It is.'

The man put his hand out, 'Eddie McDonagh,' he said. 'And these gentlemen here, Tim Heneghan and Gus Madden. Galway men all. You're most welcome. You're Catholic, are you?'

'I am,' Luke answered.

'And Irish too, by the sound of it.'

'Mayo.'

'You've pledged your loyalty?'

'I have.'

A beer was placed in front of him.

'So how's Costello doing these days?'

'Well, I'd say. As you know, his bar is in Five Points, and God knows, that's one of the roughest places on God's earth. Still, he runs a good business and keeps up with his faith. His bar is close to St. James' Church, right where the Hibernians were founded, I understand. But he's had his own tragedy too, lately.'

'How's that?' Gus asked.

'Through his brother. That was the way I got to know John in the first place. I met *Conaire* on the crossing from Liverpool to Quebec, and we worked in Quebec together, and then out to the forests for the winter. They split us up, put us working in different timber patches, and after the winter, he had disappeared. He'd told me his brother had a bar in Five Points, so I was able to trace John quick enough when I got to New York. But he'd heard nothing about *Conaire* either, and still hasn't. We're sure he would've had someone write a letter for him by now, if he was still alive. One way or another though, it was me who found John Costello while his brother never did. And I reckon *Conaire* is dead.'

'How are you finding it here, Luke?' Eddie asked.

'Damned tough, I'd say, and getting tougher. I'm well used to hard work, breaking stones, shovelling, and even working up in the forests, but I'll tell you, nothing prepared me for this. I can swing a pick right enough, but I never thought I'd have to do it lying down. And now, the strike.'

Ah, yes,' Tim Heneghan said. 'Bates and his damned strike.'

'Yes,' Luke said. 'I'd thought the hell of the mines was bad enough, but I never thought I'd regret not having to do it at all.'

'Don't we know it,' Eddie said. 'This fellow Bates, he's an idiot.'

'An English idiot,' Gus Madden added.

'It doesn't matter a damn where he's from,' Eddie said. 'He's a fool to call a strike before the Union even has a strike fund.'

'I know,' Luke said. 'They're looking for ten cents a week subscription – five dollars a year – to run the Union. They never told us how much running the Union would cost, nor how much would be left for a strike fund. The only thing I'm certain of is that there's damned little in the fund right now, and if this strike goes on, there'll be starvation in all the mining towns.'

'Bates reckons he doesn't need one,' Tim said. 'He's putting it all back on us. The Welsh will have their own arrangements, but he's reckoning the Irish can live off the Hibernians. He's got a gun to our heads, Luke. Most of the Irish are members already, and they've been paying their dues to the Order for long enough. No, Bates knows the Order is going to have to pay; he knows we've no choice in the matter.'

'But how? Who will pay?'

'We will. All the other branches here. You know how we support our own.'

'I do,' Luke said. 'I've done it myself – food deliveries, and the like in New York. But can we do it here? Food deliveries in Lackan? Christ, it's as bad as Soup Kitchens in Mayo.'

'There's only one problem,' Gus said. 'We've got damned little money.'

'And still the Union wants its dues,' Tim said.

'Little enough dues they'll get during the strike,' Gus said. 'But it's not that that worries me. If Bates is only interested in bringing the money in, and has no interest in having enough to pay anything out, what kind of man is he? Has he no sense of money at all? Does it mean nothing to him?'

'Oh, I think it means something right enough,' Eddie said. 'I don't know if what you said about English men is true, they're not all the same. But this fellow Bates, I wouldn't trust him as far as I'd throw him. Organising a Union is one thing. We've all got to hang together, we all know that. But with this Bates, we'll all hang separately, and devil a damn he'll give about it. We need money for them back home. We need money for ourselves and our children. How long, in the name of God, do you think this damned strike will last?'

'I know one thing,' Gus said. 'The owners here are tough bastards. They're not going to give in. They'll never give in. This strike will go on until they've starved every one of us into surrender.'

He walked back to the Morans' house, deeply depressed. He had brought Winnie and the baby from one famine straight into another.

As he walked up the street, he was surprised to hear singing. When he got to Morans', he saw three candles burning in the window. Puzzled, he walked in. Winnie threw her arms around him.

244

'Isn't it wonderful, Luke?'

'Wonderful! What?'

'It's over. It's all over. And we won.'

'We won?'

Ned had poured out a whiskey, and handed it to him. He raised his own.

'Here's to the Union.'

Luke sat down, puzzled. 'But...we didn't give in?'

'Give in! Not us. It was the Operators. They were the ones that gave in.'

Luke sipped at the harsh spirit. Ellen offered him water, but he brushed it away.

'The Operators gave in? After one day. I don't believe that.'

'It's true right enough,' Ned said. 'We're to have no more scrip. It's gone. No question of that. They're raising our tonnage payments by a fifth.'

'A fifth!'

'And they've caved in on the question of lien too.'

Luke remembered his puzzlement at this expression on the field in Pottsville. 'Now would be a good time to explain that one to me, Ned.'

Ned refilled Luke's whiskey.

'It's very simple, Luke. It means that if an Operator goes bankrupt, the miners have first claim. We get paid ahead of any of the suppliers, or the banks for that matter. One way or the other, they're pushing it through the Assembly in Harrisburg. It's going to be State law.'

Luke shook his head. 'I can't believe this. I've never believed in miracles.'

'Well, you've got one now. And there's more too.'

'But Bates asked for nothing more.'

'They gave it anyhow. The weigh stations. The Union demanded that a Union member should be present all the time, and check for short measure. They even agreed to that. Can you imagine it?'

He was working with Mick and Jack at the coalface.

'Shows you the strength of Union power,' Mick said. 'Didn't I tell you so?'

'I don't remember that you said anything much about it, at all,' Luke said.

'Will you stop arguing the pair of you,' Jack said. 'It doesn't matter which or whether, they gave in and we got all our demands. And who would ever have expected that?'

Luke hacked angrily at the anthracite. Then he held a spike, as Jack hammered it home. The anthracite cracked, and fell out. Luke heaved the coal out.

'I don't know. There's something too easy about this. I'll tell you, in all the years on the railways, I've never seen anything like this.'

'Perhaps not,' Mick said, 'and I'll tell you why. They had their revolution, but the government faced them down. The English – they had the power. They had an army.'

'And what are you saying?' Luke asked. 'The Operators gave in because they didn't have an army?'

'You've a point there,' Jack said. 'I wonder what would happen if they did have an army.'

'Let's not worry about that,' Mick said. 'They've no army, and we don't have to worry about things that will never happen.'

'And one thing that might,' Luke said, 'look at that crack in the roof.'

'Christ! It's getting wider. Get back.'

They moved back, and watched. Sometime later, the roof collapsed.

'That was nasty enough,' Jack said.

'And how many tons do you think were in it?' Luke said. 'None of it coal, neither. We'll have to clear all that out of here, and no payment on any of it.'

'There's our fifth for the week gone,' Jack said.

'*Arra*, no,' Mick said. 'It's little enough. Let's get at it.'

As they smashed the grey rock, and loaded it into the low wagon, Luke was thinking of other things. Whatever else the Operators had given in on; they still were not supplying enough props to support the roof of the drift. Much of what they got was rotten too. Even so, many of the miners resented having to carry the timber down and drive it into position, seeing it as wasted time. The only time that mattered was time in mining anthracite, and building up the tonnage.

And what of black lung?

They pushed the wagon into the tunnel. Jack untied the mule, as Mick tied it between the shafts of the wagon. Luke slapped the mule, and led it out. Why worry? Black lung could wait till later.

One day, Luke travelled into Scranton. Winnie came with him, carrying Liam in her arms. She looked at the shops, but bought nothing. Luke was bored, and arranged to meet her at a bar he had spotted.

While she was shopping, he went to the Chemical Bank and arranged a money order for Carrigard. Then he walked to the bar, wrote a letter to Carrigard and waited for Winnie.

When she arrived, she read through the letter.

'You make Lackan sound a lot better than it is,' she said.

'Why not? Sure there's no need to be worrying them. There's not much they can do about Lackan. We're on our own over here.'

'We are.'

'And I told them to send a pound up to your mother while they're at it.'

'She'll need it too. From all we hear, the famine is getting worse. And at least we can half afford it now.'

The Operators had kept their word. Higher wages certainly.

'And scrip abolished,' Ned said one night. 'Whoever would have believed it?'

'There's still the truck shop,' Luke said. 'Not that we have to buy there, but the supervisors sure as hell won't like it if we don't.'

'*Arra*, what can they say?' Ned asked. 'Sure they've no power no more.'

Every Saturday, the Union man was waiting at the payment desk. Dutifully, everyone dropped their dime into the bucket.

One Saturday afternoon, Farrelly approached Luke.

'Luke, we've just been having discussions with Stan Cantwell. We need a Union man to check the weigh station as agreed with the Operator. Seeing as it's mostly Mayo men in this drift, we thought it best to put your name forward. There's so much sums required on the weigh station, we'll need someone who understands figures. Would you do it?'

'I haven't thought about it,' Luke said. 'How long would it take?'

'It's a full-time job. Sure there's always cartloads coming in and going out.'

Farrelly introduced Luke to Cantwell, who offered him six dollars a week. A reasonable wage, but he quickly realised it was a safer job, carrying far less chance of black lung. He accepted at once.

Winnie was delighted. 'Six dollars, it's not bad. And at least you won't be coughing your lungs out. We'll have you around a few years longer.'

'*Arra,* hell, why would you want a fellow like me?'

Winnie slapped him playfully on the ear.

'Sure we've got to have a father to bring up the son. And anyway, you've no idea how much I worry about you every day. All of us women, always waiting for the alarm siren. You might not know it, but we're edgy all day until we see the light of your lamp coming home.'

Luke thought it better not to mention the roof collapse. No point in alarming Winnie further.

Sometime later, he attended his second meeting of the Ancient Order of Hibernians. On this occasion, Ned accompanied him. Luke spotted Eddie, Tim and Gus at a table in the corner. He joined them and introduced Moran.

The conversation was of Ireland, and famine.

'It's terrible, by all accounts,' Eddie said. 'You know well yourself, it was a full-blown failure last year. The starvation is going to get worse and worse, until at least the first crop comes in, and that's months away. And what if it fails?'

'Oh God, don't say that,' Luke said.

'There's more too. The fever is back with a vengeance. Cholera too, I'd say. I don't think the country has a chance.'

'So what can we do?' Luke asked.

'Do what every good Catholic Irishman does, earn as much as we can and send as much home as possible. Then go on our knees and pray that it'll be a good harvest.'

'Much good prayer will do,' Gus said.

'We'll have no blasphemy out of you,' Eddie said, 'Still, if it does fail, there'll be an almighty famine. We'll have to prepare for a huge flight out of the country. Food, jobs, whatever we can do. Before that we'd have to keep sending money back across to encourage them to buy the tickets to come out.'

'Do you really think Ireland is finished?' Luke asked.

'God only knows. Like I said – we can only pray for a good harvest.'

They were home late that night. Winnie was sitting at the table with Ellen Moran.

'I thought you'd have gone to bed by now, *alanna*,' he said.

He saw she was crying. 'My God, what's wrong? Is it Liam?'

Winnie shook her head, gulping.

'Liam is grand. It's the Operators that are at fault. There's posters all over.'

'Posters! But what…?'

'It's a lockout.'

'A lockout!'

'Yes,' she said. 'They've locked ye all out, and the mines are shut.'

Chapter 19

London Evening Standard. February 1849:

Imperial Parliament, London. Sir Charles Wood: He would also take this opportunity of doing justice to a nobleman, whose name had on former occasions been mentioned in this house with some reproach – he meant the Earl of Lucan – who had since devoted himself with extraordinary success to the improvement of his estates and the neighbourhood around him, had reduced his establishment, employed a large number of labourers, obtained loans of money from the government, removed a portion of his people to America, and effected very great improvements in that part of the county, the Castlebar Union, in which he now resides. The Chancellor of the Exchequer defends Lord Lucan's 'improvements' in County Mayo.

A noise woke him. Pat stared at the blackened straw ceiling of a hut. He was desperately tired. He closed his eyes again and fell asleep.

He was half woken by a savoury aroma.

'*Awake, are you?*'

He tried to waken, still remembering the vanishing dream of a beautiful woman.

'*'Tis time you ate,*' said a woman's voice.

At last, he opened his eyes.

'*That you should open your mouth too.*'

He did as he was told, and sipped as she spooned him a thin soup of cabbage. Herbs too?

She was very old. A hundred years, Pat reckoned in his confusion. She wore a faded red skirt. Covering her head was a black shawl tied underneath her chin. Even so, her hair was white, and her cheeks were wrinkled and sunken. The whites of her eyes had turned to yellow.

The rough walls of the shed were built of turf. One side had been dug away from the bog, the others built up with sods. Some rough branches held the straw roof in position. It might have been high enough for the old woman, but he knew he could not stand in the cabin.

'*They gave you a good belting.*'

Slowly, the memory of the attack came back.

'*They did,*' he said. '*There were four of them. Sure what chance did I have?*'

He was remembering where he had been, and the reason for his being there.

'*Where's my pack?*' he asked in alarm.

'*There was no pack with you when I found you.*'

'*Oh God…*'

'*I found this down the road though. Perhaps it's yours?*'

She handed him the notebook. He grabbed it, and clasped it to his chest.

'*Thank God for that. You gave me a terrible fright there; I can tell you.*'

'*It must be of great value to you.*'

'*It is.*'

'*'Tis of none to me. The writing is beyond me.*'

'*And there was nothing else?*'

'*Nothing.*'

She spooned more soup for him. He gulped it down.

'*How did you get me here?*'

'*I borrowed a donkey.*'

'*It must have been hard for you?*'

'*Indeed. You're a good weight. Not starving I would say.*'

'*Not before that. I am now though. How long was I in dreaming?*'

'*All through the night, and more. You were out cold when we found you, but you woke a while before the donkey's owner left. Then you slept again. Do you not recall?*'

'*I don't.*'

'*You took a sip of poitín with us, before you slept.*'

He shook his head in bewilderment. Was he losing his memory too?

'*But where…where am I?*'

'*Cruachán.*'

'*Cruachán! In Achill?*' How had he gotten there?

'*No. The other Cruachán. More convenient to the town of Bangor.*'

She ladled him more soup.

'*So where are you from, young man?*'

'*I'm from a place called Carrigard, near Kilduff. 'Tis over in the east of the County.*'

'*You're a long way from home so.*'

'*I am.*'

'*So why are you travelling here?*'

'*I've been sent by the people in Castlebar to see just how bad the hunger*' and fever is in this part of the County. 'Tis long I've been travelling.'

'Yes. I can see it from your tiredness.'

More soup.

'And yourself,' he asked. 'Are you from these lands?'

'Close enough. I came from Dún Flidhais.'

'Yes. I've heard of it.'

'Not many have,' she said. 'Have you been there?'

'I don't know. The knock on the head has knocked my remembering. Where is it?'

'You know Ráth Muireagáin, do you?'

Ráth Muireagáin, he thought. Rathmorgan, surely?

'I do,' he said. 'Just by Carrowmore Lake.'

'Indeed. 'Tis no great distance.'

More soup.

'So you left when you married, did you?' he asked.

She shook her head.

'I left it the time my husband was murdered. Up by Dún Chiortáin, it was. He was much into cattle rustling, so his death was no surprise. But his family thought otherwise. They held my lover might have murdered him, though they had no proof. They were angry with me, so I had to leave that place.'

He noticed she had not denied her lover might have been responsible for the murder. Nor had she denied that she had lovers.

Was it all a silly story? Nothing but silliness. Forget it all. And yet?

He still had vague memories of a dream. This old woman had once had a lover. More than one? Who knows? There was something alluring about her. Her voice perhaps.

'A hard story,' he said.

'It was. And not so easy since. It's many terrible things I've seen in my life.'

'Famine and fever?'

'Countless times. The young people, they had forgotten that. When I was only an infant, there was starvation in Mayo. When I first came here, there was famine and fever too. Every year since – the hunger. Starving people waiting for the harvest. Isn't that the way of it?'

'It is,' Pat said. 'But what of now? The last few years?'

'A terrible time. The people here starved.'

'Tell me about it.'

'What do you want to know?'

'All about the hunger and fever around Mayo. The men in Castlebar, they want to know everything that's happening, how bad it is in every part of the County.'

'Do they not know?'

'Not enough. They never have enough food nor enough hospitals for the sick. And never enough money to pay for either. Always they receive letters saying how bad things are, but they all make it worse in the telling. So they send me around the County to find the truth of it.'

'Can't they go themselves?'

Yes, why can't they? To hell with it, who cares?

'Perhaps they could,' he said, 'but they pay me for the travelling, and that pays for food for my family.'

'Yes,' she said, 'I can understand that. Still, if you travel everywhere, and if they send food on your word, then you have a mighty power.'

'Perhaps I have, but it's the truth of it I want. What has happened here around Cruachán, will you tell me?'

'I will.'

She began to talk. Pat held his notebook on his knee, but his pencil was gone, and he wrote nothing. He listened, trying to commit it to memory.

More description of starvation around *Cruachán*. More and more testimony of famine and fever in Mayo. On and on, village by village, road by road, house by house. The horror was unrelenting. From time to time, he held his hand to stop her, to check what she was saying, and remember it all.

'You've a good memory,' he said after some time.

'Sure I'm searching the depths of it for you,' she said.

He smiled. Then she spoke more. When she finally paused for breath, he held up his hand.

'And you? How did you live?'

'I had little fear of fever. When a person lives alone, they have no need to fear fever from other men and women. Fever is the big killer; they all forget that.'

'And for food?'

'It's little enough I need with the thinness of me. Turnip. Cabbage. And there are many herbs and mushrooms in the woods and all around. People are so used to eating potatoes and cabbage, they forget what else they can eat. The foods they see every day, the foods their forefathers lived on.'

Should he believe that?

Next morning, he had to leave. He was already late.

"'Tis sorry I am to see you go, young man.'

'And me to leave you,' he said.

They stood outside. Without warning, she drew him towards her and kissed him on the cheek.

'Go on now,' she said. 'Go back to your life, and forget that you ever met a half-starved, old beauty like me.'

He left, walking fast. As he went to go around a bank of turf, he looked

252

back. She was still at the door. He waved, but she did not.

He walked for some time. At length, he found a blackthorn tree, where he sat and considered all she had told him. It was essential to memorise it all for his report in Castlebar.

Memorise it? He had never asked her name, nor had she asked his. Did it matter? Perhaps not, but how could he have forgotten?

No pack. And no food. How many days walking was it back to Westport?

He went on, again and again remembering what the old woman had told him. Blight, villages, deaths. He did not stop walking until he reached Srahnamanragh Bridge. It was raining heavily. He slept under the bridge, just above the river. He was wet, hungry and cold.

Another hard day's walking brought him to Newport where he found a hayshed on the outskirts of the town. He hardly slept that night with the hunger. He knew, from all he had heard as a child, that the first two or three days were the worst. After that, the sense of hunger would fade as the body accustomed itself to not expecting food.

By dawn the next day, he had passed through Newport, and started out the Westport road. The rain had stopped, but it had turned cold, glazed ice covering the puddles. On the roadside, the frosty grass crunched under his boots. He was feeling weak, weaker than he had ever felt before. By the time the sun was high in the sky, he saw Westport in the distance. He struggled on.

The Lieutenant at the workhouse recognised him at once, and admitted him. He made his way to the administration block.

'Pat!' Sarah exclaimed. 'Would you look at the state of you?'

The Clerk came over.

'What in the name of God happened to you?'

'I was attacked.'

'Oh no,' Sarah exclaimed.

'It's all right, *a ghrá*. Sure I'm alive, aren't I?'

'Come on, I'll clean you up. Have you eaten?'

'Not for a few days.'

'Oh Pat...'

''Tis fine,' he said. 'Sure Castlebar want me to understand what's happening in County Mayo. A little hunger gives a man a great understanding.'

Sarah took him to the kitchen in the administration building. She spoke to the cook, then she sat Pat down, while she stood alongside the cook, overseeing everything.

'Here you are,' she said, a few minutes later. 'Indian corn, it's the best we could manage, but we snuck you in a few rashers.'

Pat wolfed it down, saying nothing as he ate. He began to feel a little ill, and realised he was eating too fast. He put the knife and fork down.

'So what happened to you?' Sarah asked him.

'Four lads jumped me, just outside of Bangor. Gave me a hell of a belt on the head. Knocked me out cold. They took everything. I was lucky they didn't take my coat.'

She examined his head, feeling the bruising.

'Rough enough,' she said. 'And you lost all your food?'

'I did. But I kept my notes.'

'Your notes are all you worry about! In the name of God, Pat, they could have killed you.'

'*Arra* no. It takes a lot to kill a fellow like me.'

'But still, a belt like that on the head. What happened after?'

'An old woman found me, took me back to her *tigín*, and took care of me till I woke'.

'She must have been strong enough to drag the likes of you.'

'She borrowed a donkey. That was what she told me. Even so, she was an old woman. Very old. Living on her own and well off the road. But however she did it, she got me there and she fed me. Not much more than cabbage and herb soup mind you, but enough to strengthen me up, until I was fit to go.'

He ate again. At last he finished all on his plate.

'So what about you?' he asked. 'Any great news in Westport?'

'Oh, there's news alright. The fever is killing them in terrible numbers.'

Pat stood. 'Can I see?'

'See what?'

'The fever wards, what else.'

'Pat, are you mad?'

'No madder than your mother was; or you I'm sure. So don't tell me you stay out of the wards. And any way you look at it, Gaffney has asked me to report on the condition of the County, including the workhouses.'

'God, Pat, aren't you the right *amadán*. We have to work with them, you don't.

'I do. How can I make a report otherwise?'

She glanced out the window, as if to find an answer to that. Then she jumped up.

'Fine so. Come on. Let's go.'

She led him across the Stonebreakers' Yard towards a fever shed. Dozens of men, women and children were breaking stones.

'I hadn't seen this here before.'

'I never brought you this way before.'

She opened the door.

The stink was overpowering, the result of diarrhoea and vomiting. Several inmates were spreading straw on the floor on one side, while others swept up straw on the other which had already absorbed the disgusting fluids.

They walked on to the exit at the far end. They met another man coming towards them.

'This is Dr. Lowery. All the way up from Dublin.'

The two men shook hands.

'This is terrible,' said Pat.

'Oh, you get used to it.'

'I don't know that I ever could.'

'Dr. Lowery is the second doctor here,' Sarah said. 'Dr. Donovan died in the fever last year.'

'Yes' said Lowery. 'And I'm not even sure that there's much purpose to it anymore. Typhus or dysentery, there's not an awful lot any of us can do. The main use of the sheds is quarantine – we just separate them from everyone else, and hope the fever will stop its spread. And now there's cholera on the way. So what are you doing here?'

'The County wants me to do a report on the condition of the workhouses.'

'What kind of good would that do? All we need from them is money, but they don't have any.'

He returned to his patient.

They walked back across the Stonebreakers' Yard, the sound of smashing stone echoing through his head. When they were some distance away, she stopped.

'I don't know what to tell you, Pat. I don't know what my future here is ever since mother died. I'm not paid – I never was paid – but at least while mother was alive we could live on her salary. But now, all I have is board and lodgings, and I'm not even sure how long that might last.'

'Oh God. What will you do so?'

'I don't know, Pat. A lot of it depends on the Master and the new Matron. The last Master, he hated mother while she was here. He was happy enough when she died. You see, he wasn't an honest man, and she knew that. It was all to do with the weights he was using, giving out short measure, then selling grain back to the merchants on his own account.'

'But…did no one else know?'

'Oh, they knew well enough, but they kept their mouths shut, the whole damned lot of them. And it's not just that I knew about them, but they all knew that I knew. But there's worse than that. I reckon they're giving short measure again. I can't prove it, but I know from Knockanure how the system works. Not that father or mother would ever have done that, but they would here, I've no doubt about it, and I reckon they're afraid of me. So I'm lucky enough getting board and lodgings. But what next? What else might they do to me?'

Pat's mind was spinning.

'But – you were talking about some plan for the Australian colonies.'

'Yes,' she said, 'and lucky enough I was not to be part of that, I can tell you. But it was all under way by the time mother died. If she had died earlier, I'd be out in Port Phillip now. That's assuming they ever got to Port Phillip.'

'Do you think they mightn't?'

'It's just that we've had no news yet. You know yourself, it takes three months to get to Port Phillip and three months to get back. The Lady Kennaway, the ship the girls went on, it sailed out of Plymouth for Port Phillip. It had been wrecked once before, they say. And what kind of ship is that for a three or four months' journey out to the colonies? Did it sink on the way? God only knows. No, Lord Grey doesn't give a damn about Mayo's orphan girls. All they want is to people the colonies. And sure if the girls don't make it there, what matter. One way or another, the landlords in Mayo don't have to worry about them anymore, nor pay land rates to keep the workhouses running.'

Pat was stunned.

'You know,' he said, 'You'd told me of this, but I never thought it was this bad.'

'And it's not just that,' Sarah replied, 'they're planning more sailings for the colonies now. They're intending on clearing the orphan girls out of the other Workhouses – Ballinrobe, Castlebar and, worst of all, Westport. And do you know what they're looking for, Pat? The girls shouldn't be just orphans, they're more interested in young women. For making children, God damn it, convict children to people the colonies. And best of all, they want young women with writing and arithmetic, and I'm just what they're looking for. Their only problem is that I'm over eighteen, and too old for the scheme. But that won't stop them.'

'Why not?'

'No baptismal certificate. I was born somewhere in Cork or Tipperary, and I can't prove my age.'

'But you're well over eighteen. Three, four years at least.'

'I know, but it's my word against theirs. So if I'm still in Westport Workhouse over the next months, it's the colonies for me, and the life of a convict wife, somewhere in the back of beyond.'

Pat hugged her. For some time, neither said anything.

'I can see now, why your mother would have wanted you to marry someone else. Someone with a better position in life.'

'Yes,' Sarah said, 'some nice young fellow in the workhouse office, with a chance of making Master. Oh God! I don't think I could stand it. At least you're working for the County. But how long will that last?'

'I don't know,' Pat said, 'but it's not a lasting position, and no question of it being one. I'm here on Gaffney's request to help in a crisis. And when the crisis is over, I doubt I'll be working for any damned County.'

'I know,' she said, 'and then there's the question of your family, isn't there? If we married and went away – England or America – there'd be no one to run the farm. God knows, your father is old enough as it is.'

They entered the administration building and walked along the corridor towards the canteen. Suddenly, Pat grasped her arm.

'We're still talking about marriage. Isn't that it?'

'It is,' she said. She pulled herself up, and kissed him on the lips. 'It's marriage for sure, a serious matter, with the state of affairs today. You know, Pat, I always dreamt of love and romance, and while there'll be plenty of both between us, I didn't want it to be like this. There isn't much romance in a workhouse corridor, nor with a threat of transportation to the colonies hanging over me. No, we'll have to get everything sorted first. See where we'll be living, or what we'll be doing, the both of us. Westport, Castlebar or Carrigard? Ireland, England or America? Which is it to be Pat?'

'God only knows.'

Later, as he left Westport Workhouse, he saw men and women working in a field across the way. Curious, he walked across and realised at once he was watching the digging of another mass grave. Visions of the ever-lengthening trench in Knockanure Workhouse flooded back to him. Mrs. Cronin would not have been buried in a mass grave. Or would she?

But where was her grave?

He walked over. He looked away from it but could not avoid the stink of it, nor the sound of the rats.

'*What do you want?*' a woman asked.

'*I'm looking for a grave.*'

'*You won't find it. They're all buried together.*'

'*Mrs. Cronin. The Matron…*'

'*She's the one buried over the other side,*' one of the men said. '*Come, I'll show you.*'

He led Pat along by the mass grave, and then across the graveyard to a single heap of clay. At one end was a small wooden cross, made up of two short planks nailed together. Painted on it was – 'Emily Cronin. 1799–1849.'

'*Thank you,*' Pat said, as the man left. He dropped to his knees and prayed. '*Ár n-Athair, atá ar neamh, Go naofar D'Ainim. Go dtagfadh Do*

Ríocht. Go ndéantar Do Thoil ar an talamh mar a dhéantar ar neamh...'

Our Father, Who art in heaven, Hallowed be Thy Name, Thy kingdom come, Thy will be done on earth as it is in heaven...

He hesitated. Who was he praying for? And why?

Did he still believe in prayer, anyhow? He looked back at the death trench. Thy will be done?

He stood and left.

He walked out the road towards Castlebar. Broken houses and mud cabins lined the roads. Some had been totally demolished. The walls of the fields were being demolished too. He travelled on to Castlebar Workhouse.

'Pat! I thought you were dead.'

'Close enough, Mr. Gaffney. I was attacked. They damned near killed me.'

After he had finished telling his story of the attack and his rescue by the old woman, Gaffney pressed him on what he had seen of Erris. They spoke for what Pat felt to be hours. Gaffney listened carefully, sometimes interrupting, sometimes scrawling notes of his own.

Workhouses, bogs and mountains. Evictions and death.

Pat spent the next day poring over maps and scribbling more notes.

He was concerned he might have forgotten what the old woman had told him, but his memory of her story was clear. Then he scribbled notes on what he had seen in Westport Workhouse.

When he was happy he had remembered everything possible, he started to draw up a full report, written, as usual, in his best copperplate. When he had copied it out a second time, he gave the copy to Gaffney while he went back to produce two more copies.

'I don't know what I'd do without you, Pat,' Gaffney said later. 'These reports are invaluable. You can have little idea how much.'

'So what next, Mr. Gaffney?'

'I've been thinking about that, but I'm not certain. It will probably have to be Partry. Mweelrea too. I'll have to clear it all with the Grand Jury though. Which gives you a week or so to see your family, if you want.'

'Of course. It would be a good time.'

'Why not? You've been hurt badly enough. You're exhausted too. I'll drop you a note the moment I have clearance from them. Just be sure to be back as soon as you receive my letter. I depend on you far more than you might think.'

Pat left Castlebar for Carrigard. There was no doubt in his mind now that Famine was tightening its grip. More people begging, but that was to be expected. More children with the bloated stomachs, and the fox faces. Closed cabins. Abandoned perhaps. How many had dead inside?

When he arrived at Carrigard, all the women were there – Eleanor, Sabina, Kitty and Brigid. He had not seen Kitty in months, and her condition shocked him. She was eating a bowl of oatmeal porridge.

'You should have told us you were coming, Pat,' Eleanor said.

'Sure how could I? I never knew from day to day when I'd be finished. And by the time I did, sure I knew I'd be ahead of the letter.'

Kitty had not said anything.

Eleanor ushered him to a seat at the table.

'You'll eat.'

'I'll wait till later. How's it with all of ye here?'

'It's getting better in ways. Fergus Brennan is dead, and isn't that better.'

'Fergus Brennan!'

'Kitty's husband. Or had you forgotten?'

'Kitty?' Pat exclaimed. 'What...?'

'Yes,' Kitty said. '*Fergus is dead. Died of fever, and I've been evicted.*'

Pat stared at her, hardly comprehending what she had said.

'*But what will you do?*' he asked at length.

Kitty did not reply.

'*She's moved in with me,*' Sabina said.

Eleanor was delighted to have Pat home, even if it was just for a few days. During his long journeys around Mayo, she always worried whether he would return. Starvation was worsening, and always she heard distant tales of cholera from people on the road.

But Kitty was another concern. Clearly, she would not stay with Sabina for ever.

One evening, both Kitty and Sabina came to Carrigard. Michael and Pat were smoking by the fire.

'So what will you do?' Michael asked Kitty, directly. 'Will you stay, or will you go.'

'I don't know,' she said. 'America, perhaps, but I don't have the money. And I don't want to ask it of anyone here, even if I know it would be given. Anyhow, there might be better chances in England.'

'A hard enough place,' Michael said.

'Working with Danny, it was,' Eleanor said. 'But what of Murtybeg? What do you think, Pat?'

'Damned if I know,' Pat said.

'There are better prospects than Danny or Murtybeg,' Sabina said.' There's many going to Bradford, from all I hear. The woollen mills are taking people on. There's three girls planning on leaving. The Reilly sisters, *Áine* and *Síle*; and Peg McHugh.'

'Now there's an idea,' Eleanor said.

That evening, when Sabina and Kitty had gone, and Michael had gone to bed, Eleanor stayed up talking to Pat.

'So what about Sarah?' she asked. 'What will happen now her mother is dead?'

'We'll marry,' Pat said. 'At least that's what we are intending. But I must tell you mother, she is in a very dangerous state. She's earning nothing, and with her mother gone, her only reason for staying in the workhouse is for food and lodging. Better than the inmates, mind you, but I'm not even sure how long that will last. It seems the people in the workhouse don't like her.'

'But why not?'

'The last Master was stealing from the workhouse through giving short measure on food. There's some question the present Master, and perhaps the Matron too, might be doing the same. They know Sarah knows well how a workhouse works, and she'll be the first to spot it. She's working with the Head Clerk, but if there is stealing, he'll be in on it as well. No, she reckons they want to get rid of her, and as fast as possible. But they don't want to be too obvious about it.'

'How could they do that?'

'By sending her to the colonies. They're looking for orphan girls to be sent out.'

'What on earth for?'

'The story is there's too many men out there, and they want young women to marry them. For breeding, if you like.'

'But that's dreadful.'

'I know.'

Eleanor poked idly at the dying embers of the fire.

'So what do you intend to do?'

'I'm not rightly sure, mother. Just now, I have to go to Partry, but I'll be coming back up through Westport after. I'll see how things are then. Like I say, we'd like to marry, but we might not have time for that. If she has to leave, then I'll just bring her back here.'

'Yes,' Eleanor said, 'do that. It's better than having her as a convict's mare.'

A letter arrived in Carrigard. Eleanor handed it to Michael. 'Where's it from?'

Michael looked at the postmark, 'Bradford.'

'Bradford? Who on earth could be writing to us from Bradford?'

He ripped it open.

'Murty.'

'What's he doing in Bradford?' Eleanor asked.

'They've moved there to live. The two of them.'

'Bradford,' she exclaimed. 'After we just talking about it.'

'What else does he say?' Pat asked.

'Nothing much. He's well. Aileen's well, and that's about it.'

'I'll have to tell Sabina,' Eleanor said. 'Kitty too.'

'Yes,' Michael said, 'I suppose you will. He'd certainly be able to advise them about Bradford, no doubt about that.'

That afternoon, Eleanor took Brigid up to Sabina's bar. She threw the letter on the counter. Sabina glanced through it.

'*Kitty*,' she shouted.

Kitty came from the kitchen, where she had been washing the empties.

'*What's wrong?*'

'*Aileen's living in* Bradford. *Murty too.*'

'*And we only talking about* Bradford *last night!*' Eleanor added.

'*So are ye saying I should go then?*'

Eleanor held her hand up.

'*Not quite yet,*' she said. '*First, I'd suggest we write a letter to Murty and Aileen, and explain that you are thinking of it.*'

That evening, Sabina wrote to Murty. Six days later, Sabina and Kitty appeared at Carrigard with his reply.

Sabina spoke first. '*He says that they're staying with a Mayo family by the name of* Kerrigan. *They own some sort of boarding house. Mrs. Kerrigan might be able to board one or two girls. Her next-door neighbour, the same. And there's more than that.*'

'*What is it?*' Eleanor asked.

'*He says there's a desperate call for workers in the mills.*'

'*Well, it's all clear then,*' Sabina said. '*I'll write another letter to Murty, and confirm the four girls are coming.*'

Some days later, Kitty left Kilduff with the three Kilduff girls. Sabina had given her thirty shillings for travelling, which Kitty insisted was only a loan.

Eleanor was heartbroken to see her go, but she knew there was no future for Kitty anywhere in County Mayo.

Next day, a letter arrived from America. Eleanor gave it to Pat.

'Lackan, Pennsylvania,' he read out. He opened it and passed it to Michael.

'They've left New York,' Michael said. 'Off working in the coal mines. They must be doing very well.'

'Well thank God for that,' Eleanor said.

She took the bank draft and passed it to Pat.

'Perhaps you'd drop this in to the Hibernian Bank in Knockanure tomorrow.'

So there it is, she thought, that night. *Exile, Your only answer. Is this the land You promised us? Mayo, a land flowing with milk and honey? Or four long years of torture. No milk, no honey, not even potatoes, only death. Kitty is leaving now, how it breaks my heart. What future for her, poor girl, working the machines in their mills? She has no idea of what awaits her, nor do I, except there'll be precious little milk, and no honey. The same with Luke and Winnie and little Liam. What kind of hellholes are these mines? Your punishment, but for what? And Sarah, breeding stock for jailbirds at the other end of the earth. Is this some kind of joke? No, I won't let You do that. Sarah stays, damn You. She's ours.*

Chapter 20

Telegraph & Connaught Ranger, Mayo. March 1849:
Horrible Deaths! Ballintubber! We have just been informed
that last week, a poor woman with three children, turned
out of the workhouse on the Outdoor Relief, which as
stated to us, they never got, were found dead in a lime
kiln in the townland of Culladeer, Parish of Ballintubber,
from fever and starvation, and in a decomposed state. The
police got some straw thrown over them and then covered
them with earth.

After Pat had left for Knockanure with the bank draft, a letter came from
Castlebar. Eleanor knew full well what it meant. She handed it to him when
he returned that evening.

'You haven't opened it,' he said.

'Sure it's none of my business, that's what I was always taught. Don't
open letters that aren't addressed to you.'

'*Arra* what. It's our business that's for certain. If it's from Castlebar, it's
your business.'

He slit it open.

'He's expecting me tomorrow. He wants me to travel to Partry.'

'Partry. How bad is it there?'

'Bad enough, he says, and isn't it my job to find out? But I'll tell you this,
mother, if it's anything like Erris, it's savage.'

'Erris! You've not said a word about Erris.'

'Sure you knew I was attacked.'

'I knew that much, but you never told me anything more, and never
mentioned it since you came home.'

'Ye never asked me.'

'We thought it better not to ask you, and that you'd tell us in your own
good time.'

'Maybe I didn't want telling you.'

'But I'm your mother. If it's that terrible, I'd be able to comfort you.'

'You will in time. Wait till I get back from Partry.'

*

When Pat arrived in Castlebar, Gaffney was at a meeting.

He found a map and an empty office. Partry, south west of the county. Many mountains, that was for sure.

After some time, Gaffney entered.

'Hiding away, were you?'

'I've just been studying this map. Partry is a long way.'

'It is, and I'm thinking this time you should take a horse,' Gaffney said. 'I don't think that knock on the head did you much good.'

'Are you sure, Mr. Gaffney?'

'It'd be easier for you to ride. Partry is tough enough – as much as Erris perhaps, but at least you won't have the same kind of swamp and bog as you had going up to Glenamoy. And there's many things I'd like you to do, so it won't be easy.'

'Like what?

'First, see if you can call on Father Ward in Ballinrobe. He's a most informative man.'

'I know,' Pat said, 'I've met him.

'Of course, I'd forgotten. The time you were down there last year.'

'That's right.'

He passed a letter to Pat.

'This is from the good Father. I don't know that you should believe everything that he says. Whatever you do, you must accompany him on his calls and make your own assessment.'

'Yes, Mr. Gaffney.'

'He says there's cholera in Ballinrobe.'

'I'd heard.'

'Which is a bit odd, since there's none here.'

'You think he's lying?'

'I don't know, but I'd like you to find out.'

'How in hell…'

'I'm sure Father Ward will show you. Otherwise the workhouse certainly will.'

Gaffney crossed to a cabinet and took out another map. He unfolded it in front of Pat.

'Now before you even get to Ballinrobe, there's something else. I'd like you to travel by Claremorris. I want you to get some idea of the appearance of the country after the Lucan evictions.'

'In Claremorris?'

'No. After Claremorris, but closer to Ballinrobe. Just here,' he said, pointing at the map.

'Levally?'

'Yes, and Caheredmond just after it. As you can see there's more villages in here to the side. There's been massive evictions here too.'

Pat looked at the map.

'I'd never heard of any of this. I thought Lucan was only evicting around Westport and Castlebar.'

'No, no,' Gaffney said, 'Lucan owns thousands of acres in the south of the county. A right murderer he is too. And for God's sake, don't tell anyone I said that. If he hears, we'll sure as hell never get any rates out of the bastard for the workhouse. Nor for anything else neither.'

Pat examined the map more closely. There were many villages to the east of the road, none of which he had ever heard of.

Gaffney extracted another map, and placed it on the table.

'Next point. Father Ward keeps sending us terrible stories of the mountains here – the Partry Mountains and Maumtrasna to the west. Like I've said before, I don't know how much to trust his reports, but if you can find him in Ballinrobe, he might direct you to the worst places. Can you do that?'

'It has to be done,' Pat replied, 'isn't that it?'

'It does, I'm afraid. And one more thing too. The last area I'd like you to look at is over here. When you're finished with Father Ward, it's easy enough to follow the road down here, and then up to Killary. It's after that the problem is. This area running along the coast by Killary Harbour, under Mweelrea Mountain, and on up the coast to Roonagh, Louisburgh and Westport. We got terrible reports from Louisburgh back in '47. The area was badly hit by the fever epidemic in that year.'

'Yes,' Pat said. 'It was terrible up the Ox Mountains that time too.'

'According to the Connaught Telegraph, the fever killed an awful number along the coast beyond Louisburgh, all the way to Killary. Wiped out whole fishing villages, they say. Again, what the truth of it is, I just don't know. Cavendish often exaggerates; all editors do. Not that I mind Cavendish shocking them in Dublin Castle now and again, but we must find out what's really happening. Lord Sligo is landlord for the area west of Louisburgh, but I'm not sure he'd know much, or tell us if he did. The real problem in this area is the lack of roads. All along the strip between Mweelrea and the shoreline, there's almost no roads at all. The surveyors did well in surveying it back in '38 and even the census takers got some information there, but I reckon there's many areas they did not reach. The fishermen see no need for roads when they can go everywhere by boat. There's some fields cultivated too, and I'd guess between potatoes and fish, they've enough to eat in a normal year. But what I'd really like to know is what happened to them during the epidemics of '47 and what's happening there today.'

'How would I get across without a road?' Pat asked.

'I reckon you'd be able to lead your horse across. There should be some kind of trails in the grass and heather going from one settlement to another. Going over the rocks might be tricky, but it's most important we try it.'

'Fine, so.'

'One other thing' Gaffney said, 'when you get to Louisburgh, you might see if you can find Dean Callanan. He might be a proselytiser, but what of that? Here, read this.'

He passed Pat a copy of the Dublin Evening Packet, and pointed:

The Famine years of 1846, 1847 and 1848 were halcyon years when contrasted with the dismal year of 1849! To give you a few examples of the suffering of our poor, four of one family travelled 60 Irish miles (for they had to go three times from Louisburgh to Westport) to the Westport Poor-House to seek for aid; they sought it in vain; two of the number perishing (being exhausted by famine) in endeavouring to cross the rivers; the remaining two lagged behind from exhaustion and thus were saved – saved from the water, starved on the land! Another poor man was found dead in my parish from hunger a short time since; the only property he had on him was a ticket to the poor-house; he died before he reached it! He was huddled on a horse's back, and buried in his rags in a sandbank! Frequently, I have known of two of the family lying dead in one cabin from starvation, and it causes not the least excitement in my locality. I hear parents about me returning God thanks for taking away by death their famine stricken children, their poor children who had died from the effects of hunger and cold; the sandbanks about me are studded with the bodies of the dead! Often, I have given some aid to the poor to buy coffins; for the small sums they receive from me, they bought some food, and then buried their dead in the sandbanks. The very graves in my churchyard have, in my presence, been assailed by the starving dogs! From morning until night, I am now hourly beset with crawling skeletons begging for food! The poor persons set down as entitled to outdoor relief are not this moment receiving half the quantity ruled for them! The poor in my parish ought to have received their trifle of relief for this week last Thursday. No meal has yet arrived from Westport nor is any distribution expected here before Sunday next. The recipients of outdoor relief are starving three days in the week! Such, my dear friend, are the sufferings of our poor – here now my own case. For the last year and a half, I received only £20 from the parish and I have had to pay more than £22 in poor rates and cesses in this period. PJ Callanan incumbent of Louisburgh.

John, Archbishop of Tuam.

'What do you think?' Gaffney asked.

'Sounds just like Erris. Maybe worse, I don't know.'

'Yes, it could be worse. It's most important that you talk to Dean Callanan. The local priest too, I don't know what his name is. Not that it matters. I'm sure Dean Callanan is not exaggerating. Protestant or not, you see the name under his.'

'The Archbishop?'

'McHale.'

'McHale,' Pat exclaimed. 'But sure he's Catholic.'

'He is,' Gaffney said. 'And Bishop McHale is supporting a Protestant vicar, no less. There's no arguments about proselytising or anything else either. Protestant, Catholic or Presbyterian, they're all singing off the same hymn sheet now. And about damned well time too.'

That evening, Pat wrote a brief letter to Carrigard, explaining about his plans for Ballinrobe, Partry and Killary. Then he slept.

He left Castlebar early, reached Claremorris fast enough, and rode on towards Ballinrobe. Even before Levally, there were signs of evictions. When he reached the village, he saw that there were two houses standing. The rest had been demolished. Caheredmond was the same – two houses standing. A woman was standing at one.

'*What has happened here?*' he asked, feigning ignorance.

'*The evictions of* Lord Lucan.'

'*Many people?*'

'*Hundreds. Thousands. Who knows?*'

'*But ye remain?*' Pat asked.

Her husband had joined her.

'*What business is it of yours?*'

'*Just asking,*' Pat said.

The man dragged his wife inside, and the door was shut.

He remembered Gaffney's instructions and turned to the side off the road, working his way back, parallel to the main road.

Bawn. Cavan. Saleen.

He found many shattered villages, some with no remaining life at all. Some had ceased to exist – even the wreckage of the houses was gone. At each village, he counted the houses, noting any that were left standing. Whenever he met anyone, he asked for names of evicted families, and noted them down.

Rathnaguppaun. Knocknacroagha. Ballinteeaun.

A pattern was becoming obvious. Most villages had dozens of houses before the evictions, with only one or two houses left now.

But why the remaining houses? Men were working in the fields. Some were digging ditches, some were tearing down hedgerows, but the majority were constructing dry-stone walls. The countryside was slowly being converted from one of small fields with hedgerows to one of enormous fields with stone walls, all running in regular straight lines, intersecting at precise right angles.

Cappacurry. Ballynakillew. Cloonacastle.

He stopped his horse, and sat in the saddle, watching. Stones were being taken from the ruins of one village, and carted to where the walls were being built. Here the natural hedgerows had already disappeared.

He saw a man riding towards him. He drew up in front of Pat.

'Good work, isn't it?' he said.

Pat recognised the accent as Scottish.

'It is,' Pat agreed, 'I've rarely seen dry-stone walling done so well.'

He was thinking fast. Why aggravate the man? He was here to get information.

'Yes,' the man said, 'we train them well. They work far better as employees than as tenants. They know they're lucky to be working for us, and they see how few are needed to run a farm efficiently. That's what I call improvement.'

'Is Lord Lucan the landlord around here?'

'He is,' the Scot replied, 'And Lord Lucan knows what improvement is.'

Pat made his way towards Ballinrobe. Improvement? Another word for slaughter.

He found a wrecked house. He pulled the horse in under the remaining roof and slept beside it.

As he entered Ballinrobe, it was unnaturally quiet.

He spotted a door with a white cross painted on it.

He walked on, trying to ignore the stink of the open sewer. More white crosses. Then a church. The dead body of a woman lay outside, one arm missing. He did not gag. It no longer meant anything to him.

Outside the priest's house, hundreds of people were sitting or lying on the ground, a few more leaning against the wall. He made his way through, stepping over and around them. No-one challenged him. The silence was unsettling.

The woman who answered his knock was old and very much stooped. He asked for Father Ward.

'*He's not here.*'

'*Where's he gone?*'

'*He said something about Partry. That's all I know.*'

She shut the door.

What now? Gaffney still expected a report on cholera. The white crosses might be evidence of that. If Father Ward had gone, that left the workhouse. Who was Gaffney's contact when he had brought Murtybeg to Ballinrobe to recruit navvies? Daly? Yes, Daly. That was all a long time ago.

The crowd at the workhouse gate was far less than he had expected, and he gained entry easily enough. He asked for Daly.

'*Mr. Daly's over there,*' an inmate told him, pointing to the sheds along the wall. Pat's heart sank. Fever sheds?

He entered, and was hit by a sweet-sour stench of diarrhoea and vomit. There were beds down both sides of the building, each, Pat noted, with a single patient, unlike the practice in Knockanure Workhouse during the typhus epidemic of 1847. In front of each bed was a chamber pot, many full. An inmate was pulling a trolley-load of chamber pots to the door while other inmates were mopping the floor. He stood aside as the trolley passed.

'*Where's Mr. Daly?*' he asked.

'*Not here.*'

He tried the next shed and the next.

On the fourth, an inmate pointed down the ward. '*Second bed from the end.*'

At the bed a man was kneeling beside a patient, holding his head up as he held a bottle to his lips.

'Mr. Daly?'

The man looked around. 'Yes. Who's wanting to know?'

'Pat Ryan, we've met before.'

Daly beckoned to a woman to take over the patient. She was not wearing the uniform of the workhouse. A nurse perhaps?

'Yes,' Daly said, 'I remember you. Yourself and your brother, wasn't it...?'

'My cousin, Murtybeg.'

'Whatever. You brought our men over to England for working on the railways. We've had many of them back.'

'Back?'

'The Manchester Workhouses, they had them sent back to Liverpool and shipped back here. Told us there were no jobs.'

'There were jobs right enough,' Pat said, 'but soon after there was the Railway Panic. Then there were no jobs.'

They both stood aside as the trolley came back again.

'What brings you here now? Looking for more men for jobs that aren't there?'

'No,' Pat said, 'I'm working for the County now. They've heard reports of cholera in Ballinrobe, and they want to know the truth of it. Seems you're the first town in Mayo to get it.'

'The first? Surely...'

'There's none in Castlebar, though they're reckoning it's coming. But it's here right enough. Isn't it?'

Daly gestured around him.

'Here is right, and this is just from the workhouse. The people in the town, they just die in their houses.'

'I know,' Pat said, 'I've seen the crosses.'

Abruptly, Daly took him aside.

'Do the County really know nothing about cholera?'

'Not a thing,' Pat said. 'It's like I told you, there's none in Castlebar and the Grand Jury are trying to say it's all a lie.'

'A lie! God damn it, you've seen it yourself.'

'I have, and I'm not denying it. In fact, I want to give Castlebar the truth of it all. But tell me this, is there nothing to be done?'

'There's only one treatment and that's water – water with salt in it. They've a desperate thirst, but it goes in one end and comes out the other. That's the reason for this mess. But if we stop giving them water, they'll die. And even if we do, most still die. It all depends on how strong they are. Starvation doesn't help, I can tell you. Most of those in the town will be dead soon, and it's highly infectious. If one dies, the whole house will get it. It's the police that started the system of marking the white crosses on the doors, a sort of home quarantine you might call it.'

'I know,' Pat said, 'I'd guessed.'

Daly brought Pat out of the shed, and into the Administration block. He led Pat to an office and sat him down.

'Well now, you've seen it yourself,' he said to Pat. 'It's all over Ireland, God damn it. It's killed millions of people around the world. Sure all you have to do is read the papers. It's terrible what's happened in England.'

'I know,' Pat said.

'And the papers are talking of cities losing thousands to cholera, and if that isn't a killer, I don't know what is. But it's worse here. Fever spreading like wildfire, and now cholera. What in the name of God do the County expect us to do about it? We're giving Outdoor Relief, but it's not a fraction of what we need, and the ratepayer has to pay for it all. Wouldn't be a problem for the likes of Lucan, but he'll be damned to hell before he pays a penny. Most of the rest are bankrupt, you know that as well as I do. They expect us to feed all who need feeding; they expect us to cease the sickness; and they give us blasted little money to do it with. And here it's worse than anywhere. Do you know, right here, right in this Workhouse, the fever is killing hundreds, every single week.'

Pat looked up, stunned.

'Hundreds…?'

'That's what I'm telling you. Look – we have two thousand in a work-house built for six hundred. I've written to the County, I've written to Dublin Castle – no answer from anyone. Now go back and tell that to the accursed bastards in Castlebar.'

'I will, I promise.'

'And tell them what you've seen in the town, and what you've seen in the wards right here in the workhouse.'

'It's what Mr. Gaffney asked me to do. He doesn't just want my thoughts, he wants real numbers to convince Lord Lucan and the rest of the Grand Jury.'

'As if any of them will do anything about it.'

'I don't know,' Pat said. 'We can only try. What other numbers can you give me?'

Daly stood, and took a large book from a shelf.

'There you are,' he said. 'These are the deaths, day by day, week by week, for the past twelve months. Now you can sit and look at this.'

Pat turned the pages. Long lists – Surnames, Christian names and Townlands, all totalled at the end of each day. He took out his notebook and pencil, and began copying in dates and numbers.

'And here,' Daly said, 'you can see the increase coming up to the potato harvest. Then the failure and the numbers increase again. Then the fever really took off – you can see it in the numbers here. And here's where the cholera began. And if this doesn't wake the whoresons in Castlebar, then God help us all.'

Pat had been scribbling very fast. Between the figures, he took down Daly's comments, as he described what had happened in the workhouse, day by day.

'I'm sorry,' Daly said at length. 'There's times I get upset about this.'

'I wouldn't blame you,' Pat said.

'No, I should have given it to you slower. Are you sure you got it all down?'

'Near every word,' Pat said. He passed the notebook over to Daly.

'By God, you do it fast. Accurate too. Will they see this?'

'Mr. Gaffney will,' Pat said, 'and he'll make sure everyone else does. And if the Grand Jury don't understand it, the Connaught Telegraph sure as hell will.'

Daly came around and shook his hand.

'Thank you for coming, Pat. I'm sorry I was a little rude earlier. Now go with God.'

*

Pat left the workhouse. He rode past the dogs. He turned his face away, but on the other side of the street, he saw what was left of a leg, gnawed down to the bone, a shoe hanging off the end. Two rats scurried off as he approached.

He checked the position of the sun, and went in what he reckoned might be a north-westerly direction. He was not certain though. He dismounted and knocked on the door of a cabin. There was no answer.

He led the horse to the next cabin and knocked again.

'*Who's there?*'

'*I'm looking for the road to Partry.*'

'*It's not this way.*'

'*Which way is it?*'

Silence.

He rode back to the centre of the town. He took another road, and saw a woman approaching him. As he came nearer, she pulled her shawl tighter around her wizened face.

'*I'm looking for the road to Partry.*'

She pointed in the direction he was riding.

As darkness fell, it became cold, and he looked for somewhere to sleep. He found a turf shed and stepped inside. There was a movement in the shadows.

'*What do you want?*'

'*Somewhere to sleep.*'

'*You may stay if you want.*'

He went out to tie his horse. Then there was a scream. Fever? Typhus or cholera? How could he tell? He got back on his horse, and went on.

Two more sheds had people sleeping in them. The next shed was empty. There was no turf, but a little straw in the corner. He pulled his blanket around himself and slept.

In the morning, he arrived in the village of Partry. A ragged man walked towards him, carrying a bundle of kindling. He was thin, but he carried no signs of hunger or fever.

'*I'm looking for Father Ward,*' Pat said.

'*He was here last night right enough, but I'd heard he'd gone on to Tourmakeady.*'

'Is he long gone?'

'Not so long. The sun was just risen when he left. You might catch him if you ride fast.'

'Which direction did he go?'

'Left at the crossroads ahead.'

'Was he walking?'

'Riding. You'll have no difficulty though. He's on a donkey and won't be going fast.'

Pat thanked him. He whipped the horse into a canter. He realised he had to be careful not to miss Father Ward, who might have stopped at any cabin along the road. He watched every cabin for donkeys, but there were none.

He overtook a horse and cart with a man, a woman and four children. The woman was holding a baby. All were thin, but there was no sign of fever or the extreme stages of hunger. Two of the children were sitting on crates, and at the front of the cart there were three sacks, all full and knotted tight.

He slowed to their pace and asked if they had seen Father Ward, but they had not.

'*Are ye going far?*' he asked.

'*Westport,*' the man answered.

'*And further than that, I'd guess?*'

'*America, if we can make it.*'

'*Have ye money for a ticket.*'

'*We have, but whether it will be enough, I don't know. We had held back corn from last year's crop to pay the landlord in June.*'

'He won't see that so,' Pat commented.

'*The devil he will. He can go swing for it.*'

Pat lashed his horse and went on. In the village of Cloonlagheen were two more corpses, but he did not look closer. Two miles outside, he saw a black figure astride a donkey in the distance.

'Father Ward,' he shouted. He lashed the horse on.

'Father Ward,' he shouted again. The donkey stopped.

'Who's looking for me?'

'Pat Ryan.'

The priest peered closer at him as he came up. He was wearing a patched grey soutane, ripped at the lower hem. His shoes were cracked.

'By God, Pat Ryan. I hadn't known you. What are you doing out this way again? More men for England, is it?'

'Not this time, Father.'

The donkey stumbled.

'Careful, Father.'

'I'm fine.'

They rode on, side by side. It was clear the road had not been repaired after the winter. Even where it had been repaired, the pot holes had not been levelled, and in more the gravel had been washed out.

'I'm sorry for what happened last time,' Pat said. 'I've been to the workhouse. Mr. Daly told me all about it. Many arrived back, I understand.'

'They did. Not that the workhouse could take the most of them.'

'I won't try to excuse myself,' Pat said. 'All I can say is that when we brought them to England, there was a great need for labour. Railway Mania, they called it then. Then it was followed by the Railway Panic. There's thousands – hundreds of thousands – out of work right across England.'

'A bad time for them then?'

'It was. And you'll remember my cousin, Murtybeg. It was his brother who was running the business.'

'Ah yes, Daniel Ryan, wasn't it?'

'It was,' Pat replied, 'and he couldn't take it either. He killed himself.'

Father Ward looked at him, whether in surprise or shock, Pat could not tell. The donkey stopped.

'Killed himself? I'd heard he was dead. I didn't know…'

Pat halted the horse alongside. 'It happens,' he said, 'and anyhow, I decided to come home after it. Mr. Gaffney in Castlebar, he asked me to help out. He said I was to meet with you. He was most definite about it.'

'Why me?'

'He reckoned you know far more about the south of the County than anyone else. He's seen your letters to the Telegraph. He reckons you're the one who tells it like it is. But the Grand Jury don't believe it, so Gaffney wants me to confirm everything.'

'As if it needed confirmation.'

'I agree,' Pat said. 'But if that's what they want, that's what I have to get. So if you don't mind, I'd like to ride around with you. Then I'll make a report to the County.'

'A report?'

'I've seen the letters you've been sending. They want me to see the truth of it all and report back.'

'So they're asking you to measure distress?'

Pat winced. 'Something like that,' he said, 'and before you say it, yes, it is impossible to measure, what with the cholera and all.'

'Cholera! May God damn it to hell. It's inflicting terrible destruction in Ballinrobe.'

'I know,' Pat said. 'I've seen the sheds in the workhouse. I've seen the crosses on the doors too, but I've not been inside the houses.'

'Isn't it a terrible thing for the Almighty to visit upon us now? Does he want to crucify us all? I'd always believed we shouldn't question his ways. Now I don't know. I just don't know.'

'Don't be like that, Father. It will all end. It will.'

'Yes, but when? Two years ago, we thought it was finishing, but last year the starvation was worse than ever. Fever too, seven of my priests dead…'

'Seven!'

'Close to eight. I was ill myself, but God saved me, and for what? To see all the misery that He sends us. Now cholera on top of fever. And you think it will end! It will – when we're all dead. And still no supplies from Castlebar. Four cartloads of grain once, but we've had nothing in these months past.'

They rode on.

'You know Father,' Pat said, 'one reason they're very concerned about Ballinrobe is because of the cholera. There's none in Castlebar, nor Westport, I understand. And I didn't see any sign of it in Claremorris.'

'Did they not believe me so?'

'Not yet. I've seen it in Ballinrobe though, and it will be in my report. But, like I say, Ballinrobe might be the only town in Mayo to have it yet. There'll be more though. They're preparing a cholera hospital in Castlebar, I understand, and I'd say they'll have use for it.'

They were passing a cabin. A man and a woman stood outside, thin, bare-foot and ragged. They both bowed their heads to Father Ward. He stopped briefly and gave a mumbled blessing. Then the woman was crying. Neither had said a word.

They rode on.

'Which way did you come to Ballinrobe?' Father Ward asked.

'By Claremorris. And before you say it, I've seen the Lucan villages, or what's left of them anyhow.'

'Lucan is a pig. God knows how many thousands he's evicted.'

'What happened to them?'

'Some made it to the workhouse in Ballinrobe, but damned few. The rest – they're scattered to the four winds. Or dead.'

They passed through Tourmakeady. It was quiet. Some stone houses, surrounded by mud cabins. They continued west, Lough Mask on the left, the mountains of Partry rising off to the right.

They were approaching a village. It was very quiet.

'*Bóthar na hAbhainn*,' Father Ward said. River Road.

He knocked at the first cabin. A man answered.

'*God with you, Eoin.*'

'*God and Mary, Father Peter. You're travelling?*'

'*I am. How are you and your family now?*'

'*One of the girl's in fever. The rest might live.*'

'*I'll only be a moment*,' Father Ward said to Pat. Ducking down, he entered the cabin. Pat did not dismount.

A few minutes later, they both came out of the cabin. Pat followed them for a hundred yards. They stopped outside another cabin. A man answered their knock.

'*We're looking for your cart, Dónal*,' Father Ward said.

'*Have you food, Father?*'

275

Father Ward put his hand into the pocket of his cassock and brought out two slices of brown bread. Pat saw a light dusting of blue mould on them.

'*This is all I have. There's no supplies from Castlebar.*'

The man tore one of the slices in half and began to eat it. He brought the remaining bread inside. When he came out he led them to a cart behind the cabin.

They backed the donkey into the shafts of the cart. *Dónal* strapped it tightly, and drove it out. They stopped outside another cabin.

'*Peadar Flanagan*' Father Ward whispered to Pat.

'*Two daughters and two grand-daughters gone,*' said *Eoin*. '*All four dead in an hour, they say, though I'm not sure I'd believe that.*'

A gaunt woman answered. Pat reckoned she might have been in her sixties.

'*Is Peadar here?*' *Eoin* asked. She pointed inside. Father Ward entered. Pat went to follow him.

Eoin grabbed him by his arm. '*Are you mad? It's enough for Father Peter to be risking his life.*'

'*I have to see it,*' Pat said without any further explanation. He broke free, stooped under the bog-oak lintel, and went inside.

In the corner, Father Ward was kneeling beside a man, who was moaning. He lay on a bed of turf with straws on top. A rough blanket had been thrown over him.

The blessing was given – '*Per istam sanctam unctionem...*' Through this Holy Unction, may the Lord free you from sin and raise you up on the Last Day.

The room stank of smoke and something worse. Pat stepped around to see what was in the corner. He stood on a hand. Four bodies were thrown in the corner on top of each other, a baby and a young child on top of two young women. All had bloated faces, two half-eaten away. From under the bodies he heard the screeching of rats.

One of the women's legs showed the unmistakeable signs of gangrene. Fever. Now he knew the risks he was running.

He expected Father Ward to give Extreme Unction to the four corpses, but he did not.

'We'll have to bury them,' he whispered to Pat in English.

'Oh God...'

Father Ward went to the door, and asked the other two to help. Pat was surprised when they both refused.

'*We've got families,*' Eoin said, '*and we've enough fever already.*'

Father Ward shrugged his shoulders, and looked to Pat. Pat lifted the baby and carried it out onto the cart. Father Ward followed with the young child.

They both returned to the cabin and carried the young women out in turn, holding each by the shoulders and ankles. They laid them on the cart, alongside the children.

They returned to the man. The moaning had stopped.

'Dead,' Father Ward said.

'I know,' said Pat.

They carried him out.

'*Have ye spades?*' Pat asked.

'*Hold a moment,*' *Dónal* replied. He went back to his own cabin and returned with a spade and a *sleán*. He left them inside the cart. Father Ward stood at the front of the cart, and drove the donkey. Pat followed, leading his horse, the other two men following with the woman of the house. They turned off at a small boreen and stopped at a high bank of turf.

'*This would be best, Father,*' the woman said.

Pat looked surprised.

'There's no graveyard within five miles,' Father Ward explained, 'and we're not going to carry the fever that far. It's bad enough already.'

They took the spade and *sleán*. '*Here, let ye two rest,*' Father Ward said to the other two men. He passed the *sleán* to Pat.

'I'm not sure either'd be able for heavy labour,' he whispered.

They worked for some time. When it was still less than two feet deep, Father Ward stepped out.

'Let that be enough.'

He and Pat laid the corpses into the hole. Then he stood on the edge, and gave the blessing. They shovelled the wet turf on top of the dead bodies.

Pat walked to another boghole, and carefully washed his hands and forearms. Father Ward joined him.

When they had returned the cart to the village, Pat and the priest rode back towards Tourmakeady.

'We'll have to go faster than this,' Father Ward said.

'I know,' Pat said. 'Burying bodies takes time.'

But the road had worsened. Again, the donkey stumbled, pitching Father Ward forward, but he clutched the donkey's mane and did not fall.

A few minutes later, they came to a corpse in a ditch. They looked at each other.

'No burials,' Pat said. Father Ward nodded. He stayed on the donkey, and whispered the blessing.

A mile later, they saw another body on the road. A dog had found it already. As the blessing was repeated, Pat slipped off from his horse, broke a small branch from a whinbush and rushed at the dog. He whipped it sharply across the back. The dog ran, whelping.

'You're wasting your time,' Father Ward said. 'He'll be back the moment we're around the corner.'

It was dark when they entered the village of Gortmore, but a bright half-moon lit the cabins. They did not dismount.

'*Anyone here?*' Father Ward shouted. '*Father Ward here. Can anyone hear me?*'

A door opened, and a woman came out.

'*You're welcome, Father Peter,*' she said. '*We've much need for you.*' She went back into the cabin and took a half burning branch from the fire.

'*Come with me.*'

She grasped the donkey's bridle. They came to a cabin. The mud sloped back steeply, ten or twelve feet thick at the bottom. The roof rose further up to a high ridge. It had been constructed with ancient bog oak and scraws of heather, blackened by smoke. The woman opened the door without knocking, and handed the burning torch to Father Ward. He and Pat entered.

Pat came close to vomiting. He counted seven bodies. Controlling his choking, he decided to check them for life. He went on his knees, and crawled to each in turn, watching and listening closely. He shook his head.

'All dead,' he said.

Father Ward gave the blessing once. 'I'm sure the good Lord will understand,' he said. 'There's no need in repeating it seven times.'

'I'm sure you're right, Father. And we're not burying them neither.'

'Don't worry, Pat. They'll pull the roof in on them instead. They might bury them when they have more strength, and when the bones are eaten clean.'

They went out again. Pat heard keening, though he did not know from where.

The woman was waiting.

'*Do ye have anywhere to sleep?*' she asked.

'*Nowhere. Not yet.*'

'*That ye may stay with me.*'

As they were leading the animals back, Pat hesitated.

'*Have you fever in the house?*' he asked the woman.

'*I'm alone,*' she said, '*and I don't have fever.*'

'*I'm sorry asking…*'

'*No need for that. We must all have a care.*'

When they came to her cabin, Pat went to tie his horse to a whinbush on the other side.

'*Ye'd better bring the animals in,*' she told them. '*They'll be stolen otherwise.*'

'*Are they of so much value?*' Pat asked.

'For food, yes. There's not a donkey left in this village. They're all gone for eating.'

'And if they didn't eat them, the dogs would?'

'There's no dogs neither.'

Pat thought about the reason for that, but did not ask.

'Rats so?' he asked.

'Yes, there are many rats. Too many to hunt down, and too fast in the moving.'

They brought the donkey in, but they could not force the horse under the low lintel. Pat tied it to the door jamb, and slept at the open door.

When they arose, Pat took oatmeal bread from his sack, broke it into chunks and passed it to the others. The woman filled a cup with well-water, and each drank from it before it was refilled. Then they left.

At Tourmakeady, they turned, climbing away from the lake and up the Partry Mountains.

They passed a man crawling. Pat took bread from his own sack, and tried to hand it to him. The man looked at him, but did not take it. They went a few yards. Then Father Ward stopped. He turned his donkey around, and quietly whispered the blessing.

They came to a building with windows, but most had been broken in, and the front door swung open. 'That used to be a school,' Father Ward said. 'Let's see if there's anyone sheltering inside.'

They entered. Pat saw the cast iron remains of desks, but there was no timber.

'Gone for firewood,' Father Ward said. In one corner, there was a corpse. It was far decayed, and eaten down one side. They went no nearer, and the blessing was given from a distance.

Pat knotted the door shut, and they left.

'We had over a hundred children there once,' Father Ward said. 'Now not one. Do you know Pat, five years ago, there were fifteen hundred children in eight schools in my parish? One thousand five hundred boys and girls. Can you imagine it? Now we have one school open in Ballinrobe. And do you know how many children there are attending school there? Ten!'

'Where have they all gone to, Father, do you think? Have they emigrated?'

'Emigrated! There's few enough of them could emigrate. No, they're too weak to come to school. They're dead or waiting for it.'

'So many?'

'Indeed, and that's just the children. I'll tell you something, Pat, it's places like Partry where the dying is done. I'm sure it's bad with ye around Kilduff, or even Castlebar, but I'd say it's nothing like this. Even in Ballinrobe they have some food, but up here in the wilds of Partry – nothing. Nothing since

279

Castlebar's last supplies, and nothing much before that either.'

'Nothing from the landlords neither?'

'No, the landlords don't want to know – if we even knew who the half of them were. There's very little corn here and the potatoes are gone. What's worse is the way they all crowd together. Once fever enters a village it jumps from house to house and kills everyone. You've seen it yourself.'

'I have,' said Pat, 'but it no longer surprises me. This is just the way it is in Erris too. And my brother Luke, he told me about it in the Ox Mountains, but that was back in '46 and '47. Knockanure Workhouse too. But you're right. This is worse.'

They were climbing now, following a road leading towards the higher ground. To the far right the ridges of the blackened potato ridges went higher and higher, nearly as far as the tops of the mountains, only heather and rock above.

At length, they turned off the road, following a narrow boreen across the side of the mountain. The road was rough, with more mud than gravel. Again, the donkey fell. Again, Father Ward grasped the mane, but his fingers could not hold it, and he fell sideways into the mud. He rose, rubbing mud off his soutane.

'You get used to it,' he told Pat.

Pat dismounted and they led the horse and donkey along, but still the men and animals staggered and lurched in the mud.

'A rough road,' Pat said.

'It is. A road of sorrow for man and beast.'

They came to another village.

'*Baile Uí Bhánáin,*' Father Ward told him. O'Bannan's village. Ballybanane.

There were perhaps twenty cabins, all built into the steep slope of the land. Father Ward shouted, but this time there was no answer.

Pat knocked at three doors in succession, but there were no replies. He opened each door, but all were empty.

'You needn't bother about those ones,' Father Ward told him. 'They're gone already. Dead and buried. Buried everywhere you could think – fields, bogs, ditches, it doesn't matter anymore.'

They came to a hovel, more miserable than most. There were no walls. A round roof rose from the ground, the back built into the bog. It was covered with turf. The entrance was less than two feet high. There was no door, no chimney and no window spaces.

'Willie Walsh,' Father Ward said. 'Dead some weeks back, him and the son. They were to bury them. I've blessed them already.'

'I'll have a look,' Pat said.

'No. Don't.'

But Pat ignored him and crawled inside. As his eyes became accustomed to the gloom, he spotted a blanket in one corner. He lifted it, and pulled back, choking. Underneath were the skeletal remains of a man and a child. There was nothing left of their flesh. The child looked to be hugging his father, the skulls touching at the foreheads.

Father Ward was waiting outside.

'The rats didn't leave much.' Pat said. 'Nothing more than bones.'

'There was more flesh on them when I last came. It was horrible.'

Pat saw he was shaking.

'What?' he asked. 'What was so horrible?'

'Never mind. There's things it's better not to know.'

They left. Another cabin, walled this time.

'Martin Walsh, I spoke with him a month or two back.'

The door did not open. Through a gap, Pat saw it was propped shut by a branch. He found a thin piece of wood and, pushing it through the gap, displaced the branch.

Inside were two dead men and a dead woman. There was little except bones left of the woman's body, showing through the ragged remains of her dress. The rats still squeaked around the corpses of the men. Another blessing.

Pat spotted a heap of scraws of heather in a tiny field beside the house. Knowing well what he would find, he walked over and pulled a few back.

Another corpse. Another blessing.

'Are there any left, do you think?' Pat asked.

'None.'

Pat went down one side of the boreen, opening each door, sometimes using force to break the door open, but every house was empty. He came back up the other side. The same.

'Didn't I tell you so,' Father Ward said. 'Everyone else we've buried, and that last man you found, that was Anthony Derrig. They wouldn't have had the strength to bury him. If there were any left alive.'

They crossed from *Baile Uí Bhánáin* and came to another mud village.

'*Droim Chogaidh,*' Father Ward said. Drimcaggy. The Ridge of War.

'*What war?*' Pat asked, not noticing he had slipped into Irish.

'*Who knows? Some long-forgotten brawl in the hills. It's of little matter now.*'

More empty huts. Then a larger house, built of rock and thatched with reeds.

Pat opened the door. Inside were five skeletons. Again, Father Ward gave the blessing.

'Pat Shaughnessy, Three more of them too – his mother, wife and little girl. I saw him the day he died. He said he was so hungry he could eat his children.'

'He didn't...'

'Never got the chance. He was dead the same night, I'm told. The wife and child were too. I meant to come back, but never got the chance till now.'

They spotted two dogs, scrabbling at a manure heap. They pulled out a tiny, manure-covered corpse. Pat ran at them, but they ignored him.

Father Ward grasped his arm. 'Come on, Pat. I told you before, you're only wasting your time.'

At the end of the village they spotted a saw pit. As they rode past he spotted two corpses lying in it, a man and a woman. They dismounted. Pat twisted the man's skull around. The eye sockets were empty; the face a vivid pink colour, pockmarked with black. Pat's insides heaved.

'James O'Brien,' Father Ward said, his voice flat. 'He was the last man I spoke to living here. There were only a family of three alive from eight, all the rest buried.'

'Three? There's only two here.'

'The daughter must have died since. They might have buried her already.' Another blessing.

As they crossed the ford out of the town, Pat spotted clothing caught in the branch of a tree by the stream. A dress? He dismounted and splashed down.

'Father – down here.'

It was the body of a young girl. The head was in the water. Grasping her hair, he pulled the head up, and dropped it in shock. Carefully, he did so again, and pulled the body out of the stream. He laid her on her back. The face was grossly swollen, giving the appearance of a head twice its natural size. It was a pale, yellowish white. One eye bulged out of its socket, the other was gone.

'That's what water does,' Father Ward said. 'I've seen many drowned men out the Killaries and Clare Island. A few days in the water and they swell up.'

He gave the blessing. Pat vomited.

Across the stream, was another mud cabin, more wretched than most. They led the animals through the water. Pat wiped his mouth, still dry retching.

They came to another cabin.

'Mary Kennedy,' Father Ward said. 'They were all near death when I last called.'

Pat held the reins of the horse and donkey. Father Ward tried the door, but a rope was tied through a hole in the door and around the doorframe. It was knotted tight from the inside. He took a small knife from his cassock, cut the outside of the rope and entered. Moments later, he came out again, his hand across his mouth, gagging and spluttering.

Pat left the animals and made for the door, but Father Ward caught him first, holding his arm in a vice tight grasp.

'No, Pat.'

'But I must see…'

'NO.'

Pat stood back, stunned, as Father Ward knotted the door shut. 'There are things no man should see.'

'But how can I understand…?'

'You've seen other cabins. Let that be enough for you.'

'And you?'

'I've seen too much already,' the priest said. 'I'm damned to hell this long time.'

They returned to the animals. Pat was disturbed and puzzled. What could be so awful that Father Ward could not even say it? So terrible as to damn him. It made no sense.

The priest led the donkey along. Pat grasped the horse's reins and followed him out of Drimcaggy. All around were the dead and dying villages of the Partry Mountains. Below, the houses and hovels of Tourmakeady crowded the edge of Lough Mask. The lake sparkled in sunshine, but sheets of rain were closing in from the west, shrouding the peaks of the Maumtrasna and Devilsmother range. A rainbow glimmered at the end of the lake.

He stopped. To the side, a goat track went higher, past a few cabins and up to another ridge above Drimcaggy. At the highest point of the ridge, a dead blackthorn tree clung to the edge of a high, rocky outcrop. Its gaunt limbs stood stark, sunlit against a darkening sky. He gazed at the tree, sensing the primeval power of it.

'Come on, Pat.'

'What's up here, Father?'

'Just a few cabins. There's no name to them.'

'Shouldn't we see who's there?'

'No-one lives there anymore. Hunger and fever killed them all.'

'All of them?'

'Twenty people, I don't know. The dogs had a feast, I can tell you.'

'That's awful. Did you see it?'

'Nothing much. I gave them the Last Rites a few weeks back. Not that there was much left to bless. Only a few skulls.'

'Oh God!'

'Don't let it be upsetting you, Pat. Sure it's no different to many another place. A few years' time, and they'll all have been forgotten, by God and by Man. Now come on.'

Pat followed Father Ward down towards Tourmakeady. Then the rain

283

began, a light drizzle at first, which quickly became torrential. Behind him, he heard the rolling of thunder over the crag above Drimcaggy. Soon he was drenched through. His hands were trembling, and he found it hard to grip the reins. The village of no name had frightened him. Why should it? It was tiny, just a few mud cabins, like so much of Mayo.

A simple place. A place of skulls.

Chapter 21

Bradford Observer, April 1849:

We call this an Irish question; but we are beginning to find out it is an English question too. Edinburgh, Glasgow, Liverpool, Bradford etc., have long been saddled with far more than a sixpence rate-in-aid for the support of the thousands of Irish emigrants whom idleness, crime or poverty throws upon British resources. Our labour market is thus over-stocked with shoals of destitute wretches whose misery prompts them to offer their services on terms frequently most prejudicial to the home operative. Besides all this, we are heavily taxed to maintain 30,000 troops in Ireland, whose duty is to keep discontent within due limits and enforce at the point of the bayonet the sacred duty of submitting to fate! These are no times to be squeamish about trifles. We should be ashamed to advocate spoliation, but the millions of Ireland ought to derive sustenance from their own soil; and as its present owners cannot rescue it from barrenness, there remains no alternative but to hand it over to others who should submit it to cultivation, make it feed its own inhabitants, and rescue England from the disgrace and peril to which she has been so long exposed.

The approach of cholera was slow. Its occurrence in Wakefield was followed by Huddersfield and then Bradford. Then all talk of it died away. It appeared, from all Murty could work out, that it had not been infectious. Very few had contracted it, and almost no one died.

Sinéad was not convinced.

'*They're saying it was the wrong kind,*' she told them. '*All the girls in the mill, they're talking of the big one, this time. King Cholera is back, he's killing shedloads of them everywhere.*'

Murty was not concerned. He believed that what *Sinéad* had heard in the mill had only been stories. King Cholera! Utter nonsense. If there was any cholera, it had come and gone. There were more cheerful matters to consider.

The letters from Carrigard had astonished and delighted him. He was relieved that Fergus was dead. Far more than that though, was that Kitty was coming. She had always had a calming influence on Aileen. Not to say that this was as critical as it had been. *Sinéad* too, had a soothing effect, and the work in the woollen mill, hard as it was, meant that Aileen was no longer brooding at home. He was delighted too at the thought of three other younger women joining them. He noted they were from Kilduff and the names were unfamiliar to him, since they had not attended his school in Carrigard. He reckoned he knew of their families though.

The days exhausted him beyond measure. Most evenings, he had his dinner with the family. It was at times like this that he appreciated the fact that he was lodging with a Mayo family. In many ways, they were gentle people, but with all the hardiness to survive the harsh conditions of Bradford.

Their use of language intrigued him. At home, the women always spoke in Irish. At first, Murty found it difficult to follow since he was not used to the dialect of the west of the county, but he understood it well enough and, within days, his own dialect of the language was changing.

The girls spoke English with no difficulty. This was no surprise, since they would have had to speak it in the mills and, being young, they would have little difficulty. *Tomás* Kerrigan was content to speak either language. When talking to Murty he spoke in English, sometimes in Irish, and Murty felt that *Tomás* was not even thinking of which language he was using. Sometimes he referred to *Máire* and *Sinéad* as Mary and Jane, and Murty guessed that these were their Mill names.

There was never any question of *Bríd* speaking English though. She never worked in the mill and spent all her time either at housework, or as an outworker stitching shirts on the table for the manufacturers. Murty felt that, while she might have had a basic understanding of English, she was not fluent, and, not wishing to embarrass her, he spoke mostly Irish when she was part of the discussion.

He learned that the family had left Mayo in the time of the 1840 hunger. They were not married, though as Murty noted, *Bríd* had already taken the name of her man.

'*And a hard time it was too,*' she told him. '*Four children, we had then. My youngest daughter died of fever. My oldest son died too, and he was a sore loss. He worked on the railways like yourself, travelling Yorkshire. He met with an accident, but as to what killed him, we never found out. And where he's buried, God only knows.*'

Many evenings, Murty sat at the table with *Tomás*; both men smoking their pipes and drinking whiskey. *Tomás* worked as a woolcomber; spinning being regarded as work for women and young men. As Murty soon discovered, he was a radical political thinker, something Murty had never expected among the grinding poverty of Bradford. He had been a member of the Bradford Mechanics' Institute Library for many years, where he had learnt how to read and write.

'And most important, I learnt to speak English there,' *Tomás* told him. 'That was always the first thing, knowing how to speak it, even before reading or writing it. There's many the man couldn't speak it when he first came to Bradford. You'd hear all sorts of languages being spoken in the Institute – Russian, Swedish and Polish, but German more than most. And the German speakers, they had all sorts of ideas of Unions and the rest of it.'

'The mill owners wouldn't like that.'

'They didn't,' *Tomás* said. 'But they wanted us speaking English. They didn't like all these notions the German fellows had. But sure what could they do? Stop the lectures in the Library? They didn't want that either. They needed the workers. And anyhow, reading and writing isn't against the law.'

'It's not,' Murty said. 'But I'm amazed the mills are taking on so many workers. There was talk of a crash in the markets.'

'That was last year,' *Tomás* said, 'and a dreadful crash it was too. Thousands and tens of thousands thrown out of work, right across the Yorkshire mills. Lancashire too. But then the market turned. Don't ask me why, but in a matter of a month or two, the mills were screaming out for workers. And they knew that in Mayo too. It's just like the time of the Railway Mania, when there was famine in Ireland and great want of men in England, then the Irish came over to England in their hundreds of thousands. And who, most of all? The Mayo men, of course. The men for the railways, and the women for the mills.'

'Hardly surprising, with all the evictions in Mayo,' Murty said. 'Lucan and the rest of them, it's them are driving everyone out of Mayo.'

'I know,' *Tomás* said. 'It's hard on them. Hard on you too, working on the railways.'

'Sure what choice do I have?'

'Not a lot, I'd say. It's either that or the workhouse.'

'This woolcombing, though, is it as hard as railway work, would you say?' Murty asked.

'The combers would like to say it is, but in all honesty, once you learnt the way of it, it wasn't so hard. But it hardly matters now. They brought in the accursed combing machines last year. Now, half the combers are gone.'

'Gone?'

'Gone from combing. There's still lots of jobs in the mills though. They're working as labourers, sweepers, ragsorters – all sorts of things. It's tough on them too.'

'I'd say it is,' Murty exclaimed. 'Low wages too, I'd guess.'

'Very low. But it's not just that. Now they're looked down on as the lowest of the low in the mills. It's a terrible thing for any fellow who takes a pride in his craft. Aristocrats of labour, they'd call themselves. Now they're no-one.'

'But…but what about you, *Tomás*.'

'I'm fine. I was lucky enough to stay on, and now I'm working the combing machines myself. But right now, for every job in combing there's dozens of men wanting it.'

'And what of other men's work in the mill? Would there be openings?'

'No. They don't want Mayo men pushing the wages down and bringing fever. The combers who were dismissed, they're angry as hell with their low wages now, and the last thing they want is Irish fellows working for less. No, there'd be no chance for you in the mills.'

'But you? You're Irish.'

'Ah yes, but I've been here many years. There was a time the hate was not as forceful, but this Famine has put paid to all that. They resent all the Mayo men in Bradford now. It's easy enough for the women to get work, harder for the men. And when the men get work, the hours are long. The women are held by law to no more than sixty hours a week, the young people the same. But for the men there's no upper limit, they work us for as long as they wish. And who makes all the profit? The mill owners, who else?'

'Will it ever change though?' Murty asked.

'Not until we organise. Strong Trade Unions, that's what we want.'

'Would that be possible?'

'It was possible before,' Tomás said. 'We had a strong Union once, acting for the combers and weavers. They organised a general strike, twenty thousand mill workers walked out, and thousands others joined them. All they wanted were wage increases – God knows, they're low enough – and Union recognition too. They held out for half a year, but in the end, hunger forced them back. Back in 1825 it was, they still talk about it around here.'

'I'd say they do.'

'They do. They'll never forget the '25 strike in the woollen towns. They're proud of it, and they still bear the bitterness. But where does pride and bitterness get you? We'd never organise a general strike now. The Chartists tried again in '42, and that went nowhere neither? Then the miners tried in '44, but they were starved into surrender. Another strike that'll be remembered for the rest of time.'

Murty was soon to learn more about mining in Bradford. The following Sunday, he and *Tomás* were smoking pipes as Bríd cleared up after dinner. The front door opened, and two young men entered the kitchen.

'Your new lodgers, Tommy?' one asked. 'More Irish?'

'Will ye go on out of that,' *Tomás* answered. 'This is an Irish house, ye'll have to put up with Irish neighbours. Won't ye?'

'We will right enough.'

'Two Sassenachs,' *Tomás* said, introducing them. 'Arthur and Samuel.'

'Yeadon,' the man called Arthur said. 'English and proud of it.'

'Miners too,' Samuel said, 'and proud of that too.'

Tomás waved them to the table, as *Bríd* took out four cups and filled them with a white spirit. Arthur tasted it.

'*Poitín*,' he exclaimed.

'Good God, your first word of Irish,' *Tomás* said. 'We'll make Irishmen of ye yet.'

'Not a snowball's chance in hell, Tommy,' Arthur said.

Murty discovered much about the Yeadon brothers. The first was that there were three of them. They were miners, working in the Bunkers Hill mine about a mile distant. Murty reckoned Arthur and Samuel were both in their early twenties, if that. Their parents were country people, their father working as a country labourer until the agricultural crash of the 1820s, when he had lost his job and moved to the coalmines of Bradford. Their mother, a widow now, was living in the next house, in a single room with the three brothers.

No-one had mentioned the third brother by name, and Murty did not ask.

'Nice fellows,' he commented, after they had left.

'They are,' *Tomás* said. 'We've known them for many years, well before the '44 strike. There's many in Bradford hate the Irish for that, you know.'

'For the strike? But…why?'

'There were stories of Irish scab miners. Thousands of them, they'll tell you. Some say it was Irish scab labour that broke the strike.'

'Was it true?'

'Not at all. Or could I put it this way. If there were a dozen Irish in all of the mines through the strike, I'd be surprised. But you know the way it is – the story grows in the telling, and a dozen becomes a thousand. If there were scab miners, they were brought in from Cornwall. There's many miners there, and well able to work hard, unlike the starving Irish. But the Bradford people wouldn't know the difference between the Cornish tongue and the Irish, so Irish they became.'

'So what will the miners do now? Will they strike again?'

'*Arra*, I don't know. The Miners' Association has collapsed. They were the best hope for Union power in England. They were strongest in Bradford, mind you, and the Bradford miners held out the longest, well into '45, until they were hollowed out with the hunger. Once the Bradford strike was over, the Association was finished, and we haven't heard a whisper of them since. I doubt there'll be another strike, and no wage rises either.'

'And what of Arthur and Samuel? What do they think?'

'Oh, they can tell you all about the strike. They were great Union men once. Their father was all wrapped up with Unions too before he died, long before the Association was begun even. He was some sort of Union officer once. He damned near beat it into the three of them. But now it's over. All over.'

'But what would they think of the Irish now?' Murty asked.

'Arthur and Samuel? They know the truth of it. They know there weren't no thousands of Irish scab miners, no matter what anyone says. And anyhow, we've all been friends this long time.'

One day, Murty was back working on the McCormack Cutting. He was stronger now. His wages had been increased, but he was an old man. How long could this last. He was always aware of the Edwardes & Ryan contract only a short distance away. Mayo men too, and what were they being paid? A shilling a day, if they were lucky.

And what of Murtybeg? Was he as rough as Danny? He was not certain. Certainly, Murtybeg had been a gentler lad when he was younger. But here he was, working with that Irene woman, and she was surely tough – tougher than any woman he knew. And now she owned Edwardes & Ryan. Murtybeg hated her, so why was he still working with her? Was it only money?

Could he himself work with Edwardes & Ryan again? An easy job in an office. Higher pay too, abusing Mayo labour. Working with the Molly Maguire gang? Danny had used them; he was sure of that. Would Murtybeg work with them though?

All these questions became more urgent that morning, when Roughneen appeared on the site.

'Johnny,' Murty exclaimed. 'I wasn't expecting to see you again.'

'And you might not have,' Roughneen answered. 'It was hard enough to find you. It took me an hour asking after you.'

'It's a big site,' Murty said, 'but you must have some great interest in me to go to all that trouble.'

'I have. Or should I say, your son has.'

'Be careful. You're not working for Murtybeg on this site. If the foreman spots you dossing, you'll be sacked.'

'Sure I don't work here anyhow.' Roughneen said. 'I can pretend though.'

He picked up a shovel and started work.

'So what is it Murteen wants with me?' Murty asked.

'He wants you to work with him again.'

'He does, does he?' Murty said 'Would that be his call though? He works close with that Miller woman, and she hates my guts.'

'That hardly matters anymore. Murtybeg fired her.'

'He what?'

'Fired her. Lavan was there, he saw it.'

'But she owns the business.'

'She might have. She doesn't now.'

Murty was puzzled. Was all the talk of her ownership just nonsense?

'So what now?'

'Murtybeg wants you back.'

'But I don't want to go back.'

Roughneen leaned on his shovel.

'But this work, Murty, it will kill you, and you know it.'

'Yes, Johnny, you're right, and I know you're right. It's a hard call for me to make either way. So you'll say I'm a fool, but I must tell you, I don't think I'd return. One way or another, I'd never want to work for Edwardes & Ryan again.'

'Would you not at least think about it,' Roughneen said.

'I'll tell you what,' Murty answered. 'Go and tell young Murtybeg I'm mindful of his generous offer. If I decide to work with him, I'll go over and talk to ye, and ye can pass the message on to him. But to be honest, Johnny, I don't think I could.'

Murty watched Roughneen walking back across the site towards the Colne Extension. Then he returned to shovelling muck.

In spite of everything, it had been a very hard decision for him. Might that change in years to come? Navvying was tough work for a man who had been a teacher. And teaching was a respected profession. Now he was nobody, working hard in the stink of Bradford. What would happen when he no longer could? Approach Murtybeg again, and ask for office work. No. With or without Irene, he had no wish to work for Edwardes & Ryan.

There was Aileen to consider too. She was earning money, and from all accounts becoming most able on the spinning machine. Her wages had been increased. He knew of the brutal conditions in the mills, and the long hours, though the ten-hour limit meant she worked less than the men, *Tomás* included.

He returned home that evening, carrying his shovel over his shoulder. A young woman rose from the table.

'Kitty!' he exclaimed. 'Kitty Brennan, is it? Arrived at last?'

'Who else would it be,' Kitty laughed. 'It's great to see you again.'

'*And this young lady?*' he asked, switching into Irish.

'*Peg McHugh,*' Kitty said. '*The Reilly sisters are next door; you'll meet them in time.*'

Bríd went to serve him.

'*So how are you liking it here?*' Murty asked Kitty.

'*Sure she loves it,*' *Bríd* answered for her. '*I gave herself and Peg mattresses in with Sinéad and Máire. They'll take the girls over to the mill tomorrow.*'

Murty sat and cut into a block of cheese.

'*You're looking well,*' he said. '*Ye must be tired after your journey though?*'

'*Tired enough,*' Kitty said. '*It was a long journey.*'

'*Which way did ye come? Was it out of Westport?*'

'*Not a chance of that. It was across Ireland we went, walking.*'

'*A long way.*'

'*Indeed, and far longer for me who had never even been to Castlebar in my life. 'Tis a mighty big country, Ireland. Six days crossing the country and all.*'

'*And you should have seen her crossing the Shannon,*' Peg said. '*Thought she'd drown, didn't you?*'

'*Arra, go way out of that.*'

'*She couldn't understand how it was two rivers either. No one told her there'd be an island in the middle.*'

'*Would you listen to her teasing me,*' Kitty said. '*It's fine for some. She's been working on the English harvest for years. I haven't.*'

Murty laughed. '*You've seen mighty things so,*' he said to Kitty.

'*Strange things too,*' Kitty said. '*Trains and steam boats, sure what of them did we ever have around Kilduff? Mills neither.*'

'*Well, you'll see plenty enough here,*' *Bríd* said. '*It's like you say, it'll be a new world for you, Kitty, and you're most welcome.*'

Murty finished his dinner, listening to the chatter around him.

He passed his plate back to *Bríd*, and waited until she had left the room.

'*Well tell me,*' he said to Kitty, '*what's Carrigard like?*'

''*Tis well enough,*' Kitty said. '*Pat is working for the County, as you may know, and bringing money home. Luke has been sending money back from America, but some of that has to be divided with Winnie's family up in Brockagh. Still, I'd say they've enough money to keep them going. What with Sabina and the bar too, they'll have no problem.*'

'*And what of the conditions around?*'

'*Starvation is desperate, and getting worse. Funerals every day, for those that can afford them. Bodies in the streets for those that can't. And evictions all over Mayo. Always, you see them on the roads, trying to get to*'

292

the workhouses, but sure they're not taking in any more. They say they're full three and four times over, and sure all they are is breeding grounds for fever. Mayo is dying at a terrible rate. We saw hundreds of them crossing the country, the half of them starving. It wasn't all a happy walk.'

'And cholera? Did you see any of that?'

'None in Kilduff yet. There's stories of it around Mayo, but whether they're stories or fact, I don't know. We heard enough of fever and hunger, and we crossing the country, but nothing of cholera. There were stories of it in Dublin before we left, but again I don't know how bad it might have been. Nothing like you have it here in England, from all we hear.'

Kitty and the other girls quickly got work in the mill.

'And it's as with Aileen,' Sinéad told Murty. *'Sure they know well what spinning is, and they'll work out the workings of the machines soon enough.'*

'It's hard work for ye, though,' Murty said to Kitty.

'No harder than the work of being a farmer's wife in County Mayo,' Kitty said. *'And here they're complaining of ten hour days. Sure in the summer months in Mayo, we'd be working night and day. We didn't even know what hours were, neither.'*

Murty was happy to note how much Kitty's presence had improved Aileen. There was incessant joking around the table, and sometimes Aileen smiled. Sometimes she spoke, though very little.

The Sunday following, Murty and *Tomás* began to build wooden bunk-beds in the girls' bedroom. The Yeadon brothers joined them, and the work was finished amid much banter and laughter.

It was a matter of wonder to Murty that these girls could find so much to laugh at, both at home and in the mills. Bradford too. The cholera, the stink of the sewers, even the noxious stench of the chimneys did not faze them. He had expected it would all be a shock to them, but they took it all without complaint.

Chapter 22

Wolverhampton Chronicle, May 1849:
North Staffordshire Railway. The southern portion of the main line of the North Staffordshire Railway, extending from Stone to the junction with the Trent Valley Line at Colwich, was open for passenger traffic last Tuesday. By running three trains daily to Colwich, in addition to those to Norton Bridge, the means are afforded of communicating with the metropolis 6 times within the 24 hours.

The letter from Sternberg shocked Murtybeg. He sat on the bed staring into the candle. What now? He had sacked Irene, he thought he was well rid of her, and now this. Would she end up as owner of Edwardes & Ryan after all? And if she did, would she sack him?

What other possibility was there? He had sacked her when he thought he had won. There was little doubt in his mind that she would seek her revenge in the same way. And then? All the long negotiations with the bank for nothing. All the long calculations and negotiations with Brassey and Mackenzie for nothing.

And no work either.

A thought struck him. Did the banks and the big contractors have confidence in him, as well as Edwardes & Ryan as a business? If he lost the business, he would have no money. Would they back such a man? Doubtful.

Next morning, he took a train into Manchester, and walked to the Law Library.

'Murtybeg!'

'Good to see you again, Louis, though like meeting a doctor, I'm afraid of how bad this might be. What's all this about an appeal?'

'One moment so. I'll just get the file from my locker.'

He returned and flicked through the papers.

'It's very bad news, I'm afraid. She's going after us again. Two different counts. First, she's appealing probate to the Probate Division of the High Court of Justice.'

'The High Court of Justice?'

'Yes, and I can tell you it surprised me at first. That's something that's

294

only done with large estates. And that's for a very obvious reason. At that level, you're talking about enormous legal fees. I've looked through a number of the past cases for probate in the High Court, and it's always involved top flight barristers. I don't want to be cynical, but in cases where there is a great level of doubt, it's often the party with the deepest pocket who wins. She's retained James Curzon of Curzon & Clegg as her counsel. On Rothwell's advice, I've no doubt. Curzon is one of the top silks in England, far higher ranking than Pritchard will ever be, and he will not come cheap. She knows I'm your counsel, but as for arguing a High Court case, she's banking on me having to appoint another top barrister to work with us.'

Murtybeg had gone pale. 'So we've no chance?'

'Little enough if she continues with Curzon. But it's not just that, she's threatening you with more than probate.'

'What so?'

'She wants to go after you personally on civil and criminal charges.'

'Criminal?'

'Fraud. Misappropriation of assets.'

'Misappropriation,' Murtybeg exclaimed. 'She should be well practised at misappropriation. So what can we do now?'

'There are two possibilities. Either she has indeed very deep pockets, and is prepared to gamble everything.'

'I doubt that, unless she's been involved in misappropriation herself for a long, long time.'

'Which brings me on to the other point. My very strong suspicion is that this is a bluff. She's hoping you cannot afford this. In fact, I reckon she knows it. It's like poker. She thinks you'll drop out, simply because you cannot go on. I must say, that while I have never met this lady, I strongly suspect that it is the kind of thing she would do.'

'So what would you recommend?'

'Call her bluff.'

'But I'd not be able to afford that either, would I?'

'No, just pretend you can. Take it all the way to the Courthouse steps. Many of these cases are resolved at the doors of the Court as soon as both parties realise that neither can afford to go further. In some ways, it takes a lot of nerve, because you don't know whether she will continue her bluff, but somehow I doubt she will.'

'So we pretend to go along with it. Is that it? Agree to go to the High Court, even though we know we're not going to go in?'

'Exactly, and I'll continue to deal with everything, at our agreed rate. If, of course, that's acceptable to you, Murtybeg.'

'Surely.'

He handed Murtybeg a cheque.

'What's this?' Murtybeg asked.

'Your twenty-five pounds. It was contingency only. And we haven't won.'

Murtybeg looked at the cheque in surprise.

'But we had won.'

'We thought we had. Now, let's wait until we see what happens. If it turns out it was all a bluff, then we win.'

'Oh look, Louis, that's unfair to you. Keep the money.'

'I can't.'

'Fine,' Murtybeg said, 'but I'll tell you what we'll do. I'll hold the cheque. But if we win, I would suggest another twenty-five pounds on top. Fifty total. Contingency, as you say.'

'Most generous of you, Murtybeg. But let's get back to more practical matters. What say you to a pie and a pint? My call.'

Murtybeg was a little surprised, but he decided to hide it.

'Why not?'

'Come on so.'

They left the Law Library, crossed the road, dodging carriages and carts, and went on to a bar.

'The Black Lion,' Sternberg said. 'This is for the younger crowd from the Law Library. Top silks would never eat here. Prefer to eat in private.'

Sternberg went to the bar to order, Murtybeg following. Sternberg pointed across to another table.

'See those three fellows over there – old friends of mine from law school.'

They had already spotted Sternberg.

'Nick! Is this a friend of yours?'

'Client more like. Murtybeg Ryan.'

'Oh, the Ryan case, is it? Good luck with that one, you'll need it.'

'We'll see.'

Sternberg and Murtybeg sat at a quieter table at the back of the bar.

'Now as I see it,' Sternberg said, 'the case against you might hinge on several other factors. The first is the question of the actual ownership of the business. Edwardes & Ryan was not a company, so the issue arises as to who owned it before your brother's unfortunate death. Miss Miller can claim that she and Daniel Ryan started the business together.'

'But that's not true. She only joined the business a few months after Danny had started it. He employed her as a clerk to look after correspondence.'

'But can you prove that?'

'I'm not sure,' Murtybeg replied. 'Could she prove otherwise, though?'

'Perhaps. All she would need is a letter addressed to Daniel Ryan and

Irene Miller trading as Edwardes & Ryan, and that, needless to say, might be forged. She's ruthless enough for that?'

'She is.'

'Which brings up another question. Who was Mr. Edwardes? Can we find him?'

'There was no Mr. Edwardes. It was a false name that Danny used to give his business respectability.'

'To give his business what!'

'Yes,' Murtybeg said. 'A respectable English name. Better for business, Danny thought.'

'I don't understand,' Sternberg said.

'It's just that many of the Irish contractors have a low reputation. Danny pretended that Mr. Edwardes looked after all accounts, but there was no Mr. Edwardes.'

'No court is ever going to believe that. Even if they did, another likely option is she will claim the three of them founded the business together, including the fictitious Mr. Edwardes.'

'But if Edwardes can't be found? Which he won't.'

'His third of the business might be held in trust. But in this situation, she could end up owning half of the rest of the business, and that creates another problem. If either party owns more than the other, there is a clear line of management. With equal shares, management can be paralysed, since there can be no majority decisions. Unless of course, Mr. Edwardes' trustees vote, though that's unlikely. In such a situation therefore, you would have to agree with her in everything, unless you held your nerve, and that puts you in a very difficult situation.'

'It does,' said Murtybeg.

Their food had arrived. Murtybeg cut into his pie, as Sternberg took a long draught of beer.

'Now, there's one other question I must ask you – is the business solvent?'

'It is now,' Murtybeg replied.

'Are you sure?'

'Yes, I prepared the trial balance a few days back. The business has been doing very well since Danny died.'

'But what of the time when your brother died? Could it have been losing money then? After the Railway Panic. Were his contracts profitable?'

'I don't know. Danny kept a lot to himself.'

'Could he have met all your debts in the event of a liquidation?'

'No.'

'In that case, it could be argued that Edwardes & Ryan were trading while insolvent, and that is contrary to law. Not that I'd worry about it now, since that time has passed, but if Miss Miller loses the case, she could threaten to expose you.'

'I see.'

'And it's been trading well since then?'

'Very well. We tightened up credit control and negotiated new loans with the Manchester & Salford, and since then, the business has been going very well indeed. There were other reasons, of course.'

'Like what?'

'Irene had her ways. Often, she would buy contracts.'

Sternberg looked at him in surprise.

'You mean Edwardes & Ryan have been involved in bribery?'

'Yes. I've had it stopped since she left though.'

'Thank God for that. You know, if offences have been committed, I should report them. So let's assume you never said any of that.'

'Agreed,' Murtybeg said.

'And there is one final point. This case must be taken by the possible beneficiaries, in other words those who would succeed to the business on your side, and that would most definitely include your father and mother. In fact, it might be argued that your father and mother might be the only beneficiaries. You would, of course, inherit, as their only living son, in due course, but that might be many years away.'

Murtybeg was stunned by what Sternberg had said, but decided not to question it. He realised that Sternberg had been assuming that he, Murtybeg, was taking the case on behalf of his parents as well as himself. But now it turned out that Murty and Aileen would be the owners of the business if they won, and he himself would be excluded. Why fight then, for a business he did not own either way?

But then a thought struck him. Murty had not been enthusiastic about owning Edwardes & Ryan, since he did not want to exploit starving navvies. Was he sure of that? Why ask? He had intended to write to Murty to tell him about the decision of the Probate Court, but he had not yet done this. Murty would still believe that Irene owned Edwardes & Ryan, which she did not, but might again. It was just as well he had not mentioned anything to his father. Best wait and see who owned the business when the dust had settled.

It was agreed that Sternberg would agree a date for the hearing and revert to Murtybeg as soon as it had been fixed. Then they parted.

As Murtybeg walked home from Stockport Station, a man approached him.

'Message from Gene Brady, Mr. Ryan.'

Thinking quickly, he said 'I don't know any Gene Brady.'

'I'm not lying to you,' the man said. 'I have a message from Mr. Brady.'

'Let me repeat,' Murtybeg said, 'I don't know any Brady.'

He was getting angry. There were two possibilities. A setup was one, someone was trying to trap him. It could be that Crawford was testing him, to see if he would report a Molly Maguire contact. The other possibility was that it was a real message, but in that case, it should not have been sent by Brady in this way.

'Your brother knew him,' the man said, 'and you've taken over from your brother. You know exactly who Gene Brady is. Now he will be expecting you next Wednesday morning. Your brother knew the address, but in case you don't, it is McCabe's bar in Vauxhall, just off Scotland Road, which is in Liverpool.'

'I know damned well where Scotland Road is,' Murtybeg said.

'Fine so. McCabe's bar. Wednesday morning. And be there, or, by God, you'll regret it.'

The encounter frightened Murtybeg. The more he thought about it, the more he thought that he had been threatened with death.

That evening, he wrote a letter to Inspector Crawford. He did not insert his own address. He used block capitals instead of his usual handwriting.

'Mr. B. sent me a message. He wants to meet me. What do you think? M.R.'

He did not sign it. Crawford would know who he was. He posted it to the address Crawford had given him.

Three days later he received a letter marked 'Private and Confidential' on the envelope. He opened it. This letter too was very brief.

'Why don't you go and meet him? J.C.'

For some time, Murtybeg considered Crawford's words. Then he realised the following day was Wednesday.

He decided to meet Brady, but he knew he was taking an enormous risk. He sat at his desk and began to write a letter.

'On May 8, 1849, I will travel to meet Mr. Gene Brady at McCabe's bar in Vauxhall, near Scotland Road, Liverpool. In the event of my murder or disappearance, the information should be passed to Mr. Louis Sternberg at the Manchester Law Library, and Inspector James Crawford of the Manchester Detective Police, and the said Mr. Brady should be tried for murder. Murtybeg Ryan.'

He placed it in an envelope, addressed 'To Whom It May Concern'.

He sealed the envelope, cleared the middle drawer of his desk and put it inside. Then he made a second copy.

Next morning, he left the house early.

His first stop was at the Law Library in Manchester.

'Murtybeg! I hadn't been expecting…'

'Sorry if I'm disturbing you, Louis. This is a different matter.'

Briefly, he explained to Louis about Danny's involvement in the Molly Maguire gang. He explained Crawford's request to meet with Brady, and the dangers it entailed. Finally, he took a copy of the letter and showed it to Sternberg.

'An excellent idea, Murtybeg. We may, of course, have a problem with Habeas Corpus, if your body should disappear, but I think that's a minor risk.'

'Habeas what?'

'Habeas Corpus,' Sternberg replied. 'If they don't have a dead body, it's hard to prove murder. But like I say, that's most unlikely to happen.'

'Fair enough,' said Murtybeg.

'I see you've left it unsigned.'

'I thought it should be witnessed.'

'Just what I was going to suggest,' Sternberg said. 'And we might as well have two witnesses.'

He walked across to another table, and returned with a colleague.

'This is Henry Chorlton,' he told Murtybeg. 'Another barrister.'

Murtybeg signed the letter, and Sternberg and Chorlton signed it as witnesses.

'And you needn't worry,' Sternberg told him, 'this will be kept safe. Very safe.'

Murtybeg walked to the station.

When he arrived in Liverpool, it was no different to what he had always known. Hundreds of Irish begging in the streets. The docks, the shipping and, amid all the commerce, the never-ending movement of passengers off the Irish ships. There were many recruits here for his navvy gangs, but that was not his reason for being in Liverpool.

Rather than take a cab, he decided to walk. Scotland Road was familiar to him, as of old, and Buckleys' was still there, busier and shabbier than ever. Quickly, he found McCabe's bar. He passed the scribbled address to a barman.

'I was told to come here.'

'Who are you looking for?'

'A Mr. Brady.'

He was ushered into a back corridor.

'Your name?' the barman asked.

'Ryan.'

'Your full name?'

'That'll be enough,' Murtybeg said firmly. 'If you want any more, I'll go.'

'You'll go nowhere,' the barman said. 'Just stand here and, by God, if you try to go, you'll know the consequences.'

Murtybeg stood. Very quickly, the barman returned.

'Mr. Brady will see you now.'

Brady was conciliatory.

'I'm sorry if you've been treated with suspicion, Mr. Ryan, I'm sure you know why,'

'I don't know anything, Mr. Brady. All I know is that I've been asked to be here.'

'Oh, there's reason enough.'

'There'd better be. I was approached in the street the other day by someone saying he was sent by you.'

'Yes,' Brady said, 'I heard about that.'

'If you don't mind me saying it,' Murtybeg said, 'it was a damned stupid thing to do. How in hell did I know who he was? He could have been from the police, trying to set me up. I had no way of knowing.'

Brady laughed.

'I'm sorry, Mr. Ryan. You're suspicious of the police?'

'Damned right, I am.'

A young woman came in carrying tea in china cups on a silver tray. No one said anything until she left.

'Now, Mr. Ryan. The first question is – have we met? I think we have.'

'I think so too,' Murtybeg said. 'I know we had been receiving assistance on bringing men in through the Port of Liverpool – paying off police and the like. I think I may have met you on one occasion then. Since then, we have dealt with your people directly.'

'But you didn't know my name?'

'I may have heard it since in conversation with my brother. To be honest, it didn't mean much, and until now, I'd not put the face and name together.'

Brady appeared to be satisfied.

'Well, let's leave that for now, shall we? We have other things we must discuss. But first I must say how sorry I was to hear about your brother's death.'

'Yes,' Murtybeg said, 'it was out of the blue. You knew him well, did you?'

'Well enough. But tell me, how do you think he died?'

Murtybeg was concerned about this line of questioning.

'The reason is clear enough,' Murtybeg said. 'He was run over by a train. The real question though is – how did that happen?'

'Quite so,' Brady said. 'That is what we are wondering too.'

'And who are 'we'?'

'We can discuss all that another time,' Brady said, with a wave of the hand. 'But as to how your brother died, what is your opinion?'

'From all the evidence, and mostly that of the train driver, it would look that he killed himself. The driver says he knowingly stepped out in front of the train.'

'He would say that, wouldn't he?'

'We could look at it like that, but no, I think he was right. I think Danny killed himself.'

Brady leant back in his seat.

'Let me tell you one thing, Mr. Ryan. A week before your brother's death, I was arrested. Had you known that?'

'I had not,' Murtybeg said. 'Sure how could I know? I don't live in Liverpool, and up to now, I've not known you in any real way.'

'Well, I was. And then your brother killed himself. Can you not see the two events might be related?'

'I wouldn't have thought so,' Murtybeg said. 'There were enough reasons during the crash in the money markets for Danny to be troubled. Many of his contracts were cancelled.'

'Well, there's another reason,' Brady said. 'We reckon my arrest was because of an informer, and that that informer was your brother. And he knew that we knew about him.'

'But…how can you prove that? It's utterly foolish.'

'Not so foolish, Mr. Ryan. The day after your brother's death, I was released and one of my friends, Aidan Sheridan, was arrested in Manchester.'

'But what would your release have to do with Danny's death?'

'Simple. Since he was dead, the police no longer had an informer. So the next question that occurred to them was – had your brother been murdered?'

'But what did that have to do with this fellow Sheridan?' Murtybeg asked.

'Since I was in prison and I could not have done it, the police would have thought that I might have had him killed through someone else. Hence Aidan Sheridan's arrest, following my release. They questioned him for days, but then they released him too. They had concluded that your brother had killed himself. That, at least is our understanding of matters as they now stand.'

Murtybeg stood up.

'It seems to me that you know more about all this than I do. It's very kind of you to give me all this information, but there's nothing more I can add to it.'

Brady stood and put his hand on Murtybeg's shoulder.

'Sit down, Mr. Ryan. We've more to talk about.'

'And if I don't want to talk?'

'You do. Believe me, you do.'

Murtybeg sat again.

'So what do we want to talk about?'

'Your foreman, James McManus. He was a comrade of ours.'

'I hadn't known that,' Murtybeg replied. 'Let me say though that he was, as you put it, a comrade of ours too. Not only was he a top foreman, he was also an old friend, even as far back as our school days. His murder upset us greatly.'

'And you don't think he killed himself?'

'Of course, not.' Murtybeg was getting angry again. 'He had been shot, and there was no gun beside him.'

Brady was conciliatory again.

'Fair enough, Mr. Ryan, and I regret if I've upset you. His killing upset us too. The real question is – who carried it out? Do you know?'

'I can truthfully say that I don't,' Murtybeg replied. 'There is one strong possibility though. You know, before Jamesy's death, there was a fellow running a shebeen on that site. He was beaten up and died afterwards. You know about that?'

Brady's eyes were impenetrable. 'Go on.'

'It would be a reasonable guess that Jamesy was killed in revenge. Nothing else.'

'So who killed him?'

Murtybeg stood up again. 'Look, you're questioning me, and I haven't the slightest idea. How in hell would I know? One of the fellow's family perhaps. A friend? Who knows? Do you?'

Brady dropped his eyes.

'We don't. We have our suspicions though. But the question was – why Mr. McManus?'

'Because the shebeen fellow had been on Jamesy's site. It would be a sensible guess that either Jamesy had beaten him up, or someone else had, acting on his orders.'

'On your brother's orders, perhaps?'

'Damned if I know. Not that it matters any more. Danny is dead.'

'So he is,' Brady said. 'But there is one thing I must tell you. James McManus' death had to be avenged.'

Murtybeg was unbelieving.

'Avenged? How in hell could it be avenged if no-one knew who killed him?'

'Does it matter?'

'It does. I'm asking you again – did you know who killed Jamesy?'

'We didn't. So we chose a foreman on the next site. An English fellow. We had to set an example. As much for your sake as ours.'

'For my sake! No, don't include me in this. You're saying you killed an innocent man!'

'Justice had to be done.'

'Let me repeat, Mr. Brady, not for my sake. All my foremen are possible targets now. If one of them dies, I'll blame you.'

'Which is why you need protection.'

'Protection! How…?'

'Very simple, Mr. Ryan. We will let them know that in future our retribution will be at the rate of three to one. That'll stop them. Dead.'

Murtybeg shook his head. 'And you're serious about this?'

'I am.'

'There may be those who don't care how many die. Had you thought of that?'

'No, Mr. Ryan, it would certainly work. Three to one will stop any possible payback. There will, of course, be a charge.'

'A charge!'

'Protection, if you like. You pay us for your protection, you and your workers. Let us say – tuppence per man per day. How many men do you employ?'

Murtybeg stood. 'Let me tell you Mr. Brady, there's no question of that. You stop this now, whether there is another revenge killing or not. It's bad enough as it is. And if I hear of any more killings of English foremen, or the like, you really will have an informer. And before you tell me about the fate of informers, the police will be informed in advance, and you'll be up on a hanging charge. And I will testify and see you hanged.'

Brady was furious.

'That would cost you your own life. You know that.'

'So it might, Mr. Brady. My life for yours. If I die, the police will know by whose hand. Two dead men. Not very sensible, is it?'

'And what if you disappear, here and now?'

'You'll hang anyhow. I can warn you of this. If I don't return, there are people who will know why not. The fact of my being here is already in writing, with your name, address, and the reason why.'

'The reason…?'

'Yes. I said, in writing, that I was meeting you today, and if I don't return, that you should be arrested for murder. A copy has been filed away in the Law Library, signed and witnessed by two legal counsel.'

'You damned bastard.'

'Call me what you like, Mr. Brady, but first, think it through. If I return, fine, you'll never hear from me again. If I don't, you will pay the price. If you go any further with this, you will hang for it.'

Murtybeg made for the door.

'Mr. Ryan.'

'Yes, Mr. Brady,'

'Let's forget all about it, shall we?'

'Damned right, we shall,' Murtybeg said.

He returned to Manchester, and re-visited the Law Library.

'Just so you can see I'm still alive, Louis,' he explained. 'You might hold on to the letter though, in case of future necessity.'

'Fine so,' Sternberg said.

Murtybeg explained developments to Sternberg. Then he decided to leave the matter sit, and did not write to Crawford again. For some time, he thought that that was the end of the affair.

Then, one evening, the maid told him that there was a Mr. Crawford at the door. Murtybeg went down himself, and brought him in.

'I hope to God no one has been watching this door,' he said to Crawford. 'Your just being here could set me up as an informer, you know that.'

They both sat.

'Well,' Crawford said, 'you know the reason I'm here. I'd been waiting for you to get in touch. When we didn't hear from you, I thought it best to come and see what was happening. Did you meet Gene Brady?'

'Why should I tell you?'

'You might need protection.'

'Protection from the likes of you, more like. I have committed no offence. Have I?'

'Now we're getting a little heated, Mr. Ryan,' Crawford said. 'We are trying to trap a very dangerous criminal. We were, as you know, most concerned about your foreman's murder. We know for sure that James McManus was a member of the Molly Maguire gang, as is Brady, who has already exacted his revenge. Will Brady kill again? That is what I want to know.'

'I rather doubt that,' Murtybeg said.

'And why, pray, do you say that?'

'Because I asked him not to. And if he tries it, he knows the penalty. He may threaten, but he won't do it.'

Crawford shook his head.

'I don't know what to say to that,' he said. 'You asked him – very nicely, I'm sure – not to exact his revenge. And he agreed?'

'Exactly,' Murtybeg said. 'Just so.'

'And why would he do that?'

'Because he knows that he would have to kill me first. He knows too, that he would hang for it.'

'But...I don't understand.'

'With respect, Mr. Crawford, that is your problem, not mine.'

A SETTLEMENT. Murtybeg was working late one evening. The door opened, and Irene entered.

'How did you get in?' he asked.

'Never mind.'

She was wearing a long black and grey dress lined with sequins, drawn tightly in at the centre to uplift her breasts.

'What do you want?' he asked.

'An understanding.'

'An understanding!'

'Yes. We're wasting money on lawyers, both sides. And both of us run the risk of losing. Perhaps we should cut our losses and come to a settlement.'

'Damned right, we should. But how?'

'Rothwells have been in touch. Curzon & Clegg have suggested one class of settlement that would certainly work.'

'What kind of settlement might that be?' he asked, intrigued.

'A marriage settlement.'

At first Murtybeg could not understand what she was suggesting. As it sank in, he gazed out at the rain, trying to hide his surprise.

'A marriage settlement?'

'Yes. The two of us together. It's the only way to protect the assets of both parties.'

'You're saying...we should marry?'

'I am. And it could work. Couldn't it?'

Murtybeg was thinking fast, though he felt half hypnotised by the rain-drops running down the window panes. At last he turned from the window, observing her.

She still stood erect, the taut dress outlining her figure.

'It could,' he said, trying hard to sound casual. 'In fact, it could work very well indeed.'

Chapter 23

New York Herald, March 1849:
We have to report the arrival at quarantine of the British ship
Cambria, the same vessel that put in under the protection of
the Delaware Breakwater a few days since. She brings one
hundred and fifty passengers. Since she left Ireland, seventy-
eight deaths have occurred on board, and she has now on
board fifty-two sick with ship fever.

The lockout caused a shock all across the coal patches.

Winnie's reaction was to take care of Liam, and keep on at stitching
shirts – their only form of income. At first, Luke was frustrated, roaming the
house, and hanging out with other miners on street corners. It was still cold
though, often barely above freezing, and the bitter wind made it much colder.
They stood on the lea of the shacks, blowing into their cupped hands.

One day he walked down to the Hibernian Club. Groups of men sat at
the tables, but there was very little whiskey being drunk. Farrelly was there,
together with Mick O'Brien and Jack Kilgallon. He went to join them. There
was a heated discussion.

'Sit down,' Farrelly said, 'and tell us your opinion.'

'What is there to say?' Luke said. 'It's a lockout. They want to break us.'

'And Jack here is saying it's not a lockout. It's a suspension.'

'A what?' Luke asked.

'A suspension,' Jack said. 'And it's not what I'm saying, it's what the
Operators are saying. It's nothing to do with us or the Union. They're suspending mining for four weeks.'

'In the name of God, why would they do that?' Luke asked.

'Because the price of anthracite in New York and Philadelphia is too
low,' Jack said.

'*Arra*, that's nonsense.'

'They're saying they're losing money.'

'That's only a damned excuse.'

'True or false, that's what they're telling us. They're suspending all
shipments for four weeks to drive the price up. They're saying they're losing
money on every ton.'

'Yes,' Mick said, 'we've heard that one before. It's only a way to drive down wages. They've told us that it's a choice between closing the mines and lowering wages. That's what they're going to do. And they'll starve us. In four weeks' time, we'll agree to anything.'

'I reckon you're right,' Farrelly said. 'Sure it doesn't matter a damn if the Operators get the prices back up. The railways will see their chance; them and the canal operators. As soon as they see higher prices, they'll jack up the freight rates, and the Operators will still have their excuse to push wages down. No, they gave in when we had them over a barrel, but spent the next weeks plotting how to break us. Isn't that it?'

'And what about our strike pay?' Luke asked. 'We've all paid into the fund.'

'The Union are saying it's a lockout, not a strike,' Farrelly said. 'And I'm not sure that we have a lockout fund.'

'But that's mad.'

'I know.'

Luke found it all hard to understand. All the talk of markets and freight rates had confused him. He had seen the lockout simply as a way to break the Union and the miners' resolve. He reckoned that was still true, whatever the Operators might say. But the Union's attitude to strike pay disturbed him even more.

When he told Winnie what he had learnt that evening, she saw it all as immaterial.

'We still have to eat, Luke,' she said. 'If you can't work, at least you've got a seamstress in the family. And we don't have to waste time in washing,'

'Washing what?'

'Washing the curtains every week. Or perhaps you hadn't noticed. It's not you that would have to wash them. Have you never noticed the amount of dust the breaker gives out?'

'Well, yes.'

'And where do you think it all ends up?'

'But sure we've no problem now. No breaker, no dust, no washing.'

'Exactly,' Winnie said.

Then their own coal ran out.

They scavenged the forests around for firewood. Soon the supply of dry timber had disappeared in the area. They went higher up the trail, looking for fallen trees and branches. When they found what Luke wanted, they attacked the trunks and branches with axes, cutting it into smaller pieces to carry back. But then there was nothing left there either.

'What do we do now?' Luke asked one evening.

'I know what Winnie and myself are doing,' Ellen replied. 'We're going up the culm bank. There's plenty of coal in with it.'

'You're right,' Luke said. 'But I'll tell you what, you leave that to us men, and you girls keep stitching shirts. That way we'll keep some money coming in.'

The next morning, Luke and Ned took buckets and left the house. It was still dawn, but in the dim light, the culm bank almost appeared to be moving. There were dozens of women and children around the base and all the way to the top. For a moment, he thought back on the mass graves in Mayo; the rats crawling over dead bodies. To hell with it. He would have to stop thinking like that. He worked with Ned, picking fragments of anthracite out from the stone, until they had both filled two sacks. Then they hefted them onto their backs, and returned to the house.

Soon the easy supply of anthracite on the culm bank was gone. Some of the women began to dig deeper into the bank, but already Luke knew it was useless. Always, they looked at the anthracite bank just outside the mine entrances. They were well guarded though, day and night.

Slowly, their cash ran down. There were still no contributions from the Union's strike fund. Winnie and Ellen cut back on portions in the meals, though there was no question of cutting back on Liam. In any case, he was still suckling.

'We'll soon have nothing left,' Winnie said. 'The truck shop has put all the prices up.'

'Just what you'd expect,' Ellen said, 'and still they're saying it's not a lockout.'

'And what will we do when we run out of money?' Winnie asked.

'The truck store will extend us credit,' Ned said. 'But we don't want that, do we?'

'No way do we want that,' Luke said. 'What with their prices, and their interest, we'd be paying it off for years.'

'If we'd ever pay it off,' Ned said.

One day, the shirt-man arrived. He brought in boxes of material, and placed them on the table. He was a thin-faced man, lean in appearance.

'I want you to note,' he said, 'this material is white.'

He snatched a completed shirt from the table, placing it beside the material.

'Have you washed these?'

'We have,' Ellen said, uncertainly.

'They'll need more washing back in the warehouse. That'll cost, you know. How many have you done?'

'Ten shirts,' Winnie said. 'How about you, Ellen?'

'Twelve.'

The shirt-man counted them.

'Eight cents per shirt,' he said.

'It was ten!' Winnie exclaimed.

'Well, it isn't now. There's thousands of women across the coal patches stitching. They can't take this number of shirts in Philadelphia. New York neither.'

He left. Winnie looked at the money she had received. 'What now?'

'We'll stitch more shirts. That's all,' Ellen said.

Winnie went up to the bedroom. When she came down, she handed Luke a needle and a thimble.

'Here, you'd better get started.'

Luke looked at her in amazement. 'Me! I wouldn't be able.'

'Here, it's simple. Grab the needle.' She handed him white thread. 'Now all you've got to do is put that through the eye of the needle. Just like this.'

Luke tried again and again. '*Arra*, it's impossible.'

'Well, why can I do it?'

'Because you've got smaller hands. Sure look at mine.'

Ned was laughing. 'She thinks a miner can stitch shirts.'

'And what are you laughing at?' Ellen demanded. 'Here, grab this.'

Slowly, the two men got used to stitching. Watching Winnie's fingers move though, Luke wondered how anyone could work at a speed like that. He could not even get up to half. It was slower still, trying to stitch in straight lines. On more than one occasion, Winnie took his shirt from him, and stitched it herself.

Sometimes Luke took their remaining money to the truck store, but prices had increased beyond anything he could believe. He thought of the price of grain in Kilduff during the worst days of the Famine. Was it the same now? Surely, no luxuries could be afforded anymore. Basic corn, and no meat.

He was thankful, as the four-week lockout came towards an end.

'Two days to go,' he commented to Ned.

'Yes,' Winnie said, 'and a week after that till we'll have wages.'

Then the news came through.

Ned had been out playing cards in the Miners' House.

'They've extended the lockout,' he said. 'Another week.'

Luke stared at him in utter disbelief. 'But how could they do that?'

'They just did.'

The shirt-man had not come back. Now they had no cash whatsoever.

'We can get credit at the truck store,' Luke said.

'As if we damned well want to,' Ned answered.

'As if we'd any choice,' Luke said.

He dragged himself up to the truck store. The price of corn had gone up again. So had the rate of interest. 'Thirty percent,' he gasped.

'Take it or leave it'.

Luke took it.

Winnie and Ellen had cut back to one meal a day. Luke was beginning to feel sluggish. He realised he had not met Farrelly, O'Brien or Kilgallon for a few weeks, and somehow, no longer cared.

Another week. Another extension of the lockout.

'They use big words anyhow,' Luke said. 'It's almost poetic.'

'Damn your poetry,' Winnie said, gruffly.

Luke realised she was finding it hard to feed Liam. He did not comment on it, preferring not to upset her. She was on the edge already. She had already come close to losing Liam to cholera in New York. Now they were facing starvation.

Impossible. This was the United States of America.

Stories of famine in Ireland drifted back to the coal patches, often through the Hibernian Clubs. Luke felt worse than ever. They were starving in America. How on earth could they send money to their starving families in Mayo?

Then the shirt man returned.

'Which is one good thing,' Winnie said.

They went back to stitching shirts.

'And at least there's no coal dust to be turning them grey,' Ellen said. 'But the prices in the truck store have gone up again.'

One night, the truck store was attacked. Screaming men broke down the doors and the windows. Luke saw a stream of women in the moonlight, running towards the store, and even as they came out, they were fighting over the spoils. Then the police arrived. A baton charge scattered the women.

Winnie had come outside, standing beside him. He pulled her back. She resisted, still watching the spectacle, as women were coshed by the heavy batons.

Lackan was awash with rumours. There was talk of women killed, though Luke doubted it if had really happened. A few days later though, attention turned to the coal banks. A group of women roped the top of the fences and pulled them down. This time, the police were late in arriving and the banks of anthracite were too extensive to guard. The running battle went on for two days.

'I can't understand it,' Ellen said. 'That's always been our right. The women have always taken the coal. What's wrong with them now?'

'It's the Operators, I'd say,' Ned said. 'They're trying to break us, force us into the truck store and credit forever.'

'It's not worth it,' Luke said. 'The warmer weather is coming anyhow. We'll need little enough coal for cooking. But don't worry, we're back working on Monday.'

The lockout was extended for a seventh week.

There were rumours of deaths from starvation in the remote coal patches in the mountains.

Still Luke was extending his credit at the truck store to pay for food, but even so, they were all gaunt with hunger now. He was desperate. At thirty percent interest, it would be almost impossible to ever pay back the debt. Would Liam grow to be a man, cursing his father's debts?

To hell with that. How much further could they cut back on food? One meal a day, and little enough at that.

'I'd never thought I'd feel like this in America,' Ellen said. 'This is out-and-out war. They'll not stop till they have us on our knees.'

They continued stitching shirts, often in the sputtering light of a single candle. The price had dropped to six cents per shirt.

'It's worse than Ireland,' Winnie said one night. 'We had a famine there, and what did we do? We fled across the Great Ocean to America, the land that can feed the world, and here we are, starving. These Operators, they're worse than the bloody landlords.'

'I think you're right,' Luke said. 'And talking of bloody landlords. The stories of famine from home are getting worse. There's evictions around the county. What can we do? We've no money for ourselves.'

'Borrow from the truck store,' Winnie said.

'We can't. Credit is for truck, not for cash. They reckon we'd disappear if we had cash in our pockets.'

At last, the extension was coming to an end.

'And they're saying it's for sure this time,' Ned said. 'There's no further extensions. We're back to work on Monday. We won't have to starve anymore.'

'And damned glad I'll be of that,' Luke said. 'I couldn't have taken much more of this.'

The following day was a Sunday. Luke stayed home with Winnie and Ellen, while Ned went playing cards in the Miners' House.

'I hope he won't be gambling,' Ellen said.

'I doubt if anyone will have anything to gamble with,' Winnie said.

It was late when Ned returned. He thumped the table in fury. Ellen jumped back, stunned.

'Ned, what in the name of God…?'

'The Union,' he yelled.

'The Union? But what have they done?'

'A strike. That's what they've done. The bloody Union have declared a strike.'

Chapter 24

Freeman's Journal, Dublin. May 1849:
In consequence of the low price of coal, the miners of
Pennsylvania are determined not to forward any more for
the present. The result is a falling off already of beyond
one hundred thousand tons in the supply of coal from that
quarter as compared with the same date in former years.

Luke hugged Winnie close in bed that night. Thankfully, Liam was asleep.

'How could they do this?' she asked. 'What kind of animals are they?
They're meant to be on our side. If they wanted a strike they could at least
have waited until we had fed ourselves before they starved us again.'

'I know, *alanna*,' Luke said, 'I can't understand it any more than you can.'

'They never even asked us.'

'They didn't.'

'But this Bates fellow, what kind of man is he? What game is he playing at?'

'I've been thinking about that,' Luke said. 'Either he's working for the
Operators, or he's trying to play some kind of political game.'

'Or he just hates the Irish,' Winnie said.

'Yes, that's another possibility.'

Winnie blew out the candle. For some time, she was silent, but Luke
knew she was not sleeping. At last she turned to him again.

'I don't know when they'll finish with their strike. We really are starving
now, aren't we?'

'We are,' Luke said.

'Or at best, the child will end up with rickets. Stunted growth too.
Maybe that's what they want. Short fellows to work the low drifts in the
mines.'

Luke was getting concerned. He wondered if Winnie was quite stable.
Still, no matter how he thought about it, there was no sensible explanation
for the strike. Perhaps Winnie was the one who was sound, and the rest
of the world was mad.

He slept, until he was awoken by Winnie's shout. He started up out of
the bed, realising that it was daylight. Winnie was at the window.

'Luke, come and look at this.'

He stared out the window. Right across Lackan, hundreds of men were streaming towards the mines.

'They're open, they're open.'

'Oh, my God,' Luke said, 'I'd better get moving.'

Half an hour later, he was at the weigh station. He waved at Farrelly and the others as they went down the deep drift. Six days to the end of the week, and money. Real money. Not that they should spend too much of it. It would be a year at least before they could spend all their wages again. Their first need was food, but that would still have to be kept to a low level. The reports coming back from Ireland were savage. As soon as possible, he would have to start sending money back to Mayo. If not, he, Winnie and Liam would live, but their families in Ireland would die. A deadly choice.

And the other desperate need was his debt at the truck store. Thirty percent interest. It just had to be paid off, and paid off quickly. That would not be easy. If he let it get away from him, he would never catch up.

But there were other things to concentrate on. Much of the time he was working alongside Cantwell, ordering the carts forward, placing the weights on the scales, and agreeing the results. Every evening, he and Cantwell would check the accuracy of the weights.

Mostly, the mules were led out by miners, though sometimes by young boys. Sometimes the boys were pulling the wagons on their own. This made him uneasy.

Just as disturbing, were the boys working inside the breakers, hunched or kneeling over the moving belts of coal. He was working alongside the Number Two Breaker, and in the gloomy light, he could see them picking slate and grey rock out from the black anthracite.

Another line of slate pickers was made up of old men, a few with missing legs, working alongside the boys. Few of them were as nimble in picking out the slate as the boys were.

On the third day of work, a stranger came across to Luke at the weigh station. He was wearing a long duster overcoat, made from a rough black canvas, ripped in places. A wide, black belt held it together; brown leather showing through the cracks.

'What are you doing?' the man demanded to know.

'Isn't it obvious,' Luke said. 'Weighing coal, what else.'

'And who pays you?'

'The Union.'

'Not any longer. I represent the Union here. There's a strike on, you know. And, by God, you'd better shut down, otherwise you'll pay the penalty.'

He left, without further explanation.

Another cart was waiting for the weigh station.

'What's happening?'

'It's the Union,' he told them. 'They want us to close the weigh station.'

'But why?'

'Damned if I know.'

Cantwell strode over. 'What in hell did he want?'

'He said he was from the Union, and I've got to stop for the strike.'

'The bastard. He's always causing trouble.'

'Who is he?'

'Carew. He's one of the Union negotiators.'

'A rough fellow?'

'Rough is right,' Cantwell said. 'He's got one hell of a name for trouble, that bastard.'

'That bad?'

'Worse. He was some kind of officer in the Cherokee Wars down in Texas, but he got himself court-martialled. Damned if I know what for. Even the army wouldn't have him.'

'So what do we do now?'

'Ignore him. If we stop the weigh station we'll have to dismiss everyone, and you're not going to do that, are you?'

Luke was caught. He realised he could not stop, and he kept working for the rest of the day. Towards evening, Farrelly came, leading a mule and cart.

'I'm not being paid, Martin, you know that?'

'What?'

'The Union have refused to pay me. They say there's a strike on.'

'But…'

'It's different for ye. It's the Operators are paying ye, and the Operators are back in business, but the Union isn't. They've said I'll pay the penalty if I carry on. Whatever that means.'

He decided not to mention the episode to anyone else. He could clarify all, either with the Union or the Operator tomorrow.

He went home with Ned. As Ellen and Winnie cleared the dishes, Luke sat talking to Ned about the other events of the day. No tobacco or whiskey though.

'I'm just so glad to be back at work,' Ned told him. 'Not that we're doing any great production. Seven weeks of lazing around doesn't help. Still, I reckon we'll get up our speed, and be back to normal tonnage within a week or two.'

'I know,' Luke said, 'we'll need it too.'

There was a loud knock on the door, and a shout of 'Union'.

Ned stared at Luke.

'I'd better open it.'

Two men pushed their way inside. Luke recognised one of them as Carew. Both men had pistols pushed down inside their belts. The metal glinted grey and gold in the candlelight.

Carew pointed at Luke.

'There's one. Scab labour at the weigh station.'

'Who the hell are you?' Ned asked.

'Enforcers for the Union. And, by God, you will respect the Union.'

He whipped out his gun and pointed it at Ned.

'Let's see your fingernails.'

The black grime under the nails was obvious.

'More scab labour.'

Luke was about to protest, but at that moment, two more men entered. They were both carrying clubs.

'In the name of God,' Ned said, 'is there any call for this?'

'Yes,' Carew said. 'A strike has been called, and you've refused to recognise it.'

He spun the cylinder on the gun.

'But damn it to hell,' Luke said, 'after seven weeks' starvation…'

'It's not for you to reason why. John Bates has his reasons, and you don't question them.'

'So it's back to starvation, is it? We can't…'

Carew's face contorted with anger.

'I've warned you twice already.'

He pointed the gun at Luke's head and pulled the trigger. There was a loud click. Winnie screamed. Luke staggered, only slowly realising what had happened. He touched the side of his head, but there was no wound and no blood.

'And that's only to show you what'll happen to you the next time,' Carew said. 'From now on, all the chambers will be loaded.'

He left, followed by the other men.

Luke was convulsing violently. Winnie was crying, Ellen's arms around her.

'Stay easy, Luke,' Ned said, grasping him by the arm.

'I'm sorry, Ned,' Luke stuttered. 'For a second, I thought…'

'I know what you thought. So did I.'

He sat Luke down.

'The real question in my mind is how many others have been visited? What's going to happen tomorrow?'

'Well, they can't have visited everyone,' Ellen said.

'Let's wait and see,' Luke said, stammering. 'I'm damned if I want to risk my life, and I'll tell you something, that game with the gun frightened the hell out of me. Were there any bullets in it?'

'I didn't see,' Ned said. 'I wasn't looking too close.'

'Well, neither was I. We don't even know if I could have been killed. But I'll tell you this, Ned, I'm not going to go back to work, I don't know about you?'

'How will we know what's happening though?' Ned asked.

Luke held his head in his hands.

'There's nothing to stop us going down towards the mine, see what's happening in the morning. We'll stay well back, though.'

Slowly, the convulsions faded.

When they went to bed, Winnie was crying.

'Luke, this can't go on. We've no money, and no food.'

'I know,' Luke said, 'and the only way we can get by is by getting more credit through the truck store, and you know where that leads. And they sure as hell won't give us money to be sending back to Mayo.'

'Mayo? I wonder if they're alive or dead.'

'God only knows.'

'Perhaps we should leave this accursed place,' she said, with vehemence.

'And go where?'

'Anywhere. Get you back on the railways?'

'There's damned little work on the railways,' Luke said. 'Isn't that why we're here, digging coal instead of building railways.'

'I wonder how Murtybeg is doing. Would there be work back with him?'

'There might,' Luke said. 'And to be honest, I'd take that work if I had a chance, and to hell with the rights or wrongs of it. But we don't have that choice any longer, do we?'

'Why not?'

'In God's name, Winnie, where would we get the money to cross the Atlantic?'

'But damn it Luke, we're starving. And I'll tell you this, neither the Ryans nor the Gallaghers ever starved in Ireland. You always had enough work as a clerk on the Relief Works. Pat too. Your father and my father too. You all had work, and little as it was, it was paid work. And here, what do we have? A strike. No pay from the Operators, and nothing from the Union neither. Why were ye all paying Union dues? Can you tell me that?'

The next morning, Luke and Ned walked out towards the mine. There was a group of men in front of the mine entrance and the breaker, a hundred or more, Luke estimated. Every one of them were carrying cudgels, and Luke saw that some of them were also carrying guns. Enforcers! Carew was there.

To the side were a group of police; chatting to each other and smoking pipes. They clearly had no interest in what was happening in front of them.

Luke and Ned stayed well back.

A large number of miners had gathered in front of the enforcers. For a long time, there was silence. Then Carew raised a gun in the air, and let off a single shot. There was a roar from the enforcers as they charged forward, whipping wildly at the miners in their path. The miners broke and ran. Still the police did nothing.

Many men had fallen, and the enforcers strode between them, whipping at everyone who moved.

'Nothing we can do,' Ned said. 'Let's go home.'

They described the bloody scenes to Winnie and Ellen.

'This is impossible,' Winnie said. 'They're worse than Lucan's tumblers. Good God, we called him the Exterminator. What do we call these bastards?'

'Enforcers,' Ned said.

'Not a word I'd heard before,' Ellen said.

'Simple enough,' Luke said. 'It's American for Exterminator.'

That night, Winnie went upstairs to feed Liam. Then there was a knock on the door. Luke and Ned stared at each other.

'In the name of God, who is it this time?' Ned asked.

'Let's see,' Luke said.

He went to the door.

'Who is it?' he shouted.

'Mick O'Brien.'

Luke opened the door.

'Any news?'

'They've decided to leave the battleground to us,' Mick said.

'What!'

'They've withdrawn the enforcers to the edge of the mine. They're setting up tents there, so now they're letting us take away our injured and dead.'

'Dead?'

'Only one, to be honest, but isn't it enough?'

Luke and Ned put on their caps and lit their lamps.

Winnie had come down stairs. 'What is it Luke?'

We're just bringing our injured back. That's all. Now you stay with Ellen, and don't worry about us.'

'No, Luke. No.'

'It's alright,' O'Brien said. 'They're well back. They're letting us take our wounded out. They're not going to attack us.'

'But...if they do.'

'They won't.'

Winnie was still doubtful.

'Watch for the guns, Luke.'

'We will.'

At the edge of the mine was something Luke had never expected to see in the United States – dozens of miners' lamps in the dark, moving forward and back through the area where the charge had taken place.

One man came over to them. 'Be careful, and don't vex the bastards. They're well and truly armed. Now, can you take an injured man in for tonight?'

'We can,' Ned said. 'That's not to say that we'll be able to feed him.'

'*Arra,* sure I know that. But at least you'll be able to clean his wounds.'

He showed them a man lying on the ground.

'This fellow, he's from up the Miner's House. They're all crowded out tonight. We can't leave him here though. God only knows what the bastards would do to him in the morning.'

Luke and Ned edged the man up into a standing position. He was groaning feebly, only half aware of anything. In the dim lamplight, Luke saw the blood on his face. Carefully, they walked him forward, stumbling as they tried to avoid the other wounded. At length, they reached the house.

Ellen answered to their knock.

'Quick. Bring him in.'

She laid towels on the floor, and Luke and Ned eased the man down onto it. Ellen stuffed a folded jacket under his head. Already, Winnie was heating the water.

A few minutes later, Ellen gently washed his wound.

'We'll need bandages,' she said.

'Don't I know it,' Winnie said. She produced a section of shirt-material.

'That's just what we need,' Ellen said. She took it from Winnie, ripping it sharply, and started to wrap it around the man's head.

Sometime later, the man was fully conscious.

'*Where am I,*' he asked in Irish.

Luke recognised the accent as Mayo. '*In a Mayo house, beside the mines,*' he answered.

'*There's a pain in my head.*'

'*That was from the smack on the head they gave you. The enforcers, may God damn them to hell.*'

'*Ah yes,*' the man replied.' *I remember now. It was a hard battle.*'

'*It was. They're violent men.*'

Blood oozed through the dressing.

'Over here, Ellen.'

Ellen ripped more shirt material and brought it over.

'It was a hard blow,' she said, 'but I don't think your skull is cracked. Enough to knock you out cold, but no worse than that.'

Carefully, they eased him up from the ground and brought him into Ned and Ellen's bedroom.

'But I can't be taking a bed,' the man protested.

'Arra, don't you be worrying,' Ned said, 'there's many the night we slept on the floor back in Mayo.'

As Luke threw a blanket over him, the man grasped his hand.

'Dara O'Gachain is the name to me,' he said.

'Luke and Winnie are the names to us,' Luke told him. 'Ned and Ellen here are the man and woman of the house.'

Next morning, Dara was sitting at their table, spooning porridge.

'Will you have family worried?' Luke asked.

'Not in America,' Dara answered. ''Tis the Miners' House I'm staying in.'

'And a Mayo man too,' Ned said.

'Indeed. Erris. A little village you would not know. Torán is the name to it.'

Torán Luke thought. Conaire was from Torán.

'There were evictions there,' he said.

'There were,' Dara said, 'but I'd left before that. I thought my family were all secure, and I leaving. A Catholic landlord. But you can't trust any of them. It was a desperate thing.'

'So I'd heard,' Luke said, 'but you left before it, you say? Straight to America, was it?'

'Through Quebec,' Dara said. 'I worked a winter on the Gatineau forests.'

''47, was it?' Luke asked.

'It was.'

'You'd know Conaire Ó Coisteala then? He was a Torán man on the Gatineau in '47.'

Dara looked at him in surprise. For a long time, he was silent.

'Yes,' he said at last. 'I knew Conaire well. We played together as children in Torán.'

'But is he still living?' Luke asked. 'That's my question.'

Dara shook his head; tears in his eyes.

'You knew him, then?' he asked, without replying to the question.

'Indeed,' Luke said. 'I crossed the Atlantic with him on the Centaurus. A hard ship it was too.'

'I'd heard of the Centaurus,' Dara said. 'I was on one a week after. It was only in the forest that I met up with the other Torán men. It was a hard winter too, working down on the wharves on the river. But there were six *of us, all from home, and that made it easier.'*

'*And then?*' Luke asked.

'*Then we went off on a river drive to Quebec, driving the great rafts of logs. We fell in with a bunch of Munster men, and that was our undoing. There was a riot, and Conaire was stabbed in the neck. When the riot was over, we brought him back on the raft, and so to Trois Rivières and buried him there.*'

That afternoon, they made up a rough stretcher from branches and carried *Dara* back to the Miners' House. Afterwards, Luke thought of writing a letter to John Costello in New York, to explain how *Conaire* had died. But postage was expensive. In any case, Costello would know, from length of time, that *Conaire* was dead. Why add to his grief by telling him how?

Silence in the mines. The enforcers still occupied the tents in front of the mines, the weigh stations and the breakers. The hunger deepened. Their debts at the truck store increased, and still no money to send to Mayo. Luke felt he should write, but the cost of a stamp was beyond him now. In some ways, it was as well not to. He could only lie about America. Famine in Pennsylvania! No-one in Carrigard would believe that.

All through the long days, they continued stitching shirts. By now, Ned was worried about eviction. They had not paid rent on the house in weeks. Then one day, when Luke was at the truck store with Ned, the clerk demanded to know the address they were living in. When Ned responded, the clerk checked through a ledger.

'Let's see. Edward Moran two dollars fifty a week rental. Six weeks unpaid. Fifteen dollars outstanding. Pay cash?'

'I don't have cash,' Ned said.

'Sign here for a further fifteen dollars' credit.'

Ned signed.

'Luke Ryan, a dollar seventy-five a week, by six weeks, ten dollars fifty outstanding. Sign here.'

Luke signed.

As they walked away, he kicked at a lump of slate.

'Damn them all to hell.'

'Sure what difference does it make?' Ned asked. 'We'll never repay it anyhow.'

On the way home, Luke and Ned decided to call in at the Miner's House. Farrelly and Kilgallon were playing cards, broken pieces of half burnt matches in the kitty.

'We have to use something for money, when you've nothing else,' Jack said.

Luke laughed. 'I suppose it keeps you engaged.'

Mick O'Brien had just woken up. He came across and sat at the table.

'So what's with the bold Luke? Any great news?'

'Not a lot, apart from the fact that they're adding our rent onto our debt at the truck shop.'

'Sure I know that,' Mick said, 'they're doing that to all of us. But how's Winnie and the child?'

'Hungry.'

'Silly question,' Jack said. 'But tell us this Luke, we'd been arguing earlier about the Union. What do you think this strike is about?'

'Damned if I know. I can understand a strike for higher wages, or an end to scrip. But sure we've got all those. Lien too. The devil take me, but I can't see any reason.'

'I'd agree with you,' Farrelly said, 'but the story that's coming back from the Union is that they're striking so as to stop production, and keep prices high in Philadelphia and New York.'

'Well, isn't that what the Operators said about the lockout?' Ned asked.

'Exactly,' Mick said. 'So whose side is the Union on?'

Luke sat down on the bunk beside O'Brien.

'Another thing that's been occurring to me,' he said, 'what about all this strike pay we're supposed to get?'

'Yes,' Farrelly said, 'we were wondering the same. They're quick enough taking our Union dues from us, ten cents a week, every week. There's not a penny of them come back, you know that?'

'Not that I've seen anyhow,' Luke said.

Jack had dealt the cards again, four hands now, but no-one took up their cards.

'I don't know what this Bates fellow is up to,' Jack said, 'but either he's a fool or a scoundrel.'

'I don't think there's any doubt to the answer to that one,' Mick said. 'A fellow on fifteen dollars a week...'

'Fifteen dollars,' Ned echoed.

'Isn't that what I'm saying?' Mick said. 'That's what the chairman of the Union gets. John Bates Esquire, worth three times as much as any man in this room, and that'll tell you where your Union subscriptions are going. There's only one way I can see of explaining Bates. He's an English man. More than half the miners here are Irish, whether it's Mayo or Kilkenny, it doesn't matter, and Bates has come over from England too. It's the government there, they're not content with starving us in Ireland, they want to starve us here too.'

Luke spoke about it as he and Ned walked back to the house.

'I'm not so sure I'd believe that bit about the English sending Bates over to starve us here. What do you think?'

'Total nonsense,' Ned said. 'There's only one puzzle though. If it's not that, then what in hell is he trying to do?'

Weeks later, there was a knock on the door. It was early on a Monday morning. Again, it was Mick O'Brien.

'They've gone!'

'Who?'

'The tents. They're all gone.'

Luke looked up the hill to the mine.

'Well, the cute hoors,' he said to Ned. 'They struck their tents and stole away in the night.'

'What now?' Ned asked.

His question was answered by a piercing whistle.

'Time for work,' Luke said.

Not knowing what his job now was, he went to the weigh station. Cantwell greeted him back.

That evening, Luke and Ned went to the Hibernian Club. Mick and Jack were already there. No one was drinking. Mick waved at them to sit.

'Well, what do you think of it now, Luke?'

'I'm still puzzled. They've called off the strike, we've no idea why it was called in the first place, and we've received no benefit from it.'

'They were just trying to starve us,' Mick said.

'Why on earth would they want to do that?'

'It forces us to increase our credit at the truck shop. The higher our credit goes, the more we're tied into the Operator, the more trapped we are. And if Bates wasn't working for the fellows in London, then the only other possibility is that he's working for the Operators.'

'You might have something there,' Luke said. 'I'd almost believe that.'

Afterwards, when everyone else had gone home, Luke stayed talking to Mick outside the club. It was late, but moonlit with a clear sky.

'Isn't it time you thought of serious resistance, Luke?' Mick asked.

'I know,' Luke replied. 'You've said that to me before.'

'And now you see the difference. First, we have a Union and what does that get us? Our own special famine in America. Unions are good for nothing, they've no power. What we need is a real revolution.'

'God! That's dangerous talk,' Luke said. 'Haven't we already had one battle here, and see what's happened.'

'Forget your battles,' Mick said. 'That'll never get us anywhere neither. What we need is the silent approach. Choose your man, hit when he's not expecting it, and fade back into the darkness. It's the only fighting we can do, and it's the only language they can understand. Now, will you not join us?'

'Us?' Luke said. 'The Molly Maguires, is that it?'

'Maybe or maybe not. It's not for you to know. Not yet.'

'It's dangerous talk, Mick,' Luke said. 'It's the kind of talk that could get a man hanged.'

'*Arra*, what? To hang a man, they'd have to catch him first.'

'I'll think about it,' Luke said.

'Well, think fast. You know, your work on the weigh station puts you in a dangerous position. It could be argued that you are working for the Union and for the Operators.'

'As if there were a Union,' Luke said. 'All I know is that I'm checking that Cantwell is giving us right measure. I don't even know if there's a Union any more. Come Saturday, I might not even be paid. For the next few days, I'm working for the miners, and, sure as hell, not for the Operators. After that we'll see.'

As it turned out, the Operators were paying him, though Cantwell told him his responsibility was still to the miners, regardless of who was paying. He certainly put no pressure on Luke to be dishonest, but, as Mick had said, it could well be seen that way.

Winnie had other concerns. As soon as the strike was over, reports began to filter through of cholera in Philadelphia.

'But sure it's as far away as New York,' Luke said. 'Why worry? It hasn't come up from New York in all that time, so why should it come up from Philadelphia? It's always the coastal towns, they're the ones to get it.'

Then stories began to spread of St. Louis.

'And that's as far inland as you can get,' Winnie said. 'And they're saying that thousands are dying in St. Louis.'

'*Arra*, it's only stories,' Luke said.

'Afraid not,' Ned said from across the table. 'It's a hell of a killer, this cholera.'

'More like 1832,' Ellen said. 'I don't know if it isn't worse. It's a new one. The Asiatic Cholera, they're calling it. Kills in two days.'

'Sure don't we know,' Luke said. 'Liam has had it already. And he didn't die, did he? Anyhow, he'll have resistance to it by now. No, he won't get it again.'

'Whatever about ourselves,' Winnie said.

'No,' Luke said. 'We've been exposed to it when Liam had it. I doubt we'll get it.'

'But what of myself and Ellen,' Ned asked.

'Well, that's a different question.'

Lying in bed that night, Winnie turned to him.

'This thing of Liam not getting cholera again,' she said, 'I don't believe it.'

'Just you don't be worrying about it,' Luke said.

'But I do worry,' she said. 'The time he had it in New York, I thought he was going to die, I couldn't have taken that. And I don't think I could take it again now. Not after all this starving in America. And not knowing what's going on in Mayo. How can we put up with this, Luke?'

Chapter 25

London Evening Standard. May 1849:
In the Ballinrobe Workhouse, the deaths for the past week amounted to 146, and upwards of four hundred paupers fled from it, preferring, as the account says, to die by the wayside than become victims to disease in that charnel house. The number of deaths in the Westport Workhouse for the week was 66. In some of the other Mayo buildings the mortality was equally terrible.

They followed the mountain down from Drimcaggy; the horse and donkey carefully treading around the holes in the gravel. That night, they stayed in a derelict cottage, wet and miserable. Pat found it difficult to sleep. Even when he did, he had little rest, as ghastly dreams of corrupted bodies and faces kept waking him.

Next morning, the storm had passed, and a warm sun dried their clothes. Soon, they reached Tourmakeady. Straggling groups of people were walking south along the main road. Father Ward dismounted. He crossed the road to a small family group, sitting alongside a wall.

'*Where in the name of God are ye all going?*'

'*Home,*' the man answered. '*Home to Bóthar na hAbhainn.*'

Pat thought of the wreck of a village he had seen at *Bóthar na hAbhainn*. Why would anyone go there? He said nothing.

The man's clothes were in tatters. The woman's costume was in better condition. Pat recognised it as the uniform of the workhouse.

'*But where have ye been?*' Father Ward asked.

'*The Workhouse. Ballinrobe Workhouse.*'

'*Were they not feeding ye?*'

'*They were feeding us right enough, but the cholera was killing us in great numbers. It's better taking our chances with the hunger outside.*'

The next group along the wall were from Ballinrobe Workhouse too. The man spoke of their home in Killadoon. Pat remembered the wards he had seen with Mr. Daly. The child was not moving. Trying not to stare, he tried to see if it was breathing. Killadoon? He knew from the maps in Castlebar where that was. Could they make it? The child certainly would not. And what of the mother? Gaunt and pale. Unlikely.

'*Ye left the workhouse, did ye?*' Pat asked. '*They made ye go?*'

'*There was no forcing about it,*' the man said. '*We broke out through the gates. Masses of us.*'

Father Ward went to the child, and raised his hand in blessing.

'*Per istam sanctam unctionem...*'

The man took off his hat, held it at his chest and bowed his head alongside the woman. Then he arose, carrying his dead child, and walked away.

Father Ward mounted his donkey.

'I'm just going back towards Ballinrobe,' he said. 'Would you not come?'

'I've seen enough of Ballinrobe,' Pat said. 'Anyhow, Gaffney's asking me to go back to the coast at the Killaries and follow around to Louisburgh and Westport. He says there's terrible things happened there in '47 during the fever.'

'And he's right. But he sure doesn't let up on you, does he?'

'There's work to be done,' Pat said.

'Well, if it's the Killaries you're going to, there's a good road I'd advise you taking over the mountains and down to Griggins Bridge, and then there's an easy road up to Leenane. After that it's best to go by Delphi and Killadoon. You'd find it a far rougher ride than following the coast by the Killaries. There's few enough tracks along Killary Harbour.'

'I'd guessed that. There's not much on my map. But it's the way Gaffney asked me to go.'

'Fair enough so. You'll find much more when you get the other side of Mweelrea. The schoolmasters and priests will tell you much. There's schools in Kinnakil, Gowlaun and Cloonlaur. We've a chapel in Gowlaun too. Everywhere you go, you can mention me. The churches and schools in Louisburgh will tell you everything you want to know, and a lot you don't.'

Pat mounted his horse.

'God be with you, Pat,' Father Ward said, as he raised his hand in a blessing. 'You and yours.'

Pat dropped his head. Then he pulled his horse away.

He rode, always overtaking small groups; all, as he discovered, fleeing the horror of Ballinrobe Workhouse.

There was an eerie silence. There were no other horses on the road, no donkeys either. Some groups of people spread across the road from side to side as they walked. Then Pat would ride slowly behind them, as no one parted to let him through. Sometimes he led the horse along the side of the road till he got past them.

Then he heard keening. Off the road, a woman sat beside the corpse of a man. But what could he do? He rode on.

Following a road across two passes, a lake between, he found the bridge. It was raining heavily now. He scrambled down under the bridge. There were people under the arches, some asleep. He took his pencil and notebook out of his pack and began to write. Grey eyes watched him, but no one spoke. The rain got heavier, and this time it did not let up. He slept beside them, leaving before they had awoken in the early dawn.

He rode along Joyce's River in the direction of Leenane. Families were sheltering under bushes and trees; many more in the ruins of wrecked houses.

As he passed one family group, a man came across and grasped the horse's bridle.

'We're going to Leenane, but the child cannot make it.'

Pat dismounted and helped the man put the child on the horse. They laid him across the saddle.

'He's still sleeping,' the man said.

Pat nodded, though he could see the child was dead. Together with the rest of the family, including two other children, he walked slowly towards Leenane, leading the horse with the small corpse. These people too were among those who had broken out of Ballinrobe Workhouse. The woman told of the horror of the workhouse, and Pat said he had already seen it. The couple had already lost two children to cholera.

Just before Leenane, the man indicated a boreen to the right.

'It's up here we live.'

Pat said nothing for a moment. Leenane was not far.

'It's the church you'll be needing,' he said.

There was a silence. The mother looked at him in horror, then she began to cry. Her husband took her by the arm.

'Stay easy, Caitlín. You take the children back to our house, and I'll go on with this young man to the church.'

The woman's face had crumpled in shock.

'You take her home, Seánín,' her husband said.

One of the children took her by the arm.

'Come on mother.'

When they arrived in Leenane, Pat brought the horse into the graveyard. Together with the man, he eased the child off the horse, and left it lying inside the graveyard wall.

'I'll find the priest,' he said to Pat. 'Now you go on.'

Pat saw a rat by one of the graves.

'I'll guard the child till you return,' he said.

'That God may bless you.'

The man returned with a gravedigger and two shovels. The gravedigger was lean enough. The two men began to dig.

Pat took the father's shovel. '*Here, I'll do it for a while.*'

He dug at the other end of the grave from the gravedigger. He was surprised to see that despite the man's gaunt figure, he could still dig faster than he could himself.

At length, the grave was finished. Two feet only. Why think about that? It was enough to cover any scent from the dogs. The rats might burrow down, but why worry about that?

The child's father shook his hand. '*God be with you, my friend.*'

'*And with you,*' Pat said.

He mounted his horse and left Leenane, crossing the Erriff River at Ashleigh Falls, under the flanks of Devilsmother Mountain. He rode along by the long, straggling inlet of Killary Harbour and under Ben Gorm Mountain. Still there were groups, and sometimes single men and women, heading west, very few going the other way.

He came to a split in the road and took out his map. To the right was the road to Delphi Lodge. Straight ahead, the road went under Mweelrea Mountain, still along the inlet.

Father Ward had told him of the difficulty of following Killary Harbour here. As against that, Gaffney wanted to know more about this area. Was there any point, if there were so few houses?

The map decided him. Delphi would be a long way around, so he decided to go by Killary. At the first village, Bundorragha Town, according to his map, he counted 25 houses, spread widely. Many were empty, some collapsed.

An old man sheltered under the ruins of one house. The man stared at him with grey eyes. He was desperately thin.

'*What has happened in this village?*' Pat asked.

'*The fever back in '47, wiped out the half of it. That and the hunger. And these past years, even the herring have abandoned Killary. We starve.*'

'*I'm sorry.*'

'*Arra, it's little you can do. It's not only starvation though.*'

'No?'

'*There's far more than that. Lord Sligo's men, they wished to clear the mountain for sheep, and men get in the way. They've only started, but I've no doubt they'll finish their savage work.*'

'*They will,*' Pat said.

He left the village. Then the road ran out. The horse picked its way along narrow boreens and tracks between the Mweelrea range and the edge of the inlet.

At Bunnaglass there were three houses on his map. On two, the thatch had been burned and the roofs collapsed.

An abandoned currach lay at the edge of the water, holed and ripped. There was no need for roads in these settlements. They lived for the most part off fishing, what need was there of roads?

There were none now. He dismounted and led his horse across fields with rough tracks beaten into the grass or heather, passing isolated houses and cabins, very few now. Some were occupied; most empty. Doors were swinging open on a few of the houses. From the outside, he looked into one. More corpses, one only a skeleton.

The flanks of Mweelrea ran steeply down to the water, broken rock and scree along the edge of the inlet. He considered turning back. It was already late in the afternoon though. If he did, he would take days by the other route. Warily, he continued, treading along rocks at the edge of the inlet, and sometimes slipping and sliding on the scree. Cursing himself for his foolishness, he kept moving.

Then the horse slipped, falling heavily forward. It rolled on its side and did not move. Pat examined the horse's fetlocks. There was a gash above one, but when he pressed on the fetlock bones, the horse did not react. At least he had not broken the horse's leg, but it was clear he would have to rest the animal. He sat against a rock, took food out of his pack and ate. He felt drowsy, and soon he fell asleep. When he woke, it was dawn. How long had he slept? He looked around in alarm. The horse was standing. Carefully, he went up to it. There was no sign of distress. He placed his pack on the saddle, and again began to lead it forward.

At last, he reached a group of houses. One was built of stone, but the roof had collapsed. The rest were mud.

He glanced at his map. Gubnafunshoge and Derry were marked, four or five houses in each. He saw a man trying to bring in a currach. He was very thin, and was struggling with the boat.

'*Perhaps that I can help,*' Pat said.

The man looked up in fright. '*Who are you?*'

'*You need not fear me,*' Pat said.

'Lord Sligo's *agent, are you?*'

'No,' Pat said, '*I am no agent. A man travelling, nothing more.*'

He grasped the currach and between the two of them, they dragged it out of the water. He sat on a rock, the man still standing; still suspicious.

'*Have you been fishing?*' Pat asked.

'*I have. But what of you? How have you got here?*'

'*I've come from Leenane,*' Pat said.

'*With a horse! 'Tis lucky you did not break a fetlock.*'

'*I know,*' Pat said.

'*What class of amadán are you?*'

'There's those would say I'm foolish enough. But what's done is done, and I've made my way here. But now I must go on to Killadoon.'

'It's easier travel from here.'

'Which way would I go?'

'Just follow the road to Uggool, and across the sands to Doovilra.' It was clear he did not wish to talk further.

I thank you for that,' Pat said, 'and now I will take my leave of you.'

There was no answer.

At Gublea, women were gathering seaweed from the sea and carrying it back to the tiny fields between the rocks. He guessed they were using it as manure, though he saw more drying on the roof of a cabin. Were they eating seaweed? What else was there to eat?

He mounted his horse and rode west across the side of the mountain to the village of Uggool.

More wrecked houses. More people now though; fear in their eyes. Anger too. He thought of the man's question about being an agent. Was he in danger? If Lord Sligo was clearing these mountains, these people might seek vengeance.

He reached the beach. He led the horse across the open sands, thankful at least for the flat feel of them. In places, the sand was dry, sometimes damp where the horse's prints showed clear. Then he realised the tide was coming in. He led the horse across to the dunes, continuing alongside them for some time. Then, where there was a gap, he made his way through.

To one side, where the wind had scoured the dune, he saw the hollow eye sockets of a human skull, broken ribs beneath. He stared at the skull, half hypnotised by the empty eye sockets, which he fancied were staring back at him. All the horror of the village of skulls came back to him. He felt dizzy, then paralysed by an irrational fear. The clouds were spinning.

When he came to, he was lying on the ground, shivering. It was near dark, and the moon had risen in a cloudless sky. Stars sparkled, well above the sunset. He could not see the horse. In a panic, he ran forward. No horse. He ran back onto the beach, and at last saw the horse some distance back, munching at the edge of the dunes. He followed it down and grasped the bridle. Then he turned and walked on, the horse following. He went out between the dunes, looking away from the place of the skull.

He found the wreck of a cabin, and slept beside the horse. The nightmares returned, but this time, he did not wake. Next morning, he reached Doovilra. A dozen houses, half derelict, half occupied. But at last he was on a gravelled road. He mounted the horse.

Now there were many more houses, scattered all over the countryside. As before, many ruined, some still standing. At Kinnakil, he found the school.

It was a well-constructed building with a slate roof.

He knew the schoolmaster would give him information. When he got there, he found there was no front door. There were no doors inside either, nor floorboards. All taken for firewood, no doubt.

He went out and went to the small house beside the school. The doors here were still in place, but no one answered his knock.

Gowlaun was the same. The school had been cleared of timber too, and there was no schoolmaster. He went into the church. An old woman was on her knees in front of the altar. He walked up, and she looked around in fright.

'There is no need for fear,' Pat said. 'I was just looking for the priest.'

'He's out travelling. They all need the Last Rites, both for the dying and the dead. The fever and hunger are killing many.'

'And all the other villages back the way? Fever and hunger too?'

'The same.'

'And evictions?'

'Not here. Not yet. There have been many in other villages though. We wait our turn.'

He left. It was warm for the time of year. Sometimes he saw people sitting alongside the road, a listless expression on their faces, as if they were uncaring and simply awaiting their fate. Over the following villages, the story was the same as Gowlaun. Killadoon was shattered. There were many houses, though almost all were empty now. Fever, he was told again. Some mentioned hunger, but fever was the big killer, and from all he heard it had been worst in 1847. But now hunger and fever had returned.

He rode towards Cloonlaur. He found the church easily enough, but it was deserted. He rode on, hoping to find the priest, out on sick calls perhaps. He questioned an old woman carrying seaweed.

'He's dead,' she told him. 'Caught the fever, poor man. We've had no Mass this long time. No sacraments for the dead, neither.'

As he rode, he passed women carrying rush baskets filled with turf on their backs. Most were ragged and gaunt. He offered to carry one woman's load on his horse, but she looked away in alarm and did not answer him.

At last, Roonagh Quay, with Clare Island on the horizon. The currachs were landing fish. Men lifted creels of fish out onto the quay. A group of men surrounded them, sticks in their hands. Beside them, women sold their turf at a penny a load.

There was a group of twenty people at the end of the quay, many dressed in the uniform of the workhouse. They were watching a larger boat coming in from the sea. He guessed it was the ferry for Clare Island. As they all boarded the boat, he wondered how many paid. Or could pay.

More houses and tiny villages. Again and again, he counted the houses, full and empty, and tried to estimate the numbers of people that had lived and died in these unknown places.

He came to the cabins on the outskirts of Louisburgh, followed by the more substantial stone houses of the town itself. The roads were filthy with sewage. No corpses though.

In the centre of the town, he found what appeared to be a bar. It was late now, and the sun had set. He tied his horse to an iron ring on the side of the door, and entered. In the weak candlelight, he saw three men sitting in the corner, and another behind the bar. He questioned the barman about lodgings in Louisburgh, and was glad to be told that the bar itself had rooms available. He asked about stabling, and when he was content that his horse would be secure, he returned to the bar, ordered a beer and took it across to the corner.

'If I may join ye?'

One of the men indicated an empty seat. 'You're welcome,' he said, 'if you're not travelling for Lord Sligo.'

'Not I,' Pat said. 'I've seen much fear of his agents as I've travelled. He's an evil man.'

'The gallows would be too good for him. Mind you, he was a decent enough fellow when this all started. Nothing like those other bastards, Lucan, Palmer, Gore-Knox and the rest of their breed. We were so sure young Georgie – the Marquess of Sligo to you and me – would never evict. And then he started. They say he's bankrupt, and sure he's getting nothing at all in rents. His only hope is sheep and cattle, and what kind of attention do they need beyond a shepherd to guard them from the starving? It's his only chance, they say. They say it'll never stop till he has all his tenants evicted.'

Pat guessed that the men were either cattle drovers or perhaps stronger farmers from around the town. He had little interest in that though. They spoke about conditions in Louisburgh, and the area around it. All of it confirmed what he had seen on his journey around from Mweelrea. Their account of the fevers of 1847 was almost too much to take. And now, more evictions were being planned.

The next morning, he found the Catholic chapel, but discovered the priest was out travelling the parish, and was not expected back anytime soon.

He remembered what Gaffney had told him about the Protestant vicar. He found the church, the glebe house beside it. He tied his horse to the gatepost, and knocked on the door. A very old maid admitted him to a flag-stoned hall, darkened portraits lining the walls, and sat him on an old, cushioned bench. He was disappointed to be told that the vicar too was travelling. He rose to go, but a well-dressed woman came, and introduced herself as the vicar's wife. When she learned from Pat what his mission was, she asked him into the parlour. The old woman served them buttermilk, as Mrs. Callanan spoke.

'You must understand, young man, that having a living in Louisburgh is no living at all. You know that our predecessors both died of fever. Husband and wife.'

'I had not heard that,' Pat said.

'No. We are not so long here, and it's my expectation that we will die the same way. I always thought when I was a young woman that we might suffer martyrdom for our faith. My husband was much into going on the China Missions, but they told him he was more urgently needed in County Mayo. It was only when we arrived here, we discovered why. So if there is to be any martyrdom, it won't be for our faith but for our flock. And, I might add, everyone else's flock too. It's all the same here, Catholics, Protestants or the Friends, we all work for the people and we all die, the priests more than most. What else can we do, any of us?'

For some time, she told him of conditions around Louisburgh. Then Pat explained his own mission, and Mrs. Callanan questioned him closely about the Partry Mountains and the villages around Mweelrea.

There was a sound of a gate opening.

Mrs. Callanan stood up. 'That would be my husband.'

Dean Callanan was a man of middle age, clad in a dark suit. His hair was black and long, framing a reddish face. He looked at Pat in surprise.

'Who's this?'

'A young man from the County,' Mrs. Callanan said. 'They've sent him down to enquire into conditions around Louisburgh.'

'As if they don't know.'

'And I know just what you mean,' Pat said, quickly. 'It's just that there's those on the Grand Jury who won't believe what they don't want to believe. So Mr. Gaffney has sent me down to see the truth of it all. And before you say it, I've travelled much.'

'Fair enough,' the dean said, taking out a bottle of sherry. 'What do you want to know?'

'As much as you can tell me,' Pat said.

The dean handed Pat a glass.

'Gonzalez Byass,' he said. 'Far superior to Osborne, don't you think.'

Pat had never heard of either. Gingerly, he sipped at the glass.

The dean confirmed everything his wife had said, and far more. All the clergy in Louisburgh and around it, all the way down to the Killaries were in utter desperation. He confirmed too about the letter that he had written to the Dublin papers.

'Yes,' Pat said, 'I'd heard it was strongly supported by Archbishop McHale.'

'Indeed,' Callanan replied. 'Like all the rest of us, there's no dissension any more. All we can do is try to get supplies, but now even that is impossible, so we just give the Last Rites, at the risk of our own lives. No, there is no difference here, vicar or priest, we do everything we can. That is the reason that the Archbishop supported my letter, together with many other bishops in the Church of Rome. That was why it got so much attention through the national press. It was re-printed in the London and Manchester papers too. What difference that might make, I don't know but, damn it, we'll see.'

Pat was a little surprised at the swear word, but did not comment.

Now the dean questioned Pat intensively about his experiences since he had left Castlebar. Again, Pat described what he had seen, starting with the Lucan evictions south of Claremorris. Pat's descriptions of the dying villages of the Partry Mountains horrified him, and his ride along the coast under Mweelrea Mountain surprised him.

'I never heard of any man taking a horse along there,' he told Pat. 'In fact, I don't know of anyone who's even walked it.'

'Yes,' Pat said, 'looking back, it was a silly thing to do. The horse nearly didn't make it.'

'Why did you do it so?'

'Mr. Gaffney had some interest in the area. And it looked shorter on the map. The better route would have been around by Delphi.'

'Ah yes,' the dean said, 'Delphi Lodge. You've heard about that?'

'I know nothing about it,' Pat said. 'I've never been there. Whose is it?'

'Well, it was built by Lord Sligo as a sporting lodge, but it's been in the Irish and English papers a few weeks ago, and it wasn't for its hunting or fishing. A crowd of paupers who were seeking relief here in Louisburgh, were asked to present themselves for inspection at Delphi, because the Relieving Officer here did not have his books ready. Why they were to be ready in Delphi, I don't know. Can you imagine it? It's fourteen miles to Delphi. And when they arrived at the Lodge, they were told to return to Louisburgh instead. At Louisburgh, they were told to go to the village of Cregganebane, six miles back again, before their names could be placed on the Relief Book.'

'But why?'

'The Lord only knows. But I must tell you, on the road between Louisburgh and the Lodge at Delphi, seven dead bodies were found.'

'Seven!'

'Yes, and our information is that another ten never reached their homes. And that is the price of human stupidity, or should I say human cruelty. 'Pauper Slaughter' – that's what the Freeman's Journal called it, and with good reason.'

Pat questioned the dean about the Lord Sligo evictions. Callanan confirmed all that Pat had heard, not only of the past evictions by Lord Sligo, but of those that were planned. He told Pat too of what had happened in many other villages for miles around.

At length, he stopped.

'But tell me one thing, my young friend. I've written to the County before, the Connaught Telegraph, the Dublin papers and all the rest. Why will the Grand Jury not believe me?'

'They don't want to believe you. There's men in Castlebar would deny any of this is happening. And don't say I said that.'

'Oh God, I'm sick of them all.'

'So am I,' Pat said. 'With the strong exception of George Gaffney though. He's a hard man, and a fair man. He knows well what's happening, and my reports give him the ammunition to use against the rest of them.'

When Pat left, the dean shook his hand, gravely. 'I can't say how happy I am to see you, even if I might have sounded a bit miserable. It all gets to you in the end.'

'I know.'

'Well, you just give them the facts. Hit them hard, and don't let them deny it.'

Pat mounted his horse and pulled away from the house. He followed the road out of Louisburgh, under the cone of Croagh Patrick, and so to Westport.

Chapter 26

Telegraph & Connaught Ranger, Mayo. May 1849:
What a visitation has been this devouring famine of 1846!
When, now in the fourth year, its withering career is more
destructive to life and property than in any former year
since it displayed itself in the destruction of the poor man's
food! Yes! The people are dying, and the dogs are feeding on
their putrefying bodies in the ditches! Is it any wonder the
pure air of heaven is impregnated with foul odour? Is it to be
wondered at that disease, call it what you will, is fast mowing
down the Foodless! Clothesless! Homeless! Shelterless! Poor
of Mayo?

He made Murrisk in good time. After a diversion to Murrisk Pier, he came
back to the road again, diverting again to follow the coast towards Westport
Quay. As he passed the Customs House, he glimpsed Westport House Lough.
Curious, he made his way to the lake. Beyond it, he saw what he took to be
Westport House itself, which he already knew to be the residence of Lord Sligo.

Across from the lake, the long green lawn ran down to the water. The
house itself was at the far end. It was tall, three storeys at least. A grey slate
roof topped out the house, with chimneys and many chimney pots. There was
a balustrade in the front, with more balustrades on a bridge over the lake, all
with pots of flowers, blooming red and yellow in the sunshine.

He turned away. Was it for this that men, women and children had to be
evicted, broken and killed? All part of Lord Sligo's war on the people of Mayo.

He made his way back to the Customs House and went on towards
Westport. At the workhouse, there were no people in front of the gates, only
a few sitting along by the wall. From behind him, there was the incessant
tramp of marching from the military barracks. Why was the government so
frightened of starving people?

An inmate and an infantry man were on guard, just inside the workhouse
gate. He asked for Sarah Cronin, explaining she worked in the offices. The
inmate went away, and came back a few minutes later to say that there was
no one of that name in the Administration Block.

Pat was shocked. He had not expected this.

'*Can you find out…?*'

'*It's not my business to be running messages for you,*' the man said.

Pat took a farthing out of his pocket and handed it through the gate.

'*Is she dead?*'

'*I do not know,*' the man replied.

Thinking fast, he asked for the clerk instead.

A few minutes later the clerk appeared at the gate.

'Pat Ryan. In the name of God.'

'I'm looking for Sarah.'

'I know you are. Come in, come in.'

The gate was opened slightly, and Pat slipped through with the horse.

'Is she dead or what?'

'Oh, nothing like that,' the clerk said. 'It's just the workhouse reducing costs. They say they can't afford giving her board and lodgings in the Administration quarters. She's an inmate now.'

'An inmate! Do they have her on stone-breaking or what?'

'Worse than that,' the clerk said. 'They have her working in the infirmaries. She's back here somewhere.'

He led Pat around the back of the workhouse. There was a row of sheds along the side wall, two more rows in front of them.

Even between the sheds, and in every free space, there were huge crowds of people, some standing, many more lying on the ground.

'What on earth is going on here?' he asked the clerk.

'Fever to start. Cholera too. Now if you don't mind, Pat, I've work to do.'

Pat went from shed to shed, trying to find Sarah. In many of the sheds, inmates were working at cleaning out the shit and piss, mixed in with straw, and wheeling it out of the sheds in barrows, to a heap in the top corner of the site. Outside one of the sheds was a donkey and cart, half full of bodies. As he walked from shed to shed, it followed him, picking up more dead bodies in each.

In each shed, he asked for Sarah, and it was some time before he found her, overseeing a group of inmates washing down patients. She was wearing a striped shift.

He went up to her.

'Sarah.'

She turned around in surprise.

'Pat.' She threw her arms around him, 'I never thought I'd see you alive again.'

'I know. I've been a long time gone.'

'Where were you?'

'All around the south of the County. Ballinrobe, up the mountains in Partry, along by Killary and Mweelrea and back around by Louisburgh. It all took time.'

As they spoke, two inmates passed them, carrying a dead body.

'Hold on a moment,' she said to Pat. 'I've got to watch over these. Come along and stand outside.'

The body was thrown on to the cart.

'It's near full now,' the cartman said.

Sarah looked. 'It'll take a few more.'

They went to the next shed. Another body.

Two more from the next. They were thrown sideways across the others.

The cartman took a hold of the donkey's bridle and slapped the animal on the flank.

'That's enough.'

They started moving through the crowds of inmates, dead legs and arms flapping over the side of the cart. The crowds made way, but no-one spoke. They went across by the side of the Stonebreakers' Yard, hundreds of men, women and children breaking rock with sledge hammers or hand hammers. The inmate and the infantry man opened the gate, and they made their way down the road and across to a field alongside the infantry barracks.

Still, there was the tramp of marching men.

Sarah opened a gate into the field.

'This is the workhouse graveyard,' she explained. 'Only open a few years. They had a rough time here, I can tell you. They only had the workhouse built when the hunger started. It didn't take long for them to start filling the graves.'

Through the gates of the barracks, the dragoons wheeled in formation. Why were they here? Had they been sent to County Mayo to guard dead men? Who knew?

The cart crunched along the gravel road towards where inmates were digging. They came to the edge of a new mass grave.

Pat gasped.

'Damn it,' he said. 'I thought Knockanure was bad, but this is huge.'

'And needed too,' Sarah said. 'They're reckoning on a hundred dead a week. That's what I'd heard.'

'A hundred a week! Oh God, Sarah, you can't stay here. It'll kill you.'

'Sure it's nothing as bad as Ballinrobe, is it? And you've been down there.'

'I don't know,' Pat answered. 'What I saw there was bad, but I didn't go to the trouble of seeing their graveyard. But why is it so awful here?'

'In one word Pat – numbers. Do you know how many we have right here? Five thousand inmates, and that's just what we have in the workhouse. We've rented other houses around too. We've got them pushed together, every way you can imagine. The sheds are bad enough, but all the wards have two in a bed, and the beds pushed up against each other. The same in the dormitories. One in fever, and they all have it. And now the cholera too.'

'Oh God, this is horrible.'

'It is. They got a right shock a few days ago, right here. Found a baby in the grave when it started crying. They took it out of course, but I doubt it lived long. There's many babies thrown in since.'

The inmates threw a body into the grave. No coffins now, and always, the squeaking of the rats. He saw Sarah glance across to where her mother's grave was. Abruptly, she turned away. Pat said nothing.

At last it was finished. They followed the cart towards the barracks, and halted as a squadron of cavalry came out, and moved towards the centre of Westport.

'What are those fellows doing here, do you think?' Pat asked.

'I haven't the slightest idea,' Sarah answered. 'I doubt there's anyone fit to fight them anymore.'

They followed the cart back, and stood at the edge of the Stonebreakers' Yard. Another cartload of cadavers was being filled.

'So what are you, Sarah, an inmate now?'

'Yes,' she said, 'and isn't that a terrible way to end up?'

'I'd heard something about the workhouse not being able to afford your board and lodgings with the Administration.'

'That's what they said, though I doubt that's the real reason.'

'Yes,' Pat said, 'you mentioned something before about the last Master being had up for short measures on weights.'

'He was prosecuted too. Lord Sligo had him convicted and jailed. I haven't a clue what happened to him since then. Nor do I much care.'

'But what's that got to do with the present Master?'

'He knows I'm too close to the books. Like I said, they're fiddling things somehow, whether on weights or otherwise I don't know.'

'But the clerk?'

'He's being bribed; I know that for certain.'

'But where do you eat, or sleep?'

'In the workhouse, I'm afraid. No special privileges anymore. Not that there's much to eat.'

'But – the dormitories?'

'Not so bad as most. I managed to wangle my way into the geriatric infirmary. They're all dying, right enough, but of old age, not of fever.'

'I'd never have thought of that.'

'Neither would I, but when they put me in working in the fever sheds, I worked it out soon enough.'

'And what about your uniform?'

'Oh, there's no shame in wearing stripes. In fact, in some ways it's a privilege too. When you become an inmate, they take away your own clothes, wash and press them and put them away for the time you leave. Now, I prefer this uniform. No one from outside knows me, and it doesn't matter.'

'But they still have you working?'

'They wouldn't feed me otherwise. You know what a workhouse is, Pat?'

'Of course. But the fever wards...'

'I know, and rough and all, I'd prefer the Stonebreakers' Yard, but they won't let me. I'm at the end of my tether, Pat. I know the risks I'm running. I know if I stay in the fever sheds, I'll die soon, but I can't see any way out. Even if I got out of the workhouse, I'd only starve, and there's still all the risk of fever and cholera.'

'But Sarah, you can't go on like this.'

'Don't I know it, Pat?'

He was puzzled. What now?

'And this Australia business,' he asked. 'Are they still intending you should go on it?'

'I'm not sure of that. Maybe. Anyhow, it won't be happening until the end of summer. I don't know if I'll be alive by then.'

'You always told me not to worry about you working in the sheds.'

'Yes,' Sarah said, 'but you always knew what they were like. Murder sheds, that's all they are.'

'But we can't leave you here,' Pat said. 'Marriage, but that would take weeks to organise, what with the banns and all. There's only one other answer.'

'Which is?'

'Bring you home to Carrigard.'

'Yes, I was hoping you'd say that. I'm sick and tired of workhouses.'

'I know. And mother would be delighted to have you.'

That night, Sarah slept in the geriatric ward, while Pat stayed with the horse inside the gates of the workhouse. He threw his greatcoat on the ground and slept soundly.

The next day, Sarah Cronin and Pat Ryan left Westport Workhouse. They had to recover her possessions first. Sarah returned to the women's dormitory and changed into her own clothes.

'You look much better like that,' Pat told her.

'I know,' Sarah said, 'and I'll tell you this, come hell or high water, I'll never wear workhouse clothes again.'

He embraced her. She clenched him closely. He realised she was crying.

'It's nothing,' she said. 'It'll soon be over. There's a new life coming for us.'

This time, the workhouse gates were opened for them. The crowd had grown, and three Infantry men were guarding it. They pushed their way through and walked back towards Westport. A battalion of soldiers came towards them. They stood to the side.

Their first stop was the Post Office in Westport, where Pat scratched a quick note to Carrigard, telling them of his plans, and his intent to marry Sarah. Then Sarah mounted the horse, as he posted the letter.

He came back, and took the bridle, leading the horse out of Westport.

'They'll have the letter soon enough,' he said.

'And talking of letters, what of Luke?' she asked. 'Any news from America lately?'

'They're leaving New York. All's fine with them. He says there's better chances in mining coal. They're travelling to some other town; Lackan they call it. We've no fixed address yet, but I'm sure we'll hear from them very soon.'

The scenes on the road to Castlebar had changed again. Along by Islandeady, all the cabins and houses had been fully demolished, nothing remaining except floors or rough foundations. There were stones in neat heaps, along large fields, where walls were still being demolished. Men with carts trundled across the fields, carrying rock to where new walls were being built in perfect straight lines.

'Lord Lucan,' Pat explained.

'As if I didn't know.'

'That's what he calls 'improvement'. I've seen it all over.'

When they arrived in Castlebar, they were admitted to the Union without difficulty. They went straight to the door of Gaffney's office.

'Sit here,' he told Sarah 'and wait for me.'

He knocked on the door and entered.

'Pat! We were worried about you.'

'What on earth for, Mr. Gaffney?'

'You were a long time.'

'No longer than was needed. Going around the Lucan villages, that all took time. Going with Father Ward in the mountains, you don't think he'd let me off easy, do you?'

'Not Father Ward, that's for sure.'

'Under Mweelrea has tough, no roads at all. And riding the coast from Mweelrea to Westport, there's all kinds of boreens along there. It all takes time.'

'Well. Is it as bad as they say?'

343

'Worse.'

For the first time, Pat thought Gaffney was showing his age. Or was he just imagining it? He remembered when they first met on the Famine Relief Works at Carrigard. How long had that been? Three years! Impossible. Yes, it was three years, and Gaffney had certainly aged in that time. His hair was greyer; sparser too. He had been through much, they all had, but still, his eyes showed the strength and determination of a man who only expected hard work and integrity from anyone who worked for him. He had always been like that.

'We've a meeting of the Grand Jury next week,' he said to Pat. 'We'll need your reports, and we'll need them fast.'

'I'd better get writing so,' Pat said. 'There is one other thing though, you might be able to help me on.'

'If I can, Pat.'

'My intended bride is travelling with me.'

'Travelling with you!'

'I'm taking her back to Carrigard. She will stay there for some weeks. But I don't want her travelling alone.'

'I'm sure we'll be able to put her up here.'

'Not in the dormitories, I hope.'

'Of course, not.'

'I'd be willing to pay for her board and lodging.'

Gaffney waved his hand.

'Don't be silly, Pat.'

Gaffney was true to his word. An inmate took Sarah to her room. That evening, they both had dinner with Gaffney, together with the Master, the Matron, and other staff of Castlebar Union.

When he started work, Thady was not there. He asked Gaffney about it.

'Oh, they're fostering him out,' Gaffney replied. 'A couple out the Claremorris road. Farmers.'

'They'll work him hard,' Pat said. 'Not at accounts either.'

'You're right Pat,' Gaffney said. 'What can I say though? The Union can't afford to feed him, and the Grand Jury are always pushing the numbers down. At least he'll get fed for his hard work. Young as he is, the farmer will see him as valuable and will want to keep his strength up. It's hard, I know, but it's the best thing for him.'

'It is,' Pat said.

He spent the next few days in a frenzy of writing. Again and again, he checked maps, place names and always his own rough notes. As he finished each page, Sarah began to copy them.

At the end of the first day, Gaffney came to where Pat was still working by candlelight. Silently, he took the first pages and read through them.

'Lucan is the devil incarnate,' he said.

'He is,' Pat said.

'All he tells us is that he's improving his estates. Improving! Another word for murder. And don't repeat that. Either of you.'

'On our word, Mr. Gaffney,' Sarah said.

He flicked through more of the report.

'Tell me, Pat. what of Father Ward? How do you rate his reports? Is he reliable?'

'Having seen it, Mr. Gaffney, yes, he's reliable.'

Next morning, they were joined by two younger men.

'Transcribers,' one of them explained.

Pat passed over what he had already written. By the end of the week, there were twelve copies of his report.

'I appreciate it more than I can tell, Pat,' Gaffney said. 'We'll see what the Grand Jury think of these. I'd like you to be here for the meeting. That won't be for another week though, so if you wish to take your bride-to-be back to Carrigard, now would be the time to do it. On your life, though, be back here by Wednesday.'

'I will.'

'I can't offer you a horse this time, I'm afraid.'

'I wasn't expecting one, Mr. Gaffney.

'No, but you will need something for young Sarah and her baggage. I've requisitioned a donkey for you. Just make sure it doesn't get eaten.'

Next day, Pat helped Sarah into the saddle of the donkey. He led it out of the workhouse. A few streets away, a group of ragged men and boys were throwing stones at a building on the side of the street. Glass lay on the road, most of the windows having been smashed.

'Better go around some other way,' Sarah said.

An old woman was at the corner, watching the scene.

'*What's going on here?*' Sarah asked.

'*That's the cholera hospital,*' the old woman answered. '*They're murdering people in there. Cut their throats, they do. None ever come out.*'

They went on.

'No point in disputing what she says,' Sarah said. 'They'll believe what they want to believe.'

'They will,' Pat said, 'and while they might be wrong about the throat cutting, the result is the same. I saw it in Ballinrobe. Cholera kills, and it kills damned fast. All they're doing is quarantining the people, trying to stop it spreading. Very few come out though. I wouldn't blame them for thinking they were being murdered.'

The walk from Castlebar to Kilduff nauseated him. There was no doubt about it, the starvation was getting worse. But his travels around the County had toughened him in a way he had never expected. Much like Luke in the mountains in the winter of '46 and '47. But from all he heard of Luke on his visits down from the mountains to Knockanure Union, he knew that Luke was very close to breaking then.

But Luke was in America now and Winnie gone too. He himself was determined he would not break. To hell with all that. He had done his work for now. Time to recover his senses.

Closer to Kilduff, there were all the signs of another big eviction. They saw a woman with three children in the wreckage of a house.

'*What happened here?*' Sarah asked.

'Lord Lucan. *His men came with the police. Destroyed the villages all across the foot of the mountain.*'

They moved on.

'That's terrible,' Sarah said.

'Yes,' Pat said, 'and what's even worse, Clanowen already smashed up all the villages from here up the side of the mountain some years back. God knows what's left now.'

In Kilduff two houses had white crosses on the doors. Cholera?

They went into Sabina's bar.

'Sarah! Pat!'

He put a penny on the counter. 'I'll have a Guinness and a gin.'

She poured the drinks.

'Where have ye been?'

'Well, Sarah has been working in Westport Workhouse. She's been having a rough time.'

Sabina looked towards Sarah. 'A rough time?'

'Yes,' Sarah said. 'Once my mother died, everything changed.'

'Yes,' Sabina said, 'I was sorry to hear of your mother.'

'It's good of you to say so. But up to then I'd been working in the office. Sometimes helping out in the fever sheds, but both of us knew the dangers. It killed her though. Fever.'

'But you've lived anyhow.'

'I have, but pretty dreadful it was. The Master and the new Matron didn't like me. They were trying to send me off to the colonies. Wanted all the young women to go and marry convicts.'

'I'd heard of that, but I thought it was only stories.'

'Oh, it's true right enough. Another few months and I might have gone, but they thought me better off as an inmate while I was waiting.'

'An inmate!'

'Not that it made much difference. At least we were being fed. Not much from last year when the Master was cheating on the weights. They jailed him, it didn't improve much since.'

'You're thin enough,' Sabina said.

'I am,' Sarah said, 'but I'm living, aren't I? And glad enough of it too. While they had us waiting for the colonies they put me back working in the fever sheds. With the cholera, too, I reckoned I was going to die before any chance of marrying a convict.'

'God! It must have been rough on you.'

'No rougher than on mother. And the inmates who were helping in the sheds, sure they're all doomed to die, whether they know it or not. Though I reckon they know it well enough.'

Sabina had poured herself a gin. 'The County is in a terrible way. Now tell me, what about you, Pat? What have you been doing?'

'Travelling around Partry, and working the accounts for the County in Castlebar after that.'

'Hard work?'

'It is. But forget that, Sabina, I've seen the white crosses on the doors, and we coming into the town.'

'Cholera,' she said.

'I thought so. Ballinrobe too, they have the crosses for cholera. It's in a terrible way with it.'

'It's only come here today.'

'Today. They were quick enough painting the crosses, so.'

'Oh, that was the army fellows. They don't want to be billeted where there's cholera.'

As they left, Sabina saw them to the door. Pat began to lead the donkey away.

Sabina threw her arms around Sarah.

'He doesn't say much about Partry,' she whispered.

'No,' Sarah said. 'Nothing at all. Nor ever will.'

When they arrived in Carrigard, Eleanor embraced Sarah, brought her inside and sat her down.

'We got your letter,' she said to Pat, 'and we're delighted to see the pair of you.'

'I was hoping you might,' Pat said. 'I know I'm putting someone else in on ye, but sure at least I'll be paying for it.'

'*Arra*, it's not payment we were looking for,' Eleanor said.

'Perhaps not, but it's payment ye'll need.'

She took a jug of buttermilk, and poured out three mugs. Ever since she had received Pat's letter from Westport, she had been happier than before. Now she was certain that Sarah was to be her daughter-in-law. Sarah would find it hard to adapt to the life of a poor farmer's wife, though. Still, it was going to happen, and Sarah had the strength to deal with it. She would help with rearing Brigid, and in time there would be more children in the house.

'But how was it for you in Westport?' she asked.

'Terrible,' Sarah said.

When Sarah told her the story of Westport Workhouse, Eleanor was shocked to realise that she had ended up as an inmate.

Michael entered. He greeted Sarah warmly, as he sat to unlace his boots.

'You're most welcome,' he said. 'Maybe you can put manners on that son of ours.'

Sarah laughed. 'I might,' she said, 'but I've got to corner him first, and that mightn't be so easy.'

'Go on out of that,' Eleanor said. 'You've got him well reined in already.'

Michael sat at the table, as Eleanor poured out four cups of whiskey. He raised his cup. 'And here's to the pair of you.'

The conversation continued in a light-hearted way. Then Michael held up his hand.

'So what was Partry like?' he asked.

'Don't ask,' Pat said. 'You wouldn't want to know.'

'Let me be the judge of that.'

'Look,' Pat said, 'you think you've seen famine and fever. Partry is worse than anything you've seen around Carrigard or Kilduff, I'll tell you that for sure. Tough and all as ye might think ye are, ye don't want having nightmares, and I don't want to talk about it and be giving myself more torment.'

He stood, and walked over to the open door. He stared up at the trees, as if thinking. Images kept flashing across his mind. A mud hut beside a stream and a dead blackthorn tree on a crag. He grasped the door frame, trembling, and hoping no-one would notice.

At last he turned back.

'But if ye want bad dreams, wouldn't there be enough in Kilduff already?'

'What of Kilduff?' Michael asked.

'There's cholera in Kilduff. Or hadn't ye heard?'

'Cholera!' Eleanor exclaimed. 'Surely not.'

'What are you saying?' Michael asked, disquiet in his voice.

'Cholera,' Pat replied.

'Who told you?'

'Sabina. And sure how could it not? It's all over Mayo.'

'Oh God,' Eleanor said. 'How long is it since we last had that last? Ten years, twenty, I don't remember,'

'1832,' Michael said. 'That was a terrible time right enough, though Carrigard wasn't so bad.'

'It wasn't,' Eleanor said. 'It was mostly in the towns. Kilduff got it bad then, though. Couldn't I see it myself every time I went up shopping that time.'

Michael had picked up a stick, and was drawing circles in the ashes at the front of the fire.

At last he spoke.

'Sure, maybe it's not as bad as last time, it'll be a different kind.'

'I don't know about that.' Pat said. 'Wherever it's coming from, they say it's a powerful one this time. Even worse than '32.'

'Enough of this,' Eleanor said abruptly. 'We can talk all night about terrible things, but there's better things afoot. I'm sure Pat did not bring Sarah here just out of friendship.'

Pat smiled. 'No, mother. There might have been other reasons, as you have well guessed. We are to be married. But sure you've always known that.'

'And a better daughter, I could not ask for.'

'And another mother for little Brigid,' Michael said.

Pat was concerned though. Even with his wages, it was hard enough to feed the family, and now there was one extra mouth. Still, his parents welcome for Sarah delighted him. There were better things in life than cholera, and talk of marriage distracted everyone from Partry.

But Eleanor was thinking of more practical things.

'It'll be a few weeks to the wedding yet,' she said. 'First we must have the banns read out.'

'You can leave the Kilduff side to me,' Michael said, 'I'll talk to Father Reilly. A decent man too, he'll have the banns read here.'

'I'll write to Knockanure and Westport,' Pat said, 'the moment I get to Castlebar.'

'Yes,' Eleanor said, 'that would be a good plan. I just hope people will see it as it is. It's a bad time in some ways, what with people suffering all around us, but sure life goes on, doesn't it? Luke and Winnie got married in the middle of the fevers. There were many others marrying at the same time.'

'Yes,' Michael said, 'I think you're right.'

That evening, Michael took out pen and paper and started to write a letter.

'Who to?' Eleanor asked.

'Luke and Winnie. It's a long time since they've heard from us. We must tell them of Pat and Sarah.'

'Of course,' Eleanor said. 'But what of Mayo? What can we say of that?'

'Well, we're not starving, and I believe Winnie's people are fine too. They'll want to know that.'

'They will,' Elanor said. 'And tell them John Gallagher is in England.'

'Fine. They might know already, but sure I'll say it anyhow.'

'And what should you say about the rest of the County?'

'We must be honest. The starvation is getting worse and now, the cholera!'

'Yes,' Eleanor said, 'they'll need to know all that.'

That night, she lit the turf fire in the room that Luke and Winnie used before they went to America. It was there that Sarah slept that night while Pat slept in the outshot in the kitchen.

Over the next few days, Pat helped his father around the farm, rebuilding walls along the fields, smashing rock in the quarry, and rebuilding the destruction of the winter on the roads where they still held contracts to the County.

Then it was time to return to Castlebar. Eleanor had made up a bag of cooked potatoes, cooled overnight. Pat hugged his mother and Sarah. He knew that the old friendship between them had been re-established, and the strength of that friendship would carry them through for many years, good and bad. And Sarah had taken young Brigid to her heart.

Then he mounted the donkey and rode towards Castlebar.

Gaffney rose from the desk as he entered.

'Pat, I'm most happy to see you.'

'Did you think I wasn't coming?'

'I was thinking of all sorts of terrible things about you, fever, cholera or whatever. And it wasn't just you I was worried about; I need you for this meeting with the Grand Jury tomorrow.'

That evening, Pat slept in the administration building.

Next morning, he was sitting outside the Committee Room.

'Just wait till you're called,' a clerk said to him.

He went through his own copy of the report again and again, though he was already confident of its contents.

When he entered the Committee Room, he saw there were copies of his report mixed in with a mess of papers around the table.

Gaffney was on the right-hand side of the table, two men alongside him, three more facing them.

At the top, a man sat facing down the table. He was bald on top, but with black hair all down his face – thick mutton-chop whiskers and sideburns with a dense black beard. He wore a well-ironed shirt, a bow tie and a thick black jacket. The Chairman.

Pat took the chair at the opposite end of the table.

'Stand,' the Chairman shouted.

Pat glanced over to Gaffney who just nodded. He stood.

'Who produced this drivel?'

'This is my most reliable man,' Gaffney replied.

'If he is your most reliable, you should fire the others. This man too. He's a liar.'

'I resent that,' Gaffney said.

'He talks of cholera in Ballinrobe. Have any of us seen cholera? Is there cholera in Westport? Or Castlebar? Fever perhaps. Cholera no. On what evidence, have you based these lies?'

'I saw it myself,' Pat said.

'Saw it himself. We have a medical expert now, do we? Would a man like this know the difference between cholera and common diarrhoea?'

'The difference is death,' Pat said. 'Cholera kills. Diarrhoea rarely does.'

'Oh yes, and who do we have to confirm it. A papist priest! We've know what lies they tell.'

'They're not lies,' Pat said. 'I spoke with the doctor. He knew cholera right enough.'

Gaffney raised a hand, before the other man could reply.

'Tell us about the rest of it, Pat,' he said. 'Levally and the rest of them.'

'Yes, Mr. Gaffney. Lucan's evictions...'

'Lord Lucan,' the man shouted from the end of the table. 'You'll call me by my name.'

Now Pat knew who the man was. He decided to press on.

'Yes, my Lord, I witnessed your eviction...'

'There were no evictions.'

'But I saw the villages. Levally, Cloonark, Cloonacastle, Baun, Cappacurry, Knocknacroagha...'

A man from the left-hand side raised his hand.

'You visited all of these villages?'

'I did.'

'Were you there when these people were supposedly evicted?' one of the other men asked.

'No. I...'

'Surely it is possible that the people in these villages simply emigrated, or even died.'

'It's easy to know the difference between an eviction and emigration,' Pat said. 'It's all in the way the roof is brought down.'

'So we've an expert on demolition now,' Lucan said.

'No expert, my Lord,' Pat responded, 'but I've seen Lord Clanowen's evictions being carried out in *Gort na Móna*. Just by Kilduff. I know how it's done. And Father Conway witnessed the Levally evictions in 1848.'

Lucan waved his hand with contempt. 'A priest.'

One of the other men stood.

'Before you go, this story of your travels in the mountains.'

'All fabricated,' Lucan said from the end of the table.

'Were you there?' the other asked.

'I was. Father Ward took me...'

'Another priest,' Lucan repeated.

'I believe the word of my own eyes,' Pat said. 'And I'm not a priest. Nor is Father Ward a liar.'

'This report is total nonsense,' Lucan said. 'And you know it.'

'And we wouldn't think Dean Callanan would lie either,' Gaffney said. 'And you could hardly call him a priest of Rome.'

'Yes,' Pat said. 'I met him too. And I don't think he tells lies either.'

'How do we know the accuracy of Dean Callanan's letter?' Lucan asked. 'His letter is counter-signed by damned near every papist bishop west of the Shannon. It could well be a forgery.'

'He told me he had sent the letter,' Pat said. 'It's no forgery.'

Silence.

'My Lord,' he added, with disdain.

Pat and Gaffney were dismissed from the meeting.

'I'm sorry, Pat,' Gaffney said.

'They didn't believe a word I said, and they have the gall to tell me the report was made up.'

They walked along the corridor to Gaffney's office.

'They didn't want to believe it. Maybe they've got enough problems already without worrying about Partry or Louisburgh.'

'I know.'

'I wouldn't worry,' Gaffney said, as they entered the office.

The Connaught Telegraph was lying on his desk, a note on top, underlined – 'Read This'.

Gaffney picked it up. 'I wonder who this is from. Doesn't want us knowing, whoever it is.'

He read it. Then he handed it across to Pat.

'A letter to the Editor?' Pat exclaimed 'From Father Ward?'

'Indeed,' Gaffney said. 'Wouldn't you know Cavendish would copy something like this?'

May 13 1849

To the Editor of the Freeman.

Dear and Respected Sir – it is with pain and with trouble that I thus address you, soliciting your influence with the charitable and humane people of

England and Ireland for my distressed and perishing flock. The heart cannot conceive nor can the tongue describe the frightful and awful sufferings of human nature here. A famine of four long years and the agonies of hunger, unprecedented in the annals of our Irish history, together with fevers, dysenteries, sweating, cold, and nakedness, and, to crown the climax of our misfortune, a raging cholera or plague has set in for the last fortnight. The people are withering with fear and are dying in multitudes. Deaths numerous but coffins few – buried without coffins in dykes and ditches, and many – many disfigured and destroyed by rats. In this doomed and mountainous parish, upwards of nineteen hundreds of God's creatures fell victim to this devouring famine – more than seven hundred families are wandering without a house to put their heads into. They are seeking shelter in dykes and ditches. This is the effect of the Gregory clause. Five years ago, there were fifteen hundred children attending the several schools in my parish, now there are not ten children. Where are they gone to? Famine and eternity can tell. For the last week, I witnessed many a disconsolate heart. At Bornahowna, Peter Flanagan, wife, the two daughters and two grand-daughters died within one hour of each other. A poor sight – four corpses leaving one house together.

At Gortmore, about the hour of midnight, there were seven corpses in the same house. There is wailing and crying almost in every house. At Ballybanane, Wm. Walsh and his son were found dead, entwined in each other's arms and both nearly eaten by rats. Martin Walsh, in same village, together with his father and mother, were also found dead. Anthony Derrig, in the next field dead under scraws. At Drimcaggy I found James O'Brien and his wife dead in a sawpit, and near to the place his little child drowned in a stream in the same village. But now there are no villages.

Pat Shaughnessy's two daughters, his mother, and his wife, were found in a hut dead together. There are many similar and equally distressing cases. They are now complaining before their God. On whom will we call – to whom will we make our sad complaint! Our gardens are turned into graves – our fields strewed with the sick and with the dying – our houses mouldering in dark ruins – our people naked, shivering, wandering, and craving for a grain of meal or a crust of bread. What can a priest do alone? There is no resident landlord, magistrate, or gentleman, in this extensive and remote parish. I am labouring from morning until night, and often from night until morning, in administering to the sick and dying, and helping to bury the dead, where they are melting into corruption by length of time.

I shudder and am sorely afraid at the awful and gloomy prospects before me. Three long months without any prospects of relief, except through charity.

Dear and respected Sir, in the name of charity I call on you – in the name of a suffering Redeemer I invoke you – and in the name of a perishing and dying people I implore you to speak – speak, and arouse the great and the charitable to the relief of the suffering and starving people of this doomed and perishing parish.

With feelings of profound respect, I remain your most humble and most obedient servant,

Peter Ward, Parish Priest, Partry, Ballinrobe.

'So what do you think of it?' Gaffney asked.

'Tears hell out of us all, doesn't it?'

'See the acknowledgment. It's taken from the Freeman's Journal.'

'And the date on the letter. That's the day after I left Father Ward. All the villages he describes, they're the ones the both of us visited together. He told me when I left that he'd write his own report. To be honest, I thought he was going to send it to the County here, I never thought he'd send it to the Freeman's Journal.'

'Confirms everything in your report. Now all Ireland knows of it.'

'He's leaving one out though. There was one family, name of Kennedy. Father Ward wouldn't let me in the door. It upset him something awful. He said there were things no man should see.'

'You never mentioned that in your report.'

'I didn't see inside. I'd have had to attack him to get past, and sure I couldn't do that. God knows, he was upset enough already.'

'A pity,' Gaffney said. 'There's been some ghastly stories.'

'Like what?'

'Never mind. Now I want you to do a quick errand for me. I want you to run over to the Connaught Telegraph, and get five more copies of this paper. Ask for Cavendish if you have any problem.'

Pat forced his way out through the gate. Ghastly stories, too terrible to tell. Again, the same caginess, this time from Gaffney. But what stories?

He reached the Connaught Telegraph. He had decided to ask for Mr. Cavendish anyhow.

The clerk at the door looked up in surprise.

'Mr. Cavendish? And who should I say is calling?'

'Pat Ryan. Mr. Gaffney sent me from the County.'

He waited. Then he was ushered into an office.

It was large and needed to be. Along one wall, the floor was piled high with newspapers. The other walls were lined with shelves, covered with heaps of loose papers and files. In the centre was a desk, which was covered with more newspapers and printers' proofs, all with many scribbles across them. A tall man stood behind. He extended his hand.

'Pat Ryan?' he said. 'I've seen your reports.'

'I know you have, Mr. Cavendish.'

'Not that any of us should admit that we've seen them. But you don't have to worry, they're under lock and key. Now, what can I do for you?'

'I'm looking for five more copies of last Saturday's Telegraph.'

Cavendish went to the door and whispered an instruction. He returned.

'How can it help you?'

'Well, maybe I shouldn't say, Mr. Cavendish, but the journey Father Ward describes is the one he took me on. No one will believe my word on it though. Father Ward's letter will help.'

'You were on this journey?'

'All he writes about in his letter. I saw every one of the houses and cabins he entered. It's all true.'

'And Ballinrobe?'

'In a terrible way, entirely. Father Ward tells the truth of it.'

Pat made his way back to the Union, and brought the newspapers to Gaffney.

'That's splendid,' Gaffney said. 'Let's just open them all at the letter page.'

Then he took the papers, and he walked into the corridor with Pat.

'I'm afraid I can't ask you in,' he said at the door of the Committee Room. 'You may stay outside.'

Pat could hear loud voices within. Only a few minutes later, Gaffney came out again.

'It was worth it just to see Lucan's face. Near went apoplectic he did.'

'Did he believe it though?'

'Oh, I reckon he believes it alright. Not that he'll ever admit it, nor the truth about the Levally evictions. Maybe we should ask Father Ward to write a note to the Freeman's Journal about that too.'

Pat had other things on his mind. That night, he wrote to Voisey in Knockanure, requesting that he ask the local parish priest for freedom to marry on behalf of his intended bride, Sarah Cronin, who had lived for most of her life in Knockanure. He received a letter from Voisey by return, stating that the banns would be read the following three Sundays. For Westport, he wrote to the clerk, asking that the request be passed on to the chaplain to the workhouse. Over the following weeks, he received letters from both Knockanure and Westport saying no objections had been raised to the marriage of Patrick Ryan and Sarah Cronin on the grounds either of existing marriage, or of close relationship as cousins, and enclosing letters of freedom as requested. He wrote to Carrigard to inform them, and said he would request leave in a few weeks.

He stayed on with Gaffney working on accounts. He noticed many things. Castlebar Workhouse was selling its own furniture to pay for corn. There were very few wooden beds in the dormitories now. Instead, the floors were covered with straw, where inmates were crowded together every night.

Even so, the workhouse's income was very little. The big landlords, including Lord Sligo in Westport, and even Lord Lucan in Castlebar were only paying their county rates from time to time, a point which still surprised Pat, since they could be prosecuted. On thinking about the matter though, he realised that the Grand Juries would be dominated by the big landlords – especially Lord Sligo and Lord Lucan – and they would hardly prosecute themselves, nor convict themselves if prosecuted.

Many of the other landlords were not paying at all, and some had not for two years. In some parts, he had travelled there was no record of landlords. In much of Erris there had been very little paid, and there were very few paupers in the temporary workhouse that had been erected there. The same was true of Partry. Many of Partry's poor would have made their way to Ballinrobe Workhouse, where large numbers would have died. Even the ones who broke out of the workhouse would only have lasted a short time.

One morning, he entered Gaffney's office to discuss correspondence. Frederick Cavendish was there.

'Delighted to see you again, Pat.'

'And you, Lord Cavendish.'

'I think we can forget the 'Lord' bit. There's more important matters than titles now. Have a look at this.'

He passed a newspaper to Pat.

'Father Ward has been writing letters again,' Gaffney said. '*Dublin Evening Post* this time. It's from the minutes of some relief committee he'd written to in Dublin.'

He pointed to a single paragraph.

'This little passage here. We'd like your opinion.'

Pat read –

'The heart will never conceive the appalling scenes of woe and grinding agonies of hunger. I have seen, though I did not publish the fact, the flesh of the dead daughter mangled in the mouth of her poor dead mother, four of them dead together on the same wad of straw.'

He whipped his hand to his mouth.

'Oh, Christ!'

'Pretty awful, isn't it?' Gaffney said.

'But…where?'

'We don't know for sure. There's talk of Drimcaggy, but no-one knows.'

'You travelled with him,' Cavendish said. 'Did you see any sign of anyone eating the dead?'

'I didn't,' Pat said. 'But there was one house he wouldn't even let me into. Mary Kennedy's, it was. He said there were things no man should ever see.'

'Yes, I remember you told me that,' Gaffney remarked.

'So I did,' Pat said. 'Well, that house was in Drimcaggy. Whatever he saw in that house upset him terribly, and he was a man well used to terrible things. He knew I was too. And that was what puzzled me. What could be worse than what I had already seen?'

'Could it be true, so?' Cavendish asked him. 'Could a mother eat her own children?

Pat found it hard to speak. The very question was sickening.

'I...I can't imagine it.'

'Me neither,' Gaffney said. 'Mind you, here's been rumours of this kind of thing from all around the County. I had reckoned they were only stories. But Father Ward has always been reliable in the past.'

'He has,' Pat said. 'But now...I don't know.'

Cavendish stared at him, as if mesmerised. Then he shook his head in frustration.

'Has he lost his mind or what?'

Pat hesitated. The question was a sharp one.

'He did say he'd been in fever. People picture strange things when they're in fever.'

'Had he recovered when you met him?' Gaffney asked.

'He was well enough. But he was weighed down with worries. And all the things we saw on the road; it was enough to rattle any man's wits.'

Gaffney drummed his fingers on the desk.

'Maybe he's had fever again.'

'Perhaps,' Pat said. 'God knows we were in enough cabins with fever.'

'So we might never know,' Cavendish said.

'I'm sorry,' Pat replied. 'I should have insisted on seeing inside the Kennedy house for myself.'

'Oh, it's not your fault, Pat,' Gaffney said. 'And anyhow, there might have been nothing in that house. He might be writing about some other village entirely. And even if it had been that house, it would have been asking far too much of you to witness that. No, don't you worry about it. You've done well. Very well indeed.'

Afterwards, Pat walked back to his office. His senses were on edge. The old grey floorboards screeched like never before. The whitewashed walls crowded in on him. The corridors stretched forever, their dripping candles forming all kinds of grotesque figures, intermingled with flickering images of a dead blackthorn tree. He was trembling, but he steadied himself on the wall. Then he walked to his office and began to work on accounts.

Chapter 27

Bradford Observer. June 1849:

The Sanitary Commissioners in their recent report, presented by them to Parliament, submit a mass of evidence all proving that cholera and other diseases are not contagious. The conditions of transmission and infection are an impure atmosphere and depraved physical health. The best antidotes are cleanliness, temperance, cheerfulness. As surely as magnet attracts steel, so certainly will filth and dirt develop cholera. Hard drinkers will fall the easiest prey. Incessant dread may predispose the body to take it. Let all offensive dunghills, dirt heaps, stagnant muddy pools, and decomposing matter of every description be forthwith removed.

Over the weeks and months, Murty got to know the Yeadon brothers better. He had at last discovered that the mysterious third brother, Nathan, was ill with miners' lung. Nathan had been the first of the brothers to work in the mines, starting at the early age of ten, pulling carts along the shafts. Later, he had become a miner, hacking at the coalface, until the coal dust had destroyed his lungs, and he could take it no more. Now he lay in the bedroom in the next house, waiting for death. Sometimes the brothers spoke of the workhouse as the only way out for him.

'Does it not worry ye that ye'd get it yourselves?' he asked them, one Sunday.

'Miners' lung!' Samuel exclaimed. 'That'll never catch us. Firedamp will kill us first.'

'Firedamp?' Murty exclaimed.

'One spark is enough to set it off, and bring the roof down. The men who die from the collapse, they're the lucky ones. The ones who are trapped, die in their own good time. Explosions are the killers in the mines.'

Murty could sense the defeat in what Samuel had said, and the way he had said it. It surprised him, because of what he knew of the brothers' interest in Unions.

'And what of the Union? Would they not make a protest?'

'If we had a Union, they might,' Arthur said. 'But such a Union, we do not have. The dragoons broke any chance of that in Bradford.'

'For now,' Samuel said. 'But we'll be back.'

Kitty, with her easy ways, got on well with everyone. She assisted *Bríd* around the house, most especially on Saturday nights, when it was cleaned of coal dust and smoke grime. She responded too to the bantering ways of the Yeadon brothers, teasing them about their appearance when they came back from the mines and, more important, insisting they be clean before they came into the Kerrigan house. The brothers accepted this with good grace and humour.

Cholera returned to Bradford. The outbreak earlier in the year had caused panic, but now it was said that it had been of a milder sort.

'*This is the worst one now,*' *Sinéad* said, '*the one we've all feared. You mark my words, we're for it now.*'

This time the approach was faster. Within days, neighbours in Adelaide Street had it. *Sinéad* was convinced that it spread in the mills, but she and the other women worked on, *Tomás* too. The same sense of defeat as before, Murty thought, waiting for their fate.

'*They're saying it's the Irish bringing it,*' *Máire* said one evening.

'*Arra, that's nonsense,*' *Tomás* said. '*Sure it's hitting every city, near and far, whether there's Irish there or not. Weren't they saying the same about the fever?*'

For once, Murty felt it was better working on the railways. If what the girls were saying about the mills was true, then the open air was healthier. He worried though about Aileen. Would she get cholera? Would she die of it?

As it turned out, Kitty was to be the first to get it.

When she came back from the mill one evening, she was irritable, which in itself was strange. Then she started complaining of muscle cramps.

Quickly, *Bríd* had her isolated upstairs. *Sinéad*, *Máire* and Peg brought their horsehair mattresses down to the front room, where they were stored under the dining table, to be pulled out at night and made up as beds on the floor for themselves.

Murty was concerned when Aileen took over as Kitty's nurse. For two days, she did not go to work, bringing jugs of water up to Kitty to feed her powerful thirst.

'You should have put salt in with it,' *Sinéad* told her, 'that's what the girls in the mill are saying.'

Murty was even more surprised when Aileen insisted on staying upstairs. She explained to him that if she got the disease, she would only spread it to everyone else if she came downstairs. On her request, *Bríd* prepared her meals and left them on the landing at the top of the stairs.

Dinner times were silent now. What if Kitty died? Aileen had lost two adult children already. Kitty was not family, but she was very, very close. If it came to the worst, he did not know how he could possibly cope with her silence again.

Then came the news that *Síle* Reilly too had contracted cholera, and a few days later, they heard she was dead. Murty and *Tomás*, went into the house next door, *Bríd* stayed at home, concerned that Aileen should stay too, and knowing that she needed the company, even if only from the distance of the stairs.

Murty and *Tomás* carried the coffin out with Arthur and Samuel. They placed it on to the waiting cart, and followed it to the graveyard. As they walked, two more coffins were added to the cart. They were buried separately. The four of them knelt at the graveside, as the coffin was lowered into it, and the last rites were spoken.

When they returned, Murty asked *Bríd* about Kitty.

'She'll live, I think.'

'She will?'

'I won't say it for certain. She's been long enough ill with it, but Aileen says she's getting better.'

Work continued on the Lancashire & Yorkshire. At times, Murty wondered how it might compare to other work. From all of what *Tomás* had told him though, the mills were closed to Mayo men now.

Even here on the railways, he could see how much the Irish were despised. There was always the chance of rioting between the English and the Irish navvies, but Murty, Higgins and Doyle made sure to keep well away, when any chance of it developed. While they all enjoyed the odd beer, he knew how fast trouble could erupt in the bars and shebeens around the railway works. He was surprised to discover that there was a 'company shebeen' on the works on the Colne Extension. Danny had been violently against shebeens on the works. He suspected too that Danny's involvement with the Molly Maguire gang was what led to his death. The gang had cleared the shebeens for Danny, but what else had they done? Murder?

It was tough on the McCormack cutting, but even so, Murty knew he was better off working on the Lancashire & Yorkshire. Murtybeg's works on the Colne extension had a brutal reputation. Murty reckoned that Murtybeg was working many of his navvies to death, and all for a shilling a day. Yes, he was feeding them, and some of them became strong enough to leave and work for other contractors. What of the others though, who died in the shacks, packed to the limit with men who had no other way of making a living, and no other way of gaining shelter? And Murtybeg was charging rent for these killing holes, where disease killed them faster than hunger could in Mayo. Fever before, cholera now.

No, he could not work with Murtybeg again. But was it any better where he was working now? Yes, the men were better paid. Still nothing like what they had been paid on the Leeds & Thirsk, but Murty himself was earning two shillings a day now, and while McCormack might have been doing very well out of it, he was not misusing his men to the same extent as Murtybeg was.

But what they were doing was worse. As they continued driving the Lancashire & Yorkshire through Broomfields, houses and shacks were being demolished. The tenements were disgusting. Dens of disease too, dozens of people crushed into houses designed for a quarter the number. The shacks were no better than *sceilps* back in Mayo. They were roughly constructed out of timber off-cuts by those who dwelt in them. They too only spread fever and cholera faster, and they could not keep out the driving rain and cold in the winter.

What made it worse was that this part of Broomfields was Irish. Day after day, the police cleared the tenements and shacks, batons whipping at the people if they moved too slowly. Murty knew that some of the evicted men were working on Murtybeg's site up on the Colne Extension. These were the men that were fodder for him. Soon they would be in Murtybeg's shacks, paying a rent and dying of disease. Not that that was very much different to what was happening in Broomfields.

But what of the others being evicted? Nowhere to live at all. What would happen to them? How long they would live, was an open question.

After the people were cleared, the McCormack men would move in to demolish the shacks. That was the easy work. Bringing down the tenements was more dangerous, but most of them were demolished using blasting powder. Afterwards, Murty, Higgins and Doyle would move in with their sledgehammers, smashing the remaining fragments of wall into bricks, then loading the bricks onto wheelbarrows to be brought down to the advancing railway and thrown onto the wagons for disposal.

Was this any different to how evictions were carried out in County Mayo? Was he an evictor?

Painful thinking, but what could be done? Organise an association, a union? Unionise the navvies in Bradford? Proscribe the demolitions? What chance would that have? Very little.

'You're still not thinking of unionising?' he asked the Yeadons one night.

'What good would that do?' Arthur asked.

'We could strike for higher wages,' Samuel said, at once.

'Aye, and we've tried that afore, and look where it got us,' Arthur said.

'Don't listen to him,' Samuel said, 'Next time, we'll do it proper. Just like the woolcombers did back in '25. Fetch on a general strike. Isn't that it Tommy?'

'Yes,' *Tomás* said. 'That's the way to do it.'

'But you didn't win then,' Murty said.

'We didn't,' said Samuel, 'but you can't blame that on us. It wasn't us that gave in first. But mark my words, Murty, the Miners' Association will be back; the Woolcombers & Weavers too. Not just one Association, and not just separate. There'll be many Associations, but all united in one great national union that will force the bosses to their knees. It's happened before, it'll happen again, you wait and see.'

Murty lay awake in bed that night, thinking of all he had heard. An attempt at a general strike twenty years ago, ending in failure. Another in 1842, with the same result. A third in 1844, broken. The Charter defeated. Was there no way forward?

And what of the navvy?

At the cutting the next morning, a whistle was blown as the fuse in the blasting powder was being lit. They moved back behind another house.

'I'd been talking to some fellows last night about Unions,' he said to Higgins and Doyle. 'I doubt there's much chance of it in Bradford anymore.'

'Not from all we hear,' Doyle said. 'They talk it round and round in circles in the shack, but the Unions in Bradford are finished.'

'Right across the country, too,' Higgins said.

There was a loud roar, as another house crashed to the ground. They waited as the dust cleared.

'Yes,' said Murty, 'you're right, but still we can dream. Can you imagine the look on young Murtybeg's face if we called a strike on the Colne Extension?'

'I doubt it would worry him much,' Higgins said. 'Sure there's thousands and thousands of navvies on the tramp, the half of them starving, and most of them within a hundred miles from here. If there was ever talk of a strike on the railway works, they'd all be making their way here.'

'Scab labour,' Doyle said.

'Scab or not,' Higgins said, 'a man doesn't give a damn if his belly is empty. No, all they'd suffer is a day's delay on the Colne before they'd be up to full speed again. Whatever about the mill workers or the miners, you'll never unionise the navvy.'

'I'd agree with you,' Murty said.

Still, he thought of the idea of a strike on Murtybeg's works. Unionising the navvy? An impossible dream. The navvy was there to be used and abused. Most of them were single men, with no other source of pay.

But what was he himself? A navvy too. And an evictor! What of it? He, at least, had a wife working and no children to worry about. Nessa and Danny dead, Murtybeg, a ruthless, wealthy contractor. He and Aileen could pay their rent, and eat. But what would happen when he was too old to work anymore. Would they end up in the workhouse, the same way as Nathan might? How could that happen when he had such a wealthy son?

A son? What son?

And what of the mills? One night he spoke to Kitty about it all after dinner. Aileen was already earning good wages, and from what *Sinéad* and *Máire* said, she would soon be earning more. He asked Kitty about wages in the mill.

'The spinners are up to nine shillings a week – one and six pence a day,' she told him. Loomweavers the same. Better than the ragsorters, I can tell you. Six shillings is their weekly lot. The piecers are even less, up to three shillings if they're lucky.'

'But sure no one could live on that.'

'Not if they're feeding a family, they can't. But they're part of the family. Boys and girls, and whatever they make is extra for the family. It's important, don't you see? If the child doesn't work, it's only a mouth and a mouth takes feeding, and feeding costs money. But a child has hands, and hands earn money. No, a family can't afford to have too many children not working.'

Yes, Murty was thinking. Not as much as what we're earning on the Lancashire & Yorkshire, though the work can't be as hard, and the hours are only sixty a week.

'But what age do they start them at?'

'God only knows. They're only kids, some of them. Whether they've five years on them, I wouldn't know?'

'Five years?'

'Isn't that what I'm saying? It's a hard job too, being a piecer. If a thread on a spindle breaks, the ends have to be repaired at once. The piecer goes forward and joins them, there's a knack in doing it, and the kids learn it fast. And they've many spindles to be watching, running backwards and forwards as needed. Running miles and miles a day. And near half the mill would be children. The ones who live, that is. Sure half the children in Bradford die before they make it to men or women. You should listen to the older women talking, they can tell you how many of their own have died. I reckon the most of the women started off working in the mills as children, five to ten years old, that kind of age. You can ask all the women on the looms, they'll tell you the stories of what they went through when they were young.'

'And what of Aileen, Kitty? Do you think she's able for all this?'

'More so than I might have expected,' Kitty said. 'It's the hours that hit her first, that's what she tells me. But she was well used to spinning and weaving before, so even with the new machines, she learnt quick enough. She's strengthened up too. But whatever about the long hours and hard work, it's the other women that make it easier. Us Irish, we just stick together, make our own fun. It's strange how people can laugh, no matter what. And I include Aileen in that.'

'Laughing?'

'And talking more than ever. The mill is taking her out of herself.'

'I'd say you're right,' Murty said. 'And it's not just the mill neither. It's yourself too. I don't know how we've done without you all these years. Nor how we could in the future. You've worked miracles, you have.'

On a Sunday afternoon, the unseen Nathan was taken to the Bradford Workhouse. Murty watched from the door as he was carried out on a stretcher. He heard the raspy breathing, and knew full well that Nathan would not live long.

Murty offered to help, but the two brothers refused politely, and brought Nathan to the waiting cart.

'*And we'll never see him again,*' Bríd said. '*A hard life, and him only a young man.*'

A few days later, Arthur and Samuel joined Murty and *Tomás* around the table in Kerrigans'.

'Well, how did he take it?' *Tomás* asked.

'Not so well, Tommy,' Samuel answered. 'We walked over this morning. He was upset he hadn't seen us for a few days. He's in there with all the other old miners, a ward all to themselves. Not a place I'd care to stay, what with all the puffing and panting. It's hard on him.'

'It'll be hard on you too,' Murty said, 'when you end up there yourselves. Have you thought of that?'

Arthur laughed. 'That's not for us,' he said. 'It's like I told you, it'll be a rockfall or an explosion.'

'And what of the Miners' Association?'

'In one word, dead. Dead as a doornail, no matter what Sammy thinks. What difference could they make to us? The firedamp won't go away just because the Association orders it. Nor will the rocks stop falling.'

On the McCormack Cutting, Murty always looked forward to Saturday afternoons. Sometimes, when they had been paid, he would go with Doyle and Higgins to their shack on the edge of the Works. The shack disgusted him now. But every time he visited, there was good company. The men were from home, and their high spirits and good humour never failed to lift him.

Sometimes whiskey was produced, sometimes *poitín*, but only for special occasions as they saw it. Sometimes they played pontoon, and from time to time, even poker, gambling for farthings and halfpennies.

On Sundays, he enjoyed the harangues with *Tomás* and the Yeadon brothers. They, too, were all advanced in their thinking, and in some ways this surprised Murty. *Tomás* could read and write, and while his writing might have been limited, his reading was certainly good enough for the Bradford Observer.

When Murty suggested to the Yeadons that they should learn, they scorned the idea.

'Reading isn't for the likes of us,' Samuel said.

'How can you say that?' Murty said. 'It's the only way you'll be able to beat the bosses.'

'Not in our lifetimes,' Arthur said.

He might be right, Murty thought. The miners' lung will catch them both soon enough. If, of course, a rockfall doesn't get them first. There was no way he could beat their fatalism.

This showed itself in another way.

Murty knew Kitty had come from a poor background, and was both illiterate and innumerate. One morning he took her aside.

'Isn't it time you learned to read and write?' he asked her.

'Me!' she exclaimed. 'But sure how could I do that?'

'I could teach you. And isn't it a great chance for you? Here you are, living with a teacher, and I can tell you, it would be a great pleasure for me to be back teaching.'

'But how could I pay you?'

'Sure forget about that. After all you've done for Aileen, how could I ever charge you.'

Kitty hesitated.

'Not wishing to upset you,' she said, 'but you're a man can read and write, and you're only working on the railway. Aren't you?'

'True enough,' Murty said. 'I don't have to tell you, I was long enough working as a teacher, but when the new schools came to Mayo, they wouldn't take me on because I wasn't practised their way. Same thing over here. So when I came across, I was working with Danny, and then with Gilligan's gang. I wasn't working as a labourer there, they had me on clerical work, and I was as much a part of the gang as anyone else. But that was when we worked as a gang, here we're just common labourers, and McCormack sure as hell doesn't have any more need of clerks; he's enough English ones of his own.'

'But you could look for other clerical positions?'

'I could, Kitty, but my age is against me now. And you're right, I should try. But you, you're young enough, you can do it if you want.'

'There's other reasons though,' Kitty said. 'You talk about clerical work, sure that's not for women. Irish women wouldn't have a chance in hell. You know that as well as I do.'

'Things will change.'

'Oh, but will they?'

'They will, Kitty, they will. There'll be other openings for you. Like teaching...'

'Teaching!'

'Why not? There'll be chances for intelligent women, Irish or not.'

'But teacher training costs money. And time too. Time I'd not be earning.'

'We'd find a way. But first you'd have to read and write.'

That night, Kitty came to their bedroom. Aileen answered her knock.

'Kitty child, come in.'

Kitty entered, and sat at the end of the bed.

'I was thinking of what you were saying about teacher training,' she said to Murty. *'I'd have to learn my numbers and letters first. So I'll accept your generous offer.'*

'I knew you would,' Murty said.

'But how long before I'd be able to start their training.'

'Hard to say. Five years. Could be six. It wouldn't just be writing and arithmetic. There'll be other subjects too. And examinations to take, before they'd let you in.'

'It's not easy then.'

'It's not. Every evening, every weekend we'd be working, you and I together.'

Kitty looked to Aileen.

'Has he been talking to you of this?'

'It was I spoke to him,' Aileen answered.

'You said it first?'

'And sure why not?'

'But teacher training? We could never pay for it.'

'We'll wait till that time comes. After that, Murtybeg will pay.'

'Murtybeg!' Murty exclaimed. *'Just how in hell...'*

'We'll write to him,' Aileen said.

'And what would we say?'

'Tell him Kitty is in England.'

'Arra, what. Would he even know who Kitty is?'

'He'd know, right enough. They played together as children back in Mayo.'

Murty shook his head, baffled.

'*But how could we ask him for money?*'

'*Sure there'd be no need to ask. He'll see she's living with us, and is to be schooled.*'

'*Even so.*'

'*It'll give him a chance to atone for his sins. He'll do it, Murteen will. He'll do it for his sister.*'

'*Sister!*' Kitty exclaimed, wide-eyed. '*But then…then I'd be your daughter.*'

'*As you already are, alanna.*'

Chapter 28

Manchester Courier. July 1849:

Very early one morning last week Mr. Fogg, as inspector of nuisances, accompanied by two police officers, made an inspection of the lodging houses in New Town, occupied by the Irish tramps, or wretched beings of the same station in society. In the cellar of a man named Murphy, in Bridge's Court, Newport Street, they found 15 men and women, and in the coal-hole a man and his wife, making 17 in one cellar, besides Murphy's family. In the lodging house of William Hornby, Cross Street, they found 14 men and women in one room. In another house in Back Dawes Street, they found 11 men in the kitchen, and upstairs 20; making 31 persons in a small house, besides the family of the occupier. They also visited another house in Back Dawes Street, kept by John Patten, and found 12 men and women on the ground floor, the room being 12 feet by 12 feet, and 8 feet high. In the room above there were 16 men; and in the garret, there were 18 men and women, making 46 lodgers in the 3 rooms, in addition to Patten's family. The sexes were indiscriminately huddled together, the rooms without any ventilation, and frightfully filthy.

Murtybeg's relationship with Irene changed beyond all knowing. Their desperate coupling that night swiftly saw to that. Here, at least, she yielded to him as master, though her driving urgency pushed his manhood to the utter limits.

When at last she slept, he stayed awake, watching the flickers of the street lights reflected on the ceiling. Was this the woman he had hated so bitterly? A woman he would gladly have strangled, if he could have gotten away with it. So what did he feel for her now? Love? He thought of his mother, and how protective he had been towards her. And Nessa before she had died, his own sister snatched away in childbirth. That was love. There were other women – girls too – when he was younger. Some of these he had thought he had loved, but none had lasted.

But what was this? A wild animal passion? No, it was far more than that. It was no softness, though. It was a hard way of loving, based on their ability to test each other to the extreme. Was that love? Did it matter? It was an unbreakable bond, stronger than any, and Irene was his only future.

Next morning, after their aching lust was spent, they had a quiet breakfast and returned to the office. It became evident now that Irene respected Murtybeg, far more than she had ever respected Danny. The link between them was based on another passion too – their shared ambition to make Edwardes & Ryan the top labour contractor on the railways in the north of England.

Now, he deferred to her on dealing with the suppliers to the business, where her tough dealings forced prices down to the minimum. Their smaller suppliers knew she could break them, and often Edwardes & Ryan was their only lifeline for survival.

She left the sourcing of labour to him, whether off the boats in Liverpool, or from the workhouses and slums of Liverpool, Manchester or Bradford. He also continued dealing with the main railway contractors, especially Brassey and Mackenzie. Responsibility for the smaller contractors was divided between them.

Dealing with the banks was also a joint concern, though Murtybeg played the lead role. The Manchester & Salford bank was not used to dealing with women at a high level, but he knew that Winrow and his colleagues would grow to respect Irene, and while negotiations would always be tough, he and Irene would always bring them to a profitable finish.

His relationship with his family was a different matter. His father's refusal to return to work in Edwardes & Ryan had depressed him, but it was no surprise. He knew how much Murty despised Irene. Now that Irene was his future, Murty and Aileen could not be part of his life. Danny's break with his parents had been one of the reasons for him killing himself. More and more though, Murtybeg felt that he was stronger than Danny, working closely with a hard woman who saw him as her equal. He had chosen his road in life, a choice that Danny could not make, and the need for which had torn him asunder.

His relationship with his gangers changed too. He could see Roughneen and Lavan regarded him with a new respect, almost deference. They had quickly sensed the future and were working to keep their part in it.

Of the other gangers, Gilligan seemed nervous at first. Murtybeg knew he too understood the changes taking place in Edwardes & Ryan, and he too came to respect him and learned to deal with the navvies with the same callousness.

The gangers had other concerns too. Roughneen was the first to bring it up.
'The stories of cholera,' he said.'

'I know,' Irene said, 'they say there's people dying in Manchester.'

'Worse than Manchester. The Woodhead Tunnel too. There's been navvies dying. If it gets a grip on the railways, it will spread right across the network.'

'Let's pray it doesn't,' Murtybeg said.

But it did spread. When Murtybeg next travelled to Bradford to visit the Colne Extension, he met with Gilligan. New shacks were being rapidly built.

'Are we employing more men?' he asked.

'We are,' Gilligan replied. 'We're employing more to fill in for the ones with cholera. And those shacks there, they're our infirmaries, if you want to call them that.'

'Infirmaries?'

'We have to quarantine them, that's the law.'

'But surely the Bradford Infirmary would take them?'

'Not now. There's too many cases across the city. Broomfields and Kirkgate mainly. They're trying to cut back on the numbers they're taking in the city, and they don't see why they should take Irish navvies.'

'This'll slow things down on our contract.'

'I wouldn't worry,' Gilligan said. 'Like you said yourself, there's plenty of Mayo men in Broomfields, half-starved too. No, we've no problem filling the openings.'

'Fine,' Murtybeg said. 'Just take care of yourself, Joe, we wouldn't want you ending up with cholera.'

One evening, the subject of the Molly Maguire gang arose.

'It's always been a dangerous situation,' Irene said. 'You know that Danny had been caught up with them?'

'Yes,' Murtybeg said, 'I'd known that at the time.'

'He was a fool to do it,' she said. 'They're a very dangerous gang. Danny had his excuses, of course, he only wanted to clear the shebeens off his sites, but as you know, that resulted in one death and Jamesy McManus was killed in return.'

'I know all that. There was a police investigation at the time.'

'There was. The police were looking for information from Danny, but he was terrified to give it. While he might not have asked the gang to murder anyone, men had died, and Danny thought he might hang for it. I thought a long prison sentence was more likely, but I think that terrified Danny even more. And there was an even worse problem. If he informed the police, the gang would kill him.'

Murtybeg shook his head. 'I hadn't known that he was thinking like that.'

'He might have been overstating his fears, but even so, right or wrong, he could see no way out of it.'

'But he's dead now. Surely, it stops there.'

'So you might think,' she said. 'My only concern is that the gang won't let it rest.'

'I wouldn't worry about that,' Murtybeg said. 'They will now.'

'How can you be so sure?'

'They've already made contact. Mr. Brady, that is. He wanted to offer us 'protection'. But I wouldn't have it.'

'You wouldn't have it?'

'I threatened him with hanging.'

He walked over to the desk and took out a copy of the 'To Whom It May Concern' letter. Irene glanced through it.

'Interesting.'

'Yes,' Murtybeg said. 'Brady knows of this letter. He knows too that there is a witnessed copy, filed away in the Manchester Law Library. So I told him there was no question of protection, and assured him that he would hang if anything happened to me.'

Irene stared at him.

'And you really believe he won't do anything?'

'Not now. He's a man of the world, is Gene Brady. He's not going to risk his life for a little protection money. He said as much to me. He wanted to forget the whole matter of protection.'

'And…and what of Inspector Crawford?'

'Odd you should mention that. He came around to see me, weeks after the Brady meeting. I told him that I had committed no offence. I agreed that I had met with Brady, but had not agreed to carry out any criminal act. There was nothing he could do.'

It was time to meet with Sternberg. Murtybeg wrote to him, but did not mention Irene. A meeting was arranged at the Law Library.

When Murtybeg introduced Irene, he saw that Sternberg was taken aback.

'I must say, I had not been expecting to meet you here today,' he said to Irene.

'Of course, not,' Irene said. 'Inside a courtroom would have been more appropriate.'

'I'm sorry,' Murtybeg said. 'I should have warned you of what was happening. You see, Curzon & Clegg have been talking with Rothwells, and have come up with something, which might solve all our problems and leave us with no need for further court cases.'

'No need…?'

'Don't worry, Louis,' he said, 'there will be plenty of work for you yet. You see, Curzon & Clegg have suggested that, if Irene and I were to marry, there would be no further…'

'Marry!'

'Well, why not?'

'Yes, Mr. Sternberg,' Irene said, 'and why not? As Curzon & Clegg have said, it would protect the assets of both parties. So before you think it, the next question has become a personal one between the two of us.'

'Yes,' Sternberg said, 'I can understand that.'

And more than that, Murtybeg was thinking. Sternberg could understand Irene's other attractions too, but he's too much of a professional to say anything about that.

'So the question is,' Irene said, 'where do we go from here?'

'I wouldn't like to be too precipitate,' Sternberg said. 'It will, of course, be a complex situation, for various reasons. The first thing you should be aware of, though you doubtless know already, is that on marriage, a wife's property passes to her husband. But right at the moment, we still have a case reserved in the High Court, and no judgement has been made as regards ownership yet. Also, I presume you do not, as yet, have a date for your wedding?'

'Not yet,' Murtybeg said. 'It is something we need to discuss very soon though.'

'Indeed,' Sternberg said. 'And it's probably as well it hasn't been arranged yet. We would have to consider the legal implications very closely. It is all a matter of timing.'

'Can you explain to us why timing is so important,' Irene asked.

'First,' Sternberg said, 'we must consider a pre-marriage settlement. There must be no question of intestacy this time. I don't have to tell you the complications that arose from your partner's intestacy the last time.'

'Indeed not,' Irene said. 'But the question arises now, how could intestacy come about on this occasion?'

'I doubt it could,' Sternberg said, 'particularly since, as I say, in the event of the husband's demise, his property automatically passes to his wife. It is as well to have this in writing though, stating specifically the principle of 'each to each', in other words that on the demise of either party the property passes to the other, unless of course, there are children.'

'Of course, there will be children,' Irene said. 'We must take that into account.'

Murtybeg looked at her in surprise. This was a matter they had not yet discussed.

'In due course, we shall,' Sternberg said. 'It should unquestionably form part of the pre-marriage agreement.'

He turned to Murtybeg.

'There's one most important question I must ask you,' he said. 'Since you are not as yet married, Miss Miller, legally speaking, is still our opponent in a court case. Do you wish to drop this case?'

'Yes,' Murtybeg said, 'very definitely.'

'There are other matters we have discussed in the past, which were confidential between us at the time.'

'There is no need for silence, Louis,' Murtybeg said. 'Irene is my intended. That will not change under any circumstances.'

Sternberg was scratching on a paper pad.

'Very well,' he said. 'When we spoke before, I did point out to you that your own parents, Murty and Aileen Ryan, could have had prior claim to Edwardes & Ryan. They would certainly have ranked above you personally, whatever about Miss Miller's claims regarding common-law marriage and such factors.'

'I can see that that would be an important point,' Murtybeg said. 'Certainly, they could make a claim on the business.

'Yes,' Irene said. 'But the question arises then, what is the business?'

'It has assets, surely,' Sternberg said.

'Indeed, it has,' Irene replied. 'Horses, carts, timber and suchlike, but that is not where the real value of Edwardes & Ryan exists.'

Sternberg arched his fingers, as though thinking. At last, he looked Irene straight in the eyes.

'I know,' he said. 'The intellectual property of the business is vastly more valuable.'

'Indeed,' Irene said, 'and you're one of the few men who can see that.'

'So if we were to allow Mr. and Mrs. Ryan senior to take over the business without any involvement from either of you, it would effectively be worthless?'

'Precisely, Mr. Sternberg,' Irene said.

Sternberg looked to Murtybeg again.

'But I must now ask you specifically, as my client, is this satisfactory to you?'

'Perfectly satisfactory,' Murtybeg said.

He could see a growing respect between Irene and Sternberg. He knew that she was assessing Louis closely, testing his toughness as well as his skills. It was clear that Curzon & Clegg had no future with Edwardes & Ryan. Irene had decided, and Murtybeg knew that. Louis was already thinking of a future relationship with Edwardes & Ryan, and anticipating the many bitter court battles that would be fought with suppliers, competitors and anyone else who got in the way in the years ahead. Had Curzon & Clegg foreseen all this when they had recommended Irene to a marriage settlement? Why worry? There was little need for him to talk now. Listening to Irene and Louis was far more satisfying.

Sternberg was speaking to him though.

'Would you perhaps like to make some sort of settlement with your father, once your ownership of the business is legally valid,' he asked Murtybeg.

Irene interrupted.

'That would be a decision for my future husband to make,' she said. 'For myself though, I do not feel we owe them anything, but there might be other problems. For example, would an offer of a settlement imply that there was a liability in the first place?'

'Not necessarily,' Sternberg said. 'But to avoid any such development, it would be essential to have the ownership legally established before any such settlement.'

'And how would we do that?' Irene asked.

Sternberg looked to Murtybeg again, raising his eyebrows in a questioning way.

'No problem, Louis. Go ahead.'

'Very well,' Sternberg said. 'The way to solve this predicament is very simple. We should go to the High Court, and indicate that we are withdrawing any objection to Miss Miller's claim. Then, when she wins the case, and it is so declared, she will legally own the business without any doubt, and ahead of any other claimants, such as Murty and Aileen Ryan.'

He paused.

'Or yourself,' he added.

'And then?' Murtybeg asked.

Again, Sternberg looked to him questioning, then he went on.

'It's not a matter of 'then', it's more a matter of 'before'. There is another fact I must point out to you, Murtybeg. I am still retained on your behalf, and in spite of what you say about your forthcoming marriage, I must act in your interests. I would insist therefore, before the court case goes ahead, that you and Miss Miller are married.'

There was a silence, as his words sank in. Murtybeg was the first to break it.

'I understand,' he said. 'It is clearly the sensible way to proceed.'

'I understand too, Mr. Sternberg,' Irene said. 'In fact, I would be disappointed with you if you did not give such advice to your client. I would like to declare therefore that I have no objection. I expect Murtybeg and I will be married in the next few weeks. I will make sure to have a fair copy made of the appropriate documents and have them despatched to you.'

'Excellent,' Sternberg said. 'Now, with your joint agreement, I will write to Curzon & Clegg and suggest that the court case be deferred for a few weeks. You might notify Rothwells that you have no objection to this.'

'Certainly, Louis,' Irene said.

Before their intended wedding, Murtybeg wrote to Murty, inviting him and Aileen to attend. A few days later he received a curt response from Murty, saying that Aileen would not be well enough to travel. Murtybeg thought there might have been other reasons. Could they afford the travel? Perhaps he should offer to pay for the tickets? Or was that the problem at all? Was it simply that Murty no longer wished to have any association with him? He decided to dismiss it from his mind. He had invited them. If his father did not wish to attend, that was his concern.

Murtybeg Ryan and Irene Miller were married in the Registry Office in Stockport. It was a quiet affair. Irene's mother and father attended, though. He was a quiet, inoffensive man, she a quiet, dumpy woman. Murtybeg wondered how they had raised a firebrand like Irene.

Roughneen, Gilligan and Lavan were there too. The only other one to attend was Louis Sternberg.

Afterwards they signed the registry, Lavan and Sternberg acting as witnesses. Two fair copies were made, one for the Ryans and one for Sternberg.

A wedding breakfast was held in the Wellington Hotel. Baked lamb tongues were served with tea and toast; followed by lobster sausages, pork chops and almond pudding. At first, Murtybeg was concerned that they were being so spendthrift. But what of it? He ordered a keg of ale and a dozen Turkish cigars. Danny would have understood.

The following week, Murtybeg and Irene travelled into Manchester, and walked to the Court. Sternberg was waiting outside.

'We must hurry,' he told them. 'Mr. Gilbert doesn't like anyone being late.'

They entered the Courtroom, and sat waiting until their case was called. Both Curzon and Rothwell were there, representing Irene. They both nodded to Sternberg, saying nothing.

Their case was called.

'I have reviewed all these documents,' the judge told them, 'and my understanding is that Mr. Ryan is withdrawing his case, and conceding to Miss Miller.'

Curzon raised his hand. 'If I may, m'lud?'

The judge nodded.

'Miss Miller, as you call her, has changed her name this morning. She is now to be known as Irene Ryan.'

'Irene Ryan? In God's name, why?'

Sternberg approached the bench and placed a copy of the marriage certificate before the judge. The judge ran his eyes down it, frowning.

'Mr. Curzon? You have seen this; I take it?'

'Yes, m'lud,' Curzon replied. 'In fact, it was we who suggested this course of action to Mrs. Ryan. We are proceeding with Mr. Sternberg's consent.'

'So, if I follow this correctly, Edwardes & Ryan is to be conceded to Irene Ryan.'

'Indeed.'

'And through her, it would then pass to her husband, Murtybeg Ryan. Is that your understanding, Mr. Sternberg?'

'It is, m'lud,' Sternberg said.

He shook his head, half in admiration.

'Nice one, gentlemen. Very nice. And my congratulations to both of you, Mr. and Mrs. Ryan.'

It was late when they returned to Stockport. The maid had already gone to bed. Carefully, Murtybeg lit the candle at the door, and led the way upstairs. He lit two more candles in the bedroom.

Then she embraced him tightly. He pushed her back and threw her on the bed, pulling her dress high. Afterwards they lay on the bed gasping.

'My God,' he said, 'you could kill any man.'

She laughed. 'I doubt that. You're a tough fellow, Murteen Ryan, I'll grant you that. Tougher than your brother ever was.'

'I'm sure he was well able,' Murtybeg said.

'He was, right enough, but still, I frightened him, and a woman has to know who's in control. It's the same with every breed of animal.'

'You're not saying...?'

'Not in everything, I'm not. In business, we're equals, and always will be. Already we're working for the top contractors in England. Soon we'll be railway contractors ourselves, no matter what Brassey or Mackenzie might think. And by the time we're finished, we'll be the top railway contractors in the north of England. You see if we don't.'

Chapter 29

The Mountain Sentinel, Pennsylvania. June 1849:

We learn, although unable to get the entire particulars, that the Irish engaged on the Pennsylvania Railroad from below Union Furnace in Huntingdon County, to Antis Township in this county under the several contractors have been engaged in the most serious riots during the past week. A large body of Irishmen met in mortal combat, armed with rifles, muskets, pistols and bludgeons of every description as their weapons, creating terror to the peaceable inhabitants, and wounding, and we believe, taking the life in some instances, of the different combatants. They also destroyed by burning and tearing down several shanties, and assaulted Mr. Gillespie, a contractor, so severely, that his life has been despaired of for several days.

As Luke soon discovered, he no longer had a position in the weigh station. Since he had never been paid by the Union for that work, it made no difference.

During his weeks there, he had developed a working relationship with Cantwell, which was courteous, if not friendly. He suggested Luke return to work down the mine with the other men.

The mood at the drift was one of sullenness. Farrelly tried to put a good face on it, but in the end, the Union had achieved nothing. Wages dropped again. They were still slightly higher than before the Bates Union was created, but it was hardly worthwhile, after the losses they had all taken during the strike, without any strike pay.

Luke felt that McGlinn might have been happy to see him back inside the mine, not necessarily because he wished to work with Luke, but more because he had resented that Luke was in a superior position, and now had been brought back to earth. He said little though, and his silence told much.

Life in the coal patches was returning to normal. And the coal dust was back.

'I never thought I'd miss it,' Winnie said. 'What with all the scrubbing and all? I'll say one thing though, when there's dust, there's food.'

'There is,' Luke said.

Slowly, very slowly, they began to put on weight. Luke was still concerned about his debt in the truck store. Could he ever send money to Mayo again? What was happening in Mayo?

Winnie was still concerned about cholera.

'Well, let's not worry about it,' Luke said. 'It hasn't crossed the mountains yet, and from what all they're saying in the mine, it's not going to either.'

'Why not?'

'There's a cholera line. Cholera doesn't cross mountains. As long as it's on the other side, we're safe.'

The next day, news came through of cholera in Wilkes Barre.

'You said it was impossible,' Winnie said.

'Sometimes, the impossible happens,' Luke said.

But by that time, they had other matters to consider.

The Operators closed the mines again.

As before, the same excuse was given. The prices in New York and Philadelphia were too low, and a stoppage would force the prices up. This time it was stated that the stoppage would be for two weeks only.

Winnie was shattered.

'How could they do this again?' she asked. 'Do they want to starve us all?'

'Looks like they do,' Luke said. 'Still, since you ask, the reason they're giving is that the prices in the market are too low.'

'Too low?'

'That's what they're saying. And it's said that the stoppage will only be for two weeks.'

'And should we believe that?' Winnie asked.

'If it's true,' Luke said, 'we might just be able to make it. At least we're all better fed, after four weeks of working.'

'But what on earth are they looking for?' Ned asked. 'Is it just to drive us back to the truck shop again? Push our debt up, interest on top, and make sure we can never get out of it?'

'I think that might have something to do with it too,' Luke said. 'And at least the weather is warm. We won't have to go around scrabbling for coal in the culm bank. That's for sure.'

They waited. There was no suggestion of an extension this time.

'The seventh of July, that's what it's looking like,' Ned said.

Then came an announcement of a picnic.

'A picnic!' Winnie exclaimed, when Luke told her. 'What? Where?'

'Down in Pottsville again. Fourth of July. Independence Day. A miners' jamboree, that's what the Union is calling it.'

'Damn the bloody Union,' Ned said, 'there's no way any of us are going for picnics with the Union. We can't eat, and they're having bloody picnics.'

This time, no one from Farrelly's gang went to Pottsville. On the following day, the news of the picnic came through.

The Union had declared a strike. Again.

'They want to support the Operators,' Ned told them. 'It's only for five days.'

'Five days!' Luke echoed.

'Five days too long,' Winnie said. 'What in the hell are they trying now? What's this about supporting the Operators?'

'They're agreeing with them,' Ned said. 'The Union, they're trying to support the market. They reckon the less anthracite going to New York and Philadelphia, the more the price goes up.'

'That's mad,' Winnie exclaimed. 'All they're doing is dragging out the Operators' Lockout. Can't they see that?'

'They can see it right enough,' Luke said, 'but they don't give a damn, do they? They're on the side of the Operators. All they want is to screw us into the ground.'

As the lockout was coming to an end, stories filtered back to Lackan about a miners' march.

'They're making damned sure the Union strike is obeyed,' Luke said. They're beating the hell out of any miners who've gone back to work, that's what we're hearing.'

'But who are these people?' Winnie asked. 'Why in the name of God are miners starving their own?'

'I don't know the answer to that.'

This time, the mines did not re-open when the Operators' suspension ended. Once again, the enforcers appeared in front of the mines and the breakers.

'It'll never stop,' Winnie said.

Luke went to the truck store to buy food. He was stunned to be told he had no further credit. Neither had Ned.

Winnie stared open-eyed at him, when she heard the news.

'I suppose you're going to tell me it's a good thing we're not increasing our credit.'

Luke shook his head.

'The baby is starving,' she said.

'I know.'

'What are we going to do?'

'What can we do, Winnie? Wait out the strike, it's all we can do.'

'Yes,' Winnie said, scornfully, 'and then I suppose the Operators will declare another Lockout, isn't that it?'

Luke shook his head.

'There's no word of it, let's not worry about what hasn't happened.'

But the strike did end. A few days later, the tents disappeared again.

'And thank God for that,' Winnie said. 'Bad cess to the whole bloody lot of them.'

But the hunger went on. They had to work another week, before they were paid. Luke was weak with hunger, and knew the others were too. They sent fewer wagons to the weigh station, as their tonnage dropped.

At last they lined up to be paid. Two dollars.

'What's this?' Luke gasped.

'Lower output,' the clerk answered.

'I know that, but not this much lower.'

'Your credit is bad,' the clerk said. 'We're starting your repayments.'

Farrelly took him by the arm.

'Come on Luke.'

'Damn it,' he said as he walked away, 'They get us every way. There'll be interest on that too.'

Winnie stared at the coins, when he returned.

'We knew it would be lower,' Luke told her. 'We weren't making the tonnage with the hunger, and they're taking repayment for the truck shop too.'

Ellen put her arm around Winnie.

'Come on, dear,' she said.

Winnie broke away from her, and ran over to Luke.

'What kind of country is this?' she cried. 'The Operators starve us; our own Union starves us. Will there be no end to it?'

She beat his chest, sobbing.

'Once this is over, we will not starve. Never, Luke. Do you hear me? We will never, never, never starve again.'

Walking to the mine one morning, they discussed it all.

'They've declared a victory,' Farrelly told them. 'The Union say we've won.'

'Won!' Mick gasped. 'What in the name of God have we won? Starvation, that's all we've won.'

'This fellow Bates though, what class of man is he?' McGlinn asked.

'Sure he told you himself what he is,' Mick said. 'He said the Union has the same interests as the Operators.'

'Damned right it has,' Luke said. 'Famine, that's the only thing he wants. And does he care? Fifteen dollars a week, that's what he pays himself. And all these payments for the Union, where did that go? We saw none of it, did we? What's happening to all these Strike Funds they told us about?'

'Bates took his money out of it,' McGlinn said.

'Sure he did,' Mick said, 'but even fifteen dollars a week, wouldn't go through that amount of money.'

'Maybe he's giving it to the Operators?' Luke said. 'After all, he's told us he has the same interests.'

'Doubt that,' McGlinn said. 'Even Bates wouldn't go that far.'

As they soon discovered, Bates could go further. A long way further. The news came through from Pottsville and St. Clair.

'Bates has disappeared,' Farrelly told them. 'Vanished off the face of the earth.'

There was a shocked silence.

'And the Union funds?' Jack asked. 'Are they to be returned to us?'

'Now what do you think?' Farrelly said. 'Why do you think he's disappeared?'

'But...but how could he do that?' Luke asked.

'Oh, it's done easy enough,' Farrelly said.

'Have they a warrant for his arrest then?' McGlinn asked.

'Sure what good would that do,' Farrelly said. 'All he has to do is disappear out west, out to one of the Territories, and he'll never be found.'

'Like where,' McGlinn asked.

'Minnesota perhaps. Oregon Territory if he can get that far.'

'So there's no union now.'

'No.'

'And there's the English for you,' Mick said. 'Never trust an Englishman, they'll always betray you.'

That evening, Luke joined the other men in the Miners' House. Farrelly produced a bottle of *poitín*. 'And that's the end of the Unions in the coal mines,' he said. 'We'll never see them again.'

'Not true,' Jack said. 'The next time we have a Union; it'll be headed up by an Irish man.'

Mick shook his head.

'*Arra*, you're wasting your time,' he said. 'Unions have no power. It's real men you want when you're taking on the Operators. Fellows like Bates too. There's only one way to deal with the likes of them.'

He met Luke's eyes. Yes, Luke thought, I know what that means. Is he right or is he wrong? There's the question.

When he returned to Morans' that night, Winnie told him that she was expecting another baby.

'That's wonderful,' he said, not really believing that it was.

'I don't know if wonderful is the right word,' Winnie said. 'We'll have to feed him, and how are we going to be able to do that? Would they declare another lockout, or a strike?'

'At least they won't declare a strike,' Luke said. 'The Union is gone.'

'Gone!'

'Bates is gone too. Took all the money with him.'

She stared at him in shock.

'And what do we owe at the truck store? Half your wages will be going on that.'

'I know,' Luke said as he put his arms around her. 'We can only do the best we can.'

'Yes,' Winnie said, 'go back to Ireland. Starve with our own people, isn't that it?'

Luke shook his head. 'I don't know,' he said. 'I just don't know.'

The following day was Sunday, and they went to Mass. The doors were shut, militia outside. Luke spotted Farrelly.

'What in the name of God is going on, Martin?' he asked.

'Cholera,' Farrelly told him. 'They've forbidden public meetings.'

As they left the church, a cart passed by. It was drawn by two horses, and was creaking heavily. It carried a load of long, rough-built crates.

'Coffins,' Farrelly exclaimed. 'There must be a dozen of them.'

They watched, as it went past the church and on past the cemetery.

'Where are they going?' Luke asked.

'Damned if I know,' Farrelly replied. 'Wherever they're going, there's a lot of them.'

Winnie said little, until they parted from Farrelly.

'Didn't I tell you it was coming,' she said. 'So much for your cholera line in the mountains.'

'How do you know it's cholera?'

'How do you know it's not?'

That afternoon, Luke walked to the Hibernians. He was surprised to see it was still open. Perhaps it did not rate as a public meeting. Mick O'Brien was there with two other men who Luke had never met. He bought a beer and joined them.

'Always delighted to see you here,' he said to O'Brien.

'Well, why not? It's a fraternal organisation, isn't it?'

'It is,' Luke said, sipping his beer. 'And that's your reason for joining, I'd guess.'

'Of course. What else could it be?'

'Never mind.'

O'Brien was angry. 'Some of us have the courage, you know,' he said.

'You're saying I don't.'

'I thought you had. But you still won't join us.'

'The Molly Maguire gang, is it?'

He saw the other two men flinch.

'Whatever,' O'Brien said. 'The fellows in Mauch Chunk have the guts to fight. But what about Lackan. Not a stir out of anyone.'

'Look, Mick, I'm just not interested in violence.'

'It's not violence, it's resistance.'

'That's what they tried in Ireland last year, and look at where it got them.'

'The Rebellion, is it? The Young Irelanders, sure they didn't have it in them. Too soft, hadn't the least idea how to run a rebellion.'

'Who does?'

'We do. The Irish American fighters. The Brotherhood. Next time there's a rebellion it'll be run from here. Right here.'

'In the coal fields?'

'Yes. But in Ireland too. We'll show them the way. Show the English the price of the Famine.'

'We'll be a long time waiting for that,' Luke said.

Farrelly and Jack had come in, and were drinking at the bar. Luke went to join them, leaving Mick with the other two men. Neither had said anything.

Farrelly greeted him.

'We were just talking about those coffins we saw this morning.'

'What about them?' asked Luke.

'Jack says they're digging a trench out the Scranton Road.'

'A trench?' Luke exclaimed. He remembered well the stink of the trench at the back of Knockanure Workhouse. Could it be as bad as that?

'I saw it myself,' Jack said. 'They're digging it six or eight feet deep and there's coffins three and four high.'

'Would they have call for that?' Luke asked.

'From what I saw, they had,' Jack replied. 'Cholera, they told me. There were carts coming from all directions at the crossroads. There must be cholera in all the patches, up the hills and everywhere else. Scranton too.'

Luke thought no more about Mick and his talk of resistance. He was certain the Hibernians were not involved in violence, though as Costello had said, it was impossible to be certain that all members thought the same. For a while, he considered reporting Mick to the Hibernian board, but knew well that he could not do that.

A few weeks later, Mick told him that he was going to Mauch Chunk.

'For a picnic,' Luke asked him, scathingly.

'No,' Mick said, 'more like a convention. Would you like to join us?'

'Not enough money, Mick,' Luke said. 'I've still got to feed Winnie and the child, and another coming too. I couldn't possibly make it.'

When Mick returned a few days later, he said nothing about his visit and Luke dismissed it from his mind. When he came home that evening, Ned was at his dinner.

'Did you hear the news from Mauch Chunk?'

'Some kind of convention?' Luke asked.

'A convention is right. Half the town has been burnt down.'

'Burnt down?'

'Yes. Arson they're calling it.'

That night he lay awake in his bed, thinking of it. Were the convention and the fire linked? What kind of convention was it anyhow?

He decided at length that he was becoming too suspicious. He turned over and went asleep.

The price of the Famine became clearer, when a letter arrived from Carrigard.

'What does it say?' Winnie asked.

'Well, there's two letters really. The straight one is from father. The family are all well, love and best wishes from mother, Brigid and Pat. Your mother's written to them to say that she is well too, and the last she heard from your father was the same. His work in England is hard, but he's sending some money back.'

'He's in England?'

'That's what he says.'

'Harvesting or railways?'

'He doesn't say.'

Luke could see she was downcast. It was frustrating being weeks away from Ireland. News was sporadic, and partial.

'So what else?' she asked.

'Well, whatever about our own families, the hunger's worse. He's talking about hundreds dying, all around Kilduff and Carrigard. Brockagh is in a terrible way. The mountains too.'

'I don't know what to make of it all,' Winnie said. 'Happy that our people are fine. I feel guilty about that though. Mayo is in a terrible way. You know it and I know it. Do you think he's telling the truth about themselves and my mother though?'

'I wouldn't worry, *alanna*. If they were hungry we'd know all about it. Father's not one for holding that back, your mother neither, I think. There's cholera in the county though. Kilduff is in a bad way with it, though there's none in Carrigard yet. And from all they say, Pat is having a hard time, travelling around Mayo and giving reports back to the County. Father says he won't even talk about it. Whatever though, he's earning money still, and they're living off that.'

'Does he ask for money though?'

'He doesn't, and thank God for that. Pat's still earning, and whatever it is, we'll just have to assume that they have enough to be living on. God knows, we've little enough, and with all we owe up at the truck shop, there's little we can do.'

'I know,' Winnie said. 'So what's the other letter?'

Luke smiled.

'Father must have given it to Sabina to post in the village. She's written another letter across father's. She says she's well, and they're all still meeting every week. Fergus is dead, she doesn't say how. Kitty's been evicted, and she's gone over to England. She's staying with Murty and Aileen in Bradford, and working in a mill. Would you believe it?'

'That's some good news, anyhow.'

Soon, stories of beatings began to circulate in Lackan. At first it was one of the Kilkenny foremen who was beaten with cudgels, but no bones had been broken. A week later though, one of the Welsh foremen was beaten.

'And a hell of a beating it was too,' Ned told them. 'He's in the hospital, one shoulder broken, two ribs cracked, they say his skull is cracked too. It'll be some time before he works again.'

Again, Luke was thinking of Mick's invitation to join 'the resistance'. What did it really mean? More and more, he began to think that these beatings were associated with O'Brien's resistance.

Other stories began to filter in from further afield. A breaker boss attacked in Minersville. Two foremen stabbed in St. Clair, one died. An Irish miner was stabbed in St. Clair too, in revenge for the other stabbings, it was said. He died too.

Then a breaker boss was killed in one of the remote mountain patches.

'Knifed in the neck,' Mick told him. 'Choked on his own blood. That's what the story is.'

Yes, Luke thought. The Molly Maguire gang, who else?

One morning, Farrelly crawled up to where Luke was working with Jack and Mick.

'Just wanted to let ye all know. I was talking to Cantwell this morning.'

'What did he want?' Luke asked.

'You know they're opening the Number Three Breaker in two weeks' time.'

'They are?'

'Yes, and they want a contract gang for the loading and unloading. And do you know what the best part of it is? The Kilkenny fellows don't want the job. Reckon it's unskilled, which it is. So we're taking it instead. But I'll tell you, we're going to be in the open air, and even if we have to work some of the time in the breaker, it'll be far cleaner than in here. And with all that good fresh air, we'll live longer too. It's up to the Kilkenny fellows if they want to die younger.'

'Dead right, it is,' Jack said. 'Their decision.'

'Better than that,' Farrelly said. 'We can shovel standing up. And sure what does it matter if the Kilkenny men think it's unskilled? At the rate we work, we'll be making more money than most of them.'

'More money?' Mick asked.

'They're offering a dollar forty-five a wagon.'

'Not bad,' Jack said.

'Not bad indeed. Shovelling coal, sure it's no different to shovelling gravel and mud on the railways. My reckoning is, knowing you lads, we should be able to get up to seven dollars per week, per man pretty sharpish.'

'A hell of a lot better than four dollars,' Jack said.

'Yes, you'll be able to send more back to Mayo. And God knows, they'll need it.'

Luke was intrigued by the breaker – the steam-driven rollers smashing the coal, the screens grading it, and the breaker boys picking out the grey slate and rock.

The gang's work varied, sometimes feeding the unbroken anthracite into the rollers, sometimes taking the unwanted slate and rock from the breaker to dump on the ever-growing culm banks, and sometimes taking the sorted anthracite from the bins down to the railcars. They were paid on the basis of each railcar filled, or, further back the operation, each mule cart load of unbroken anthracite or waste loaded onto mule carts. Either way, they worked fast, and, just as Farrelly had anticipated, their earnings soared.

'So much for unskilled work,' Jack said one day. 'We're damned near earning as much as the Kilkenny fellows now.'

'Keep it up,' Luke said. 'We were working faster than this on the railways. It won't be long until we're earning far more than them.'

'And God knows we'll need it,' Mick said. 'Pay off those bastards in the truck store.'

Two weeks later, Luke was working beside Mick outside the Number Three Breaker, loading anthracite onto wagons.

'Not much different to England, is it,' Mick said. 'Remember working like this along the Great Western Railway?'

'They were good days.'

'Yes, and us among the highest paid on the railways.'

'Still, seven dollars a week isn't so bad.'

'If we can make it.'

'Farrelly thinks we can.'

Mick leaned on his shovel.

'I don't know whether we can or not, we'll see at the end of the week. But one way or another, there's not many can work like us on the wagons. There's many older men here wouldn't be able to keep up the pace. And I'd pity any man on four dollars a week with seven children to feed. Sure they'd be starving.'

'They would,' Luke said.

'And worse, fall behind in their payments to the truck store. Once you do that, they have you for life.'

A boy came out of the breaker, leading a small anthracite wagon, drawn by two mules.

'And there's your way out,' Luke said. 'If a man can't earn enough, he gets his lads out working.'

'And what are they paid?' Mick asked. 'A dollar a week?'

'I'd say you're right,' said Luke. 'A dollar a week at eight years old. Some life. But what can we do?'

'Never mind.'

They worked on.

Eight or nine years old, Luke was thinking. How many on the Famine Relief Roads would have been that age, or even younger? Digging roads for pennies a day, and the mark of hunger on them. The fox faces. The hanging bellies. At least they weren't starving here, but they were only children. Many were deformed, stooped like old men from long hours bent over the coal. Why weren't they at school? What of Liam when he grew to their age? Accidents were common. Cholera was not the only way for children to die.

He decided to stop thinking about it.

Chapter 30

The Sunbury American, Pennsylvania. August 1849:

The Last of Earth. The Irish have been grievous sufferers by the prevailing disease, as might be expected from the mode of life of vast numbers of them, their poor accommodations, improper diet and exposure. Three or four miles east of Williamsburg there is a Roman Catholic cemetery where great numbers of them are interred. The grounds occupy about three acres. They have been used for interments for about two years. Already the whole space is occupied by graves yet bodies are still interred there in great numbers. The grave-diggers told us that for the last two months, there had been an average of more than 100 interments a day. During an hour and a half that we remained there, 25 bodies were brought in and interred. The graves are dug about eight feet deep and several coffins are piled upon each other, with a layer of earth between – the upper coffin being within three feet of the surface.

One Saturday, Luke accompanied Farrelly to the office to collect the weekly payment. Rapidly, Luke checked through the figures.

'One moment,' he said to the clerk. 'This figure for the shovels we bought is wrong.'

'It's what you signed for.'

Luke pulled a sheet from his pocket and laid it down in front of the clerk.

'These are the exact figures I signed for at the Store. Six dollars fifty for the shovels. Perhaps you could check them against the figures you have.'

The clerk went to a cabinet, took out a ledger and checked through it.

'Well?' Luke asked.

'You're right,' the clerk said. 'Anyone can confuse a six with a nine.'

Cantwell had come across. 'Do we have a problem?' he asked the clerk.

'Nothing much,' the man said. 'A minor miscalculation.'

'Fine,' Luke said, 'but we've another error on the top here. Sixty-three wagons. $1.45 a wagon, isn't it? A total of $91.35.'

'How can you be sure?' the clerk said.

'Just give me a piece of paper and a pen, I'll show you.'

Luke wrote the figures out carefully. Cantwell was listening.

'Now,' Luke said, when he had finished, 'if we make the deductions and divide among fourteen men.'

'I suppose you're going to give me that figure too?' the clerk said.

'$6.06 per man.'

'Write it out.'

Luke did.

The clerk passed on the new calculations to the cashier beside him, where the gang were lined up. He began to pay each in succession. Luke wondered why this was necessary, and why the gross amount could not be paid to Farrelly direct. Perhaps they did not trust him.

There was a man standing across from the table, watching. He wore a cutaway coat with high cravats on his shirt. He walked across to the pay desk.

'Who's this?' he asked Cantwell.

'Luke Ryan,' Cantwell said.

'You compute well, Mr. Ryan,' the man said. 'Did you do all those calculations in your head just now?'

'I did,' Luke said.

'Amazing. And you write well too. What else can you do?'

Luke went to speak, but Farrelly spoke first.

'He can manage men. Men and boys. He's done it before.'

'Has he, by God?'

They were dismissed.

'Why did you say that?' Luke asked, as they left.

'Look,' Farrelly said, 'I'm already managing a contract gang. That fellow, he's Sugden.'

'Sugden!'

'He runs the mine. The Mine Boss.'

'I know who Sugden is.'

'If we're lucky he might ask you to run another contract. Who knows?'

'Why would that be lucky?' Luke asked.

'Look, think it through. How many other Irish men are there around? None of them run their own contracts except us, and almost none of them can add or subtract, far less multiply. They need their own gangs, these fellows. The Operators won't allow Unions anymore, so how else can they make a better living. They need a good foreman of their own. It's your own people you must think of.'

*

A few days later, a man came to the wagons.

'Luke Ryan,' he shouted.

'Here,' Luke shouted.

'Mr. Cantwell is looking for you.'

'For what?' Luke asked the man, irritably.

'The sack, what else?' the man answered. 'Why do you think Cantwell would want to see you?'

Luke walked towards Cantwell's office. The man ran after him.

'Not that way, he's over at Head Office. Come on.'

They reached the Head Office. Luke was ushered into a room. Both Sugden and Cantwell were sitting at a desk.

'I'd ask you to sit, Mr. Ryan,' Sugden said, 'but the furniture…'

'I understand,' Luke said. He stayed standing. Perhaps Farrelly was right. A gang of his own?

'How did you learn to calculate like that?' Sugden asked.

'Back in County Mayo. My uncle ran a school.'

'Taught you well, it would seem.'

Luke said nothing.

'Tell me,' said Cantwell, 'Farrelly says you've managed men?'

'I have.'

'Many?'

'Two hundred. Four hundred at times.'

'Four hundred!' Sugden exclaimed.

'I was running gangs on the Relief Works back the winter of '46.'

'Relief?'

'Famine Relief,' Cantwell explained.

'You'd hardly be well-liked for that!' Sugden said to Luke.

'It was a tough time, right enough,' Luke said. 'Caught between the bosses and the people. Like you say, it wasn't always easy. Many's the time the gangs blamed me for whatever happened, but sure what could I do? One thing I'd say, I made sure they all got paid, living or dead. Whether they got it, or their widows and families got it, I paid them, but they hated me for it.'

'Ideal so,' Sugden said. 'We're looking for a man well used to being hated.'

'Hated?'

'Look, if you're used to managing men, you'll know that decisions have to be made, and enforced. The enforcement is the important part.'

Enforcers?

'You're right,' Luke said, 'but…'

'We're looking for a Breaker Boss over at Number One. We need a man who'd not back down in the face of intimidation. Would you take it?'

'But why…?'

'Dai Lloyd has gone,' Cantwell said. 'Gone to California, prospecting for gold. Damned fool.'

Luke hesitated, thinking quickly of many things. All that Winnie and he had spoken about, being trapped on a miner's wages. A future for their own children. But what of his days as a supervisor on the Famine Relief Works, despised by his own people. An enforcer? Which was most important? The past? Or the future?

'Twelve dollars a week,' Sugden said, noting his hesitation. 'With a house of your own. Rent free.'

Still, he wavered. The famine in Mayo was getting worse. He had increasing commitments to his own family and Winnie's family. What choice was there? The silence dragged.

'Fifteen dollars,' Sugden said.

'I'll take it,' Luke said.

Winnie was stunned.

'Breaker Boss? But they're tough fellows, aren't they? How many Irish Bosses are there here?'

'None. Maybe that's why they want one now.'

'Better at keeping the Irish in line?' she said. 'Just like Danny was.'

'I don't know. There's one problem, though. We'd be leaving our own people.'

'Who are…?'

'Farrelly and the fellows, they're our people. Kilduff and around. Do you think they'd understand?'

'I don't know. That depends. But what are they offering you?'

'Fifteen dollars a week.'

Winnie staggered against the bed.

'Fifteen dollars! That's impossible.'

'That's the rate. Guaranteed. No need for piecework. And a house too.'

'A house too?' Winnie gasped.

'Rent free.'

'I don't believe you.'

'It's what I'm telling you? They want us to move in over the next few days. So now what?'

'We take it.'

'That's what I told them,' Luke said. 'But Farrelly and the rest, I don't know if they'd understand. And I know damn well what Mick O'Brien would think.'

'Yes,' Winnie said, 'but it's not Mick O'Brien I'm thinking of. It's my family. One child, and one coming. You know what all the other families are like around here. Most all of them in pawn to the truck store, and in debt for years, or forever. Isn't that the way of it?'

'It is,' Luke said.

'And what of what we owe the truck store? We'd never be able to pay it off. Even as a miner, we'd be leaving it for Liam to pay when we're dead and gone. What chance in life would he ever have? This is our chance to break away from all that, Luke. Our own place to raise a family. Money to school our children, and money to send back to Carrigard and Brockagh. Who do we think of first? The other fellow, or our own families here and in Mayo. I'll tell you the answer Luke. We go with our own families. We cannot – we will not – let our children starve again.'

The reaction from the gang was different.

'Well by God,' Farrelly said, 'I thought you might be a foreman, have a gang of your own, but a Breaker Boss, I'd never expected that.'

'Nor had I,' Luke said.

'Will you take it?' McGlinn asked. 'Abandon all your own people?'

'Sure how could I not,' Luke said, 'it's my own people I'm thinking of. There's starvation back in Mayo, and my own family need the money, Winnie's family too. Isn't that thinking of my own people?'

'And are we not your own people?'

'You won't be working for me, one way or another,' Luke said.

'No,' McGlinn said, 'it's other Irish fellows who'll be working for you. You'll be grinding their faces into the dirt, you and your like. Just like the supervisors on Famine Relief. Give them a taste of power, and they can never stop.'

'I'd advise you very strongly against taking the job,' Mick said. 'It's very dangerous.'

'How's that?' Luke asked.

'Why do you think Lloyd left Number One?'

'Gone hunting gold,' Luke said.

Mick snorted. 'That's what they told you?'

'You got a better reason?'

'He got another coffin notice, that's the reason. He was a Breaker Boss, and that was enough. He got the message too, and cleared to hell out. He knew he'd be knifed if he didn't. Now they want you in, and you know why? Because everyone else is terrified to step into his shoes at Number One.'

Luke was still torn about his acceptance of the position. What O'Brien had said was true.

The more he thought about it, the worse it seemed. A coffin notice? The Molly Maguire gang? Or could it just have been some miner with a grudge against the Breaker Boss? O'Brien himself? Could he be that extreme? Did all the other men in the gang think the same as O'Brien did?

One thing was true though. In becoming a Breaker Boss, he would no longer be one of Farrelly's gang. Being promoted to a position on a level with Farrelly would be one thing. Now he would be senior to him. Miners did not mix with Breaker Bosses; that was for sure. And no Breaker Bosses in this part of the coal fields were Mayo men. English and Welsh certainly, Kilkenny men maybe, but Mayo never.

He thought back to his days as a supervisor on the Famine Relief Works in County Mayo. His work there had been crucial, but no one else saw it that way. During the Famine, the supervisors were utterly despised, almost as much as the Landlords' agents. Could they not see that no supervisors meant no wages at all, little as they were? No, they could not. Always, Luke had been forced to hard decisions. Deciding who would be entitled to work on the Works meant, in a backhanded way, deciding who would not, and that was a death sentence for many families. It gave him a power he had never wanted. Sugden knew that too, when he had offered him the position. A man who was used to being hated. Would it be true here too?

He had worked on the weigh station for a few weeks. While he was there, he had not been hated. He had been supported by the Union and the men. Having one of their own at the weigh station ensured there was no short measure, and they knew Luke was fair. Some may have thought that he could have tipped the weighbridge in their favour, but most knew that he could not, and in that way, he would have lost his position. But that had only lasted a few weeks. Now, after the collapse of the Bates Union, there were no miners checking the weights at the weighbridge, and the miners distrusted the foremen.

He was surprised when Farrelly supported him.

'I know what Mick has been on about,' he told Luke one night, 'but don't pay any heed to him. He's not a bad fellow in many ways, but he thinks he can take on the Operators and win.'

'Would that he could,' Luke said.

'We may dream. But we have to live out the reality of it. Lloyd was a bastard, that's why he got the coffin notice, I've no doubt, but it's like when you were on the weigh station. If you're seen to be fair, the men will respect that. What Mick might think of it is another matter, but sure you can ignore him.'

'You think so?'

'Just think of this. What do you think Mick would have done if it was offered to him? Would he have turned it down? Like hell, he would!'

In the end, the most vital factor was his own family, and that meant there was no real choice at all. The experience of hunger in America had shocked Winnie. Never again! As Breaker Boss, he would have fifteen dollars a week, with no rent to pay, and he could pay off the debt at the truck store. And Liam would be educated. He did not know how, or as what, but it would be done, and Liam would never be a miner, far less a slate picker.

And Mayo? Starvation right across the County. Cholera too, he had no doubt. Pat was working as a clerk in Castlebar, but how long would that last? Then his family's survival would depend on him, and, now the hunger in the mines was over, he would have to ensure his own family survived any future famines or fevers. Brigid would be schooled, but she would need more than basic schooling. And what other children would there be in Carrigard? He remembered Sarah. A good woman, that was for sure. Would Pat continue working as a clerk or would he take over the farm in Carrigard? He would just have to wait and see. But, one way or another, there would be more children, and those children would have to be schooled. And the blight would continue year after year after year. It was too powerful to be stopped, how could it be? One way or the other, the cost of feeding and schooling the family would have to be paid, until they all abandoned Mayo.

On his first morning in the breaker, Cantwell asked him into his office.

'I'd like to congratulate you on your promotion,' he said. 'It's a great move up in the world for you, and none deserving it more. You mightn't know it, but Sugden was gobsmacked when he saw the way you could reckon in your head. There's not many who can do that, you know.'

'I don't know,' Luke said. 'Couldn't he have taken me as a clerk? That would have been easier.'

'Maybe he could have, but he reckoned you were better qualified than that. I won't say he wasn't already thinking of having you as Breaker Boss, but when you said about managing four hundred men, that decided him for sure and certain. Damn it Luke, there's few men in the mines who've ever done that.'

'You might be right,' Luke said, 'and he was surely right when he said about taking the hatred from them. It's rough, I can tell you, when four hundred men hate you like that. Not just men, mind you, women and children too. And worst of all, the dying. Forcing them to work in the snows and the winter winds on the mountains. That was terrible, and it wasn't even the worst of it. What was far worse were the selections, deciding who would work and who would not. Christ, we were paying them starvation wages, and even so, they fought like savages for the right to work. Working for pennies was one thing, working for nothing was death. Can you understand this?'

'I'd heard of it around Kilkenny,' Cantwell said.

'Kilkenny! That was nothing like Mayo. Sure, it was places like Kilkenny the starving people made for, when they hadn't the money for England or America. They knew they could get work on the harvests in the midlands, and God knows, that was better paid than the Famine gangs in Mayo. I know the hunger and fevers would have killed them around Kilkenny too, but it wasn't a fraction of what was happening in Mayo.'

'It won't be like that here.' Cantwell said. 'There's no starving here...'

'There was a few weeks back.'

'That was the Union.'

'And the Operators too,' Luke said.

He realised, that if he was not careful, he could talk himself out of the position.

'But sure that's in the past,' he said, 'and let's leave it that way. Like you say, this isn't Ireland.'

'It isn't,' Cantwell said, 'and there's one other thing too. Don't forget you'll have good foremen under you. They're the ones who'll have to take the aggression, not you. They'll be looking to you for orders and decisions, and you're the one who'll decide how the breaker is run.'

They left the office and walked towards the breaker.

'One other thing,' Cantwell said. 'I was telling Celia about you. She thought perhaps you and your wife might like to join us for dinner come Sunday? Salt pork or hog maw, she hasn't decided. What do you say?'

'We'd be delighted, Stan.'

Luke found his position as Breaker Boss more difficult that he had expected.

His first problem was that he had only worked on mining and loading wagons before. But there were many other activities in a breaker. Assembly yards, thawing sheds, the breaker itself, the screening line, the picking lines and the water recovery unit. The operation of the giant conveyor belts, feeding the anthracite to the breaker fascinated him. The continuous operation of the breaker itself intrigued him too. He soon began to understand that his own idea of a breaker had been very limited.

As Cantwell had said, he discovered that the important part of managing the breaker was to have reliable foremen. He thought of the many foremen who had worked for him in the mountains of Mayo during the savage winter of 1846 and 1847. Men like Winnie's own father. He had to work hard to win their respect, and that would have been impossible without his years working on English railways, and working in his own father's quarry in Carrigard. He would have to win the respect of these men too.

The working men were not as easy to manage as starving men on the Famine Relief in Mayo had been. Their appearance was less disturbing perhaps, but they were tougher than the gaunt scarecrows in the Ox Mountains, and more liable to dispute Luke's orders, or those of the foremen. For the most part, Luke left the foremen to manage them, though from time to time he had to settle disputes directly.

The men in the single contract gang loading the breaker wagons were tough in other ways. They reckoned their ways of filling it were none of Luke's business, provided the work was done. Thinking back on his work with Farrelly's gang, he thought this might well be true, and left them alone, dealing only with their elected foreman. His relationship with the man was straightforward. Every Saturday the account was agreed. Luke ensured there were no mistakes in the account, and there was never any dispute between them.

The boys in the breaker disturbed him more than ever, now he was responsible for them. At least the breaker provided shelter, but a dollar a week? It was more than what children had been earning on Famine Relief, but not by very much, and he himself was earning many times more.

He had thought that he could better their lives, but now he knew that he could not. This was how the breakers worked all across the coal patches, and always would.

On the weekend, they moved to the new house, well above the mine and the breaker. Luke found it a relief. While no one had directly attacked him, many of Farrelly's gang were now hostile. At least they did not work at Number One.

When they arrived, they spent much of Sunday arranging their possessions, and rearranging the company furniture. At last, Winnie flopped down on a sofa.

'God, I'm tired.'

'Me too,' Luke said.

'Sure you're always tired.'

'I know. It's not easy being a Breaker Boss, I can tell you. They're hard men.'

'Yes, I can understand that. Just like Farrelly and the boys. They were never ones to take nonsense.'

'No, but I never thought I'd be the one to be giving out nonsense.'

'I didn't mean it that way,' Winnie said.

'I know, my love, but you know what I mean. And I'll tell you something else. They've got young lads working on the slate belts, picking out the stones. They're only children.'

'I know,' Winnie said, 'I'd heard about that kind of thing.'

'It's just like working in the mountains in the Hunger. What kind of people are we?'

'At least they're not starving.'

'That's true, but damn it, Winnie, that's not what we came to America for. The breaker is breaking young lives.'

'Do you want to quit?'

'Of course, not. I'd be frightened to quit, now we've got it. But that's a bad reason. Give me some good reason, Winnie, something to make me believe that it's all worthwhile.'

'But what are we doing this for?' Winnie asked. 'You've got to think of that.'

'Well, you tell me,' Luke said. 'Why are we doing it?'

'So we don't starve. Our families neither. Look at you. You're on fifteen dollars a week. We won't starve, no matter how many children we have. And we'll have the money for their lessons too, Liam and the rest of our sons and daughters. If your mother and the other women can talk about sending Brigid to teacher training, just think what we can do with our own.'

'They're expecting to perform miracles, mind you,' Luke said.

'Yes,' Winnie said, 'but don't forget we'll be part of the miracle. Even when the Hunger is over, we'll still be paying for Brigid. And proud to do it too.'

That evening, they dined with the Cantwells. Celia Cantwell was a pleasant Kilkenny woman, and Luke knew she and Winnie would get on well. That would make it easier for Winnie to settle into Lackan, and find new friends. She would know the better shops and schools in Lackan, Scranton and Philadelphia.

Yes, he had made the right decision for Winnie and Liam, but even so, he had left his friends behind, and there was no way back.

They had already begun to pay off his debts at the truck store, but there were other things that were more important. The truck store could wait. When he received his first salary as a breaker boss, he made his way into Scranton, and went to the Chemical Bank. There he bought a bank draft.

'And they'll need it,' he said to Winnie that evening. 'My people and your mother.'

'I know,' Winnie said.

He wrote a letter to Carrigard.

Ryan Family	Lackawanna Street
Carrigard	Lackan
Kilduff	State of Pennsylvania
Co. Mayo	United States of America
Ireland	

My Dear Father and Mother,

First, I must say how sorry I am that I had not written to you before. Times were much harder here in Lackan than I had ever expected. The mine owners locked us out, and when the lockout ended, the Union went on strike. We had no wages for months, and were hungrier than I had ever expected to be in America. Still, I am sure you don't want to know about my troubles, having enough in Ireland. The strikes are now over, and this money should help ye through these hard times.

Things have changed very fast for Winnie, Liam and myself. You can imagine what a mighty relief it was for us when the strike ended and we had wages again. Within a few weeks though, the mine boss came to me and offered me a new position. He had seen how fast I was with my figures, and when he heard that I had been a ganger back in Mayo, with large numbers of workers under me, he asked at once whether I could do the same in Lackan. So now I am a Breaker Boss, on $15 a week, far more than I ever thought possible. You might wonder what a breaker is. It is where they break the large lumps of coal as soon as they come out of the mine, and then sort them out into different sizes for houses, or for mills. The mine has given us a house of our own, just for the three of us, soon to be four, with no rent. So as you can see, our state of affairs has changed from near starvation to having very good pay.

We have heard much of the hunger in Ireland, and I know apart from yourselves, Mrs. Gallagher will need some of this. I would consider it a favour therefore if you could send some of it on to her – perhaps a quarter – and Winnie would be thankful for this too.

And what of little Brigid? Is she going to school yet? This money will surely help.

In your next letter, you will tell us what you know of Winnie's family, as well as what Pat is doing, and how Aunt Sabina is holding out. We send our love to all of you.

I remain, your loving son,

Luke Ryan.

As he soon discovered, there were other complexities in the breaker. Many of the Irish could not speak English, and he was lucky to find a Mayo man from Inishturk who had spent years in the mines in Bradford.

There were no Welsh in the Number One Breaker now, and few English. Some of the other workers only spoke German, especially the older men working as slate pickers, men who had never learnt English, and never would. Even among the other German speakers, Luke discovered there were other complexities. They came from different places – the Rhineland, Bremen, Alsace and Baden. These meant nothing to him, until the day of the riot.

When it came, it was among the German speakers only. Luke had no understanding what had caused it, and never found out. This time, the Irish stayed well out of it, though there were mutterings about allowing poor emigrants into the coal patches. There was no militia now, and Luke had to wait until the foremen had brought the riot under control. No deaths, as it happened. A few broken limbs, but what of that.

He thought of the riots in the Canadian forests. On the Gatineau, they had to keep the French and Irish apart, but it did not always work. He remembered the savage riot between the French and the Irish that winter. Blood on the snow. Axes were far more vicious than knives. There were men along the St. Lawrence who would never work in the forests again. It all seemed so long ago.

As he left the breaker one night, it was stormy, rain lashing at him in the rising wind. He walked alone, hunched into the gale. There was no one else around. It was difficult to follow the line of houses in the dark and rain, but at length he came to his own. A candle was lighting in the window. He stepped inside.

'There's a letter for you there, Luke,' Winnie called out from the kitchen. He turned back to the dresser.

'Who is it from?'

'I don't know, my love. I didn't open it.'

He slit it open. Winnie, still drying a plate, came across to him.

He took out the single page, and unfolded it. It had a rough sketch of a coffin with a cross drawn on it. Beneath the cross, a rough hand had scribbled the words: Luke Ryan RIP.

Chapter 31

Tuam Herald. July 1849:

On Saturday last the churchyard of the Neale Parish, near this town, presented the awful and revolting spectacle of the remains of a human being partly devoured by dogs, and the head removed from the body. It appeared that the deceased was a pauper of the district, for whom a coffin was given by the Relieving Officer, who also (as I understand is the custom in such cases) sent home some of those people on the Outdoor Relief Lists to have the remains of the poor man interred; but those unfeeling wretches did not take the trouble of digging the grave half the depth of the coffin, and merely threw some loose scraws over it: in which state it was an easy prey to the dogs of the country. Mr. D. O'Connor of the Neale had the remains collected, and re-interred, and reported the circumstance to the proper quarter.

Eleanor sat at the table, kneading the dough for brown bread, as Sarah read out Pat's latest letter.

'*At least he's alive,*' Eleanor said.

'He is,' Sarah said. '*I'm just hoping he stays out of the fever sheds.*'

'*You're worrying too much.*'

They finished the loaves, carefully placed them in the pots hanging off the cranes, and Sarah swung them over the fire.

'*How can I stop worrying, mother. I can hardly sleep. I keep waking up in the middle of the night, thinking of them. And it's not just Pat. It's my own mother too. She was always in the fever sheds, and look what happened to her.*'

'*He'll live, though. You know it.*'

'*I don't know. What worries me too is that they might send him around the County again. It was hard enough on him; we both know that. But what happened? Do we know any of that? Why will he not tell us?*'

Eleanor knew it was time to feed the hens, but she no longer had the inclination. Winnie was gone, Liam too. And Brigid would go in time. But Sarah would stay, she was sure of it. And Sarah's children, when the time came.

At length, she stood up and started to mash the corn for the hens. There was little else she could feed them, since even potato skins were no longer to be found. She took Brigid out to the yard, but the hens frightened her. She took her up in one arm, holding the pot in the other, and had Brigid throw whatever corn there was to the hens. This, at least, provided fun for the child.

They went back inside. She took two empty pails.

'*Going to the well?*' Sarah asked.

'*I am,*' Eleanor said. '*You just stay and mind Brigid.*'

'*That's what you always say. This time, I'm coming. We'll take Brigid with us.*'

She took two pails from the corner.

'*With two of us, we won't have to go too often.*'

She went out. Brigid followed Eleanor, grasping her skirt tightly.

There was a time Eleanor had looked forward to going to the well. A time when the women clustered around, gossiping and laughing. It was different now.

Nor was it just a matter of hunger. As she approached, the women quietened. One was coming back along the track to the road carrying a pail of water. Eleanor opened the gate for her, and greeted her. There was no answer.

Eleanor and Sarah filled their pails in silence. After the storm in 1839, a low wall had been built around it to keep back the boggy soil and rushes. The water was crystal clear, unlike the brackish water stagnating around. At the bottom, it bubbled up through grey flinty clay.

No one else tried to greet them.

They started out for the house, carrying the buckets, Brigid still grasping Eleanor's skirt. Yes, Eleanor was thinking, why should they talk to us anyhow? All this time we've lived, right through the worst of the hunger. Luke working as a supervisor and Pat as a clerk and Michael even working the quarry. The Ryans had had enough earnings to see them through it, and now that hunger had returned, Pat was working, and Luke was in America. Still she had to ration the corn and oatmeal, but others had little to ration. Or nothing.

And these women? Women she had known all her married life. All of them had buried some or all of their children through the hunger. Husbands too. And many of the women would die too over the next months, she was certain of that. Yet none of the Ryans had died through hunger or fever, and she was determined that none would. But there was a price to be paid. When it was over – if it would ever end – there were families who would never talk to them again.

In many ways, she felt guilty about this but decided there was no other way. Her first loyalty was always to her own family, whether in Ireland or America, but Ireland most of all. No matter what, the family would have a future. Brigid most of all.

'They're quiet, aren't they, mother?'

'They're always quiet. We lived, all of our family lived, while all around us they were dying. They're saying with the road building in '46 and '47 we were making more money out of Famine than we had before. Supervising, clerking and running the quarry, it was probably true enough. But we were given our chances, we had to take them. If we didn't, the family would be dead. And it's the very same now. Let's just hope the potatoes are as good as they're looking now.'

'So what comes first?' Sarah asked, 'the family or the neighbours?'

'The family always,' Eleanor said. 'Not that that means just us. Sabina too, though with the bar, she's hardly starving. Murty and Aileen when they were still here, though again they had the money from Danny.'

'True enough,' Sarah said. 'Do you think though it would have been possible to have done more for the neighbours?'

'With the way it was during the hunger; sure how could we do that alanna?'

'No wonder they won't talk to us,' Sarah said.

'And they're not the only reasons,' Eleanor said. 'Us taking the Benson's farm, their quarry too.'

'But the Bensons had gone.'

'True enough, and of their own accord too. They weren't evicted. But people never see it that way. There's terrible bitterness about evictions, and now they're saying that the Bensons were evicted. Not true, but that's the way it will always be remembered. And we'll always be seen as land grabbers.'

'But there were others...'

'There were,' Eleanor said, 'and there'll be more yet. Many a family living in a mud cabin would be delighted to rent a farm with a good stone house. It's happening already, and there'll be many more. They'll know the truth of it, and they'll talk to us again. Give it time.'

'Did Kitty see us as land grabbers?'

'No, but Kitty is a rare girl. Such ambition for Brigid, and she not even her daughter. And that kind of ambition will cost money, don't forget that. Your child too, there'll be more money needed there too.'

'I don't know where we'd get money for all that?' Sarah said.

'There's many ways of getting money, Sarah. Pat is working...'

'For now.'

'True for you, but there's other sources too. There's Luke. Luke will send money, I'm sure of it, and if he doesn't, Winnie will do it for him. And *there's Murtybeg, don't forget Murtybeg. He will surely give us money.'*

'Money from Murtybeg,' Sarah exclaimed. *'Blood money, is it? I remember the time – last year, was it – he came over to Mayo looking for inmates from the workhouses to work on the railways in England, at wages that were little better than what they paid them on the Famine Roads. He's a tough man, Murtybeg is, no doubt about it. Even in Westport Union, I heard about him. There's many that would prefer to die in Mayo than go working with Murtybeg. And there's many that were sent with him from the workhouses ended up back in Mayo again. The fevered ones, Murtybeg wouldn't have them when they arrived, and the* Liverpool Union *sent them straight back to Mayo. Did you know that?'*

'I didn't,' Eleanor said. *'Not that it surprises me though.'*

One Sunday, Sarah went with Eleanor to the byre to kill a chicken for dinner. Eleanor grabbed it by the legs and carried it along, wings flapping. She did not wring the neck, she simply held the head down, placed the handle of a spade on its neck, put one foot on the spade and brought her full weight down on top of it. At first, there was no movement, then the legs ran wildly, slowing to spasmodic quivers, until the chicken was truly dead. Sarah retched, but did not vomit.

She was quiet for the rest of the day. At first, Eleanor was concerned about her. Could she kill a chicken? Could she really live this life? But why worry? The death pit in Knockanure must have been worse, and the fever sheds in Westport that had killed Sarah's own mother. No, Carrigard was Sarah's future, and the future of her children.

Far more important now was the potato crop. They had been watching it for some time. Early on, the stalks and leaves were showing healthy and green, but then signs of blight began to appear.

The next few weeks were ones of high anxiety. Michael spent every night in the potato patch, guarding the potato ridges. The weather continued bright and dry. The hay was going to be a good crop, the corn too. But what of the potatoes? And what of Luke? Still no news.

Pat decided it was time to go home to Carrigard. He already had the letters of freedom from Knockanure and Westport, and he would have heard from Michael if there was any problem with Kilduff.

He explained the situation to Gaffney.

I must congratulate you, Pat,' he said. 'You and Sarah. She's an excellent woman and you'll go far in life with her.'

'I would say so, Mr. Gaffney,' Pat said. 'My only concern is getting married at a time like this. I need to take a few days off, but I feel guilty at doing so, seeing what's happening in the workhouse.'

'No,' Gaffney replied. 'It is more important now than ever. For Mayo and for Ireland, we must never give up. There will be a time that this will end, we will need children to carry on.'

'I'll be back as fast as I can. I'm sure you've more for me to do?'

'We have, Pat, but if you drive yourself too hard, you won't be any good to anyone. Your wife, the Union or County Mayo. You must take a few days off for your own sake.'

Pat left Castlebar, walking.

There were the usual horrifying scenes in the town and on the road. Nearer Kilduff, everything had changed again. Where he had known dozens of houses, there was now only one, and it was still being built. A solid two-storey house, well mortared. The straight cut rafters on the roof had been finished, and were now being overlaid with grey Welsh slate. Already, cattle were grazing in large fields. Some fields were many times the size of the farms they had replaced.

Where all the evicted people had gone. One thing was certain, none of them could afford emigration. Very few of them could have gotten into Castlebar or Knockanure. For the rest, he had seen scavenged bodies and skeletons on the road. He had no doubt there were many more hidden under the *sceilps* and in the bog holes on the Mountain.

When he reached Kilduff, he knocked on the door of the house beside the church. An old woman answered. She was gaunt, and half toothless.

'I'm looking for Father Reilly,' he said.

'Father Reilly is hearing confessions. Father Flynn may see you.'

'No,' Pat said, 'I'll wait for Father Reilly. You can tell him Pat Ryan is waiting.'

He was shown into a living room, an oaken table in the centre with six oaken chairs. Around the room were four armchairs and two couches. The armchairs had a floral damask cloth on them, ragged in places, and faded from age. The couches were covered in brown leather, cracked in many places.

He sat down. A few minutes later, Father Reilly arrived. 'I'm sorry holding you,' he said to Pat. 'Confessions, though there's not many of them these days. And God knows why they come anyhow. Expecting me to give them penance, as if they hadn't done enough already.'

'I understand,' Pat said.

'So you're to be wed then? Your father came to see me, bringing your bride-to-be with him. A good woman, I would say, and God knows, we'll need them in the years to come.'

'I know.'

'I understand she was brought up in Knockanure.'

405

'Yes,' Pat said. 'As they might have told you, her father and mother were Master and Matron of the workhouse.'

'Still, a hard place for a girl to be raised, even if not as an inmate.'

'It was,' Pat said.

'You know we'll require letters of freedom from Knockanure as well.'

Pat took them out of his sack. 'I have them here.'

Father Reilly glanced down at the documents. 'Well, that concludes our official requirements. Now, as to timing, I'll be travelling the Mountain tomorrow. The Last Rites, you understand. Far too many people dying.'

'And dead already I'd say,' Pat added.

Father Reilly nodded. 'And awful it is too. They bury them everywhere.'

'I know.'

'Tomorrow so, but early,' Father Reilly said, 'unless there's many you intend to invite?'

'No,' Pat said, 'that'll be fine. It'll be my family only.'

'Fine so. As soon as the sun is above Nephin.'

Pat returned to Carrigard. Sarah threw her arms around him, crying. When Eleanor hugged him, there were tears in her eyes too.

'Well, you made it,' Michael said.

'I did. Did you think I wouldn't?'

'We'd been hearing terrible stories. Fever, cholera and the rest of it.'

'All true. But there is some better news. I dropped the letters of freedom into Father Reilly. We're to be wed early tomorrow.'

'Tomorrow,' Eleanor exclaimed.

'Why not?'

She hugged him again. 'You're right,' she said. 'There's no point in waiting. Sure young Sarah'll be a great help around.'

Pat took five sovereigns out of his pack. 'And this might help too.'

Eleanor took the money. She took a stool across to the dresser and placed the money on top, well out of sight.

'It'll have its uses,' she said.

'But what of the money I've been bringing, and what Luke is sending back?'

'We've got to last through to the harvest,' Eleanor said. 'Weeks away yet.'

'And what if it fails?' Sarah said. 'What if the potatoes fail again?'

'We'll deal with that when it happens,' Eleanor said.

After Michael and Eleanor retired, Pat and Sarah sat up late, talking.

'So how's Castlebar,' she asked. 'Has anything changed?'

'There's no cholera in Castlebar yet,' Pat replied. 'Fever, right enough, just like the rest of the county.'

'The same as killed my father back in '47 so, and he didn't even work in the fever sheds. I was always terrified of my mother being there, in Knockanure and in Westport.'

'Sure what choice did she have?' Pat said. 'It was her job.'

'And what about you?'

'I'm not working in the fever sheds.'

'Thank God for that too. But it's too late for my mother, and now I've no way back to Westport. No way back to the workhouse. And no harm either, I'd say. They've killed my father, they've killed my mother, and I'm even afraid they'll kill you if you visit them too often. I'll tell you this, Pat, I'll never forget the fever of '47 and all it killed in Knockanure.'

'I'll never forget that either. It was a terrible time in the workhouses.'

'And now that's all behind me at least. You're my family, my love. You and your mother and your father, and, like we said, it's a farmer's wife I'll be, so I'd better get used to it.'

'A hard life, being a farmer's wife,' Pat said. 'Didn't I tell you so?'

'And a lot harder it would be without your mother,' Sarah said, 'and sure that at least was something I knew since I first met her here. You know as well as I do that there would have been no marriage between us except for the knowing that your mother would soften things. It's very different to Westport.'

'So how is it so different?'

'In every way,' Sarah replied. 'There's a famine on, and we might be grateful that we don't suffer like those around us, but hunger is something I've never felt. I've been too soft.'

Early next day, Pat Ryan and Sarah Cronin were married in Kilduff. The wedding was attended by Michael, Eleanor, Brigid and Sabina.

They returned to Sabina's bar, and sipped whiskey. Eleanor dipped her thumb in hers, and gave it to Brigid to suck. She looked for more.

'Now look what you've started,' Pat said. 'She'll be looking for whiskey for the rest of her life.'

'I know,' Sabina said. 'It'll be the ruination of her.'

'Arra no,' Michael said. 'It won't be whiskey she'll be drinking. We can't afford that class of thing. *Poitín* will do her well enough.'

'That's worse,' Eleanor said. 'With the price of it, she'll be drinking it all day!'

They returned to Carrigard, and they spoke of the quarry, the farm and the prospects for the potatoes.

After some time, Eleanor tapped Michael on the shoulder.

'Are you forgetting what night tonight is?'

Michael looked puzzled. 'What's that?'

'The first night of their marriage,' she said.

He slapped his knee.

'Of course. And we shouldn't be going on with gloomy talk like this.'

Sarah stood.

'Come on, Pat.'

He followed her into the corridor, his heart pounding. She opened the door. When they were inside, he embraced her and kissed her fiercely.

She pulled herself away – 'No. no, slowly.'

They kissed again, this time more gently. She started to open his shirt, and slowly he began to open the buttons of her dress. After a few minutes, they were on the bed together, kissing, caressing, and embracing.

Afterwards they lay exhausted for a long time, not speaking. Later they made love again. In the morning, yet again.

'Three times a night,' she said, 'it's the right bull you are.'

'It takes two. A good heifer is needed too.'

She laughed. 'It's worth it all for this.'

He raised himself up and leaned his cheek onto his hand, looking at her.

'You had me worried yesterday. It's not just the hunger, is it? It's more than that.'

'Arra, it's nothing,' she said. 'Nothing more than we knew was going to happen anyhow. Sure amn't I used to a different life, isn't that it? I've been living in an institution all my life, with very little hard work expected of me, beyond pushing a pen and adding sums. Sometimes I'd do a little bit of cooking for my mother and father, but most of the time we were fed by the Union, served hand and foot by the inmates. We never wanted for anything. And it's not as if the cooking with your mother is hard. I've learnt quick enough. But digging the turf, that's harder, though your mother's well able for it, twice as fast as me. Maybe they should have put me on the stone-breaking at Westport.'

'You can still joke anyhow.'

'Sure why not. But I'll tell you this, hard and all as the turf is, digging for the potato planting will be a lot worse. Did you know your mother can keep up with your father in any kind of work? Sure, she's a gentle, loving woman, but by God, Pat, she's tough. But still, I can't help feeling homesick. My own mother, in a grave thirty miles away. And I miss the office too. I lie awake thinking that I'll never be writing and adding again. I never thought I'd miss that.'

'There's things that'll make up for that,' Pat said.

'Like what?' she asked.

'Our children. Brigid too. That'll give you plenty to be thinking about.'

'You know the one thing I find really unbelievable is Brigid. They're determined she'll go all the way to teacher training college.'

'Sure what's wrong with that?' Pat said, 'isn't that the best calling for any girl. Unless, of course, she wants to be a nun?'

'You're right in that,' Sarah said, 'but it's just the sheer strength of mind of the women here that amazes me.'

'And don't forget, it'll be the same for our children too.'

'But where on earth will we find the money?'

'Luke, perhaps and...God only knows where else, but we will find it Sarah. You'll see.'

Pat spent the next few days working with Michael, smashing stones in the quarry and digging turf too. Sometimes Sarah or Eleanor joined them. Yes, Sarah was slower than either of them, but far faster than he had expected from what she had said. And at night, she showed no sign of being worn out.

On the Monday morning, he prepared to leave. He hugged Sarah close.

'And it's sorry I am that I must leave so soon,' he said. 'The County is waiting for me, and ye'll be waiting for my wages.'

Sarah squeezed his hand.

'Don't you be worrying, my love,' she said. 'I'll be well taken care of.'

He left. Sarah and Eleanor stood on the road, waving.

Married and separated, all in a few days. To hell with it, another few weeks in Castlebar, and he could take leave again. Gaffney would understand.

Chapter 32

Reminiscences of my Irish Journey in 1849:
Human swinery has here reached its acme, happily. 30,000 paupers in this Union, population supposed to be about 60,000. Workhouse proper cannot hold above 3 or 4000 or them, subsidiary workhouses, and outdoor relief the others. Abomination of desolation; what can you make of it! Outdoor quasi-work: 3 or 400 big hulks of fellows tumbling about with spades, picks and barrows, 'levelling' the end of their workhouse hill; at first glance you would think them all working; look nearer, in each shovel there is some ounce or two of mould, and it is all make-believe; 5 or 600 boys and lads, pretending to break stones. Can it be a charity to keep men alive on these terms? In face of all the twaddle of the earth, shoot a man rather than train him (with heavy expense to his neighbours) to be a deceptive human swine.
Thomas Carlyle, British historian and philosopher, discusses Westport Workhouse in 1849.

When he returned to Castlebar, he went directly to Gaffney's office.

'Pat – good to see you back again. The wedding went well?'

'Very well, Mr. Gaffney.'

'Excellent. I reckoned you'd needed a break after Partry. That was a terrible time for you.'

'Partry was savage,' Pat replied.

'And Carrigard?'

'Not like Partry, but bad enough. There's starvation all around it, and plenty of it. But it should be easing soon.'

'Yes,' Gaffney said, 'and we're keeping a close eye on the potatoes, I can tell you. There's many are digging them too early, but how can they wait? No sign of rotting though. I think even Partry and Erris will be better than they were. Too late for thousands of people though, but what can we do? And even now there's still people starving. Those that hadn't planted enough, we can't forget them.'

'I know,' Pat said.

'You heard the workhouse here is bankrupt?'

'Yes, I knew there was some question of that.'

'Even so, I'd like you to stay on a while. Not that Lucan will like it, but let me deal with that.'

'So where do you want me to go now? Mr. Gaffney.'

'Nowhere. To be honest, I could do without you, if I really wanted to. At least from the point of view of travel. But now Dublin Castle is looking for all sorts of new reports. I think they're still worried about the potato crop, and they're getting the Royal Irish Constabulary to assess the crop everywhere, so they'll be doing whatever travelling is needed. But we need someone to compile a proper report for County Mayo as those figures come in. They'll miss a lot, I'm sure. Will you do it?'

'Of course.'

'Even so, I must warn you that your position here may not last the end of next month or so.'

'I know, Mr. Gaffney, I'd always understood that.'

'So what will you do? Go back to England?'

'I would, if I could, to be totally honest with you, but my father in Kilduff, he's running two farms now and two quarries. He's over sixty, there's no way he can go on like that. My brother is in America, so all it leaves is me. If I stayed on here, we might be able to hire a man to work with him, but otherwise, I'm afraid it's my duty.'

Over the following weeks, Pat worked on the potato crop assessments as well as correspondence from all over the County. Many he replied to directly, more he referred to Gaffney.

One morning he left his office, carrying letters for Gaffney's approval, and others for discussion.

As he came into Gaffney's office, he saw a stranger.

'There's a man here I'd like you to meet, Pat,' Gaffney said.

Pat walked over as the man stood up.

'Pat Ryan?'

'Yes.'

'Charles Gavan-Duffy, Pat. I'm delighted to meet you. Mr. Gaffney here has told me a lot about you.'

'Mr. Gavan-Duffy is the proprietor of The Nation,' Gaffney said.

'The Dublin paper?'

'That's right,' said Gavan-Duffy. 'You've heard of it?'

'Of course. Who hasn't?'

'We've had a little trouble with the government about it from time to time. They've seen fit to proscribe it. But don't worry. We'll have it up and running again, soon enough.'

411

An inmate came, carrying mugs of tea on a tray. He offered milk but all three men refused. The man looked suspiciously at Pat and Gavan-Duffy and walked out.

'Mr. Gavan-Duffy is trying to assess the condition of the country himself,' Gaffney said. 'He's been a few weeks on the road now. You can tell him about Mayo yourself.'

'It might be as well to hold on a few moments,' Gavan-Duffy said. 'Wait until we get Mr. Carlyle. I think he should hear some of what he might have to say.'

'Mr. Carlyle?' Pat asked.

Gaffney went to the door and shouted at one of the inmates to find Mr. Carlyle.

'Yes, a certain Thomas Carlyle,' Gavan-Duffy said, sipping at his tea. 'A Scot, but also one of England's greatest philosophers and a top rate historian with it. A great man, I understand. He's travelling Ireland with me trying to find out everything he can so as to tell his English friends about it.'

'What Mr. Gavan-Duffy is saying is true enough,' Gaffney said, 'but as he knows, there's another side to Mr. Carlyle.'

'How's that?' Pat asked.

'I've been travelling Ireland these past three weeks with Mr. Carlyle,' Gavan-Duffy said. 'He reckons we're all a pack of lazy ne'er-do-wells and we're the cause of the famine ourselves. All he can see is lazy beggars, closes his eyes to the starvation. But sure you'll see for yourself.'

The door opened.

The man who entered was tall, with wavy black hair, greying in parts. It was combed over from the right, half covering his ears above a white wing collar. Pat reckoned him at fifty years or so.

'Well, Mr. Carlyle,' Gavan-Duffy said. 'A loving heart is the beginning of all knowledge, eh?'

Carlyle looked sourly at him.

'One of Mr. Carlyle's quotations,' Gavan-Duffy said. 'On which grounds our friend, Lord Lucan must, by now, be a most knowledgeable man.'

Pat went to speak, but Gaffney raised his finger to his lips.

'You're just so blind, Duffy, you cannot see it,' Carlyle said. 'I've seen Lord Lucan's improvements with my own eyes, and they will do more for the people of Mayo than your Young Irelanders ever did, or ever could, for that matter.'

'Through evictions?' Gavan-Duffy asked.

'It's not the evictions you should be looking at, it's the improvements that follow from them. You've seen it too, though you seem to forget it. Lucan is draining, he's building, and he's harrowing his land to make it produce more.

And how could that be done with nothing but lazy, priest-ridden peasants? No, they have to be cleared, and for their own good too. Lease the land to men who are able to work it.'

'Scots, no doubt,' Gavan-Duffy said.

'Yes, Scots. Lucan is leasing it to Scottish farmers who are well able to farm it in the best possible way. And there's any amount of employment on the farms for any of your peasants who aren't too lazy to take it.'

There was a pause. At last, Pat spoke.

'And what of Ballinrobe?'

Carlyle looked at him, puzzled.

'Our young man can speak, can he? Ballinrobe? Have we visited it, Mr. Duffy?'

'Near enough,' Gavan-Duffy said. 'It's not too far from Claremorris.'

'And what of it,' Carlyle asked.

'Well, if it's Lord Lucan you want to know about, it's there you'll see his improvement,' Pat said, laying emphasis on the last word. 'I've seen his improvement. Wrecked villages, starving people. What kind of improvement is that?'

'The starving people are not Lord Lucan's fault,' Carlyle said. 'Nor should they be any concern of his. His only concern is to improve the land so that these beggars can be given employment.'

Pat made to rise, but Gaffney placed a hand on his arm.

'Shush, Pat, just listen. You can give your opinion later on. I promise.'

'So what solutions might you offer then?' Gavan-Duffy asked. He was smiling, and Pat wondered whether it was through derision.

'Simple, Carlyle replied. 'In the first place, if your newspaper had encouraged proper husbandry and encouraged the peasants to respect those who can show them how it's done, then that would be a beginning. That, and some respect for the British Crown, instead of provoking them to useless rebellion.'

'Yes,' said Gavan-Duffy, taking a notebook out. 'I'll certainly bear your recommendations in mind.' The look on his face was one of derision now, Pat was sure of it.

'Please do so,' Carlyle said.

'And how should I teach them to eat, when the blight has destroyed their food?' Gavan-Duffy asked.

'Like I said, if they weren't so damned lazy, there would be no famine. All they want to do is live on their potatoes, no work involved. That way they can live the autumn and winter in their filthy cabins, doing nothing. Look at Scotland...'

'There's famine in Scotland too,' Gavan-Duffy said.

'Only in the Highlands. Look at the Lowlands. There, the farmers don't depend on the potato for their very existence. They plant corn – a far more reliable crop and one that involves more labour too, but the Scots aren't afraid of hard work.'

'An interesting opinion,' Gavan-Duffy said. 'In the first place, corn cannot feed Ireland's population. It takes up too much land.'

'Your over-population is not my concern, Mr. Duffy, that's the fault of the government that allowed it.'

'The British Government?'

'No, Dublin Castle. And what's their solution? Feeding the lazy. Encouraging paupers to spawn more paupers. And what do the young gentlemen of this country want? A rebellion, against the only country that can show them how to live.'

'So you'd depend on corn, would you?' Gaffney asked. 'How much destruction of the corn crop have we seen?'

'Not as much as the potato, that's for sure,' Carlyle said.

'So that's the solution, is it?' Gavan-Duffy asked.

'Better than any solution of yours,' Carlyle replied. 'What answer do you have? Half the population of Mayo are paupers. It'd all end in cannibalism if it wasn't for the support of our empire. Look at the workhouse here. Look at Westport. Men breaking stones, just like you had them on the roads. Swinging hammers as slow as they can, pretending to work. And what do you get from that? Human swine, that's all.'

'Swine?' Pat asked.

'Yes, swine. I've been through Westport Workhouse, shown every part of it. A human swinery, that's all it is.'

Abruptly, Pat jumped from his chair. He crossed the room and slapped Carlyle violently across the face.

'Pat, for God's sake…' Gaffney shouted.

Carlyle rubbed his jaw.

'By God, you'll pay for that.'

Pat left the office, slamming the door.

He went back to working on reports and assessments, but found he could not. Then Gaffney came in.

'Pat, what in hell possessed you?'

'He deserved it, the bastard.'

'I'd agree with you there,' Gaffney said, 'but we can't treat him like that.'

'And what's that Gavan-Duffy fellow doing with him?'

'Taking him around to see famine. He was hoping it would soften his heart.'

'Soften his heart…'

'Yes, and get him to write of it in England. Gavan-Duffy's a nationalist as you know, Young Irelander too. He was arrested last year after the Rebellion.'

'So what's he doing with that bastard?'

'Carlyle asked for someone to show him Ireland, Gavan-Duffy thought it would work out well. He'd read Carlyle, and from his writing and philosophy you'd think him a decent man. No, it wasn't Gavan-Duffy's mistake, that's for sure.'

The door opened. Two policemen came in.

'Which one's Ryan?'

'I am,' Pat said.

Without further comment one policeman tied Pat's hands behind his back, and hauled him away. He was brought down to the Stonebreakers' Yard, shoved roughly onto a cart, and driven through the crowd at the gate, the soldiers forming a line against the crowd. Then they took him to the County Jail.

They were admitted through a steel door, beside the main gates. Pat had only ever seen the building from afar, over the high wall. What he saw now was a grey granite building with a grey slate roof, turreted battlements on top. He reckoned them as ornamental. It was not as if a prison would ever be besieged.

They brought him across the yard, where there were prisoners breaking stones. Another Stonebreakers' Yard! For what?

Above the main entrance to the building, there was a large clock. One of the policemen saw him looking at it.

'You needn't be worrying about that now,' he said. 'You'll only be measuring time by the passing of the days.'

They came to another locked door in the side of the building. The turnkey who answered wore a black uniform, crumpled and dirty. There was a sweet odour. Fever? Pat was sure of it. No cholera though.

The turnkey led them down along the corridor and stopped outside a door. One of the police untied Pat's wrists. He was pushed into a cell. It was gloomy. There was one single window, high up the wall, admitting light. There was a stink of shit and piss, but no smell of fever. One thing to be grateful for perhaps. The door slammed behind him.

Through the semi-darkness, he saw three men, all in prison uniforms.

'What are you doing here?' he was asked.

'Arrested for assault,' he answered.

'Assault...'

'A Scottish gentleman who came visiting.'

'Come to steal our land, was he?'

'Not him. Only getting others to do it.'

415

He lay back on a bunk.

'*And ye? What are ye doing here?*'

'*We're here to get fed.*'

Pat sat up again.

'*To get fed?*'

'*Well, we can't get fed outside, so isn't it better to come to the jail and live?*'

Pat shook his head.

'*Makes sense, I suppose.*'

'*It does. There's a trick to it though. Whatever crime you commit must be good enough for a few weeks in prison, but not too good, or you might be transported, or hanged. Michael Flanagan, he stole a sheep. Transportation he got. Van Diemen's Land. We'll never see him again.*'

'*And ye? What kind of crimes must ye commit?*'

'*Give a soldier a thrashing. It's enough for jail, but they've little enough respect for their soldiers, so they won't transport you. Everyone knows that.*'

Pat was surprised, though he said nothing.

'*And what about the stone yard outside?*' he asked. '*Are they not working ye?*'

'*They are right enough,*' one of the men answered. '*Ten hours a day smashing stones, with a break for food and rest. We'll be back on soon.*'

'*And what when it's dark?*'

'*A few braziers to keep us going.*'

A short time later, Pat was out in the Stonebreakers Yard himself. He thought how ironic this was. All the times he had been in Workhouses he had seen other people breaking stones.

It was not difficult though. The men worked very slowly. From time to time, the wardens shouted at them for being lazy good-for-nothings, but the men ignored them, and worked on in silence.

They returned to the cells. The stink was frightful, but he slept well, in spite of it.

He found the next few days hard enough. Not that breaking stones was hard, but the slopping out system disgusted him. Crapping and pissing in a cell with three other men. He was concerned about fever, and even cholera, but the men in his cell showed no signs of either, and he could only smell it as they passed by the infirmary wards from their cell.

On the third morning, Pat had slopped out with the others and gone to breakfast. Stirabout porridge. He never got to eat it.

Two warders came to his table.

'Up.'

A handcuff was put on one of his wrists, linking him to one of the warders.

'Where are we going?'

'To the Governor's office.'

'What for?'

'Who knows? You haven't been tried yet?'

'Not yet,' Pat replied.

'Assaulting a gentleman like that. Maybe they'll hang you.'

'Don't frighten him,' the other warder said. 'You didn't kill him. Transportation, that'll be enough of a sentence for the beak to give you.'

Transportation? That would be the end of the farm in Carrigard. How long could Michael keep working a farm with two quarries? The two women might help, but still, it would not be for long. Would they be evicted? And Sarah. Married for so short a time, and now this.

How long? Twenty years in the colonies? Would he ever come back? Would Sarah wait for him? The irony of it struck him strongly. She could end up being married to a colonial convict after all, but oceans apart.

They came to a door. The warder unlocked the handcuffs and knocked. Pat was pushed inside. Gaffney was there.

'So this is the fellow?' the man behind the desk said.

'One of my best workers,' Gaffney said. 'We can't do without him.'

'Well, Mr. Carlyle has not preferred charges, and from all I hear it's doubtful that Mr. Gavan-Duffy will.'

'They're both gone to Sligo,' Gaffney said. 'We'll not hear from them again.'

'Which leaves you as the only witness, George.'

'Of what?'

'Of what, indeed. Now, if you'll just sign here. And here.'

Gaffney signed. Then he and Pat walked back to the Union building.

'That was foolish, Pat'.

'Don't I know? Still...'

'Yes, still. I know what you're thinking, and you know what I think too. But Carlyle has left, and we won't be hearing from him again. Lord Lucan might be a different matter.'

'He knows?'

'Of course, he knows. Carlyle told him. It caused a hell of a row at the Grand Jury meeting. Lucan was insisting you leave, but I told him to go to hell. He was threatening to close the workhouse, but the other fellows wouldn't have that. The bastard's paying damned little of his County Rates, so what say could he have in the matter. Still, it was a close-run thing.'

'I'm sorry.'

They returned to the workhouse and went to Gaffney's office.

'The other thing I must tell you, Pat,' Gaffney said, 'is that even if we've

417

faced Lucan down, your employment isn't going to last long anyhow.'

'Sure I knew that.'

'Yes, well, I'd say early September is the limit. God knows, I'd like to have you here in a permanent position, but there's no way we can do that. The workhouse can't afford it. There's talk of a great crop of potatoes, so they're saying I've no need for extra staff. Mind you, there's talk of blight too, but we're praying it doesn't spread. If it does, the workhouse will be pushed to the limit, which means even less money. So one way or another, you've only a month or so.'

In many ways, his work was easier now, in that he did not have to travel the County, but Gaffney was well aware of what the workhouse needed, and was trying to get as much as possible out of him while he was still in the office. He spent long days and nights on reports, correspondence and even drafting rough maps to show where the worst 'distress' was.

At last, the time came to leave Castlebar.

Gaffney called him to his office. He opened a moneybox and counted out several coins.

'At least we can pay you. It'll help for the next few months.'

'It will,' Pat said.

'And good luck to you from here,' Gaffney said. 'In spite of what Lucan might say, you've done a great job. I'm heartbroken to see you go, but still, in the time you were with us, you did great things for County Mayo.'

Pat left the office. He went to his bed and took his bag of possessions with him, then he crossed the Stonebreakers Yard and left Castlebar Union.

In the months that Pat was away, Sarah and Eleanor developed a close relationship, looking after Brigid, and running the house. But then, the blight came.

Sarah, who had gone to Kilduff to buy corn, was ashen.

'I saw it in two fields,' she said. 'Not much, mind, but in Dillon's they're saying it's all over the county.'

Eleanor went cold.

'I don't believe it,' she said.

'That's what they're saying,' Sarah said.

Blight again, Eleanor thought. *If it really has returned, the country is finished. So are we. Already, we've little enough money left. And still no word of Luke.*

When Michael came in, the women told them of the blight.

'Strange,' Michael said. 'There's surely not the slightest sign of it here. Where did you say, you saw it?'

'Just coming into Kilduff,' Sarah said. 'There were two fields on the right.'

'That's near a mile away,' Michael said.

'Yes,' Eleanor said. 'Could it come closer though?'

'I don't know,' Michael said. 'My fear is that even if we don't see it, the potatoes will rot after we've dug them.'

'Let's pray they won't,' Eleanor said.

She had cut back on the size of the meals she was cooking. She hoped no-one noticed.

Next time, she went up to Kilduff to buy corn, she glanced across into fields. She saw the blight in the distance, little enough, but still there. If there had been much less, she reckoned Sarah would not have been able to see it. She guessed it had not spread.

She bought corn in Dillon's. The other women were silent, and she did not ask any questions.

The tension increased.

At last, the time came to dig. Michael, Sarah and Eleanor went to the first ridges, Michael carrying a spade, Eleanor a knife. There were still no signs of blight on the leaves.

Michael dug into the ridge. Eleanor scrambled in the dirt, grasping the potatoes.

'They're big enough anyhow,' she said. She looked at the eyes of the potato. No purple. Carefully, she cut around the eye. The potato was white. Then she cut straight through it. No blight.

'And pray to God it stays that way,' Michael said.

They filled two sacks. Michael carried one down to the house on his back, Sarah and Eleanor carrying a second one between them.

They washed potatoes and peeled them. Again and again, Eleanor cut through, looking for blight. Michael came over and squeezed one of the potatoes.

'They're good and hard. These ones won't rot.'

Now, it was back to hard work among the potato ridges, digging out all the potatoes and carrying them back to the house. Every night, one of them stood guard over the field.

They were stored in the loft over the kitchen.

The first day, Sarah ate too much, not realising that her stomach was unused to it. She vomited. But it no longer mattered. The potato was back and there was plenty of it.

When it was finished, and the last potatoes were stored, they sat at the table. 'Let's see your hands,' Eleanor said.

Sarah held her hands out.

'They're toughening up well, that's for sure.'

'Carrying the water from the well,' Sarah said.

'Yes. And you were able to work good and hard digging out the potatoes.'

'Digging potatoes is a lot tougher than digging turf, that's for sure,' Sarah said.

When the potatoes were harvested, it was time to harvest the corn and hay. Corn for rent, and the hay to feed the animals during the winter.

Sarah and Eleanor were out threshing one morning, when Sarah stopped and doubled over, gasping. She walked to the corn barrel at the edge of the threshing ground, and held on to it.

'*What's wrong,*' Eleanor asked in alarm.

'*I'm feeling sick,*' Sarah replied. '*I've had it these past three days. Always at the same time.*'

'*Well, one thing's for certain, you shouldn't be out working.*'

Eleanor led her back to the house, and sat her at the table.

'*At this time of the morning too? There's one thing that could be.*'

'*I know,*' Sarah said, '*and I've missed my bleeding too.*'

'*Well, sick or not, this is a great surprise,*' Eleanor said.

'*Don't tell me you didn't expect it.*'

That evening, Pat arrived in Carrigard.

'Pat!' Eleanor exclaimed, 'you're back.'

'I am,' Pat said, 'back for good.'

Sarah stopped dead in front of him.

'For good!'

'They won't be needing me anymore.'

'What's that you say?' Michael asked.

'The workhouse can't afford it. And anyhow the Grand Jury is reckoning there's a good harvest. If there hadn't been a good harvest, I'd have left soon for lack of money, and if there had, there'd be less call for me. But sure didn't we know all of this already.'

'We did,' Eleanor said. 'But still, we were hoping.'

'So was I. One way or another though, I was lucky working so long. Lord Lucan himself, he wanted me sacked earlier.'

'Lucan? He wanted you sacked?'

'That's what he wanted, but he didn't get his way. I spent three days in Castlebar Jail, though, but Gaffney got me out.'

'Three days in jail,' Sarah exclaimed. 'What in God's name for?'

'Attacking a man!'

'But...who?'

'A Scot, by the name of Carlyle. England's greatest philosopher they say. His philosophy of love leads him to believe that the Irish are lazy swine. Believes the Irish caused the famine all on their own. If we worked as hard as the Scots, there'd be no famine.'

'But isn't there famine there too?' Sarah asked.

'Only in the Highlands, I'd heard,' Pat said, 'and he thinks the Highlanders as lazy as the Irish. He visited Westport Workhouse too, Sarah, just so you know. He described that as a right human swinery, nothing but lazy people swinging sledgehammers at stones.'

'That's not lazy,' Eleanor said.

'I know. So I slapped him across the face. Hard.'

Eleanor poured four cups of *poitín*.

'You're a damned fool,' Michael said.

'I know,' Pat said, 'and you're not the first to say that. I know too I shouldn't have let my temper get the better of me. But I don't regret it. The bastard deserved a better beating.'

'So? No wages from you,' Michael said. 'They're not building roads now neither. No need for Relief Works with the potatoes looking so good. And Sarah's mother, dead. There won't be any earnings from there either.'

Sarah was crying.

'It shouldn't be money you think of, Michael, and the poor woman dead,' Eleanor said, her arm around Sarah's shoulder. 'And sure there's a good crop of potatoes too. And corn. We'll have enough to eat, and pay Burke his rent too. There's not many people around paying rent yet, I can tell you.'

'And what if the blight returns?' Sarah asked.

'That's a year away,' Eleanor said. 'It's a great harvest this year, anyhow,'

'I'll say it is,' Pat said. 'I've been seeing it as I was travelling. All the way from Castlebar to Kilduff, potatoes good and healthy. Less begging too. And no bodies on the road, thank God. And when the potatoes are back, the fever will lessen too – the fever and cholera both.'

'You might have the right of it,' Michael said, 'but it doesn't lessen the fact that you've lost your job.'

Pat looked away. 'And what of Luke?' he asked. 'Wasn't he sending money back, with the great job that he had?'

'*Arra*, what,' Michael answered. 'Sure that was months ago. We haven't heard from him this long time.'

'But when…?'

'Six months, I'd say. Could be more.'

Eleanor stood and took Michael's elbow.

'Sure that's nothing,' she said. 'We can't be expecting him to write every month to be telling us what's happening. Can we?'

No one replied.

Do I really believe that? she thought. *He'll have heard enough of the hunger in Ireland, and if he was earning good money, he'd have sent more back by now. This Lackan place sounds fine, but if it was that good, we'd have heard from him. He must be dead. Oh, may the devil take it. I'm only working myself into a fret. He'll write soon, that's for a certainty.*

But what of Pat? There's more pain there. And a deeper silence than before. There's things we'll never know; things he'll never tell us. Not me, not Sarah, no-one.

That night, Sarah told Pat that she was expecting a baby.

'That's wonderful news,' Pat said.

'It is. Except, of course, that'll we'll have to feed the mite, and like your father says, that won't be easy. So what do we do now? Have you go to England? At least you'd get wages there.'

'Sure,' Pat replied. 'Working with Murtybeg, and a woman like Irene. Yes, I'd have work, grinding men into the dirt. No, I'll never work with Murteen again, and anyhow I'll have to stay and take care of the farm, even if there's damned little earnings out of it. What else can I do?'

'I don't know. What else is there? Have us go to join Luke in America? We don't want that.'

'We don't, and even if we did, father is getting old. No, my love, Luke going to America has trapped us here, and we'll just have to put up with it. I might have some chance working on the English harvest next year. It's what all the lads around here do.'

'But they don't pay much, do they?'

'It'd be enough to pay the rent, though I'd have to leave ye and father to look after the harvest over here.'

'That mightn't be so hard as you might think,' Sarah said. 'We managed it well this summer, didn't we?'

Then the letter arrived. Eleanor spotted the stamp at once.

'Sarah,' she shouted, 'it's from America.'

Sarah opened it, and the bank draft fluttered out.

'Well, thank God for that,' Eleanor said. 'Now what does he say?'

Sarah glanced through it.

'Let's see…there's been a lockout…and a strike… They've had no wages!'

'No wages!'

'That's what he says. They've been hungry too…'

'Hungry! In America!'

'But wait…he's a new job…some kind of boss…fifteen dollars a week!'

'Fifteen dollars? I don't believe it.'

'And a house of their own. And we're to send some money to Winnie's mother. And hold a little for Brigid.'

'I knew it,' Eleanor said. 'I knew we could depend on Luke. Not only for Brigid neither, for your baby too when the time comes. And we'll never go hungry again.'

That afternoon, Sabina came to the house. They showed her the letter.

'*That'll sort a few things out,*' *she said.*

'*It will, won't it?*' Eleanor said.

'*And only two weeks till school opens.*'

'*Hear that, Brigid,*' Eleanor said. '*School. Won't it be great?*'

'*School,*' said Brigid. '*I want school.*'

Sabina laughed. '*She wants school, and she not even knowing what it is. She'll go far.*'

'*She will,*' Sarah said.

'*And she won't be the only one,*' Eleanor said.

'*What do you mean?*' asked Sabina.

'*Sarah here. She's expecting.*'

Sabina swung around, and hugged Sarah.

'*Oh Sarah, I knew you would. Another child that'll go far in life. So what will it be when it grows up?*'

'*Shouldn't we wait till it's born?*' Sarah said.

'*Arra, not at all,*' Sabina said, a hoarseness in her voice. '*Sure we can plan now. If it's a little girl, she'll follow Brigid to teacher training college. Isn't that it?*'

'*And if it's a little boy?*' Sarah asked, mystified.

'*University.*'

Eleanor looked across from where she had been peeling the potatoes. '*University!*'

'*Yes,*' Sabina said.

Silence.

'*Do you think it's possible?*' Sarah asked at last.

'*Of course, it's possible. Everything's possible when you have the money.*'

'*But not if it's a girl,*' Sarah said. '*They don't allow them into Universities.*'

'*Isn't that what I said?*' Sabina said. '*If it's a girl she'll be a teacher. If it's a boy, it'll be University.*

'*And what will the child do at University?*' Eleanor asked, intrigued.

'*Medicine? Law? Who knows?*' Sabina said.

'*And what University?*' Sarah asked. '*Trinity won't allow Catholics.*'

'*Shush a moment,*' Sabina replied. '*There's other Universities. Queen's*

College *in Belfast. I hear they're taking Catholics.'*

'Queen's College,' Sarah whispered. *'You really think…'*

'Sure why not?' Sabina said.

'But how do you know all this?' Sarah asked.

'Stephen Martin. He's one of the teachers in Kilduff School. A Belfast man himself. I know him well through the bar.'

'But how would we pay for all this, with Pat not working?' Sarah asked. *'Would Luke handle all that, if Pat couldn't?'*

'I'm sure he will,' Eleanor said.

'I don't know,' Sarah said, *'A lot of it depends on the potato now. Is the blight really gone? We saw already, the amount that was around. Not much, but it's not gone. It's been doing that before, playing cat-and-mouse, great harvest one year, and when you plant everything you can the next year, it destroys it all.'*

'You've the right of it,' Eleanor said, *'but sure how do we know for sure? It's hard to plan ahead, but we have to do it. Aren't they going on with the new schools, right through the hunger and fever?'*

'Yes,' Sabina said, *'though there was talk they'd be stopped during the fevers. Not that they ever did.'*

'Nor ever will,' Eleanor said. *'So our babies will be schooled for free for the next six or seven years. After that, we'll depend on Luke, and we can forget Murtybeg.'*

'Wait till Michael hears this one,' Sabina said. *'I'd love to see the look on his face.'*

'Or the sound of his voice,' Eleanor said. *'Can you imagine him?* 'Mad. You're all mad…'

That evening, the women told Michael of Sarah's pregnancy, never mentioning their plans for the baby.

'We'll wait till the little one is born,' Eleanor said to Sarah, later. *'That'll be time enough to talk of Universities.'*

But time passed fast enough in other ways. One Sunday evening, Sabina came to take Brigid to Kilduff. She and Eleanor walked the child along the road.

'School tomorrow, Brigid,' Sabina said.

'School. School. School…' Brigid answered.

When they arrived, they took Brigid up to the third floor, well above the bar. Sabina had already heated the room, and made up a small bed. They tucked the child in, and within moments Brigid was asleep.

'And there was me thinking she might be upset,' Eleanor said.

'Arra, not at all,' Sabina said. *'Sure little ones like that get used to anything. Another few weeks I'll have her serving in the bar.'*

424

'*The devil, you will,*' said Eleanor.

'*Sure she has to learn her numbers. What better way?*'

'*I swear; I'll kill you if you do.*'

Sabina laughed. She poured out two whiskies.

'*The potato is back,*' she said. '*There's better times coming.*'

'*There are,*' Eleanor said. '*But when?*'

As she walked home, it was a still night, cloudless and clear, with thousands of stars. To the north, the sky was rippling with red and green, stretching all across the Mountain and on as far as Nephin.

The question still echoed through her head. *When will it end?*

Will it ever end?

They died in their thousands and their hundreds of thousands. All the suffering, the screaming pain, the grisly dying and the bodies scattered over mountains and bogs. Why did You do it? Was this the price that had to be paid? Your price. For what?

The coming years, what are they to bring? More of the same? More famine, more fever, more dying, more death. Enough to send the people fleeing; escaping a blighted land.

No different to before. Michael's brother, sixty years past or more, he died before Michael could even know him. Michael's mother and father both died too with the fever that came with the hunger, long before the cholera of '32. The same cholera that killed so many of my children. Since then, fever in every year, more dead children. They paid the price. I paid the price. For what? For living? Or for the crime of motherhood?

Luke and Pat are still living, but how many did not? My only daughter and my first son, they died. And more? Yes, five more who only lived a few days. Seven of my children dead, but did You care? They were innocent, but they died anyhow. All of my daughters, most of my sons. Two left from nine. Your price again. Why complain? You do it to all of us mothers. Mothering is nothing but burying children.

A hard life, but not hard enough for You. Did we ever think it would turn into this? Famine and fever, the most savage sacrifice, the heaps and trenches of stinking bodies. All the wretched aftershock of our never-ending war with death. And for what? No reason given, only the infinite silence of the endless Void.

And all these new schools they gave us, teaching our children. Yes, we needed them, but still wasn't that what destroyed Murty's school and forced him to go to England? What is he now? Nothing more than an Irish navvy. And Aileen too? Once proud to be the teacher's wife, now she's only a navvy woman, working with Kitty in a Bradford mill. We should have expected that; we should have known the spinning and weaving machines would make the mills and kill off the outworkers on the farms. So now that they've got their big cities instead, Aileen can work in the mill, and Murty can work out his old age as a labourer on the railways. Is this the way it was meant to be? Is this their future? The future You made, the future You wanted. Is it?

Danny gone too, and dead. Dead from his own fierce ambition, thinking he was a hard man, but he wasn't. All we heard of him in England, the cruel brutality of a man who never cared for Mayo. Yet he was willing to pay for Brigid's schooling. Paying for his own sins perhaps? Who knows? He's dead now. He alone knew the agonies that drove him to it, and the price he had to pay. Your price.

Are they the same agonies as Murtybeg must suffer? Or can he conquer his own conscience, caring nothing for anyone? Little Murteen? Cruel and pitiless? I'd never have believed that of him. But now? All England needs from Mayo is cheap men for navvying, and cheap food to feed the English people. Is Murteen the one who will squeeze the price from County Mayo? How will he justify the pain he'll cause? Does he even know the pain he'll cause to himself, and the price You'll claim from him?

And Pat? I'd always known he would be the farmer. Michael said it was to be Luke, but Luke had the travel in him, whether he knew it or not. But Pat stayed in Mayo, surveying the County, and him not even able to talk about it. Few Famine Roads to be built now, that's for sure. But the workhouses are full to overflowing, no money to feed anyone, and thousands starving and sickening. Wasn't that what he saw? All the hunger and fever in the mountains and along the seacoast – men, women and children dying; and the rats and dogs tearing at them; living or dead. A county crucified.

Was it any different to what we saw here? He never said; he can never share what he saw, and he never will. His pain goes on and on. Your price again. The price of silence.

We had thought he would work with the County, but he lost his standing. Why worry? It was either that or the farm. Michael can't stay farming on his own, he's too old. Didn't I know that? We can't depend on Carrigard anyhow. County Mayo is broken. Your price? Who cares? Do You?

Sarah came with Pat, and she'll have children. But what did she suffer to get here? The Workhouse. She never talks about it either. More silence. She suffered, but her lot was better than the thousands of others who worked and died in the workhouses and the fever sheds? Yes, she lived, and she'll bear my grandchildren. You want my thanks for that? Never. I owe You nothing.

Still, her children will calm me. But for how long? How many of her children will stay and starve in Mayo? Will their future be one of famine and fever too? Or will they travel the world; banished from the farm and scattered across the face of the earth? Yes, they'll work the railways and mines of England and America; they'll break the alien rock, and eat the alien dust.

Little Brigid will be a teacher, no doubt about that. Already Sabina treats her as a daughter. But how I'll miss her. Yes, Sabina will bring the child back every Friday, but every Sunday I'll walk her back to Kilduff. Soon she'll walk it on her own. She'll do well, we'll make sure she does.

But what of Luke. He never told us of what he had seen when he worked in the mountains with the Famine Relief. The horror had touched his mind, and terrified him until he saw the Unseeable. Was it all inside his head? Who knows? He never told us. He never wrote of the fever ships either, but all the stories coming back over the Great Ocean told us enough of that. Did the terror follow him to Quebec and America?

What matter? He's gone, and Winnie followed him, taking Liam too. He's a Breaker Boss now, well paid, a man to respect. But what of all the others who must go to America? Cheap labour for American mines. And Luke, overseeing the lowest paid, the ones with the shortest lives left to live? But still, he remembers us and pays for our food and Brigid's future. A good son? Yes, a good son, but a hard taskmaster of men.

Is that the way, or is our way better? Dreaming our dreams, farming our farms and schooling our children. Yes, we can do it, the potato is back, but how much we'll still depend on Luke. There is no other way. We'll take his money, and his way will be our way, his strength our strength.

His guilt our guilt? His terror too?

Oh God.

Glossary of Words, Places and People

Acushla: Darling.

A ghrá: My love.

Alanna: Dear child. My love. From *A leanbh* (child).

Amadán: Fool.

Arra: Implies 'No' or 'don't be silly'. From *Aire* (care).

Biddy: Short for Brigid, but sometimes used as a slang word for a maid.

Boreen: A narrow road or track. From the Irish *Bótharín*, a little road.

Brassey, Thomas: The largest railway construction contractor in the Victorian era.

Bridget: Anglicised version of Brigid, also used as slang for a maid.

Bytown: Original name of Ottawa before Federation in 1867.

Camboose: Either living quarters for lumbermen, or the open fire inside it.

Carlyle, Thomas: Scottish philosopher and historian.

Cavendish, Lord Frederick: Proprietor of the Connaught Telegraph.

Clochán: A tiny settlement of primitive houses.

Connaught Telegraph: Abbreviated name for the Telegraph & Connaught Ranger newspaper.

Creel: A large wicker basket for holding fish or turf.

Crubeens: Boiled pig trotters. From the Irish *Crúibín*.

Currach: A boat made of wooden slats, covered in several layers of tar.

Drift: A horizontal tunnel in coal mining.

Eejit: Idiot. From the English word.

Emmet, Robert Addis: An American politician and nephew of the Irish patriot, Robert Emmet.

Gavan-Duffy, Charles: Irish Nationalist. Founded The Nation newspaper. Later premier of Victoria.

Gossoon: Boy. From the Irish *Garsún*, and originally, Old French Garçun (modern Garçon).

Grá: Love.

Hoor: Irish slang, mostly for a crafty fellow who is not to be trusted. Not related to 'whore'.

Jocks: Scots (derogatory).

Lackan: A fictitious coal mining village. Like Avoca and Avondale, the original is in County Wicklow.

Lucan, Lord: George Bingham, third Lord Lucan. Mayo's largest landlord. Known as the Exterminator.

Lumper: A large potato.

Mauch Chunk: Original name of the town of Jim Thorpe. Renamed after the 1877 Molly Maguire trials.

Molly Maguires: A nineteenth century Irish terrorist group.

Musha: Indeed. Probably from the Irish word *Muise*. Mainly used by older women.

Outshot: A bed built into the inside of a wall, often in the kitchen.

Piseóg: Superstition or a superstitious story.

Poitín: An illicit spirit distilled from potatoes. Moonshine.

Port Phillip: Now Melbourne. Located in Victoria, which had been part of New South Wales.

Rath: The remains of an ancient fort or settlement. There are about 30,000 in Ireland.

RIP: Requiescat in Pace. Rest in Peace. An epitaph.

Sassenach: An Englishman. From *Sasanach* in Irish, i.e. Saxon.

Sceilp: A primitive lean-to shelter made of branches and sods.

Shebeen: A small or unlicensed bar or pub. From *Síbín*. Still in use in South Africa.

Sleán: A special spade for digging turf.

Spailpín: A seasonal or migrant harvest worker.

Sláinte mhaith: Good Health, as in a drinking toast.

Taffs: Welshmen (derogatory).

Ticket-of-leave men: Ex-convicts, released on condition of good behaviour.

Tigín: A tiny house.

Townland: A rural sub-division of land.

Trawneen: Something of little value. From *Tráithnín*, a blade of grass.

Turf: In Ireland, peat dug from a peat bog for burning as fuel.

Union: In Ireland, the body running the Poor Law. Also, a workhouse. Not related to Trade Unions.

Union: In Britain, a workhouse or a Trade Union. The Miners' Association was a Trade Union.

Union: In the USA, a Trade Union, such as the Bates Union.

Whisht: Hush. Silence. Be quiet. From Middle English.

Young Irelanders: Revolutionary group behind the 1848 Rebellion.

If you enjoyed *Cold is the Dawn* don't miss
The Killing Snows and *The Exile Breed*